Praise for *The Midcoast*

"A propulsive crime saga . . . Andrew has something in common with Nick Carraway . . . and like a roughneck Jay Gatsby, Ed Thatch is driven to his life of crime. . . . Brimming with keen observation not just of the landscape but of dialect and class distinctions and all the tiny, vital particularities that make a place real . . . *The Midcoast* is an absorbing look at small-town Maine and the thwarted dreams of a family trying to transcend it."

—LEE COLE, *The New York Times Book Review* (Editor's Choice)

"One of the most anticipated novels of the year."

—*Town & Country*

"Home is atmosphere, description, trees, and coastline, but it's also solidity and safety, a sense of knowing and understanding a place. *The Midcoast* suggests that home is also other people—the ones we love, but also the ones we envy."

—LYNN STEGER STRONG, *Maine* magazine

"[White's] writing sucks you in from the first page."

—*Portland Press Herald*

"This is a story about friends, and neighbors, and the strangers who secretly live among them. . . . Cozy and chilling!"

—*CrimeReads*

"Channeling Balzac ('Behind every great fortune is an equally great crime'), White . . . dredges up the long-submerged origins of the Thatch money in this dark social portrait of a small Maine town."

—*The Millions* (most anticipated books of 2022)

"Don't rush this one. Savor it."

—*Publishers Weekly*

"White's first novel is a corker, well plotted and paced and with just the right elements of suspense . . . a fine debut."

—*Booklist*

"*The Midcoast* is a suspenseful, funny, and chilling exploration of the costs of pursuing the American dream. Adam White expertly weaves an intriguing uncovering of small-town secrets with a propulsive family drama. . . . A perfect summer read about a perfect vacation haven."

—ANGIE KIM, author of *Miracle Creek*

"*The Midcoast* is an insanely good novel, compulsively readable, with a growing feeling of menace and catastrophe that becomes almost unbearable. Elegantly written, with vivid characters and an intricately realized setting, this is a stunning debut from a writer we will certainly hear from again. I highly recommend this book."

—DOUGLAS PRESTON, #1 bestselling author of
The Lost City of the Monkey God

"Vividly drawn and movingly told, *The Midcoast* is a searching, honest, and evocative portrait of human relationships, hometown secrets, and the hidden machinations of privilege. Adam White's debut enthralls, a modern classic from a bold and insightful new voice in fiction."

—ALEXANDRA KLEEMAN, author of *Something New Under the Sun*

"*The Midcoast* is a brilliant, ferocious debut novel about ambition, class, and crime in coastal Maine, simultaneously propulsive and nuanced. Adam White brings his powerful gifts to bear on a story that speaks directly to our troubled moment with eloquence and heart. After this, Vacationland will never look the same."

—ANDREW MARTIN, author of *Early Work*

"*The Midcoast* expertly weaves sharply realized scenes and a profound sense of empathy into a plotline full of tension, resentments, and dangerous secrets. In White's talented hands, we understand how virtues like love and loyalty can still lead us to a sea of vices. . . . A wise and powerful debut!"

—STACEY SWANN, author of *Olympus, Texas*

"Gripping."

—*Down East*

"A compelling story of young love, ambition, police corruption, drug trafficking and house burglaries: the dark underbelly of the idealized Maine life to which summer vacationers flock."

—*Mom Central*

THE MIDCOAST

THE MIDCOAST

A NOVEL

Adam White

HOGARTH | LONDON · NEW YORK

2023 Hogarth Trade Paperback Edition

Copyright © 2022 by Adam H. White
Book club guide copyright © 2023 by Penguin Random House LLC

Published in the United States by Hogarth, an imprint of Random House, a division of Penguin Random House LLC, New York.

Hogarth is a trademark of the Random House Group Limited, and the H colophon is a trademark of Penguin Random House LLC.

Random House Book Club and colophon are trademarks of Penguin Random House LLC

Originally published in hardcover in the United States by Hogarth, an imprint of Random House, a division of Penguin Random House LLC, in 2022.

ISBN: 9780593243176
Ebook ISBN: 9780593243169

Printed in the United States of America on acid-free paper

randomhousebooks.com
randomhousebookclub.com

2 4 6 8 9 7 5 3 1

Book design by Susan Turner

For Erin

THE MIDCOAST

PROLOGUE

BACK WHEN I LIVED OUT OF STATE, PEOPLE ALWAYS USED TO GET
excited when they found out where I was from. They didn't meet
all that many Mainers—I was like a moose descended from a log
cabin, wandering their backyard, eating their shrimp—and wondered if I was from anywhere near the town where they'd gone to
summer camp or cruised in their custom sloop. Sometimes I was,
sometimes I wasn't, but Maine is a large state with more coastline
than California, I liked to point out, plenty of old gray villages
like the one I grew up in, plenty of places to get lost or hide,
especially when socked in by a heavy fog. Maybe they'd heard of
Damariscotta if they'd ever taken a vacation to the Midcoast, but
they tended to pronounce the name wrong and then ask what it
meant, and I would say either River of Little Fishes in Abenaki
or something Scottish, we weren't really sure. If they asked what
the town was known for, I would have said brick-making, then
ice-shipping, then oysters and this one little gallery that sells lobster buoys painted to look like political figures, but this was all

before Maeve and I moved back home and bought our *coastal charmer with a view!,* a listing so pyritic that its author, our realtor, met us at the door mid-apology and with a referral to a rodent removal service.

Before my return I was still telling that old joke, whenever I needed to explain where I was from, about the local who has to give directions to a visiting urbanite. "You can't get the-yah from he-yah," says the Mainer, which tells you a little about the roads and highways on the Midcoast, a little more about the shotgun wariness that'll greet you on so many overgrown front porches, and a lot about the granite breakwalls between those who've been here for generations and those who've landed more recently, within the past century or two. I am one of these newer arrivals, not a true Mainer—if your parents are from elsewhere, you don't count, even if you moved to town at age three—but at least I'm not a tourist. We all scowl at the tourists. They ascend as one big traffic jam every summer and presume to know the place just because they've rented a cottage with bunk beds and weathered a gentle nor'easter. The other day I saw a couple in matching sunglasses lingering in front of the Sotheby's, gazing at a flyer full of homes, one of which belonged to the Thatches, our town's wealthiest family; when I overheard them indulging in the fantasy of moving here year-round, imagining Maine as *the way life should be,* I found myself wishing I had some *other* flyer with pictures of the peeling shack Ed Thatch lived in as a child, or the trailer he and his wife Steph moved into when they were only eighteen (or our own drafty ranch, for that matter), just to show these dreamers what they might find if they ever arrived in the off-season and ventured down the wrong dirt road.

To move on from any of these dirt roads was supposed to be impossible, but then the Thatches did just that, moved from *there* to *here*—well past here, actually. Steph loved to remind us of their early days, all the hard work and long hours that had put them on this different track, and it's not that we didn't believe her, just that we'd heard it all before, heard it plenty. But every small town has its own running dramas, its own local celebrities (there's a set of twins that's been calling our high school basketball games since the big playoff run in '89, and there's a mussel farmer who wears a bodybuilding getup in every parade—we think because mussel and muscle are homophones—and he's been doing it since I was in college). So I guess I always assumed I'd return to the Midcoast, *if* I returned, to find things basically where I'd left them. And most things were. Just not the Thatches. Which was fine. They were off in the distance, nothing to do with us, their rise and fall like a rolling swell tumbling down the coast.

People do move here for the views. Ours is of the salt bay, partially, but also of our neighbor's three-car garage and a pyramid of algae-covered lobster traps. "The real deal" is how our realtor described the neighborhood, meaning that what we'd see through our windows was mostly the slowly revving engine of Mainers going nowhere. Unless there's a fog. Then there's nothing to see, only what everyone else can see, only what's right in front of us.

BUT IT WAS A SUNNY day in May the last time I saw Ed, one year ago now, when I, Maeve, Jack, and Jane went to the Thatches' house to attend "A Reception in Honor of Amherst Women's Lacrosse." That Ed and Steph had somehow given life to and sent into the world a freshman midfielder on the Amherst women's lacrosse team had never stopped seeming completely implausible, and yet we all knew Allie's story—this was the daughter—because Ed would give you the lowdown any chance he got. You'd be walking out of the post office or into the natural foods co-op when there'd be a loud honk and you'd look up to see Ed hanging out the driver's side of his Silverado, banging a flat hand against the door. "Hey, Andy! Two goals against Tufts! She's on some kinda roll!" And before you even had time to congratulate her, or really him, he'd be thundering down the low brick canyon of Main Street, past the art gallery and the butcher shop, both of which leased from him.

Our family was late getting to the reception so had to park on the shoulder of the gravel driveway, way up by the main road, behind a chartered bus and a steep line of out-of-state SUVs, their rear windows papered in Amherst Lacrosse stickers, Nantucket beach permits, and faux-European circle decals designed to make MV and OBX look like legitimate nation-states. Back when Ed and I had worked as teenage dockhands at the Pound, Ed would have called this visiting herd *Your kind of people, Andy,* but he's the only one who ever called me Andy, and I always resented the characterization—perhaps because it fit. I had gone away to Exeter, then Dartmouth, played lacrosse at both stops, roomed with Virginia aristocrats who now arrived at reunions with full-time nannies and made a show of matching any and all donations to the scholarship fund.

I thought I understood, then, what we were getting ourselves into. The women's lacrosse team would get feted and fed the day before its big game against Bowdoin College. There would be chicken parm and Gatorade. Dads would get sloshed and lean a little too close and deliver pointed musings about the way the team *ought* to be run, who should be getting more of a burn, who should be riding more pine. They'd be wearing shiny polos with their country clubs' emblems on the breast, pastel belts embroidered with whales and three-woods. The moms would be overdressed in whatever summer attire had just arrived in the boutiques of Wellesley or Annapolis, and they would ask the players about their girlfriends, or in this case boyfriends, or maybe it didn't matter anymore.

But as we steered our kids between the Thatches' garage (formerly a farmhouse) and the house (formerly a barn) and made our way onto the backyard (really a long shimmering meadow that humped down to the river over a series of small hills like an off-season ski slope) it became clear that Ed had taken the concept of "pre-game reception" in a whole new direction. What we were stumbling into was more like a spectacular Midcoast-themed carnival. There was a train of folding tables dressed in purple gingham tablecloths, a trailer-length grill blowing smoke into the sky, and a massive white tent strung with yards and yards of hanging lightbulbs. There was even an inflatable lobster the size of an elephant (where had Ed procured it? I had no idea. I assumed he must have stolen it from some boarded-up state fair). Someone had wedged a lacrosse stick in the lobster's left claw, and visitors were taking pictures of each other standing next to it as if they had slain the poor thing. The rest of the meadow was overtaken by players, parents, and coaches, all of them wearing purple.

"Can we play in the bouncy castle?" Jane asked, our daughter, seven years old at the time.

"What bouncy castle?"

She pointed in the direction of an overinflated lobster trap—another carnival prop I never could have conceived of—bursting with children, all flopping around and jamming each other's heads between the pontoons.

"Yes," Maeve said. "But bring your brother. And don't touch anyone if they look sick. Like if they have a runny nose, stay away."

"Stranger danger!" Jack said, age six.

"That's something else, Jack," Jane said.

"You're something else, *Jane*."

"Go," Maeve said. "Have fun."

The kids ran at the trap, and Maeve and I headed for the tent. We passed a table at the edge of the lawn, where I picked up a brochure proclaiming Damariscotta to be Maine's "Vacation Haven" (Steph Thatch's new marketing slogan, part of a rebranding effort, more on this later), and then we waded through the small clusters of guests, saying hello to anyone we knew—our accountant, our kids' pediatrician, our sheepish realtor—all of whom looked a little confused by the surrounding festivities but willing to go with the flow in exchange for an open bar—until a man wearing a Hawaiian shirt over a turtleneck, the school superintendent I soon learned, corralled our marital unit and asked my permission to talk shop.

"About what?" I said.

"No, no," he said, "with Maeve."

Maeve runs a not-for-profit called EduVerse that empowers students to write poems about their own lives (here's a stanza I found on the kitchen table recently: *So many seagulls around the parking lot / It's like a party for seagulls / If you have a bike you can bike right through em / But they'll just fly away / They'll be back to eat your trash someday*), and once the superintendent had thanked Maeve for all the fine work she'd done in the county's middle schools, he asked her how she might feel about expanding the program. Maeve would be very interested in expanding the program, she said, squeezing my hand in silent apology. This felt like my cue to slip away for a beer, so I waited until the superintendent wasn't looking and mouthed *Good luck* to Maeve who mouthed *Get me something, too*, so I mouthed *Okay, what?* and she mouthed *White wine, actually, no, I could go for a beer* and by now the superintendent was looking again, so I said, out loud, "I'm on it," and went hunting for the bar.

I found it in one corner of the tent, next to a raised platform where Maine's most famous all-white reggae band was just starting to plug in its amps. The bartender handed me two Shipyards, both wrapped in purple cocktail napkins with the Amherst crest on one side, crossed lacrosse sticks on the other, and I thanked him and apologized because I didn't have any cash for a tip, before following a trail of tiki torches down toward the river, where the fog was just beginning to snake along the shoreline, drafting north from the ocean. All of this land I had gazed upon many times, but always from the river, always from someone else's boat. The house was high on a hill. Pines lined the northern flank of the meadow. Birches lined the southern flank. The grass was freshly mown. There was a new dock. I was hoping to take a look at Ed's old lobster boat, recently converted into a pleasure cruiser with roaring twin engines, rumored to hit speeds northward of fifty knots, this overhaul, in total, rumored to cost northward of two-fifty—

But I never made it that far. Instead I ran into Steph Thatch. Ed's wife. Our mayor. Town manager was her official title, but she called herself the mayor, and we all followed suit, feeling like the difference was trivial and she'd pretty much earned the right anyway. She was marching up from the dock, rising through the grass in black rain boots and tight blue jeans. She wore a gray flannel shirt and a down vest, the better part of a dead coyote serving as a hood. The garments were trimly cut, unzipped or unbuttoned to her freckled breastbone, her brown hair bedazzled with blond highlights. She said hello and asked if I had seen her husband, which I hadn't.

"Well, either we launch this thing or we don't," Steph said.

"Which thing?"

She pointed to the steaming, barrel-shaped smoker where the Dodwells, a brother-sister catering duo, also operators of the town's only taxi, were prodding at a mound of wet seaweed.

"You see any lobster?" Steph asked me.

"I can't tell from here."

"That's because they're still in the river," she said. "Ed insisted on supplying them himself."

"As he would," I said.

Steph looked dubious.

"Since he's a lobsterman," I added.

"Of course he's a lobsterman. Was a lobsterman. He wears a lot of hats, you know. He's been busy. This reception means the world to him. It's nice you're here. Great turnout, actually. I just worry he takes too much crap."

"Takes it, or takes it on?"

"Takes it on."

I had no idea if this was true. Ed struck me as the kind of rural titan who's come far enough in life to turn himself into a man of leisure, but perhaps that was only in my own dealings with him, which mostly concerned Allie's lacrosse career.

"He and Chuck already filled three traps and put them in the river," Steph said. We were standing in the steepest part of the meadow, so she had to brace a hand on her uphill knee to hoist herself to my level. "We're supposed to go out on the boat, and the girls are supposed to help them haul the lobster. I should have stopped him. It's just too much."

I looked at a few of the young women, talking and laughing with their parents. "I bet they'll enjoy going out on the water," I said.

"Oh, they'll love it," Steph said. "But only if we go now. Otherwise, we've got issues." She looked behind her at the sky, which was continuing its sweep toward gray, and then she waved at a woman in a periwinkle cashmere sweater, who waved back. "Who the hell are you," Steph muttered through a smile, just loud enough for me to hear, before taking off in the woman's direction, calling as she went, "We didn't know if you'd make it!"

I sipped my beer. The challenge would be to drink just one. I wasn't worried so much about getting drunk, although I probably would, more about putting on weight, which I already had. Right around then—as I turned my gaze upon the other men in the field—I realized there was a service I could provide, a way to contribute to the gathering. I would search the premises for Ed, let him know that his presence had been requested.

At first I couldn't find him anywhere. He wasn't in the meadow, wasn't in the tent, wasn't amongst any of the boosters. Perhaps he was in the house—the hulking former barn with deck appended to the river side, shingles new enough to hold only the slightest shade of ash, trim painted forest green. Steph had hired contractors from up the coast, blasted out all the old stable walls, pumped the roof full of skylights. I liked the look quite a lot.

The inside, too. This I saw as I cupped my hands to the glass doors on the deck. I was impressed by the openness and vastness of it all. From background to foreground: an industrial-strength kitchen, a high and wide stone fireplace, a living room carefully decorated in rustic antiques—black metal, raw wood, antler chandelier, vintage telescope, vintage map of the Midcoast. On the coffee table was a live—no, a stuffed—fox in an action pose, facing me and snarling. The voices of the party were beyond earshot now, so behind me I heard only a gull, the wind, and what sounded like a murmuring brook. I couldn't detect any movement inside, but then I noticed a presence, an almost completely still presence, something—or someone—who didn't quite fit. Ed. Wherever he went, the ocean went with him, and I could sense it, even through the glass: the salt in his beard, the mud beneath his nails. He was sitting in a chair in the middle of the room, in his socks, rubber boots upright next to his feet, leaning back, his hands on the squared-off leather arms. His head was cast downward, possibly at the table next to his chair, but with his hat blocking my view, I couldn't tell for sure. I was about to knock on the glass when he shifted his gaze toward mine. For a moment we eyed each other through the door, and I felt caught.

"Hey, Ed," I said, sliding the door open.

"How we doing, Andy."

"Doing well. Thanks for having us."

I was expecting him to say something more, but he didn't, so I stood silently and he sat silently as the band launched into a cover of something familiar. They were down the hill and out of sight. "Enter Sandman" set to a reggae beat—that was it.

"Quite the party," I said. "Allie's team looks good. No wonder they're kicking ass this year."

"Yuh," he said. He spoke with a heavy Maine accent, a guttural dialect that inflected even the shortest of phrases.

A moment passed.

"Steph's looking for you," I said.

This got Ed moving, but only slowly. He reached across the armrest and flipped what looked like a manila folder from open to shut. He pulled on one boot, then the other, and pressed against the arms of the chair to lift himself to a standing position, stiffly at first, then loosening up, like a bear hitching itself onto its hind legs. I'm not short, but Ed had me by a couple inches. He was always looking down from beneath the visor of a cap, an oily thumbprint on the bottom of each brim. Since I'd known him, he'd regularly worn what you might expect from someone who grew up on the southern tip of the peninsula with a UFO-sized satellite dish in the front yard and a deconstructed snowmobile in the back—diesel-stained jeans, hooded sweatshirt, dirty baseball cap—but on this day, the hat and hoodie matched, both purple, both with AMHERST LACROSSE printed in bold white letters across the chest or crest. The sweatshirt had been knifed at the collar to make room for a thick black beard. I had thought he'd be jovial today, excited about the reception—it was as close as the Thatches would ever come to a debutante ball: his daughter, their family, officially accepted by the suburban elites who'd been paying private school tuitions and club team fees since their daughters were all in kindergarten together— but that wasn't the vibe.

He came to the door and removed the second beer, the one intended for Maeve, from my grip. He raised one eyebrow as a way of showing gratitude, then slugged the whole thing. When he was done, he burped and said, "You sure Steph was looking for me? Not EJ?" EJ was Ed and Steph's son, Allie's older brother.

I thought back. Steph had definitely been looking for Ed. "She said Ed," I said.

"That's good."

For another long moment Ed didn't say anything, and I thought we might have reached the end of the conversation, but then he said, "Now, Andy." He turned toward me. "What the *hell* kind of name is Trip?"

I was at a loss and told him so.

He repeated himself, but *Trip* meant nothing to me. "Trip?" I asked. "With one *p*?"

"Don't know," Ed said. "You're the English teacher."

This was true enough, but it was in my capacity as lacrosse coach that I had come back into contact with Ed when I returned to town, and I couldn't remember any other instance when he'd acknowledged the other half of my job title.

"Hang on," he said, frowning, thinking back. "Yuh. It was one P."

"Okay, so most likely, that's a diminutive form of 'Triple.'"

"Triple?"

"Yeah, like, 'the Third,'" I said. "For example, your son is Edward, Junior, and therefore—"

"No, he ain't. He's Everett Joseph. People just think he's a junior."

"Oh," I said. "Well, if he were a junior, you could call him Chip, like 'Chip off the old block.' And if he were a third, you could call him Trip. And if he were a fourth—" I hesitated. "Actually, I don't even know what you would call him then."

Ed scratched at his beard but no longer looked interested in discussing thirds, fourths, fifths—none of the above. For whatever reason, my etymology lesson had set him at ease.

"So who is he?" I asked.

"Who's who?"

"Trip. The person you just asked me about."

Ed smiled and put his hand on my trapezius muscle, squeezing hard enough to make me wince. "Must be about them lobsters," he said. It took me a second to gather that he was referencing the original premise of our conversation—why his wife might have been looking for him—but before I could respond, he removed his hand from my neck and walked right by me; past the inlaid hot tub (this had been the source of the brook-like noises, I now realized, also the source of the previously undocumented chlorine odor) and down the stairs to the meadow, disappearing into the crowd and the fog.

The weather had overtaken the grass by then, muting the forms of the parents and the young women who in their purple sweaters and pullovers had spread across the field and under the tent as naturally as a dash of wild lupines. It was the type of ghostly dusk that comes to the Midcoast every spring, a swirl of smoke and light, the river air at once warm and chilling, weather that can fill the sky with a sense of change—what kind of change, I can never tell.

Somewhere in the back of my mind, the paternal clock ticked—I should check in on the kids and find Maeve another beer—but instead I found myself glancing inside the house, then out at the fog, then back into the house.

I'm not sure what gave me the courage to go inside—perhaps I felt invisible, shrouded by the weather—but the next thing I knew, I was sliding the door closed behind me, and then I was alone in the Thatches' home, standing next to a waist-high vase of pussy willows.

I began to work my way around the great room, passing the windows overlooking the meadow, the fireplace, then a table topped with framed family photos (EJ as a thirteen-year-old with an overgrown crew cut and a blank stare, oblivious to the laser show going on behind him; Allie in a purple headband with a lacrosse stick resting on her shoulder; the whole family on Ed's boat, rails gleaming in the sun, everyone dressed in suits and summer dresses). I peeked into the kitchen, as spotless and dimly lit as an after-hours showroom, and eventually made my way toward the center of the space, beneath the high oak beams, around the taxidermied fox on the coffee table, angling between the couches arranged in a U before the fireplace. Above the fireplace was a flat-screen TV and above the flat-screen was a massive moose head with towering antlers and glassy black eyes.

Next to Ed's chair was a table with a copper top. On the table was a manila folder, which I had seen Ed flip shut. Thick block letters on the folder read LINCOLN COUNTY SHERIFF'S OFFICE OFFICIAL DOCUMENTS, and underneath was the department's circular seal.

EJ Thatch, Ed and Steph's son, was an officer with the Damariscotta Police Department, not with the county, although the distinction wouldn't have occurred to me at the time. I just assumed the folder came from EJ. Family business. Definitely not my business. But I couldn't help myself. Whatever was inside the folder had been occupying Ed's mind, and I wanted to know what it was. I don't know how many of my neighbors would have done what I did, but I'm sure they all would have felt the urge. It wasn't just the open bar that had brought us to the reception, after all. We weren't friends with the Thatches. The Thatches didn't have friends.

Using only one finger, slowly lifting the edge of the folder—as if the fewer digits I employed, the less guilty I might be—I splayed the file open on the table. Inside were several photos. Eight by ten. I turned over the first and saw what used to be a sedan. It was parked in a lot, an abandoned mill in the background, half the building's windows missing, graffiti at the base of every smokestack. The pavement beneath the sedan was blacker than all the other pavement. The car's frame was charred and collapsed upon itself, shrunken like a dead insect. It was a police photograph, so evinced a perceptible, almost blatant, disregard for composition. The car was nearly centered in the photograph, but not quite. The horizon line was off by a few degrees. The light was too bright.

I flipped to the next picture, and the next. The first showed the trunk of the car. The second showed the backseat. In each case, I had the impression that what I was looking at was nothing more than the burned-out husk of a vehicle. Everything was black and shapeless. But then I noticed a little pink in each photograph. Flesh. The skin of a burn victim, peeling off a skull or a clavicle. Now I could see: The car contained two bodies, both incinerated. I couldn't tell whether either soul had been dead before the flames had hit the skin, but it wouldn't have changed how I felt about the pictures; the sight was horrific, and I could sense almost viscerally the moment when the fire had sucked whatever last breath remained from the lungs.

I couldn't look a moment longer—I regretted ever setting foot in the house—so I shut the folder and took a step back; I did it quickly, barely thinking, as though the photographs themselves were generating unbearable heat.

AN HOUR LATER I WAS in the meadow, helping my children learn to throw and catch a lacrosse ball, half my mind still stunned by the images, when I heard sirens up the hill. I looked to the driveway—we all did—just as a line of state police cruisers burst from the woods, lighting the fog blue, then red, then blue.

1

WITH MY PARENTS' ARRIVAL ON THE MIDCOAST IN THE WINTER OF 1978, my dad became the only orthopedic surgeon in the county, which made us one of the richest families around, although to be "rich" in Damariscotta is to be middle class almost anywhere else. None of the locals have, or had, much money. We lived in a two-bedroom cottage, and my parents shared one yellow Volvo in those early days. Once I was old enough to go to school, my mom started going, too, studying art in Portland, accounting in New Hampshire, then forestry in Vermont. After she earned her degree, she found a job organizing weekend retreats hosted by a Penobscot named Jerry Crowfoot, the type of boondoggle where you made lodgings out of pine boughs, stripped deer hide from the carcass, ate like natives ate, et cetera. They made you camp next to a paper mill and you had to pretend you couldn't see the smokestacks or smell the sulfur. I was always bored. I mean, all my childhood—I begged for siblings, pleaded to move back to the suburbs of Boston—but especially on those Indian weekends.

During one of the retreats, one that my dad was also forced to attend, he and I made a lacrosse stick out of branches, buck intestines, and straw. He had played lacrosse, like I would someday, at Dartmouth. Neither of us expected the stick to become anything more than ornamental, but somehow it could throw and catch without completely turning to tinder, and I still have the stick—it hangs on the wall of my classroom, between the whiteboard and the window.

As we played catch—I must have been seven or eight—my dad said, "I'm sorry your mom and I have been fighting so much."

This was not something I had noticed, so I didn't respond. I just threw the ball back in his direction. He caught it.

"Anyway, you don't have to worry," he said. "We'll figure it out."

"Okay," I said.

The assumption was always that I'd stay in Damariscotta and attend Lincoln High School, but Lincoln didn't have a hockey team and I was outgrowing my club team in Augusta, so during my freshman year, I started applying to boarding schools and eventually gained acceptance to Phillips Exeter Academy. As a way of celebrating, my mom and dad told me they were getting divorced—although the coeval nature of our family's upheaval and my departure was, I'm pretty sure, a coincidence. I repeated my freshman year at Exeter, which put me on a different trajectory from my friends back home, and after that I always felt a little out of sync with everything I left behind, everyone who stayed on the Midcoast, like a severed trap marker that comes and goes on the tides, never finding the old block that once tied it to the river-bottom—not that I ever really missed the feeling of being chained to a place.

After the divorce, my mom took the position of general manager at a general store overlooking the South Bristol Gut, the narrow waterway that links our river to the one to the east. South

Bristol is populated in the winter almost entirely by lobstermen and their families, but in the summer it's close enough to Christmas Cove to semi-support the kind of store my mom ran— a place that sold imported cheese, charcuterie, *The New York Times*, wine that wasn't necessarily named after its varietal. I helped her there on summer afternoons, digging out ice cream, filling out crossword puzzles, and reading books like *A Farewell to Arms* and *Catch-22*, novels my favorite English teachers had recommended at the end of spring classes. Did I complain about the indignity of working for my mother? Yes. Yes, I did. But even then I had to admit—only to myself, obviously—that life could be worse because at least I was allowed to sleep in—

But then I caught a bad break: Tracey Thatch, Ed's mom, had her knee replaced. By my dad. Apparently he—Dad—had been observing my pathetic work ethic and so by the time he stopped by Tracey's hospital room in mid-June for a routine post-op consultation had already determined that his son's employment would be bargained off as a thank-you to the Thatches for allowing him to bill them for his services. The Thatch Lobster Pound was where my dad always stopped to fuel up his fishing boat, and it sat on a petrified forest of sea-stained pilings, on the other side of the harbor from my mother's general store, staring across like an old cranky seagull drying its wings. My dad knew precisely how convenient the new arrangement would be. And I understood, even then, that a real job, a hard job, was supposed to forge something substantial in me.

ON THAT FIRST DAY, I reported as a bleary-eyed fifteen-year-old to a disjointed collection of gray buildings that toppled down the harbor bank and leveled out at the dock. Dawn hadn't even happened yet. The pier was wide enough to hold trucks that would back across the planks, load up, then drive straight to Boston or New York or anywhere else on the planet that featured Maine lobster on the menu. The Thatches owned the Pound and had for generations, but it was Ed—the elder of Wade and Tracey's two sons, a tall boy who wore tie-dyed T-shirts and baseball hats you could only get if you sent away the required number of proofs-of-purchase from cigarette cartons—who pretty much ran the place. He was lanky then but already strong. He could toss ninety-pound crates around the dock the way I could throw baskets of dirty laundry downstairs to the basement.

On the morning I met him, there was no sun; the only light at the Pound came from a piss-colored lamp bolted atop the end of the pier. I found Ed in the process of coiling the diesel hose. "Andy, right?" he said.

"Andrew."

He finished making a perfectly circular stack of hose. Then he kicked it to make it pounce open and untangle like an angry snake.

"Now you do it," he said.

"Do what?"

"Coil her up."

"How?"

"Didn't you just watch me?"

I took the nozzle and started winding it in a circle, but it was rigid to my touch and wouldn't go where I wanted it to.

"Nope," he said.

I tried to wind it in the other direction.

"Still nope."

"What am I doing wrong?"

"The whole damn thing."

He took the hose, coiled it again, taking pains to demonstrate how one ought to make a twisting motion with every loop, and then he told me it was time to blast out the bait shed.

Once inside the walk-in freezer, I stood ankle deep in a pool of blood and salt, shivering in my borrowed rubber boots as Ed tipped over the half-full barrels of redfish. It was the foulest room I had ever set foot in, all that waste redolent of a grisly mass homicide, but when I glanced across at Ed, he was grinning back at me while hosing a spray of clean water into a pool of roiling bloody water. "Hope you ate breakfast," he said. Then he shoved over a full barrel of bait and watched the guts splash onto my jeans and all the way up to my fleece. "Sorry bout that, Andy."

Eventually Ed taught me how to bend at the knees while lifting lobster crates off the boats, and how to patch these crates when their wooden slats busted loose, but he always acted aggrieved by my perpetual ignorance, as if these skills were ones I should have intuited as an infant, so I despised the lessons and I despised the job, every moment of it. That Ed could work for hours on end for such paltry wages, at the age of, what, fourteen or fifteen, taking breaks only to patrol the river on his little skiff and haul his own traps without ever once bitching about the crappiness of it all, I took as evidence that there was something seriously wrong with him.

Naturally, I began devising ways to minimize my hours at the Pound. After my sophomore year, I started staying at school to work as a gopher at the hockey camp, spending more and more time away from home, the academic year plus the middle of the summer. And after my junior year, I decided I couldn't handle another round of grunt work, so in June of '92 I went to the Pound and told Wade Thatch that I regretted the decision already, but it was time for me to retire.

"Ed handles the dockhands," he said.

"Well, okay, but—"

"You gotta talk to Ed."

So I went looking for Ed. He was seventeen then. He had reached his full height, his shoulders straight across, his arms lean as rebar.

"I don't think I can work this summer," I told him. It was early morning, and I had found Ed by the water, smoking a cigarette, fixing a hatch in the dock that served as portal to the briny underworld.

"Going back to New Hampshire?" he asked, cigarette nodding as he spoke.

"I am, yeah. Just doesn't make sense—starting here when I have to leave after three weeks. Probably easier for you if you just find someone who can work the whole summer."

Ed slammed a final nail into the dock, then stood straight with hammer still in hand. He tugged at the brim of his cap and looked out at the harbor. The sun was warming the backs of the birches on the far side of the South Bristol Gut, and as soon as it rose above the tree line, the morning would get hot, you could feel it.

" 'Magine," Ed said.

'Magine was a local derivation of "I imagine that's so," but Ed always said it flatly, possibly sarcastically. Which made it hard to respond. Especially when I had already said all I needed to say. So we stood in silence, until the alarm on the swing bridge began to clang and echo across the waterway. I looked over the lobster buoys and between the fishing boats to the bridge. The road was slowly splitting apart and swiveling open, making way for a sport boat that gurgled into the harbor on its own rippling wake.

The boat arced toward the dock, growing larger and larger, louder and louder, her stern sliding into view. She was called the *Reel Beaut II,* and she hailed from Falmouth. She wasn't a big rig, but there were twin outboards on the back which filled the whole channel with a steady rumble until the hull bumped into the dock and the helmsman cut the engines. He was in his midforties, wearing old leather Top-Siders, blue jeans, a Harley-Davidson T-shirt. He had a long black ponytail. On the stern, ready to toss us a line, was a girl about our age with a deep tan that seemed otherworldly, the kind of skin you never see in Maine. She was wearing a Baja jacket with stripes the colors of a Jamaican flag and cut-off jean shorts that were shorter than their own pockets. Her hair was gathered in a loose ponytail, and everything about her looked thrown together, as though she'd just slid out of bed.

"Hello?" she said, holding up the docking line.

"Yeah, hello," I said.

"Are you gonna catch this or what?"

"Well, that's a pretty loaded question."

"What?"

On the one hand, I didn't want to work at the Pound, or even look like I was working at the Pound. On the other, it was unspeakably rare that a strange young woman arrived in our part of the universe and engaged in conversation. "Actually," I said, "yeah, toss it to me."

"Fine, weirdo, here it comes." She threw the line and it hit me in the face; I gathered it and tied it to a cleat.

Ed watched me secure the knot, making sure I did it right, and then asked the man—the girl's father, I assumed—how he was doing.

"Oh, we're doing fine," the man said. "This morning's a real beaut, ain't she?"

"Your dad has a catchphrase?" I whispered to the girl.

She ignored me.

"Mind filling us up?" the dad asked.

"Don't mind at all," Ed said. But he didn't budge. Instead

he swung his gaze in my direction, waiting, daring me to work. "How bout it, Andy?"

The sun had crested the tops of the trees, and the girl was taking off her Baja layer, the tank top underneath getting caught in the process and lifting up and exposing her tan belly and a belly-button stud and even the bottom of a purple bra cup before she realized what was happening and tugged at the shirt to get it back in position.

"All right," I said to Ed. "Just this once."

Ed asked the man if he needed anything else, any ice for his coolers, and the man said a half-dozen bags would be great, thanks, so Ed went up the ramp to the office, leaving me alone on the dock with the girl and her dad.

I flipped the lever on the pump and uncoiled the hose effortlessly; it had only taken me two full summers to master the pull-and-twist technique. Then I dragged the hose over to the intake valve on the boat's gunwale, unscrewed the cap, and started pumping.

"That kid's your boss?" the girl asked. She was looking up in Ed's direction, even though he'd vanished inside the shack where the ice machine was.

"Who, Ed?" I asked.

"Is that his name?"

"Yeah."

"Ed's your boss then."

"More like a former colleague."

"Sure," she said, blowing at her hair.

The pump was clicking away, its numbers spinning upward. "So you're from Falmouth?" I asked.

"Yup."

"You go to Falmouth High School?" I asked.

"Yeah. Or did. Going to Lincoln in the fall. We're moving."

"Are you?"

"Yup."

"Why?" I asked.

She took a deep breath, and—even though this conversation was not going particularly well—I could tell I'd finally broken her. She'd be forced to explain herself using a full sentence now, maybe multiple full sentences. "My dad just inherited the Schooner," she said. "You know the restaurant at the end of Main Street in Damariscotta? That's ours now. He wants me to work there."

I nodded, trying to decide if she was speaking with a Maine accent, thinking she did, changing my mind, changing it again. Her r's and ing's sounded just slightly blunted.

"You're around all summer though?"

I may have hit the word *all* a little too hard because she arched a brow. "I'm not," she said. "This is like a last-day-we're-together, father-daughter bonding trip. We're going fishing. Which apparently can only happen if you wake up at four in the morning."

"And then where do you go?"

"New Hampshire. That's where my mom lives."

I couldn't believe it. She was going to New Hampshire. *I* was going to New Hampshire. "I go there every summer, too," I said, "and my parents are also divorced. Which is unrelated, but yeah. Crazy."

"What's crazy?"

"Just the coincidence."

"Oh."

"I work at a hockey camp," I said.

"What?"

"The Exeter Hockey School. That's why I go to New Hampshire."

"Ah."

I allowed for any follow-up questions—there weren't any—
and then asked where her mom lived.

"Keene."

I had heard of the town but didn't know where in New
Hampshire it was. "Is that close to Exeter?"

"I don't think so."

"Exeter is also where I go to school."

"Got it."

For the next few minutes we waited silently until the pump
clunked to a stop. "Well, I guess this is goodbye," I said.

"Don't we have to pay?"

"Yes. You do. Sorry." She gave me two twenties and I ducked
into the shed. I opened the cash box, but there was no change.
They were the day's first paying customers. All the fishermen
paid on credit. I stepped back outside, held up the twenties and
said, "I just have to make change."

"You do that," she said as I jogged toward the ramp.

Ed was trudging downward from the office, in the direction
of the boat, and we passed each other at the halfway point. He
was holding seven or eight bags of ice, his forearms bulging at
the veins. "I'm just getting change," I said.

"Ruthless," he said.

I made it to the main building, climbed upstairs to the office,
went looking for either of Ed's parents but instead found Chuck,
Ed's younger brother, fifteen years old, about to enter eighth
grade with a full mustache, powering through a set of biceps
curls, hoisting a twenty-five-pound dumbbell from waist to chin,
over and over. He had red hair and one long eyebrow that dipped
in the middle and made him look constantly angry, which he was.
I told him I needed to make change for a customer. The office
was really just an unfinished attic, and the roofline went down
and met the floor on both sides. The windows were more like

skylights, but you could see out the front, to the parking lot, and out the back, to the dock.

"Thought you weren't working this summer," Chuck said.

"Who told you that?"

"Ed."

"How?"

"How what?"

"Did he already tell you that I wasn't working this summer?"

"He's smart like that." He went to the desk at the center of the attic and handed me the cash box. "Smarter than you, I bet."

I counted out the appropriate number of bills and coins, mumbled my thanks, then hustled to the stairs, through the office, across the pier, and down the ramp. But when I landed on the dock, Ed was standing next to the boat, talking with the girl, who suddenly looked a lot more interested in making conversation. I stopped running. The girl handed something to Ed, which I assumed was a tip (my tip!), and then he pointed to the east, where the sun was growing brighter above the horizon, a subtle glow spreading across the ocean. Ed spoke loud enough for the father to hear him over the engines, which were gurgling away again: ". . . and if you head out toward Monhegan, when you're just about to the lighthouse, you'll see Inner Duck Rock poking out of the water. Right beyond that's where you'll find the best stripers this time of year."

I arrived behind Ed holding $7.50. He turned, held out his hand. I gave him the money. He gave it to the girl.

"Much appreciated, Ed!" the father yelled down.

Ed touched his hat brim and gave the boat a push. I wanted to yell *Wait*—but if anyone had asked me *For what?* I wouldn't have been able to come up with an answer. The father saluted and cut the wheel, making a big loop through the harbor, and then several long minutes later the boat was shrinking between the rocks and the pines and the girl was looking back in our direction. I waved while Ed lit another Camel. "Better get ready for that bait truck," he said.

And so I helped him get ready for the bait truck. It seemed pointless to argue. I would quit when it was time to go to hockey school.

THAT LAST SUMMER AT THE Pound, all I had to do was survive three weeks of working as a dockhand, then I could go to New Hampshire, and then a year after that I'd be off to college. I felt so close to finally escaping Maine, to launching into the real part of my life. There was nothing left for me to do at home. We had three radio stations on the Midcoast, and only one of them played anything new, the worst of pop. There were things we lacked that I didn't even know I needed: conversations about art, diversity in worldview, people of color. I was getting some of this, plenty of this, at Exeter, but I was anxious to keep going, to make good on the call to greatness that every guest speaker reminded us of in our morning assemblies.

Perhaps because I was getting better at daydreaming myself into some other existence, the June days passed slowly but not quite as slowly as they once had; the crates felt a little lighter than they used to, and I barely even noticed the bait shed's murder stench anymore. So I was feeling satisfied and on the verge of freedom when, on my last Friday as an employee of the Pound, I went to collect my paycheck in the office. Ed tossed it on the desk. He was leaning back in a metal swivel chair, yellow foam bursting from the cushions.

"See ya in August," he said.

"I doubt that."

"Well, see ya next summer then."

"I think I'm done here, Ed."

"That's what they all say."

"Who's 'they'?"

"You know."

"I'm the only employee who's not related to you by blood or marriage."

"Maybe you'll marry my sister."

"Do you even have a sister?"

He did not, but before he had a chance to confirm or deny, give me whatever bullshit answer he wanted to give me, we heard a loud noise outside, like a small car crash. We looked through the open front skylights and saw that a post office vehicle was parked next to the mailbox, actually touching the mailbox, which was off-kilter, apparently as a result of the collision. I watched as the postman leaned out of the Jeep and stuffed the mailbox full of letters. He seemed unaware that he'd rammed anything, or maybe this was simply his modus operandi.

"Dammit," Ed said, dropping his feet to the floor. I figured he was upset about the listing mailbox, so his next move surprised me: He yanked open a desk drawer, removed a small package, and bolted for the door.

"What's that?" I asked, but he was already bounding down the stairs.

By the time I made it outside, the Jeep was chugging over the hill, trailing a brown cloud of exhaust, and Ed was cursing at it.

"God fuckin dammit," he said.

"What's the matter?"

"Wanted to get this package in the mail. That mailman never frickin waits."

"So bring it to the post office," I said.

"Chuck's out on the water and my folks aren't home. Can't leave the place unattended."

I shrugged. "I can bring it to the post office for you."

He eyed me, deciding on something, maybe how much he trusted me, probably not much.

"It's no big deal," I said. "I pass it on my way out of town."

"No, you don't."

"Close enough."

He scratched at his chin. He hadn't grown the beard yet, but perhaps he was already planning to. "All right," he said finally, "but this is important, Andy. Don't fuck it up."

"I won't fuck it up," I said, holding out my hand. "It'll be my final duty as employee of the Thatch Lobster Pound. I'll do it with pride."

He deliberated for another long moment, then handed me the box. It was small and light and wrapped in what used to be a paper grocery bag. I tossed the package along with my paycheck through the open window of my car.

"Careful," Ed said.

"I will be. Don't worry." We shook hands. "It's been a pleasure working with you, Ed."

"*For* me," he said. "You worked for me, not with me."

I WOULD HAVE STOPPED AT the post office in South Bristol, but Ed was right—it wasn't on my way—and I figured I could just drop the package in the mail when I got to Damariscotta. My windows were rolled down, the summer heat whipping in. I had to crank the volume to hear my Zeppelin tape over the wind. As I drove, I opened my paycheck, made sure I hadn't been shortchanged,

then glanced at Ed's little box. It was covered in stamps, and in
the top-left corner was Ed's name and the address of the Pound,
and in the middle of the package, it said:

> Stephanie LeClair
> 7 Woodland Ln
> Keene, NH 03431

At first the name and the address meant nothing to me, but
then I looked again—*Keene, NH*—and nearly drove off the road.
I recognized that town! I had never heard the name Stephanie
LeClair before, but I knew exactly who she was. Who she had to
be. The girl from the boat, the *Reel Beaut II.*

As I guided my car back between the lines, I tried to think: As
far as I knew, Ed had never met this girl—Stephanie, as I thought
of her then, Steph as I think of her now—before she arrived at
the Pound that day. I had been the one who did most of the talking, at least until Ed and I swapped places. And yet somehow he
had procured her name . . . and engaged in some kind of long-
distance correspondence with her? I picked up the package and
joggled it. The box made no noise. Nothing rattled.

On the dock, she had given something to Ed. In the moment,
I had thought it was a tip, but no, it couldn't have been. No one
doles out a tip before they've received their change. It must have
been a note with her name and address.

When I reached my driveway, I meant to continue on to the
Damariscotta post office, but I didn't. Instead I turned toward
home, and that night I started packing for hockey camp. I put
Ed's piece of mail in my duffel bag, telling myself I would send
it when I made it to New Hampshire. But that's not what I did.

———

THE PROBLEM WAS THAT AS soon as I arrived at camp, I stopped thinking about Ed or the package for Steph. Working in the dorm, skating late at night with the other counselors and coaches, I had too much on my mind to remember to finish the job I had promised to do. I shoved the box in a drawer when I unpacked all my clothes, then buried it under a sweatshirt that I rarely wore. Through July, then August, I lived my own life without thinking about Ed's until, one cool night toward the end of camp, I went digging for that sweatshirt and found the package. So much time had passed since Ed had given it to me—I suppose I felt guilty, but also that what was done was done. Stephanie LeClair was never going to get her present, if that was what it was. I held it for a moment, wondering what was inside, wondering why it was so light, and then I carefully unstuck the strips of tape and unfolded the brown paper flaps. I removed the lid of the box, the smell of the gift hitting me right away—like an old ship. A sweet smell. Inside was a piece of brown string. Twine. Ed had made Steph a bracelet.

My first impulse was to squeeze the jute in my hand, really squeeze it, like I could crush the thing into nonexistence, but all I managed to do was smear some wax into my fingertips. It was just a bracelet. Something small. And yet it brought about a feeling I mistook for derision. I shoved Ed's gift in my pocket, and then, on my way past a dumpster outside the hockey rink, I chucked it over the steel wall and heard it tap against a bag of trash. Which only made me feel worse. The bracelet *was* a big deal, at least to Ed—on some level, I knew this already—and now, all these years later, I can see why I allowed myself to get it wrong at the time: Ed had done well in a way that I never would have expected him to. His imagination had surpassed my own. He had proven that he could make something out of very little, whatever he had on hand, and when that's how you make something, some piece of you always goes into it, ends up deep in the fibers.

2

AFTER COLLEGE, I DROVE TO CALIFORNIA WITH MY DAD, DROPPED him off at LAX, and started sleeping on a friend-of-a-friend's couch, waiting for a Swedish personal trainer to move out, waiting to take his room. I lived in Santa Monica, close to the ocean, not far from the mountains, and lied my way into a job waiting tables at a Thai-inspired steak house. By day I worked on the novel I'd begun as an undergrad and soon landed an agent— actually an assistant to an agent—which was exciting for a minute or two, but the novel didn't sell, probably owing to the long musical interludes set in a fraternity basement. The screenplays didn't sell either. One of them was called *A Predilection of Things Past*. A producer friend told me it didn't feel like a movie. Or anything, really. Now I was turning twenty-seven and finding stray white hairs on my chest, and I could see myself working in restaurants forever, blissfully walking my dog (which I was yet to acquire but planned to acquire if all else failed) on the beach and drinking coffee with my neighbor every morning while gossiping about our other neighbors. But this sounded like a lonesome journey, and I could still hear all those guest speakers in Academy Hall calling us to greatness, so I applied to MFA programs and gained acceptance to an unranked art school in Manhattan (one year later, on the second try).

The plan was always to move back to LA after graduating, but one night in New York I was leaning against a folding table serving as an open bar when a poet wearing a leather jacket, or maybe a pleather jacket, arrived at my side and asked if I had a pen. I did have a pen. It was in my hand. I was making notes on a damp manuscript, revising a passage from a barely fictional short story about going hiking in Big Sur and getting poison oak everywhere—hands, face, nuts, *everywhere*. We were at the writing program's monthly reading salon, held in the design department's studio, so surrounding us was a ring of tall black windows and limbless mannequins. A skinny young novelist in a Mets cap was reading at the front of the room, and I was leaning against the bar because I had just had surgery on my foot and couldn't put weight on my right leg, but the pose may have accidentally made me look rebellious, like I had only shown up for the booze, like I had driven here in a Trans Am and wraparound shades.

"I'll give it right back," she said.

So I let her have the pen. It was from a Marriott where my dad and stepmom had stayed on a recent visit to the city, some of the letters smudged by sweat. Now it read: RIOTT.

"Why is it wet?" she asked.

"I'm sweating."

"Yeah, it's hot."

"And I'm reading next."

"Oh." She wiped the pen on her jeans, just above a large hole where I could see her thigh. The pleather jacket was cracked, and her hair was held up in a blond or brown bun—hard to tell

under the low studio lighting. She looked at me hard, not breaking eye contact, and placed her hand on my wrist. "You'll be
okay," she said.

I wanted to believe her—even if she had no idea what I was
about to read or if I was any good or if I had any kind of crip-
pling fear of public speaking, which I did. My heart had been
thumping all evening. We'd taken the same cross-genre lecture
on narrative point of view, this poet and I, and had accidentally
looked at each other once or twice when the professor's voice
cracked in excitement. I had looked away quickly. Now she was
standing right next to me. It really was hot in the studio. She took
off her jacket and tossed it on the table.

"Can I grab some paper, too?" she asked, biting the pen.

I tore off a corner, then watched as she scribbled a note.
Before long she'd filled up the scrap, and she tried to keep writing
on her left forearm, but it was too humid for her skin to take the
ink, so I tore off another corner, and she finished the note there.

"What are you writing?" I asked.

"I don't know," she said. "Probably nothing. Probably crap."

She folded the two scraps of paper and slid them into the
back pocket of her jeans. Both pockets were torn, a small swatch
of lavender underwear filling the hole in the denim on one side,
her poetry filling the hole on the other side.

She looked me over, then asked what happened to my foot.

"Surgery," I said.

"Why?"

"Old lacrosse injury."

"Ugh."

"It's all right—I was just running in from the faceoff wing
and—"

"No, I meant, 'Ugh, you played lacrosse,' but it's okay—we
all have our skeletons."

When she returned the pen, our fingers touched. "Maeve," she said.

"Andrew."

People were clapping now. My turn to read. I gathered my crutches, said goodbye, and limped to the front of the room, ready to read about my full-body rash.

WE WALKED TO SCHOOL TOGETHER, went to poetry readings, lived on a boat on Block Island one summer. I never moved back to LA. Instead we moved to Boston when I was offered a job by a prep school desperate for an English teacher who could coach two sports. Pretty soon we started having kids and couldn't afford Boston anymore. It's hard to raise a family in one of the country's most expensive cities on only a teacher's salary, a not-for-profit director's salary, and the handfuls of cash Maeve makes whenever a lit mag publishes her poetry (a sampling of recent titles: "Bread-Winning," "Indolent Man," and "Driving Down 95 into a Blue-Pink Sunset That Reminds Me of X"; I try not to take it personally), so we started thinking about moving even farther north, somewhere with a lower cost of living and community barn raisings, somewhere that might accept the grant Maeve had received for her poetry as a down payment on a house.

We were in the car—I don't remember where—maybe on 95, maybe the sunset was bluish-pink. I was driving. Maeve was in the passenger seat, looking through the window. Now I remember. We were driving past the many Dunkin' Donuts of Saugus, Mass., the kids passed out in the back, Jack only an infant. This was six years ago.

"We should just move to Maine," Maeve said.

I didn't love the idea of heading home, but Maeve made all the right points about living close to grandparents, free babysitting, an abundance of nature, so before long I was interviewing for a position at Lincoln High, and Maeve was researching any and all organizations on the Midcoast that sounded similar to the one she had been working for in Boston. There were none. This was good. No competition. Within weeks we were making an offer on the house by the salt bay. Several months after that, we were on our way through New Hampshire, heading over the bridge, passing the WELCOME TO MAINE sign that would once again signify a return to the homeland.

OUR INITIAL INTERACTIONS WITH THE Thatches came shortly after the move, with our clothes, books, bikes, lamps, and blenders still in their boxes, the walls of our bedrooms still rimmed in blue masking tape, rat traps on the lookout in every corner. Maeve was the first to make contact, this connection initiated by my dad, who by then had retired as an orthopedic surgeon but still served on the hospital's board of trustees and still roamed the hallways, making sure all the watercolors he'd painted and donated to the surgery wing were hanging straight. "If you want to get anything done in this town," he told Maeve, "there's only one person to talk to."

"Oh yeah?" she said. "Who would that be?"

"Steph Thatch."

We were in the old garage, stealing furniture for our living room as my dad supervised.

"Steph Thatch?" I said, holding an intricately mechanized folding chair built in the '60s, trying to place the name. It sounded vaguely familiar. "Is she related to Ed Thatch?"

"Married to him."

"*Married* to him? Wait—is this the Steph whose dad owns the Schooner?"

"Yup."

"And they're married?"

"Yup. They're like our own little power couple."

"But this has to be a joke," I said. "You're kidding, right?"

"I'm not."

"Huh," I said. "Wow."

"Wow?" Maeve asked me. "Why wow? Who is this person?"

"No one really," I said. "Steph moved here after I went away. It's just—I wasn't expecting Dad to say her name. Not as a person to know."

"*The* person to know," he corrected.

A few days later my dad sent a follow-up email to Maeve, cc'ing Steph, who replied in blue all-caps: WELCOME TO MAINE!! HAPPY TO HELP. She introduced Maeve to the principal of Great Salt Bay, the school I had attended from kindergarten through eighth grade, and then connected her with all the other elementary school principals on the peninsula and the district's superintendent.

Still, when an invitation to attend "A Celebration of Ed and Steph's Life Together" was extended just a few weeks later, we assumed it had been sent by accident. It was one of the first pieces of mail we had received, welcome-to-your-new-home coupons excepted. The invitation's stock was remarkably thick, the black ink rising from the paper like candle wax.

"Look," I said, holding up the card. "Your new BFF wants us to come to her party."

"Which BFF?"

"Steph Thatch."

"Let me see that," Maeve said. I handed her the invitation and she scanned it. "Yeah, see," she said, shaking her head, "she didn't invite me. Her husband invited you."

"Ed Thatch would never invite me to a party. He doesn't know who I am anymore."

"Well, it had to be him. Because this party's supposed to be a surprise for Steph. Says so right here. She doesn't even know about it."

ON THAT SATURDAY, WE DROPPED the kids off at my mom's and arrived at the Newagen Inn at 3:29, only a minute to spare. The inn is white, two stories, black shutters in neat rows. It sits atop a grassy hill overlooking rows of pines, a line of granite, then waves, then ocean, then islands. I was wearing my wrinkled cotton slacks and a linen blazer. Maeve was in a blue dress. She'd done her hair in two narrow braids, pinned them in back. We were cutting between oddly arranged picnic tables, each topped by a pastel runner, a large vase, a small geyser of wildflowers. There were bartenders in bow ties behind a table draped in white, shuckers in denim bibs getting ready to crack open a couple thousand oysters. It was a more staid—but every bit as elaborate—model of the lacrosse reception we would attend several years later.

"Good thing you made friends with Steph Thatch," I said as we walked down the hill beneath the inn.

"Or you stayed friends with Ed."

"Either way," I said, gesturing to the nearest flower arrangement, "this is insane."

"Is it?"

"Yeah—for around here? Totally over the top."

"I thought you said they don't come from much."

"They don't."

As we walked toward the gazebo that overlooked a flat strip of grass serving as gangway for the dock, I tried to count all the guests but soon gave up. It really did look as though all the county's residents, everyone other than Ed and Steph and their

two kids, were already in attendance. We made our way to the
back of the crowd, and a couple of older women who had the
floral-printed air of platonic life partners soon informed us that
the Thatches were on their way from South Bristol, riding in
the *Miss Stephanie,* and we could see the gray hull, once it was
pointed out to us, lifting and chopping through the swells. Word
traveled that Ed had convinced Steph that she should dress up
because he had hired a photographer to take family photos in
front of the inn on his newly refurbished boat. People passed
along the message as though Ed were some kind of sly old fox—
although the cover sounded pretty flimsy to me. Steph's mother,
who seemed to be in charge, raised her hands and told everyone
to quiet down please. Her bangs were split, half up, half down, in
a style that remains inexplicably popular in rural New England.
She glanced to sea, eyeing the boat as it sideswiped the dock,
then addressed us all. "Now when they come up the stairs," she
said, loud enough for those in the back to hear, "everyone yell,
'Surprise!' then start clapping like crazy."

"Oh," I said, under my breath, "so that's how a surprise
party works."

Maeve smiled but told me to go easy. We were guests here,
she reminded me, and we didn't know any of the others.

"I think I do though," I said. "I've just forgotten who they
are. That guy looks familiar. So does that guy. And I think that
other guy was a total asshole in fourth grade."

"Maybe you should have a beer," she said.

I decided she was right so snuck away to the bar, ordered one
IPA, one pinot grigio, and by the time I had returned to Maeve's
side, the Thatches had already tied their boat to the dock and
made their way up the stairs. Steph was wearing a linen shift with
a cashmere sweater tied around her shoulders. Ed was wearing
a beige suit and a sky-blue tie. I couldn't remember ever seeing

him without a hat on—this was a first—and the sun was bright enough on his side of the gazebo to narrow his eyes to a full squint. The beard was new to me, but from a distance, everything else about him looked the same. Neither his build nor his stride had changed in the twenty or so years since I'd last seen him. His son EJ was in a matching beige suit and matching tie, also squinting hard, but that's where the resemblance ended. EJ had no beard, his hair buzzed tight. He must have been about twenty at the time, not quite as tall as his father, but burly. His shoulders looked ready to burst through the seams of his jacket. Judging by the coat's buttons—all three fastened, even the bottom one, which strained to contain his lower abdomen—I'd venture to say that suits weren't a regular part of his wardrobe. His sister Allie, however, looked much more at ease. She was in a linen dress, like her mother. She was slender and walked with an athletic, almost bowlegged gait.

"Surprise!" everyone yelled.

Steph stopped, put her hands to her mouth, and started laughing, but the timing felt off—wouldn't she have sensed our presence as she made her way up the stairs?—and I wondered if she had known about the party all along. As we cheered and whistled, Ed stood behind his wife, pointing at her with one hand, asking us to make some noise with the other hand, flapping it up and down like a linebacker about to make a goal line stand. This was all for Steph, he seemed to want us to know. I couldn't tell if she looked exactly as she had when I first met her, or if I had just forgotten what she looked like as a teenager.

"Has she had work done?" Maeve asked.

"I don't know," I said, clapping but, with beer in hand, not producing much noise. "I don't know what's going on right now. I'm very confused."

A steel-drum island band began to play, the oysters were laid

on ice, a line formed there and at the bar, and within the hour I
was running into an old schoolmate, then another, then another.
This was the one looming function of the party I had been dread-
ing all week long, but now that all my former acquaintances were
telling me about their lives and showing me pictures of their children, I found that I was having a pretty good time. Our social
circle in Boston had been mostly limited to friends who, like us,
worked in education or academia, but now I was beginning to
imagine a more heterogeneous existence, drinking mudslides out
of the blender and telling off-color jokes with all kinds of people
who did all kinds of work. I heard myself volunteering to help
an old classmate on his lobster boat, subbing as a sternman if
he ever needed one. Then there was the second baseman on my
Little League baseball team, now a yoga instructor; Maeve and
I signed up for his vinyasa class. With another former classmate
I discussed the timeless tradition of hunting, and before long
we were agreeing that preservation and environmentalism were
really one and the same, and on these grounds, we ought to consider sportsmen when we go to rewrite the gun laws.

"So when are you planning to bring home a moose?" Maeve
asked, once we finally had a moment to ourselves, in line for the
steak-and-lobster buffet.

"When I feel like it," I said.

"Will you be purchasing a gun?"

"No."

"It's okay if you want one."

"I don't want one. Because I don't need one. Trevor's teaching me to bow hunt."

I began to load my plate, and it occurred to me that I didn't
really know what we were celebrating—Was it Ed and Steph's
anniversary? It must have been—but the specifics didn't seem
to be of concern to anyone else, so I moved on and focused on

the immaculate spread: filet, lobster, potato, clams, corn, corn bread . . . I piled a little of everything high on my plate until the paper began to buckle, and then Maeve and I found a picnic table with two open spots and, as fate would have it, the two guests we sat next to were Cammie Sweet and her husband Colin. I had gone to grade school with Cammie, always a year ahead, but didn't recognize her until she said my name, then introduced herself. As we became reacquainted, a few details started returning, among them that she had gone off to Amherst College—by coincidence the same school that Allie Thatch would one day attend—and when I asked her what had happened next, she said she'd graduated as an art history major, moved to New York, worked for an art gallery, then a branding agency where she slung razor blades and toilet paper, met Colin, had kids. Now they were reaching the point we had reached not so long ago, wondering if proximity to the trappings of city life was worth it if you never had the time or resources to take advantage.

They were yet to make the move (that was still a few months away), but they had come up for the event and taken a room at the inn, thinking they might hit a few open houses while in the area. As Maeve and Cammie spoke about local real estate, Colin turned to me and said, "You're friends with the Thatches?"

"Oh," I said. "Not really."

"Your wife then."

I laughed. "Not really. Sorry. We're just not that close. I worked a summer job with Ed in high school."

Colin gazed out at what was starting to look pretty idyllic in the late afternoon light, and I got the sense he was performing some kind of calculation, trying to decide how curious he should be. Colin is an okay guy, I can say now, for a wealth manager who attended Princeton and who has no problem identifying as socially liberal and fiscally conservative, and by okay guy, all

I mean is that he and I can stare at a grill together and drink decent beer and talk about how the meat's looking without too many long pauses. The placement of the picnic tables. Maybe that was what he was looking at. They weren't as haphazard as I'd thought. We were arranged in concentric rows, like orchestra seating, with the Thatches' table serving as our stage or pit. Ed, situated dead center, one arm resting on the back of Steph's chair, was staring back at us from an elevation, not so much as a ruler but as a lighthouse keeper, searching the oncoming waves for any sign of trouble, anyone who might be failing to have a good time.

"We've been having a lot of conversations about cost of living," Colin said.

"I bet," I said, stuffing my mouth with lobster.

"And what might be cheaper in Maine."

"Like huge parties."

"Like childcare. But yeah. Apparently also parties. Do you know how they're paying for this?"

"I don't," I said.

The family was seated entirely on one side of the long table, facing the rest of us, with Ed and Steph in the middle, grandparents to either side, and the two kids at the end closest to our picnic table. EJ was whispering something to Allie, and she was laughing. He had a highball in front of him, and he kept sliding it toward his sister, offering her a drink, and she kept sliding it back.

"What's he do?" Colin said.

"Ed?"

"Yeah."

I thought about it. "Not sure. Last I knew, he was a lobsterman. Steph runs her dad's restaurant."

"Cammie said they don't come from much."

"They don't."

After dinner, I unhitched myself from the bench, told Maeve I'd be right back, and wandered down to the cliff that overhung the ocean. I was a little drunk by then, and the time seemed right to spark the joint that had been waiting in the pocket of my blazer. I shielded it from the wind, lit it, took a hit, then stood by myself on a slippery shelf of white rock. I had been vaguely aware of the surf all afternoon, but now it was all I could hear. The cliffs were atomizing each wave, sending a fine mist into the air. The sun was sinking toward the horizon but still warm. A big roller dashed up a rocky chute, tumbled, slid toward me, and exploded. I finished my beer and, I don't know why, threw it into the next wave and watched the bottle smash into the rocks.

When I turned, I was looking at the dock, roughly a hundred yards away. Between the dock and the rest of the party were several scraggly pines, their branches thinned by ocean gusts. Tied to the dock was the *Miss Stephanie*—Ed's boat—and the sun was sparkling off the varnish and every stainless-steel rail. The hull looked freshly Awlgripped. The deck was trimmed with what looked like fine teak. It was, hands down, the nicest-looking lobster boat I had ever seen.

Ed was in the boat, talking with three people. By the red hair, I assumed that one of the men was Chuck, although it had been over two decades since I had last seen him. There was another man, the only sitting member of the party, who looked much older. His posture seemed to suggest poor health. I didn't recognize him. The fourth person in the boat I did recognize but couldn't place. She was wearing a bowling shirt, her hands tucked in the pockets of her cargo shorts, standing with a wide stance.

I wouldn't have thought anything of the scene, probably wouldn't even remember it, except that, just before I looked away, Ed glanced upward, toward the party, and waved at someone.

I followed the trajectory of his gaze to where one person was standing alone at the top of the bluff, next to the gazebo. It was Steph. Too great a distance stood between me and her to read the expression on her face, but the way her body was angled, her hands gripping the rail, led me to believe that she was upset about something. She didn't wave back. Instead she turned and walked away. For whatever reason, that gesture, or lack thereof, marked the end of my good time. The weed might have been a bad idea, I don't know.

I went back to the party, found Maeve, and we left soon after. On the way home, I realized that I hadn't thanked Ed or Steph, hadn't even said hello.

3

IT DIDN'T TAKE LONG FOR CAMMIE AND COLIN TO BECOME OUR CLOS-
est friends. We had plenty in common, all new to the area and
therefore regarded warily by the locals, even if one half of
each couple had grown up on the Midcoast. We had kids who
were about the same age, similar academic backgrounds, all
that time spent beyond Maine's borders, and—perhaps most
importantly—a shared fascination with Ed and Steph Thatch.
Cammie had been friends with Steph—only briefly, senior year
of high school—and she and I both felt as though we'd missed
some crucial plot point in the intervening years. Should we have
expected change? Maybe, but no, not in Damariscotta, not like
this. So after a couple bottles of wine, we always began trading
theories, wondering whether they'd done something we couldn't
see, maybe racketeered or extorted their way to the top, but only
Colin knew what these words meant, and the more grounded the
conversations became—talk of cash flow and tax code—the less
enjoyable I found them, so I always tried to steer us into more

dastardly waters, and then I was accused of making too many jokes.

It was on one of these nights, as dinner was winding down, that Cammie said she'd been trying to decide if she should tell us about this one night in college, a story about Steph, something that took place when Cammie was a senior at Amherst, only it didn't really answer any of our questions, it was just something that had happened. Our kids were watching *How to Train Your Dragon* in the living room, and we could hear the sound of a fireball incinerating a castle. We all told Cammie that she *had* to tell the story now, and when she said it might take a while, I reminded her that there was still an hour left in the movie and an unopened bottle of wine in the kitchen.

"Okay," she said, "but just keep in mind: I really did like Steph."

We all agreed to keep it in mind, but Cammie must have sensed some skepticism because she started explaining *why* she liked Steph, saying that Steph was smart and wanted to get the hell out of Maine but also liked to do stupid stuff like ride in the back of a truck and shotgun beers. "I was never a big drinker," Cammie said, "always too scared that a college would somehow find out and reject me before I even applied—but that made me a good designated driver, so I got invited places, and people wanted Steph to come along, too, because she was the hot new girl in school, and Ed would get an invite, reluctantly, because he and Steph were a couple. All the preppier guys were just biding their time, I think, waiting for Steph to come to her senses and dump the lobsterman and start dating one of them, even if it was never gonna happen."

"Why not?" Maeve asked.

"Just not what she was looking for. What they were offering was something that might have appealed later in life—security and stability or whatever—but Steph must've figured that she'd have plenty of time for all that. And she *liked* Ed. I'd catch her staring at him when he was doing nothing in particular, just cracking a beer or wiping his brow. But then other times she'd yell at him, and he'd yell at her. And then they'd make up. And then they'd make out. It was hard to look away. This one weekend someone decided we should all go to the Farmington Fair because they wanted to see those cars—what do you call it when the cars crash into each other?"

"A demolition derby."

"Right, a demolition derby, so I drove everyone in my parents' minivan. Ed drank too much coffee brandy on the way up and tried to win a stuffed animal for Steph at one of those carnival booths where you knock bottles off a ledge with baseballs, and he kept throwing the balls harder and harder, but he kept missing." Cammie pushed her glasses up her nose and squinted into the candlelight like she was doing her best to see this distant memory, or maybe just cataloging all the scuffs in our table's chipped veneer. "Ed didn't win anything," she went on, "so Steph, who'd also been drinking, started badgering the guy running the game, saying it was all rigged, even though Ed hadn't hit a single bottle. The guy told Ed to get control of his girlfriend, and Ed told him she could do whatever she wanted, but the guy disagreed—I think he might have even said, 'Put a muzzle on her' or something—so Ed started reaching into the booth and grabbing baseballs and firing them at the guy, telling him to give Steph a Goddamned bear, meaning one of the teddy bears, and the guy kept refusing and ducking the baseballs as he called security, and then we all ran over to the grandstand and hid in the crowd and watched the cars get in accidents for the rest of the night.

"On the way home, Steph puked in the backseat of the

minivan, probably because she was wasted, although I've always wondered if it was also because she was pregnant. But the other thing I remember about that night was sitting in the bleachers, watching the derby, and it was getting cold and the sun was going down, and Steph had her head on Ed's shoulder, like they'd just gone through some serious ordeal together. Which was ridiculous, obviously. I thought that at the time. But also I felt jealous. And when I looked at everyone else, I got the sense that they were watching Ed and Steph, too, feeling pretty much the same way I did."

"I have a question," Maeve said. "Do we know when, exactly, Steph got pregnant?"

"Early," Cammie said. "Really early. EJ was born in the spring of '93, right at the end of our senior year at Lincoln. But Steph didn't know right away."

"Why'd she keep it?" Colin asked.

"That's just her choice," Maeve said.

"Doesn't mean Colin can't ask," I said.

"I'm not saying he can't ask."

"Was she Catholic or something?"

"No," Cammie said.

"Mormon?"

"No."

"So what was it?"

"She just couldn't do it," Cammie said. "Or didn't want to."

"Or Ed convinced her," I said.

"Right."

"But I thought this was a college story," I said.

"It is," Cammie said. "Right. It is. So four years go by. I'm a senior and haven't really had any contact with Steph. Once she started to show"—Cammie gestured to her belly—"she kind of dropped out of the picture. I feel bad that we didn't stay friends, but getting knocked up in high school was just so foreign. None of us knew what to do with it. So I was pretty surprised to get a letter from her a few years later, out of the blue. It was all about EJ, being a mom, how much fun she was having but how it was so much work, and how Ed was doing really well as a lobsterman but sometimes he was out to sea for days at a time, and then the letter started getting kind of dark, and it talked about how her back was always sore and how she felt like she was missing out on certain parts of life, and then toward the end of the letter— I got the impression that this was not something she had reread, it was so full of spelling errors and just so completely all over the place—but at the end she gets all sunny again and says by the way, I'm passing through Amherst in two weekends and thought maybe I could stay with you for a couple nights.

"Well, *that's* a weird request," Cammie said, "coming from someone I haven't really stayed in touch with—but it felt harder to say no than to just suck it up and play host. The weekend she had picked was Amherst-Williams, which was a big deal on campus, even if I didn't really care about any of the football games or anything. I told her to come on down. She wrote back telling me which bus she would be on and said she couldn't wait to see me. I told her I'd meet her at the station."

STEPH AND I WERE SITTING in her home just a few months ago when I asked her about the events of that weekend, the story Cammie had told us over dinner several years prior, but Steph wouldn't let me finish. She shook her head and started giving me her version, how she'd written the letter to Cammie on a whim, and how actually she'd written several of these letters, but Cammie was the only one who'd written back. She was speaking the way she did as mayor in town halls when she was correcting some disputed record, and she kept recounting details that I think were meant to contradict Cammie, but eventually it became clear that Steph's version was basically the same as Cammie's, even if her story ended a little earlier than Cammie's, before the final scene. Both women described their relationship in similar terms. There were a few scattered discrepancies but nothing out of the ordinary. Steph had always been a good storyteller. She knew how to connect. She liked to speak with her hands in the back pockets of her jeans, and it didn't matter what the subject was—could have been the school budget or plans for a new sewage plant—she always started with some tale from the early years, maybe the time she got so pissed at Ed for storing a hundred pounds of live lobster in the trailer's bathtub that she started throwing them all out in the yard only to discover that Ed was planning to barter them off for a new bed for EJ.

It must have been around that time, EJ outgrowing the old crib, the family outgrowing the trailer, that Steph received Cammie's reply. When it arrived, she called in sick to the restaurant and started packing an overnight bag, feeling guilty about it, not that guilty. She just needed a break. She'd been parenting every day, working every night, for three years, over which time EJ had grown to the height, almost exactly, of most of the furniture in the trailer. He had a cowlick, and you would see it sliding behind a table, knifing toward unseen prey, and then you'd hear a lamp crashing on the couch or the contents of a drawer landing on the linoleum. On the morning she left for Amherst, EJ woke her up at the usual hour and ate three Eggos in three minutes and then burped and sidled up to the television, smearing syrup all over the screen as he stared at his own reflection.

Ed drove Steph to the library in Damariscotta, where the bus stop was, but when they got there, EJ refused to leave her lap and Ed had to scrape him off and promise to let him drive on the way home to avert a tantrum.

"Not actually though," Steph said.

"We'll be fine."

"I'm driving, Mommy," EJ said, standing on his dad, hands on the wheel.

Steph kissed Ed quickly, told EJ she loved him, and then as she closed the door, she heard Ed tell EJ that he had to ride in his car seat until they got to their road, and EJ started to say, "No, no, no," but by then Steph was headed for the steps of the library and telling herself not to look back and not to worry about her husband or son until they picked her up on Sunday.

She took the bus to Boston, then Amherst, staring out the scratched windows, watching the autumn sky rewind itself like a nature film played backwards, sun blazing through the clouds, leaves leaping onto trees, hills bursting into flame, her own sense of time reversing, too, until she felt more and more like her younger self, on her way to something new, anticipating the unknown. When she arrived at the Amherst bus stop, Cammie was there to meet her, as promised, wearing a cotton sweatshirt over a denim dress and wool leggings.

"Steph LeClair!" Cammie said, smiling. "You're really here. I can't believe it." They hugged on Pleasant Street, in the center of town, under a purple-leafed tree. The sky was its own kind of clarity—orange at the horizon, neon blue overhead, stars already.

"*You're* really here!" Steph said. "You *live* here. This place is amazing."

"Well, I live on campus—this is just the town."

"Even better. Oh, and also," Steph said, "it's Steph Thatch now, not LeClair."

"Steph *Thatch*, right. My mistake."

"No big deal." Steph looked around. She had never seen a town like this one—so clean, so organized. "I'm really excited to see what your life is like," she said. "That's why I wrote you."

"I'm glad you did."

"Yeah."

"And you had that other thing," Cammie said, "so it all worked out."

"What other thing?"

"You said you were passing through."

"Oh, yeah—I mean, that's just a figure of speech though."

"Is it?"

"Uh-huh. So what's the plan for the evening? I could use a friggin *drink*."

Cammie laughed and looped her arm through Steph's and began leading her south toward campus, asking about life as a mom.

"Oh, it's all good," Steph said.

"Ed's looking after the kid?"

"His parents are. Ed says he has to go out on the water with his brother Chuck because the weather's right for a 'big haul.'"

"What's a big haul?"

"Just a whole bunch of lobsters, I guess. He's gotta go on his trips if I'm gonna go on mine."

"Trips like this?"

But Steph was a little too enthralled by the town, all these cute little design flourishes, to respond. In Damariscotta, the post office was just a charmless brick thing topped in single-window apartments, whereas in Amherst it was free-standing and flanked by big screaming eagles on giant stone pillars. There were trees planted in the sidewalks, and there was a small park at the end of Pleasant Street. Even the sidewalks' curbs had been carved from fresh granite rather than crumbling asphalt. Steph took note, feeling observant, like a diplomat who was also a spy, an emissary of the Midcoast sent to learn about the way things were done behind enemy lines.

As they walked onto campus, the dusk turned to night, the air chilly but relative to the Maine night before, downright balmy. The campus glowed silently, the quad nearly empty under blooming white stars.

"Where is everyone?" Steph asked.

"Pre-gaming, mostly."

"What's pre-gaming?"

"Really?"

"Really."

They stared at each other.

"You don't have to make me feel stupid about it," Steph said.

"Sorry. I wasn't trying to make you feel stupid. It's just—" Whatever Cammie was about to say, she seemed to reconsider. Instead she said, "Basically pre-gaming is just what you do before you go to the parties."

"When do people go to the parties?"

"I don't know, eleven?"

"Wow."

"Yeah, pretty late. So right now everyone's in their dorms listening to music and getting ready and taking shots or whatever. Or if you're a jock, I guess you're wrestling each other and—"

"What's that?"

"Wrestling?"

"No, that building."

Cammie looked to where Steph was pointing, to the brightly lit windows framed by ivy. Gazing up through the glass, Steph could see the heads of students, and above them, chandeliers.

"That building?" Cammie asked.

"Yeah."

"That's dining hall."

"Oh," Steph said. "Seriously?"

Cammie smiled and said, "Come on," pulling Steph onward,

taking her on something like a college tour. They climbed the hill to the freshman dorms, and Cammie pointed out her old room, now home to some other freshman who was at this moment experiencing her first Amherst-Williams weekend and who was listening to loud music—maybe rap, a genre Steph had heard of but rarely actually heard—that thumped down the hill and across the old campus. They walked onto the bluff that overlooked the playing fields, stretching flat and black for what looked like miles toward the woods.

"That's the soccer field," Cammie said. "In the spring, it's the lacrosse field."

Cammie kept walking, but Steph stayed behind to take in the dark fields for a moment longer. As her eyes adjusted, she could make out the soccer goals, then off to the side, stacked next to an equipment shed, orange square-framed nets, which she assumed were lacrosse goals. From somewhere in the distance came the smell of firewood. Steph tried to imagine life here, life as a college senior, eating in a dining hall and having someone else cook for her and clean up after her and being able to go to classes just to *learn* about stuff and then losing her virginity to some college boy in a dorm room instead of some lobsterman in a skiff, not that Ed was really her first, but she couldn't do it, or not yet. This, she decided, would be her mission for the weekend—to get to the point where she could imagine being where she was.

THEY SLIPPED INTO THE COMMON room and onto a stiff couch upholstered in dark wool. Cammie's friends were mid-conversation, speaking in English but making very little sense, their dialogue full of strange references. Everyone drank white wine out of a box. Occasionally those closest to Steph asked her questions, but as soon as they learned that she wasn't in school anywhere

("I'm taking a break from the academic world," Steph said in a hoity-toity voice, checking to see if Cammie thought the voice was funny, but apparently not), they had nothing else to ask her about. Steph and Cammie were handed plastic cups filled just beneath the brim, and Steph gulped hers—finally!—as she tried to follow along.

"Anyway," a boy with a buzz cut and wire-framed glasses said. "You can't compare the people we're talking about—the new-wave guys and then, um . . . fucking what's-his-name."

"Fellini?"

"No. Or sure. But they're not motivated by any kind of commercial imperative, is my point, whereas our directors feel the need, as dictated by the studios, *by the way*, to bring in an audience, and that changes everything."

"For the worse."

"Exactly."

"Or for the worst."

"Either one."

"No, but which is it?"

"Depends on the degree of badness, I guess."

"But would you say 'took a turn for the worse' or 'took a turn for the worst'?"

"I just told you. It depends on how bad the turn is. Jesus. But look, if you step back and examine the arc of, like, human storytelling, it makes no fucking sense, you know? Why are we all of a sudden trying to turn what used to be a pretty pure enterprise into something that's all about action figures? I'm not anticapitalist but—"

"It's like McCarthyism, right?" said one of the girls. Steph tracked the voice to the girl's back. The girl had turned away from the rest of the group while she refilled her wine, and she must have been listening to the conversation without watching it.

"What?" asked the boy with the buzz cut. "I mean, yeah. Sure, Heather. Exactly."

"What are they talking about?" Steph whispered to Cammie.

"Movies."

Steph turned back to the group, trying to figure out if these people were geniuses, if all the references were a kind of mating game for the highly educated. "If we're gonna talk about movies," she said to Cammie, "I have some thoughts on *Pretty Woman*."

"Please don't."

Steph raised her hand, like an eager student in a classroom, but Cammie grabbed her wrist and pulled it down.

"I was just kidding," Steph said, draining the rest of her wine.

One of Cammie's male friends, who wore a cardigan and chimed in on the conversation every now and then, comparing whatever was being said to something going on in the music world, kept turning around and winking at Steph whenever the tone of the conversation became contentious. But Steph had no idea what these winks and eye rolls were meant to convey. Were they sharing a joke? Did he not see the ring on her finger? Was a diamond not something a college kid would notice? Ed had presented it to her in November of her senior year at Lincoln, after she had informed him that she was pregnant, the same day he showed her the trailer. That Ed had found a way to procure a ring and a place to live made her think that she had seriously underestimated him. In a way, she wished he hadn't given it to her. It had made it so much harder to say no. For a while there, like a year or so, that ring's luster had outshined the truth of their circumstances, made her think they had money when they absolutely did not. Except when they did. Things would get worse and worse and worse, and then all of a sudden they'd get better.

It was hot and dry in the common room, but when Steph

looked to Cammie for some sign that they could go soon, she found her friend nodding at a point made by one of her friends.

The boy in the cardigan turned back to Steph and winked again.

"What's the matter?" Steph said. "You got something in your eye?"

"Uh," the boy said.

"Didn't think so." Steph turned to Cammie. "I have to use the bathroom," which was universal girl code for we both need to go to the bathroom right now and talk, but Cammie didn't respond. Instead she pointed at the door. So Steph finished what was left of her second or third cup of wine and exited into the hallway.

In the ladies' room, Steph peed and wondered why no one had written anything entertaining on the walls of the bathroom stall, then went to a sink, looked in the mirror, and splashed water on her face. Under the twitching fluorescent lights, her skin looked startlingly pale. The wine was making her feel a little fuzzy, but not in a good way. If this was how college kids liked to have fun, Steph wanted no part of college—she was glad she'd missed it. The water was beading up on her face, and as Steph reached for a paper towel, she heard heels on the tiles behind her, and then a girl walked to the next sink over and placed an open makeup kit on the steel shelf above the sink. While dabbing at her face with the paper towel, Steph couldn't help, between dabs, sneaking in an appraisal of her neighbor. She was dazzling, this girl. Her lips looked wet with gloss, and some kind of glitter frosted the round peaks of her cheekbones. Big gold hoops dangled from her ears.

The girl glanced at Steph and smiled. Then, though she tried to be subtle about it, she did a double take. Steph's plainness must have horrified her. Steph looked back into the mirror, saw what the girl had seen. Next to the blond-streaked shiny thing, Steph had all the pizzazz of a whitewashed wall. She was wearing a plain cream-colored Oxford with a wrinkled collar, buttoned all the way to the top, and stone-washed jeans, which were honestly pretty damn cute—Ed didn't even know she owned them—but which were tucked into rubber, fleece-lined galoshes that were making her feet sweat now that she had escaped Maine's frigid early winter.

"Hey," Steph said, "this might be weird but . . ."

Without looking over, without even breaking eye contact with her own mirror, the girl said, "Yeah, help yourself."

"You're sure?"

"Yeah, it's cool." The girl took the mascara wand away from her eyelashes for a moment and blinked twice. She slid the makeup kit down the aluminum shelf, toward Steph.

Steph opened the pink bejeweled box and inside saw every shade of everything.

"Are you a prospie?" the girl asked. She finished applying the mascara and moved on to rearranging her breasts in the bra.

"A prospie?"

"A prospective student."

"Oh," Steph said. "No. Just visiting."

"Yeah, I guess you look older. I thought maybe you were like a transfer prospie."

Steph smeared blue eye shadow over her lids and purple lip-stick on her lips. She plucked a few stray hairs from her eyebrows, then a few more, then a few more. She dusted her cheeks with rouge.

The girl looked at Steph in the mirror, saw what she'd done, and said, "Oh, whoa."

"What?"

The girl laughed. "Nothing. Just—you look like you're ready to par-*tay.*"

"I am."

The girl laughed again.

"Whose friend are you?" the girl asked.

"Cammie's."

"Cammie?"

"Cammie Sweet," Steph said.

"Ohhh—Cameron. You mean Cameron. She's the one who wears denim dresses. I know her." The girl puckered her lips to study their sheen.

"I just met all her friends for the first time," Steph said.

"Yeah, so . . ." the girl paused—fixated on something in the mirror, "hate to say it, but those kids are bru-tal." She turned to look at the door, to make sure nobody was approaching. "I mean, I'm sorry you weren't born cool, but no need to take it out on the planet. You want some mascara?"

"Yup." Steph applied mascara.

"Also, how about wearing your hair down tonight?"

Steph looked in the mirror. She never let her hair down at the Schooner because it was against health regulations, and she kept it up at home because EJ would yank, just out of reflex, any free locks that swayed within his grabbing radius. "Good call," Steph said, and then she unbound her ponytail, cranked it over to the side, and started twisting it into a side pony.

"No, no, just—*down*," the girl said. She held Steph by the shoulders, turned her so they faced each other. "Can I do something?" she asked.

"Depends."

The girl smiled, then unbuttoned the top button of Steph's shirt. "That okay?"

"Yup."

"I'm Megan," the girl said. Steph let her unbutton the second button, too, revealing a miniature silver buoy on a chain, a gift from Ed.

"I'm Steph."

"You're pretty, Steph."

"Thanks. Oh, you know what else I wanna do?" She unbuttoned the bottom two buttons of the Oxford and tied the two sides of the shirt together at her belly button.

Megan laughed so hard she had to brace herself against the sink. "You're funny," she said. "Whoo." She gathered herself and grabbed her makeup kit and snapped it shut. "Going to the Owl later?"

"Yeah, I think so," Steph said.

"Cool, see you there."

"See you there."

When Steph walked back into Cammie's suite, the conversation trailed off midsentence. She could feel their eyes on the open V made by her unbuttoned shirt. Cammie didn't like it, Steph could tell. But screw her. Steph felt good. Sexy. She asked Cammie if they might be going to the Owl later.

"What?" Cammie asked flatly.

"I heard it's the place to be," Steph said.

"How do you know about the Owl?"

"Everyone knows about the Owl."

Cammie said she would take it under advisement, but first they should go to this other house party that was more their speed. She reached for her jacket and shrugged it on without discussing the matter further.

At the house party, in a living room strung with red chilipepper lights, Steph pushed through the coeds to a keg in a back corner and a sophomore who was willing to fill her a red Solo cup full of spumy beer, one for Cammie, too, but when Steph looked up, Cammie wasn't there. Steph circulated through the crowd, looking for her friend. She drank her beer, then Cammie's beer, then went back to the keg for two more. She wandered around drinking the beers for what felt like an hour. She kept standing on her tiptoes to peer across the milling heads, and then this one time someone waved at her. Megan! The girl from the bathroom! Steph waved back, hoping one of Megan's friends wasn't standing behind Steph, also waving. But Megan came straight to her, hooked her arm through Steph's, and began introducing her to people whose names Steph would never remember. A thick fog had begun to obscure her short-term memory. She hadn't drunk like this, for fun, in too long. "We need to keep an eye out for Cammie," she told Megan.

"Sure," Megan said.

"I mean Cameron."

"Sure."

"And her really *cool* friends."

Through Megan, Steph met boys who parted their hair and wore khaki pants and played varsity something or other. Megan was from Manhasset, Long Island, and Steph started introducing Megan to random partygoers, most of whom Megan already knew, as Megan, her friend from Manhasset, as if Megan were the one visiting Steph. At some point they went to the Owl, a fraternity that could exist off-campus but not on-campus according to some stupid rule, and Steph laughed out loud at the leather chairs and the old composite pictures of boys in blazers in the empty "great room." The party was downstairs and it was too loud to hear anything. Guns N' Roses played, then some more rap music that Steph didn't recognize. The girls were constantly surrounded by boys. None of them noticed the ring on Steph's finger, or didn't mention it anyway.

Steph was having a wonderful time visiting her friend Megan, and told everyone so.

"I thought I was visiting *you*," Megan shouted, and they laughed and touched their cups together and drank, which was a private joke they had invented at some point, pretending the cups were champagne flutes. Steph couldn't remember when they had come up with the joke, or who had originated it, but when they were handed shots in plastic glasses that said *Daytona Beach* on one, and *He shoots, he scores!* on the other, they pretended that these, too, were made of crystal and contained something fine and bubbly.

There was one boy, either Brendan or Brandon, who was probably the funniest-looking, most handsome young man Steph had ever seen. He was a rugby player from Maryland in a long-sleeved polo. Steph laughed abruptly when he said he had gone to Choate, as if she should know the place.

"I'm sorry," she said, holding his forearm for support, his biceps against her breast, "but I have no idea what that is."

"It's okay," he said. His smile was full of perfect teeth. "It's just my high school." He had dozens of freckles and a real dimple in his chin.

"It's so loud in here!" Steph said.

"There are quieter places."

"Like *where*?"

"Like upstairs."

"In the 'great room'?"

"Above the great room," he said.

"Do you think my hair looks okay?"

"I think it looks great."

"Because I was thinking about wearing it like *this*."

She pulled it over to the side.

"Looks pretty either way," he said.

"You're just being nice," Steph said, letting go of her hair. "What's 'above the great room'?"

"Other rooms."

"What kind of rooms?"

"I don't know, the kind with beds and desks."

"People don't actually live here, do they?"

"I live here."

"You would," Steph said, and she looked into his eyes and started laughing again. She held up her left hand and pointed at her ring because she sensed, for some reason, that the time had come. Etched into the band was a braided design, like swirling ropes.

Brendan or Brandon asked her if it was real.

"I think so," Steph said. She looked at it. She had to admit—it looked a little fake tonight. "I don't know how my husband got it," Steph said, as serious as she had been all evening, "and I don't wanna ask." Trying to sound sober was making the room waver and rotate on its axis, and talking about the ring brought something dark into the basement, something that lurked for now just in the periphery while it waited for the room to spin toward it.

"You're hot," the boy said.

"Well, thank you," Steph said. "You're hot, too."

She looked around for Megan but didn't see her. Everyone in the loud basement wore a strange happy face. Except for one person. It was Cammie.

"Where have you been?" Cammie asked.

"Here," Steph said.

"Okay, well," Cammie said, glancing at the boy, "we should probably go, don't you think?"

"Now?"

"Yeah, I think so," Cammie said. "I mean, unless you want to stay. It's really up to you."

"Then why are you giving me a hard time?"

"I'm . . . not?"

Steph turned to the boy. "Hard time, right?"

He shrugged.

"See?" Steph said to Cammie.

"I just want to make sure you know what you're doing."

"Oh, I get it."

"Get what?"

"Because I'm so dumb, right?"

"What?" Cammie said.

"I'm so dumb, I can't make my own decisions?"

"That's not what I'm saying."

"And now you're mad."

"I'm not mad."

"Yes, you are. I can feel how mad you are. It's palp-able."
Palpable was a difficult word to say, especially at this point of the
night, but Steph thought she might have nailed it.

"Um," Cammie said, "I'm a little hazy about what's going
on right now, so can we just clear the air?"

"Oh great, now she wants to clear the air."

"Yeah, look, I'm not sure what you wanted from this trip.
I thought you came here to visit me, but your letter was a little
weird, to be honest, and we haven't really been in touch, and
then you disappeared. And now you're standing really close to
Brendan—"

"Brandon," he corrected.

"Brandon, sorry. But listen, if this is what you came here to
do, then fine. I don't really know you well enough to get in your
way."

"Yeah, but this should be me visiting me at *my* school," Steph
said. "Did you even think about that?"

"What?"

"I should be visiting myself here."

"Okay."

"Why do you get this and I don't?"

"I don't know, Steph. I worked hard. I'm sure you did too,
but—"

"But ol' Steph fucked it up."

A moment passed. Cammie looked at Steph, at the boy, back to Steph. "I'm not here to pass judgment," she said finally. "But I am tired, and I am going home. You're welcome to come back with me."

Steph shook her head. "Honestly?" she said. "Your friends kind of suck. I feel sorry for you. You're basically missing out on college."

Cammie looked at Brandon and said, "I do know who you are, Brandon, just for the record," and then she left the basement. Steph felt herself teetering. Someone jostled her from behind.

"Are you okay?" the boy said.

"Yup," Steph said. She was okay. She was fine. "Brandon," she said, like his name was a new discovery. It really was too loud in here. She had already forgotten about the exchange with Cammie and wanted to find her. She wondered if she owed her an apology. She told Brandon that she needed to get out of the basement, right away if possible.

They went upstairs to a slanted hallway filled with people staring out from doorways. It was quieter on this floor, but not by much. The only way to make it really quiet was to go into Brandon's room and shut the door, and even then, you could still hear all the sounds—just muffled and distorted. Somehow the bass from the ground floor was making it all the way up the old brick walls.

"So this is *mi casa*," Brandon said. His "casa" was small. The bed was on stilts, just high enough to provide clearance for a little love seat. One wall was covered in a blue tapestry with a zooming red paisley pattern. Steph landed on the love seat, face-first. Dust puffed out. This was as tired as she had ever been. Even with her eyes shut, she saw the zooming paisley pattern. "My back hurts," she said.

Brandon sat beside her and started rubbing her lower back. "It's all EJ's fault," she said.

He worked his hands higher, lifting up her shirt and eventually unstrapping her bra. "Is this helping?" he asked.

"Mmm," she said.

He rolled her onto her back and she lay against the armrest. The stuffing had been battered and rearranged for so many years that her head rested on a worn layer of fabric that did nothing to soften the underlying wood frame—but it hardly made a difference. She could fall asleep like this. She felt Brandon removing her galoshes, thank you very much. She didn't want them on anymore. Then his fingers were unbuttoning her jeans, and she held his hand for a moment, stopping him, but then letting go because he was just being considerate and honestly who wears pants to bed? He unzipped her fly and tugged the jeans down. Each pant leg got stuck on its corresponding sock, so he had to pry the pants off, trying to be gentle, but then tugging hard while gripping her ankle tightly. He lowered himself to her chest, and he smelled like some kind of department store cologne, and he kissed her lips, and she kissed back, and it felt strange, she thought, because it was like Ed didn't have a beard anymore, and this thought had the effect of stiffening her whole body. She went rigid. "Wait," she said.

Brandon recoiled. He pushed up. His face was a foot above hers, hovering. Steph's eyes were open now, but Brandon was close enough to look blurry and kind of cyclopsed. Also, when her eyes had been closed, the lights had gone out, filling the room with purple shadows.

Brandon placed his hand on her cheek, his thumb on her bottom lip. She took his thumb in her mouth, thinking maybe she should bite it; at first the nail tasted bitter, but then it only tasted like her own saliva. And instead of biting the thumb, she sucked on it, then reached up, pulled on his collar, brought his mouth to hers. She reached under his belt and brought him out. He was already hard.

"Let me get a condom," he said.

Steph shut her eyes and listened to the bass from the basement. One of the paisley things was dancing in her eye, and then the boy was back and Steph heard him spit, then felt him start to enter her, wearing the rubber, and it felt painful in the way that remorse can make every part of your body feel something deeper than any kind of happiness. It was painful but didn't hurt. No one should go an entire life without feeling pain like this, Steph thought. She untied and unbuttoned her own shirt so that Brandon could suck on her breast and be all those boys and all those men and all the second loves, third loves, and heartbreak, all the drunken college hookups and sex without consequences, all the cities and singles, all the good dates and bad dates, the hundreds of men tapering into one, sturdy, permanent man. She didn't want to be on her back anymore, so she pushed at Brandon's shoulders, shoved him onto the floor, climbed on top, and let her hair fall around him. And then she held him, pulled him back inside, and kissed him as hard as she could.

"STEPH WAS A DISASTER THE next morning," Cammie said. "We had breakfast before she left, and she was crying, telling me what happened, full of guilt, then justifying it, then beating herself up again. She caught the next bus out of Amherst. And that was it. I didn't hear from her again for a long time, not until she reached out on Facebook."

I'd refilled Cammie's wineglass two more times while she spoke but realized now that I'd been listening so intently that I had forgotten to drink any of my own wine or water—as though

I'd been the one doing all the talking. The kids were passed out in the living room on couches and beanbags. I had been dimly aware of their movie ending, of a credits song playing, of the ensuing calm.

"God, I was the worst," Cammie said, staring at her empty glass. "The whole premise of Steph's visit was bullshit, and she was clearly using me, but I could have been a little more attuned."

"Attuned to what?" Colin asked.

"I don't know, her circumstances."

"Yeah, but if you were more attuned," Maeve said, "she might not have gotten what she wanted."

"Which was what?" I asked.

"I'd say more or less what she got."

I arched an eyebrow.

"Oh, come on," Maeve said. "I'm not saying Steph went down there to let some guy have his way with her. She wouldn't have been that honest with herself anyway. All I'm saying is—" And then Maeve hesitated, taking one big breath in the way she always does when she doesn't like some new train of thought. "I don't know," she said. "I just think some people have nights where it seems like the whole point is to get drunk enough," and I could tell she was making sure not to look at anyone in particular, "not to care what happens next."

4

ABOUT A YEAR AFTER WE MOVED BACK TO MAINE, THE LINCOLN HIGH principal called me into her office—along with coaches from the girls' lacrosse team, the field hockey team, and both soccer teams—to discuss a proposal for a new playing field. Apparently a wealthy member of the community had volunteered to spearhead the effort and wanted to break ground as soon as possible. I was all for it and figured I'd be able to lend some expertise, having worked at a school in Boston with not one but two turf fields. But when I walked through the door, I saw, of all people, Ed Thatch standing near the small conference table, wearing a black cap with a white *L* embroidered over a pair of lacrosse sticks. I had been given no such hat, not even as a reward for piloting the boys to a 7–9 record the previous spring. All the other coaches had arrived ahead of me, so they were either exchanging greetings with Ed or taking a seat.

"Andrew, this is Ed Thatch," the principal said.

"I know Ed," I said.

We shook hands. His beard had gone gray around the chin, but his eyes were still blue and sharp.

"How we doing, Andy?"

"Doing well, Ed, thanks. Good to see you."

I took a seat at the far end of the table, under a fern, and waited for some kind of explanation. I knew that Allie Thatch, Ed's daughter, played for the girls' lacrosse team—as a freshman, she was already turning into a standout—and I knew that Ed had done well for himself, but I couldn't connect the one with the other.

"Ed's here to talk about renovating the field," the principal said. I looked around to see if anyone else was sharing in my bemusement, but if they were, they weren't showing it. They were all listening expectantly, some with hands tented on the table, some ready to take notes.

"Yuh," Ed said. "Now, I been making some calls and what we need is this artificial surface—it's fake grass with rubber pellets called FieldTurf."

Ah, I remember thinking. *Well done, Ed.* I thought I was finally beginning to understand: Ed must have found his way into the contracting business, maybe extricated himself from the fishing business entirely. But then Ed went on to explain that all the more competitive schools in the state had already made the transition to synthetic surfaces, and he had looked into how much the renovation might cost, and he was willing to pay for most of the field—and a new set of bleachers, a scoreboard, and stadium lights—if we promised to use his crew and let him break ground that spring. By then the fern and my neck were on intimate terms, and I was swatting at it, shifting in my seat, sensing that my place at the table—in the corner, adjacent the flora, far from the head—was maybe not intentional but certainly telling.

"You won't believe who our wealthy benefactor is," I told

Maeve that night. She knew about the meeting, knew I'd been excited about it.

"Ed Thatch," she said.

"Who told you?"

"Wait, was I right?"

"Yes."

"Lucky guess."

"Maybe it's just not that unlikely."

"It's not," Maeve said. "They have a lot of money, and their daughter plays sports, doesn't she?"

"I guess I just can't reconcile this new Ed with the old Ed. You know those movies where they have a child actor in the flashbacks but the kid doesn't really look like the adult, so it's confusing?"

"Yeah, but when they have the forty-year-old pretend to be in high school, it's just as bad."

"It's even worse."

Maeve was washing vegetables in the kitchen. The plan, when we moved in, had been to renovate this part of the house within the first year, but then we ran out of money, so the kitchen remained untouched—the preserved living quarters, Maeve had joked, of a mediocre writer who'd died circa 1998. Faux-maple laminate was very popular then, as was wallpapering your kitchen with illustrations of things you might find in said kitchen—grapes, pumpkins, spatulas, you name it. I was still in my coaching gear, black Lincoln hoodie on, whistle around my neck, so if anyone had looked through the window, they might have thought I was giving Maeve instruction on how to properly rinse an heirloom tomato.

"We have to talk to Jack," Maeve said, bringing the vegetables over to a cutting board. "He bit another kid."

"Which kid?"

"They didn't tell me."

"Why'd he bite him?"

"I don't know, I think they were haggling over a toy, but the point is, no matter what the other boy did, Jack's not supposed to be biting other kindergartners."

"Right."

I went to the fridge, found a beer, cracked it open, and tried to think about Jack—what to say, what to do.

"On a Tuesday?" Maeve said, nodding at the beer.

"Not just any Tuesday."

"I thought you weren't drinking on the weekdays."

"I'm not, but this is all very stressful."

"Jack?"

"And the meeting."

"Why the meeting?"

"I don't know," I said, taking a long sip, staring at the pantry. "I guess I just thought they'd ask me more questions about turf."

WHEN I FIRST STARTED AT the prep school in Boston, I was asked to teach English, coach freshman hockey, and serve as an assistant coach on the varsity lacrosse team, but when the head coach left for a boarding school, I was promoted, and then, owing very little to myself and mostly to a little cadre of talent that all hit puberty at the same time, we started to win some games. In the year I took the helm, our team earned a share of the league championship, and in my last season in Boston, we went undefeated. I was interviewed on the field after the final game by some recent journalism grad as I held two-year-old Jane in my arms and as she kept yanking the brim of my hat in different directions. I had a sunburn and felt full of everything I'd ever wanted, like the place I was in may have not been the place I'd been trying to get to but only because there was no way to find it, no way to know of it, without making several wrong turns—wrong but fortuitous—on the path to some *other* place.

I missed being in that dim spotlight when we moved to Maine, and there were no club teams to coach in the summer, so I found myself with more idle time, more time that could have been spent writing if I hadn't let myself drift so far from the practice. I needed some way to fill the days, so in my second summer back on the Midcoast, I volunteered to serve as the school's liaison to the project Ed was financing, the construction of what would eventually be christened Thatch Field. "Liaison" was the emptiest of titles though. Any real decision had to be approved by our principal and rubber-stamped by a committee of budget overseers who I think worked for the county or maybe the state, and Ed's construction crew (yes, he did have his contracting license, although I never saw him onsite) had their marching orders from the architect. I went to the school all that summer and donned my hard hat while more important people pointed at various things—where the light towers would go, where the handicap ramp would attach—and since I was adding nothing by bearing witness to all this industry, I ditched the clipboard one day, picked up a wheelbarrow, and started hauling loads of gravel from this pile to that pile.

By day three, the crew had started to give me actual tasks, and at the end of the afternoon, they tossed me a Budweiser from the cooler in the back of the truck. I had dirt beneath my nails, sweat in my underwear, but this isn't a story about learning to love manual labor. The minutes always passed slowly, and my mind went to dark places (I remember thinking a lot about the irony of working with Ed once again, or really truly *for* Ed this time, since I never saw him), but I did enjoy feeling as though I'd done something at the end of the day, as though I'd justified sending the kids to farm camp during my summer break, maybe even earned my beers.

By the end of August, the plot of land designated for the field had been laid with small pebbles, then the foam-like foundation, then the turf, and the bleachers had been assembled and the lights had been wired. Everything was ready. Just before the school year began, we had another meeting in the principal's office, during which we mostly congratulated each other and planned a naming ceremony. Ed was there, and I glanced at him when my boss thanked me for all the "sweat equity" I'd invested in the stadium. Behind his beard, Ed was either smiling or smirking, I couldn't tell.

It was just a moment after I left the office that I heard him call my name. I stopped and turned. When he arrived at my side, he clamped a massive hand around my neck and said he wanted to pick my brain. Given the hold he had upon my upper vertebrae, it was hard not to take him literally; I imagined him yanking brain tissue from my skull with one of those metal barbs designed to rip meat from a lobster claw.

"About what?" I said.

"About college." Ed let go of my neck, slapped my back, and started power-steering me down the hallway in the same direction I'd been heading in the first place. "My daughter Allie's got her sights set on playing at the next level. It ain't a stretch either. She can play."

"Good for her," I said, meaning it. "You should be proud."

"Yuh, she's determined."

"That's great."

"Even if there's some people who think it's long odds."

"Well, as long as she's having fun and doing what she wants to do," I said, "then hopefully she'll be happy, no matter how far she takes it."

"What she wants to do," Ed said, "is play college lacrosse."

We had reached my classroom, so I stopped, and Ed looked inside, perhaps seeing that old lacrosse stick hanging on the wall.

"This is Ms. Ringle's room," he said.

"It was."

And then he said, almost musingly, "She made a mistake."

"What kind of mistake?"

"Told me I had potential."

"I would have said the same."

"Well, what she shoulda said was that I was the dumbest hick she'd ever taught. Then I woulda gotten all As."

"Oh, I see," I said. "Light a fire."

"Allie's built the same way. Tell her she can't do something, she's gonna keep busting her ass until she does it."

Behind Ed were the diminishing lines of beige lockers, the dim fluorescents overhead. It occurred to me then, as perhaps it should have well before, that Ed's investment in the playing field had much more to do with his daughter's own success than any desire to give back to the community. I'd grown used to this kind of parent in Boston; I just hadn't expected to encounter it here, not in the form of my old colleague from the docks, the lobster-man in rubber boots and a camo hoodie.

"Did you know," he said, "that you're the only kid from this town who's ever played lacrosse in college?"

I knew this but couldn't tell if he meant it as a compliment or an insult.

"You could show me how," he said.

"Show you how to what?"

"How to get Allie a spot."

"Oh," I said, "well, there's really no way to game the system," although this wasn't quite true. College rosters were full of young men and women who came from households with lax walls and live-in tutors, and every prep school and club team in the country pitched their access to top-tier programs as the principal return on a parent's investment.

"Let me take you to lunch," Ed said.

"Allie's only a sophomore, isn't she?"

"She is," he said, "but they say you gotta start thinking about this stuff wicked early."

He wasn't wrong, and it seemed harmless to accept the offer—harmless except in that it bruised my ego, the implied imbalance of a free meal—so I found myself agreeing to the date. We exchanged phone numbers, Ed shook my hand, and we said we would see each other soon.

Which we did. And then we saw each other the next month, and the next month, until these meetings became something like a tradition. They were always at King Eider's Pub, always at the same booth in the corner, always on the same subject: Allie Thatch's burgeoning lacrosse career. In the beginning, Ed knew nothing. I had to explain what a NESCAC school was, what an SAT was, what to expect from a summer recruiting tournament like FLG in 3d. He was a visual learner, I discovered, so I brought hard copies of charts and lists, which he would examine, not saying much. At the end of our lunches, I would always thank him, but he would insist on thanking me instead, and I found that I was looking forward to the sessions, even once Ed's knowledge began to surpass my own. After a few months, just as I was beginning to run out of resources, he surprised me with his own sheath of printouts: rankings of schools he'd found on the web, emails he'd received from coaches, flyers for recruiting showcases.

Sometimes it could feel like he was pushing too hard, and I wanted to do right by Allie, as I would have for any of my student-athletes, so when Ed would suggest hauling her to a seventh summer showcase, I would remind him to beware of burnout, and when Ed suggested a school that I didn't think was a good fit, I would try to guide him elsewhere. At one point he wanted to send Allie to a prospect day at a Division I school with a very successful program. It wasn't all that far from Maine, which was important to Ed—he would have preferred all the schools to have campuses on the Midcoast—but I warned him that this particular college tended to attract kids who were well meaning but sheltered, born of extreme affluence and privilege.

"Yuh," Ed said, "that all sounds good."

"No, what I meant is that it's just kind of a narrow worldview there," I said. "I guarantee you ninety percent of that lacrosse team goes on to work in finance. They brag about it on Twitter."

"What happens to the other ten percent?"

"I don't know—tech?"

"So they all get good jobs."

"They all earn plenty of money."

"There you go."

I let it pass, having done my best, and was relieved when Ed stopped mentioning the school, presumably because the coaches had stopped expressing interest in Allie. Mostly what I did during these lunches was listen and nod and feel satisfied that I'd done my job as teacher, given my student—Ed, I mean—the necessary tools to venture out on his own. He kept using me as a sounding board, well after I'd lost my original utility, and I kept drinking a few too many IPAs for the middle of the day.

Obviously, there were times when we'd said all there was to say about Allie's options or the lacrosse world in general, and in these interludes of silence, I thought about asking Ed how it all came to be, how he'd made it happen. Whenever I worked up the courage, though, Ed's phone always seemed to buzz or the check always seemed to arrive. It's possible that he could sense what I was trying to do and found ways to keep me from doing it, I don't know, but eventually I stopped looking for the right moment and decided that it wasn't meant to be.

5

OF COURSE, NONE OF OUR FRIENDS OR NEIGHBORS KNEW ANYTHING more than I did, not until that reception for Amherst Women's Lacrosse when the cops showed up and stories began to hit the papers. Cammie and Colin came to our place just a couple weeks later, early June, for an emergency dinner. We had so much to discuss. *The Boston Globe* had just published a big "This Is What We Know" timeline, and everyone wanted to break it down. The earliest listed event was in the early '90s and involved a big yacht called the *Neptune & Mercury*. I would have been a senior at Exeter then, so I wouldn't have heard about it, but my father insists that the boat's arrival caused quite a stir around town. Million-dollar sailboats just didn't make it all the way up our river all that often, especially so late in the season. The boat was from Rhode Island and was ninety-two feet long, built in Holland, owned by an investment banker with a home in Newport, but it was the banker's son and daughter-in-law, a lawyer and his wife in their early thirties, hailing from the western suburbs of Boston, who had been cruising along the Midcoast at the time.

On their first night in town, they took the inflatable dinghy in to the Schooner, had dinner, stayed late for drinks. On the second night in town, they did the same thing. It was on this night that Ed steered his Whaler up the darkened river, cutting the engine as soon as he rounded the buoy that marked the edge of the harbor, and rowed himself to the yacht's transom. I don't know exactly what he was looking for, but by then he knew Steph was pregnant, and his family had been telling him to let her go, let her make her own decisions, and they had also reminded him, trying to reassure him, take the pressure off, that he couldn't even afford a ring to put on her finger or a roof to put over her head. This was young love that was meant to burn bright and fast and then fade away, they told their son, and just because Ed and Steph had clipped the wick beneath the flame didn't mean she couldn't recover, no matter which choice she made, and get back on the track that she was bound to follow, off to college and then to a suburb of some midsize city where she'd marry a business-man and have the family that she'd always been destined to have.

Ed said nothing to his parents, but when he imagined Steph raising their kid on a golf course with some slacks-wearing exec-utive serving as stepdad, he also imagined stuffing the guy in a weighted bag and drowning him in the nearest water hazard. There had to be a way to prove his parents wrong, but only if he did something bold, if he found a way to show Steph that he was worth more than even his own family suspected. So on that night, the *Neptune & Mercury*'s second in Damariscotta, Ed climbed into the yacht's cockpit. He went down the ladder and past the galley. There was a panel of red lights casting a glow across all the bunks, and Ed glanced inside each chamber until he found himself in the master cabin. Next to the bed was the wife's jewelry. It's standard practice to take off all rings and necklaces when on a boat because they can get caught in the rigging and sever a finger, so it was all there, her necklaces, watch, earrings. Ed took only what he needed and left everything else behind. According to the article in the *Globe*, the ring he stole was worth $30,000, which must have shocked him when he found out what he'd taken. But I doubt he felt remorse. Stealing that ring would have been like speeding on the way to the hospital with Steph in labor, the kind of crime that's not really a crime when all you're doing is what's best for your family.

Next to the timeline in the *Globe* was a sidebar about Ben Thatch, Ed's father's cousin, fifteen years Wade's senior, who'd passed away shortly after Maeve and I moved back to town. I knew who he was—he lived by himself in an old farmhouse on the river and had an antiques store on Main Street that sold furniture, jewelry, local knickknacks, the kind of place where a pine-scented candle was always overpowering the senses. I can't say if he was the one who told Ed how dumb it would have been to give Steph the ring without altering it, how many eyebrows it would raise around the county, or if Ed arrived at that conclusion on his own, but regardless, the ring Ed stole was not the one, not exactly, that he gave to Steph when he proposed a few weeks later. Ben had dismantled the original, removing the large central diamond and the four smaller stones from the platinum band. He fenced the diamonds through an antiques wholesaler and returned the band to Ed, swapping out the monstrous keystone for a much smaller diamond. To make the band whole again, Ben soldered in a length of white gold. This is the ring that Ed gave to Steph. Ben assured him that no one would ever recognize the band without the diamond, and no one would ever see the part of the band that wasn't platinum, and he was right—no one ever did.

AFTER THE RECEPTION, THE WHOLE state, it seemed, was obsessed. I was, too. I started thinking back to every interaction I had ever had with Ed or Steph, and then I started jotting down all those recollections in a notebook, then another notebook. At some point, I found myself standing in the pantry, too distracted to remember what it was that I'd come there to eat, probably a cookie or one of the kids' fruit snacks, when suddenly I decided that the pantry really ought to be a home office. A writer's office. For me. By the afternoon, I'd torn out all the shelves, brought a pair of sawhorses and a piece of plywood up from the basement to make a desk, and duct-taped a corkboard to the wall next to the narrow cracked window, our neighbor's garage forever blocking what would have been a nice little view of the woods. I printed out maps and articles and tacked them to the board, and then when I ran out of room, the wall.

Soon I was conducting casual interviews, asking friends and neighbors if they knew anything I didn't or had any color to add to our understanding of Ed and Steph's lives. And then one day, on a whim, I called Steph's cellphone. She didn't pick up, so I left a voicemail, saying I was working on a book about her family (which I wasn't, not yet) and wondering if she might be willing to give me her side of the story. I thanked her, hung up, then moved on, never expecting to hear back.

In the afternoons, I started going for long jogs around the salt bay—I needed to after sitting in a narrow pantry all morning— and then I spent the rest of the day making calls to local sheriffs and reporters, anyone whose name had shown up in the papers, but I'm not an investigative journalist and had no idea what I was doing. Nobody wanted to talk. I asked my dad if he knew anyone, and he connected me with a gnarled old barnacle on the island of North Haven whose carpal tunnel my dad had repaired fifteen years prior. This lobsterman named Walt spoke in the most classic Maine tradition, a true lilt, and as soon as I asked him if he knew anything about the Thatches ever coming up to the island, he interrupted and said, "Ya know, it's a funny thing—you're the second person who's called me asking that very question."

I said, "Oh, did the police reach out?"

"No, no," Walt said, almost dreamily, "it was a fella from up around this way who lives in some far-flung region now, I can't remember which. I know his folks, and they put him in touch."

"When was this?" I asked.

"About three, four years ago, I'd say."

And so I had a lead, although it's hard to call it a lead when all you're doing is calling someone who's already done the work for you.

THAT TRIP TO AMHERST COLLEGE had left Steph feeling unsettled, ashamed, and then resentful, and this little angry seed began to grow and grow until its branches overtook every part of her and Steph felt stiffened in revolt against the life she'd made for herself, or against anyone who might judge her for living this life, anyone who might presume to know what the rest of it had in store. She went to the library and started checking out every kind of book— romance novels, spy novels, biographies, memoirs, history books, cookbooks—anything in print, but the reading began to feel pointless and scattered, so then she started requesting brochures from universities around the state, and she read and read until finally she pushed herself away from the kitchen table one night and came over to the couch. She looked down at Ed and said, "I have to go back to school." She wanted to study civics, she said, and she would need a car because she and Ed had been sharing his truck ever since the transmission fell out of her mom's old Camry.

"Yuh," Ed said. EJ was sitting next to him, running a plastic truck up and over his thigh. "Guess I'll just have to work a little harder."

"Well," Steph said, "let's talk about that. I'm ready to work harder, too."

"Nah," Ed said, turning back to the TV. "I got it."

"Ed—"

"Don't even worry about it."

"Well, I worry about it because I don't want to end up in the Goddamn poorhouse—"

"That ain't happening," he said.

"It's not? How do I know it's not happening?"

"Because I got it."

"How?"

"Well, you're asking for it, ain't you?"

His boots were on the coffee table, which was littered with little paper balls. He did have a point. Anything Steph had ever asked for, Ed had given her in the end, this was true, but she didn't like the implication that she was being *gifted* an education, that she needed his permission or even his help to earn a degree.

"What's with the trash?" she said, waving at the balls.

"Not trash," Ed said. "Gravel."

"We're playing dump truck," EJ said.

"Sounds fun, honey," Steph said, before swinging back to Ed. "So since when are you good at this?"

"Good at what?"

"Accounting. Math. Numbers."

"Got us a place to live, didn't I?"

"You got us a trailer," she said, arms crossed.

"Which is a place to live."

She didn't say anything.

"I'll get you a car," he said.

"And tuition?"

"That too."

"What if I want a pony?"

"You got it."

"Or a personal assistant?"

"You want a personal assistant, tell your mom to get her ass back to Maine."

Steph took off her glasses—she wore glasses to read now—and said, "I'm filling out the applications then."

"You do that."

Steph was about to walk away, but then she paused and kissed Ed on the cheek, just above the black beard, and then she put a hand on his chin and turned his head so she could kiss him on the mouth. EJ was still playing with his truck and making rumbling engine noises, so Ed went back to watching the game, and Steph went back to the kitchen and applied to every public institution within a two-hour radius. A few months later, she received a letter congratulating her on her acceptance to the University of Southern Maine in Portland, and a few months after that, she began to transfer all that intensity from the library books to her textbooks. Any energy not spent waiting tables now went into studying her notes, typing her papers. She and Ed kept trading off the parenting duties, or if they both had to work, EJ watched *Ninja Turtles* on the floor and ate Golden Grahams straight from the box.

Ed was helping Steph, and Steph was helping Ed. Whenever he had to go away for a day or two on a big haul, she would look after EJ, no questions asked. The price of lobster was always in flux, Ed had told Steph, so whenever demand was high, he and Chuck had to spend extra time on the water, outworking their rivals, raking the ocean for every last bug. This was how they could get ahead, Ed said, and Steph felt genuinely moved by how much he was doing on their behalf, as if these efforts were what he'd given her to replace the simple movements—cracking a beer, Cammie had said, or wiping away sweat—that used to make Steph forget where she was and dream crazy dreams. Later, when she would run for town manager, these years would be described as foundational in her origin story, the stump speech she insisted on making at every baked bean supper: While she was taking classes, Ed was hauling a living out of the river, the gulf, all those coves and inlets.

On only one occasion did Steph have to say no. This was June of 1998, and Ed was heading out the door, early in the morning, around four, ready to head up the coast. Steph ducked out of their room with eyes half-shut and said, "You have to take EJ."

"I can't take EJ," he said.

"I have an exam," she said.

After three years of classes at USM, Ed had thought she was done with exams, thought she was working on one last thesis to earn her BA, but apparently not. He was about to mount a protest, but Steph turned around and went back in the bedroom and shut the door.

He called his parents, but they said they had to work at the Pound—*someone* had to hold down the fort while their sons disappeared for the day. Ed considered calling Steph's father Raymond, but Raymond was ill-equipped to babysit on his own and wasn't likely to answer the phone so early in the morning.

So an hour later, Ed and EJ were in the boat with Chuck, heading east, and Ed was peering into the wet dawn, checking his instruments, checking the radar. They always left the dock at the same time as the other lobstermen, their buckets full of bait.

They kept a hidden string of traps stocked with live lobster so that when they returned to the dock, they had something to show for their efforts. They beefed up their engines and entered lobster boat races all across the region. Ed had purchased the boat from his father, painted her the color of mist, and christened her the *Miss Stephanie*. They didn't care about winning the races. The competition wasn't important. What was important was making good time on a run up the coast, getting home before anyone noticed they were missing.

On the morning they went to North Haven, the air was gray, the type of brumey dawn that came to Maine frequently—ideal conditions for a big haul—but not nearly frequently enough. Ed glanced backward at his son, who was standing by the bait barrels as the boat bucked over the swells. Ed needed to keep his family away from his business, but so too did he need to provide for that family. He had made sure Steph could go to school without taking on loans, and he had also made sure she could make the one-hour commute to her classes. He should have bought her something cheap, something used, but she deserved better than that. She deserved a brand-new Camry, and the monthly payments tended to pile up. The only way to stay ahead was to ship out every time the weather rolled in, every time the fog hit the coast.

BY SEVEN-THIRTY, ED, CHUCK, AND EJ were entering Penobscot Bay. The boat was close to North Haven now, the water shallow enough for lobster buoys to reappear. Ed slowed down and Chuck went to the bow with the decoy boat license and a roll of duct tape. He spread the gray mat with the fake numbers over the real license, then tore a length of tape with his mouth and ran it along the edge of the counterfeit strip. The silver tape, similar in color to the hull, would blend in for anyone looking from any kind of distance. On his way back from the bow, Chuck stopped at the wheelhouse, where the *Miss Stephanie* flew a yellow-and-pink buoy amidst the tangle of antennae. Chuck swapped out this buoy for a black-and-white one. Then he went to the transom. Stowed in one of the stern hatches was another gray mat, this one bigger and rolled like a scroll. The second mat, once Chuck unfurled it, had enough surface area to cover both the boat's name and her port of origin. When Chuck was done, the boat was called *Arianamaria* and she was from Casco Bay—believable, yet, they hoped, thoroughly unmemorable.

"What's Chuck doing?" EJ kept asking.

"Making sure no one bothers us," Ed told him. "Lobstermen don't like it when they think you're trying to take their lobsters."

"But we're not, are we?"

"It's just easier this way," Ed said.

They had ventured into the narrow thoroughfare between North Haven and Vinalhaven, idling between the lobster traps as Ed scanned the houses above the bank. He could just make out the blurred outline of a long, big-windowed cape perched on a hilltop.

"Take the helm," Ed told Chuck, and then he grabbed the binoculars and studied the property around the house. Trees had been removed from this stretch of shoreline centuries earlier, and in place of the woods, a tightly mowed lawn rolled down from the road, through the fog, around the house, around a vegetable garden, around boulders, around white Adirondack chairs clustered in pairs, toward a long pier. They waited, the boat slowly rocking from port to starboard and back again. A half hour passed. As the morning began to warm, the smell of the ocean rose in the mist. EJ pulled his backpack out from down below. He unwrapped a Fruit Roll-Up and smashed it into his mouth, using his hand like the tailgate of a garbage truck to slowly crush the Roll-Up down his throat. Once he swallowed, he reached for a second Roll-Up and started to unwrap it, but Ed figured one was enough—Steph didn't want EJ eating too much sugar all at once—so he removed the snack from EJ's hand and shoved it into his own pocket. EJ started to protest, but Ed shushed him and said they had to be quiet in the fog so they could hear the other boats.

Ed went back to watching the house. And other houses. And the weather. Chuck kept the boat in one spot, near a floating tessellation of seaweed, ready to move the *Miss Stephanie* away, into the fog, toward another trap, if another boat ever came near.

Finally Ed saw a garage door go up on the right side of the house. A Mercedes station wagon emerged from the door, mounted the driveway to the road, and headed west toward town.

"All right," Ed said. "Let's bring her in."

ONCE CHUCK AND EJ HAD deposited Ed at the municipal dock, Ed humped away from town on an unstriped road. The house was on Waterman Cove, just beyond Fish Point Ledge. He carried a bucket, a clammer's rake, and a waterproof black duffel bag containing bolt-cutters, a crowbar, and a ski mask. Yellow daffodils in long green weeds lined the ditches along the road, the colors muted by the gray.

A mile north of town, with his legs beginning to sweat small streams into his boots, Ed arrived at the cape he had seen from the water, the house he had scouted earlier in the season. He'd brought Steph on that trip, rented bikes and told her he wanted to take her riding for the day. She'd loved it, said they should do it more often, said it was the most romantic thing he'd ever done.

He gave the house a long look as he approached, checking every window for signs of movement, seeing none. The garage had two big doors for cars and one smaller door for people. The car doors were sealed shut. Ed tried the knob on the smaller door at the side of the garage. Also locked. He circled toward the harbor side of the house, stepped onto a cedar-planked patio, looked around him, behind him—but saw no one. A long line of tall windows faced the harbor, positioned to let the southern light in. Ed cupped his hands over the first window and peered into a sunroom, recessed and separated from the living room by two long stairs. Everything was still. A bird warbled, and a line knocked lightly against a flagpole. Ed knocked on the door. No response. He turned the knob and yelled, "Hello?"

Still no response.

Now he began working quickly, removing his hat, reaching in the duffel bag, pulling out the ski mask, yanking it over his head, rearranging the holes so that he could see and breathe.

In the living room, Ed found a bookcase loaded with trophies shaped like sailboats. He snagged a silver cup and a small platter, and by now he had found so many similar items on similar shelves that he knew what the engravings were, that they were the names of regattas, races from one port to another. He tossed everything in the clam bucket, anything valuable—even an antique-looking clock and an honorary medal with the seal of some kind of academic society—and left only the framed photograph that showed the family of seven gathered around two of the Adirondack chairs on the lawn, everyone wearing white linen, the children in sweater vests, the father with a mustache as thick as a Western sheriff's.

Ed kept moving, hustling to the dining room, straight to an old armoire, pumping open drawers from the bottom up. The lowest drawer held place mats. Ed slammed it shut. The second drawer: all napkins and tablecloths. He closed that drawer, too. In the top compartment he finally found the silver, rows and rows of it, all heavy and polished. He dumped it into the duffel bag: forks, cutlery, serving spoons, a tea set. Ed took as much as he could, then jogged for the stairs, passing a row of portraits as he went upward, photos that showed the children growing older and bigger. The stairs doubled back and took him to a low-ceilinged hallway. Ed went left. He made it all the way to the end of the hall, to a bedroom. He stepped across the threshold, ready to make for the dresser by the dormer window.

And then he heard something to his left, from behind a closed door. A shuffling sound. Then a flushing toilet. Ed stood still. The door opened, and an elderly man stepped out and looked straight through Ed's ski mask. The man was frozen, locked in a kind of action pose. He was in his eighties, hair and mustache thin and white. Slowly, Ed recognized the man. He was the father from the family picture downstairs, several decades older.

"What are you doing?" the man asked Ed.

"Nothin," Ed said. "What are you doing?"

The old man wore red pajama pants and matching pajama shirt, but his pants hung below his waist. Ed glanced outside but saw nothing other than a sky that had turned infinitely blue. Which meant that Ed—and the boat—were now very exposed. He needed to run. But this man was a witness—Ed couldn't just leave him here.

"Are you taking me to breakfast?" the man asked.

"No," Ed said.

"They were supposed to take me to breakfast."

"Well," Ed said, "I gotta put you back in the bathroom, then you can go get breakfast." The man pivoted and did as Ed instructed. Ed hadn't expected him to comply so quickly and without protest. "Hang on," he said. He inspected the bathroom, checking for portable phones or other ways to communicate from inside or anything else—a secret panic button or a trapdoor maybe—that might do Ed in. But he didn't see anything of the kind, no windows through which to crawl, nothing but a toilet and a sink and a bathtub. "All right," Ed said. "Why don't you go ahead and sit on the toilet."

The man was about to sit, but the lid was up, so Ed stopped him and put the seat down.

"Now do it."

The man sat, performing a three-point turn on his arthritic joints to maneuver himself into position. His pants still hung on his hips. "Good," Ed said. "Now I'm gonna leave you here and I need you to—"

"You always leave me here," the man said.

Ed scratched at his beard through the mask. "All right, fine then," he said. "Blame the guy who always leaves you here."

Ed grabbed the door and was about to slam it shut, but the man asked him where he was going.

"Where I usually go," Ed said. "You need anything while I'm out?"

The man shook his head.

"What's your name?" Ed asked the man.

"Frank."

"Okay, Frank, tell me this—when does the rest of the family come home?"

"This afternoon."

"What about breakfast?"

"Huh?"

"I thought they were taking you to breakfast."

"You said that, not me."

Ed looked over his shoulder at the blue window, back to Frank. "What do you need between now and then?"

"Nothing."

"You take drugs?"

"No."

"Prescription drugs, Frank."

"Oh. No."

"All right," Ed said, "I can't leave you with your pants down, so pull em up."

Frank tugged at the drawstrings of his pajama bottoms. He wasn't making much progress, so Ed helped him.

"You got anything to eat?" Ed asked.

"I don't know."

Ed patted his own pockets until he found the Fruit Roll-Up, which he handed to Frank. "You need water, you got the sink," Ed said.

"Okay," Frank said.

Ed told Frank to sit tight, the rest of the family would be back soon enough, and then he turned to go.

"Have a nice day," Frank said.

"Yuh," Ed said. "You too, Frank." He closed the door and went to lock the bathroom door, but there was no lock, not on the outside, so he looked around the room for something to use as a barricade, then hurried to the bed. Bright sunshine was bursting through the dormer window now. The bed had a heavy frame, the headboard and footboard both peaking at the corners in round knobs. Ed pulled on the front knob, then the back knob, moving the bed an inch at a time toward the door. When he had the bed halfway there, he threw his shoulder into the frame, shoving it as tight to the wall as he could, sealing Frank in the bathroom.

Then he sprinted for the stairs, bounding down to the living room, digging in the duffel bag for his walkie-talkie as he went, running clumsily in the orange overalls and rubber boots. He charged out the back door and onto the patio, the sun hitting him like a spotlight as he remembered to sling the clamming rake over his shoulder. He looked nothing like a clammer. Clammers don't run. He tried to slow himself down but only ran faster. And he was wearing the ski mask. Clammers *definitely* don't wear ski masks. He ripped it off, threw it in the bucket.

"Chuck," he said into the walkie-talkie. A stream of static greeted him. He depressed the button again and said, louder this time, "Chuck!"

The walkie-talkie crackled. A voice came through: "Dad, it's me!"

The lawn was wide open. All the fog had disappeared above this island, the other island, all the islands. Ed was hurtling through the wet grass toward the sparkling water. He tried to cling to the rake and walkie-talkie with one hand while the bag slid down from his shoulder to the bucket full of tools and silver trophies. "EJ," Ed said urgently. "Give the walkie-talkie to your uncle. Now!"

He issued orders as soon as he heard Chuck's voice: Get the boat to the house a mile west of town, the one with the long dock and the big lawn.

To the west, beyond the mouth of the thoroughfare, beyond the bay, was the endless ocean. The wind was picking up, and the only clouds were narrow and high, back toward home. As Ed hit the pier, he heard and saw the *Miss Stephanie* thundering from behind the trees to his left, approaching the dock, arriving just as he came down the ramp.

He hopped the gunwale and went straight to the cabin, dropping his tools, the bucket, the bag, stepping out of his rubber overalls and boots, shoving them in with everything else. "Go, Chuck," Ed said.

"What happened?"

"Nothing."

"Are we fucked?"

"No."

"Uncle Chuck said fuck," EJ said.

Chuck steered the boat away from the dock, and Ed watched the house from the top step of the ladder as they moved into the waterway. He didn't see any movement in or around the estate. Everything remained sunny and still.

Down below, by the sink, they kept a cooler. Ed opened it and reached in for a beer. He cracked it and drank the first half right away, the beer cold enough to sting his throat on the way down, and then he moved back up the stairs, onto the deck, as Chuck picked up speed. A dash of cold salt water sprayed over the bow and rained down on Ed's hair. The boat was plowing through the steady waves, engine whining as the props lost hold, then growling as they dug back into the water, and EJ was standing by Ed's side, looking upward.

"Hold this," Ed said, handing his son the beer. Then Ed hoisted him onto his back. EJ wrapped his arms around Ed's neck and held the can below Ed's beard. Ed took a step toward the stern and looked beyond the white foaming wake, back to the big cape house, as the boat left it behind. There were no flashing lights, no alarms sounding.

"Let's finish that beer," Ed said to his son. EJ tipped the open can toward his father's mouth, and Ed drank, but then the boat hit a wave and he nearly lost his balance. They had reached the west rim of the thoroughfare and were entering the bay where the waves turned into great big swells. Some of the beer spilled and dripped down Ed's beard.

"You missed, Dad," EJ said.

"That's all right. You can put the can down now."

But EJ didn't drop it in the boat. He threw it. Ed turned to see the beer can hit the water, landing weightlessly—

And it was at that moment that he noticed the red lobster boat. She was rising on a swell, the captain and his sternman standing above the transom, arms crossed, staring back at him. The boat's stern said NORTH HAVEN, ME. It continued to rise on the swell until the wave rolled out from underneath the hull, and then the boat leveled out for a moment before slowly dropping down. All Ed could hear was the roar of the *Miss Stephanie*'s engines. A gang of seagulls floated above the red boat, waiting for bait to get pitched to sea. But the ship's captain and sternman weren't tending to any traps, so the seagulls weren't getting what they wanted. The men stood on the stern, staring at the *Miss Stephanie*. Both men had their arms tucked in their bibs.

"Chuck?" Ed said. "Give her a little more gas."

The Thatches' boat reared up and its wake kicked higher. Ed kept his eyes on the shrinking red boat and the two lobstermen on its deck, not daring to move until the *Miss Stephanie* was safely into the bay and the other boat had vanished behind the waves. Finally Ed lowered EJ to the deck and peeked over the transom, running a hand over the duct tape, making sure the false name and port of origin were still in place.

WHEN FATHER AND SON RETURNED to the trailer that afternoon, Ed sat EJ down in front of the TV and went to the shower. He ran the water, waited for the brown stuff to cough itself into the drain and turn clear, then stood beneath the sputtering showerhead. A moment later, the door opened and he felt a draft. He knew it was Steph, but she didn't say anything right away, so he pulled the plastic curtain aside.

"Hey," she said.

"Hey."

"Got some news for you." She was standing inside the door, leaning against the frame.

"This about the test?"

"What test?"

"I don't know—the one you said you had."

"Oh," she said. "Right. No. I said exam. But I didn't mean the kind you're thinking of."

"What kind was it?"

"The kind you have at a doctor's office."

Ed turned the shower off, and Steph handed him a towel, which he snaked between his legs. "Everything okay?" he asked.

"Not really."

He waited.

"I'm pregnant again."

"Well, congratulations," Ed said. He stopped toweling himself for a moment and smiled, just barely, not sure if it was the reaction Steph was looking for. "That's good news."

"Not exactly."

"Don't you want another?"

"Of course I want another. A baby brother or sister for EJ? Yes, I want that. But Ed"—she shook her head like she couldn't believe her husband, how hard it was to get him to say the things she needed him to say—"you're not supposed to say 'congratulations' when you're the father."

"Oh," Ed said, "big deal."

"It *is* a big deal. We don't have the money for another kid. Don't have the space. Look at our house—it's a Goddamn tuna can."

Ed looked around the bathroom.

"I didn't mean 'look at our house' literally," she said.

"No, I know, but I hear ya," he said. "I can fix it."

"Fix what?"

"The trailer."

"You can't *fix* the trailer," she said. "The problem is that it *is* a trailer."

"So we'll get a real house."

"How?"

"I don't know yet."

"So I'm just supposed to trust you?"

He thought about that for a second, then went back to drying himself with the towel.

"Yuh," he said.

"Yuh?"

"I'm gonna make it work."

But she wasn't letting him off that easy. She was doing her best to frown, to remain skeptical.

"What?" he said, throwing his towel on a hook, watching it hold, then not hold, then slide off the hook and onto the floor. "I got this."

And, somehow, he did. Two months later, after a few more big hauls, the family moved out of the trailer and into a two-story, three-bedroom house in Bremen—one village north of the Pound, two miles closer to Damariscotta.

THE DETAILS OF THAT DAY on North Haven have been pieced together with the help of a bank investigator (let's call him Nate) who, several years ago, was looking into the unnatural death of his younger brother, reading police files and interviewing locals, when he stumbled upon records of the burglary. At first, the case didn't stand out. It was only one of many that Nate looked at briefly before dismissing. He couldn't see any connection between the break-in at the big cape and the death of his brother. He had died of a drug overdose, and Nate was only going through the motions of a real investigation because his parents had become fixated upon finding "the evildoers" who had sown the seeds of their son's demise. They wanted to know who was bringing all those pills to the region, they said, so that they might spare the lives of other sons and daughters. This was how they planned to grieve. Nate never expected to find anything that the police hadn't already found, but, in deference to his parents' wishes, he took a few days off from his job in Delaware, made the trip up to the Midcoast, and began looking into the matter. If nothing else, his parents seemed pleased to have him home.

What we discovered last summer, when everything came to light, was that the drugs were finding their way to the coast—and to northern New England, even some parts of Connecticut and New York—on boats piloted by the Thatches and their crew. This was the enterprise they moved on to once Ed decided that the income derived from looting houses was not enough. The papers have depicted Chuck as the muscle, Ben as the brains, and Ed as the glue that held everyone together, and while that's all true, basically, it also undersells how important Ed's vision and ambition were to the operation. It was Ed who convinced himself that his family needed more than it had, and who pushed the gang into deeper and deeper waters after a half decade of successful, nonviolent, relatively harmless larceny up and down the coast.

Recently I read an article in the *Press Herald* reporting that after years of steady decline, drug use amongst young Mainers was once again on the rise. According to this study, nearly a quarter of high school students said they had been sold, offered, or given an illegal drug on school property over the past year. I hope all we're talking about is a little pot. But I know there's plenty of meth in Maine, and for a while, there seemed to be an abundance of bath salts, too. These two substances weren't moved by the Thatches (not, I presume, because they had any moral clause that prevented them from running this type of contraband in from Canada, but rather because it could be so easily manufactured closer to home, rendering the Thatches' services unnecessary). At first, Ed and his crew brought only marijuana around the border. Then they discovered a hankering for khat, the loose leaves chewed for cannabis-like effect favored by the Somali immigrants who had settled in Lewiston, of all places, as part of a government immigration strategy. Then the Thatches started bringing in cocaine, ecstasy, and, at the end, heroin. This last substance has been blighting all our state's small cities and villages for at least a decade now. Earlier I alluded to that *other side* of Maine, the one that Ed came from, the one that I did not come from, and at first it was easy for some of us to assume that this was the only part of the state adversely affected by opioids— but of course that wasn't true.

Last month the *Bangor Daily News* published an obituary written by a man who had been married to a woman who had been raised in relative privilege near Augusta. Her mother was a state legislator. The obituary detailed the woman's problems, starting in high school (private, for what it's worth) when she first started to drink. It wasn't long before she was showing signs of addiction. At various points, she had been convicted of shoplifting and soliciting. She had spent four years trying to get sober, in and out of methadone clinics. She lived with her cat, Bullwinkle, and loved to share videos of the big fella via social media. Her favorite food was chocolate-chip-cookie dough. She had green eyes and liked to change the color of her hair. Her body was found behind a parking garage by a seven-year-old girl.

I doubt this obituary, the details of the woman's life, would

have concerned the Thatches—or, for that matter, any of the
people they did business with. They saw addicts as a demo-
graphic. As a market to be tapped. Customers wanted what they
sold. So they sold it. Most of it went through Lewiston. This was
always the less sophisticated end of the supply chain, run by a
man they called Lew, short for Lewiston, out of the back of a
liquor store. The Thatches didn't ask questions about where the
product was sold, but they did have one rule: None of it was ever
supposed to make it back home to Lincoln County.

With some luck, Nate the bank investigator eventually connected the dots between the North Haven break-in and his
brother's death, but he never went to the police, so after his name
surfaced during my own research, once I'd tracked him down
with the help of my dad's old patient and recorded his story, I
asked him one last question, why he'd kept his findings to himself.
When he told me that he thought the police might consider his
evidence too flimsy, I said nothing but didn't fully believe him,
something about his overly confidential tone. Nate might have
picked up on my skepticism, though, because he quickly noted
that he was *also* hesitant because he had a family to get back to in
Delaware, and the time spent in Maine had already put enough
stress on his marriage. There was a pause on the line—the mention of family seemed to stir something—and then he reminded
me of the only condition of our interview, that I would change
his name if my book ever went to print.

BY THAT POINT, I'D DECIDED that I really was writing a book. At
first it had felt like just the easiest way to explain what I was
doing—to others and to myself—because otherwise all that time
in the former pantry staring at maps, reading articles, construct-
ing detailed timelines and tacking them to the wall might have

been cause for concern. But also, the timelines weren't *entirely* devoted to the Thatches; one of them in fact detailed events from my own life. I posted it right above the lamp so that I could keep track of whatever I was doing whenever the Thatches were doing whatever they were doing, making some big move hundreds or thousands of miles away from wherever I was at the time. It shouldn't be this hard to keep track of your own life, I know, but I've never been good with dates, and I was so slow to accomplish anything, at least in comparison to the Thatches, the divergences would seem almost too unbelievable if I didn't have them all jotted down on paper. While I was waiting tables in LA and living without health insurance and getting drunk on Mondays, Ed and Steph were moving into the house in Bremen and bringing their second child into the world, a daughter they named Allie. And while Maeve and I were settling into Boston, still using birth control, Allie was already seven years old, and EJ was already *thirteen years old*. Maeve and I were struggling to figure out how to leave the student life behind and become adults—and maybe we were a little delayed in that respect, or just cautious in the way most of our peers have been slow to embrace the big institutions of marriage and parenthood—while Ed and Steph were busy hustling their daughter to elementary school, their son to middle school, neither parent more than a step or two ahead of their children on the same developmental curve. I can't imagine. It'd be like trying to write a guidebook to a city you've only just arrived at for the very first time.

6

EJ WAS ABOUT TO GRAB HIS BIKE AND RIDE TO CHUCK'S APARTMENT above Wade and Tracey's garage when his dad turned from the couch and said, "Your mom reminded you about drugs night?"

"What?" EJ said. He was tangled in his hoodie, the neck over his head, arms in a knot.

"Drugs night," Ed said.

As part of the county's D.A.R.E. program, EJ and his peers were supposed to perform skits about substance abuse—tonight, this was true—but EJ wasn't sure how his dad had found out about it or why he was bringing it up now. Usually EJ rode his bike to Chuck's, spent the night, saw his folks the next day, no big deal. Everyone seemed to appreciate the extra space. Because they needed it! They'd moved to Bremen in order to give everyone their own rooms, but then EJ's mom had converted one of these rooms into a home office, which she also used for doing exercises with a big plastic ball and writing open letters about the state of Damariscotta's Main Street to *The Lincoln County News,* so EJ had to bunk with Allie, making him the only kid he'd ever heard of with a little sister for a roommate, with wrestling figurines living in a dollhouse and volcanic geodes bookending a series of chapter books about young feminists.

"D.A.R.E.'s canceled," EJ said.

His dad had been sitting with boots on brown velour ottoman, watching a swarm of hockey players chase a puck across the screen, but now he sat up a little straighter. "That's not what your mom said."

"Well, it should be canceled," EJ said. "It's the most hypocritical night of the year. All it does is tell you which drugs make you feel this way, which drugs make you feel that way. It's like, Hey, thanks, now I know what kind of high I want. Plus, half the crowd will be buzzed, and Chief Hunt's an alcoholic."

"Not anymore she ain't."

"She's still an alcoholic," Steph said, coming down the stairs from her office. "She just stopped drinking."

"Either way," Ed said, "we're going." He stood from the couch.

"We?" EJ said.

"The whole family. Put your sweatshirt on."

"I'm trying."

"Allie, get your coat!" Ed yelled.

"This is so random," EJ said.

"This is not random," Ed said. "Not random at all."

So then EJ was staring out the back window of his mother's car, the inside of the window coated in cold dew. He dragged his fingers down the glass, making a squeaking, rubbing sound, leaving marks like the kind you might find on a prison wall. It *was* random, what his father was doing, but that's just how Ed was, like a zombie you think is dead but who keeps reanimating and trying to attack you with hugs, noogies, and presents, a video game here, a digital watch there. EJ didn't need presents. Presents were okay, actually. He didn't hate the presents. It's just that, according to lore, his family was poor. Until it wasn't. Until it was again. His dad liked to *talk* about working hard, and yet he never seemed to actually work all that hard, and yet he *had* worked hard enough— apparently—to purchase the Lobster Pound from EJ's grandpa, the Schooner from EJ's other grandpa, three lobster boats from various retired fishermen, and, as of this fall, several apartments above the post office in Damariscotta. Why did the family need apartments? They didn't need apartments. They already owned a house. What they ought to have bought was a bigger house, or at least a storage unit so they could clean out all the old junk from the garage—lobster gear, flowerpots, tennis rackets—and convert it into a more acceptable living situation for their teenage son.

He clawed at the window again.

"EJ, that's enough," his mom said. "You're gonna drive us all crazy."

"I feel sick," Allie said.

"That's because you're reading in the car," EJ said.

"I like reading in the car."

EJ glanced over at the book, a novel about a girl who uses math to solve disputes between classmates, to see if it was the same book she'd been reading yesterday. It wasn't.

"Mom," EJ said. "We should get Allie an iPod."

"A what?"

"An iPod. So she can listen to books in the car."

The car went silent.

"That's actually a very good idea," his mom said.

"You could get it for her as a birthday present or something."

"Yuh," his dad said. "We'll do that."

When EJ looked at his sister again, she was smiling back at him. Two of her teeth were missing. "Thank you," she whispered.

"I just don't want you to puke on me," EJ said, "that's all."

They arrived at school late. Parents and siblings had already assembled in the ale-colored light of the gymnasium, dressed in thick layers of fleece, flannel-lined jeans, rubber-soled boots. Prevailing wisdom said it hadn't snowed yet because Maine was too cold this winter, the air too raw to crystallize. EJ stood hidden behind the edge of the curtain, feeling the first tremors of serious anxiety. Chief Hunt, who ran the county Drug Abuse Resistance Education program, was in the back of the gym, and Mr. Matt, the school counselor, directed the skits from the far side of the stage, nodding encouragement, mouthing the lines delivered by his students, arms crossed but with one hand in the air, pointing at his chin. He had a background in theater. Seventh-graders stood before the audience, looking around, looking lost. Mr. Matt whispered, "Action." The kids began to act like drug dealers, like students who wanted to get high, like their future selves returning to reveal how much hair had fallen out, how many troubles had befallen their lives.

EJ's group was next. He felt panicky. It was not only that he had stage fright. He didn't have stage fright. Only a little. The larger issue was that he hadn't learned his lines because he didn't think his parents would make him come tonight. That wasn't quite true. He had tried to learn his lines, over and over, in the shower, in his head, singing them aloud—all the ways Mr. Matt had taught the students—but the words wouldn't stick. If EJ stepped out there, he would have nothing to say. He would stand in the lights and everyone would stare at him until they started to laugh and laugh and laugh. His father would pull his hat down over his face. His mother would do that thing where she slowly squeezed the bridge of her nose with her entire hand, like she was trying to remove her face. And so—to spare his family—EJ left the gymnasium and walked down the empty hallway under the flickering lights and past the bulletin boards, out the front door, into the parking lot.

THE NIGHT AIR WAS FRIGID, the birches on the far side of the parking lot pale and knobby. They rubbed against each other like toneless wind chimes. Then the wind strayed off toward the river and left the lot to the kind of quiet you were only supposed to hear in outer space. From the rows of parked cars behind EJ a dog barked, the bark muffled. EJ turned. He saw Chief Hunt's K-9 cruiser and, in the backseat, a German shepherd, nose pressed wetly against the window. EJ, thinking the dog looked like it wanted out, found a large rock at the edge of the parking lot, told the dog to back away, and started smashing out the window. It didn't fully shatter upon the first blow, so EJ had to hit the glass three or four more times. The dog barked, then cowered, then barked between strikes. When all the glass was gone, the dog jumped through the window, as if this were something he and EJ had been planning all along.

EJ didn't know what else they were planning, so he walked toward the soccer field, frost twinkling into nothing as it fled from the ambient light of the school. The field was uneven and hard. Eventually EJ found a stick. He and the dog played fetch. He fully expected to be caught. He told himself not to care. He wished it were possible to commit this kind of crime *and* return everything to its rightful place afterward, glue the shards of glass to their window frame, put the dog back where it belonged. EJ threw the stick. The dog chased after it, disappearing into the darkness, then came back with the stick in his mouth. In the cold night, EJ awaited his fate. He wouldn't mind if it showed up soon. Then it did show up, wearing a brown sheriff's uniform and a wide-brimmed hat.

"Are. You. Shitting. Me," Chief Hunt said, trying to sound like she wasn't winded. She shined a Maglite on EJ's face, so he visored his eyes with a flat hand. All he could see was the outline of the hat, her wide shoulders.

I SHOULD MAYBE POINT OUT that Chief Hunt was no longer really the chief of police in Damariscotta (or anywhere else) and hadn't been since the late '90s when she drove her squad car into a gasoline pump. She had hit the terminal at fifteen miles an hour, hard enough to rip the hose off the pump and knock her license plate off-kilter. She got out of the cruiser and walked into the store to buy cigarettes, which was all she wanted anyway (gas hadn't even been a part of her plan for the evening), but her nose was bleeding. When the clerk pointed this out and expressed his concern, she said, "Fine. Never mind then. I'll smoke something else," and left the store. She went to her car, backed it away from the station, and drove home. If she had hit something other than a gas pump—a tree, for example—she probably would have gotten away with it, but the impact had incurred enough property damage to involve the service station's insurance company, and there was surveillance tape of the whole incident. The insurance company didn't seem to care that she was chief of police.

In a matter of weeks, Hunt had resigned that post and taken a sideways demotion to sergeant in the county sheriff's office. They assigned her to the K-9 unit and presented her with the leash to a Belgian shepherd named Cliff. It was mandated that she attend AA meetings, too. Everyone knew the whole story, but most people with Damariscotta roots still called her "Chief" out of habit. EJ didn't know her as anything else. He watched her in the school's administrative office as it was suggested—not by her, by the principal—that EJ might spend two days by her side, learning to respect authority. This would be his penance for skipping out on the skit.

"And the broken window?" the principal asked.

"He'll pay for it," Ed said, glaring at EJ.

"With what?" EJ asked.

"Your allowance."

"I don't have an allowance."

"EJ," his mother said, "this is no time to be fresh."

WHEN EJ TRIED TO RIDE his bike to Chuck's that night, his mother told him he wasn't going anywhere, that he was grounded for a month. Unfair, EJ said; he was just trying to give his sister a little space. He would never be able to sleep that night, feeling as guilty as he did about the events of the day, and he didn't want to keep Allie up all night. This argument seemed to soften Steph, just for a moment, but then she said, "If you go to Chuck's, you're grounded for *two* months. And no more video games."

"Fine," EJ said. "I don't even like video games anymore."

And then he grabbed his bike, flipped on the light, and pedaled away.

By the time he arrived at Chuck's, he was already regretting the decision. Usually he liked staying there, liked that Chuck's girlfriend Mary-May wore cut-off tie-dyed shirts and boxer shorts and loved to bake, but now he felt doubly guilty. He had walked out on his family twice in one evening. It was like every time he put a stick of dynamite down his own pants, he had to shove a grenade down there, too, to blow up the dynamite. He watched Mary-May as she worked in the kitchen, his arms folded on the counter, head down, cheek smooshed against a forearm. Mary-May always made two batches, one for adults, one for EJ—brownies, cookies, cinnamon buns, you name it. As she mixed, she listened to Van Halen, and as she baked, she listened to Van Morrison. The warm scent of butter and herbs filled the whole apartment. Well, not herbs. Marijuana. Chuck and Mary-May thought he didn't know, but he knew. Once he'd asked Mary-May where the special ingredients came from, and she said, "Oh, your dad or your uncle, here or there," and when EJ said, "My dad doesn't cook," Chuck had come into the room and said, "What are you, a cop?"

IN THE MORNING, EJ SLID the blow-up mattress behind the bathroom door, pulled his sweatshirt on, and took two brownies from the baking pan marked *EJ*. But then—making sure no one was looking—he removed two brownies from Chuck's pan, then replaced them and aligned them just so, smoothing the edges so they fit with the others. On a Post-it note, Mary-May had written Chuck's name and drawn a little arm making a big muscle. The joke was that Mary-May only liked Chuck because of his guns, and whenever she gave them a squeeze, she would put a hand to her forehead and pretend to faint. Her baked goods were his spinach—Power Brownies, they called them. EJ had been swapping out Power Brownies for several months now, once a week on average, just to see if anyone would notice, which they never had. Typically he just walked around with the brownies—or buns or muffins—in his hoodie for a couple days, daring himself to take a bite, throwing them out when they finally got hard. Today, though, he vowed to eat them. *Before* they got hard. Way before. Soon. Whenever he worked up the courage.

The radio was on in his mother's car as she drove him to the sheriff's office in Wiscasset, and someone called the rock station's morning show impersonating President Bush, which made the hosts laugh like they were getting paid to laugh as hard as they could.

"These people are deranged," Steph said, turning the volume down.

It was stuffy in the Camry. The sun was cutting a hole through the trees and sucking the color from the pavement.

"I don't know what to do with you," Steph said.

"Just drop me off." They were crossing the bridge to Wiscasset, approaching the railroad tracks, the narrow Main Street. He knew she meant something else but didn't know how to respond. They were almost to the sheriff's office, which was connected to the jail, built from the same batch of bricks.

"Please be nice to Chief Hunt," Steph said.

This made EJ not want to be nice to Chief Hunt, although he couldn't say why.

"You know we believe in letting you make your own decisions," Steph said.

"I know."

"You keep making the wrong ones."

"I know."

"So that's what we need to work on."

"I know, Mom. I'm sorry."

They reached the parking lot. Steph pulled in next to the K-9 cruiser with the missing window. "I love you, EJ," she told him.

"I love you, too," he mumbled.

"And I know you mean well, but I'm really worried about you."

"I'm worried about you, too."

"What?"

"I don't know," he said.

What he meant was that he didn't want his mom to worry about him, that her worrying made him feel so much worse.

He walked inside the station and found himself alone with

Chief Hunt. She told him to sit across the desk and watch her do paperwork.

"Everyone thinks police work is all guns and solving murders," she said.

"Not me."

"Well, good."

THERE'S A WOMAN I'VE TRACKED down named Leah Wickersham, a political consultant who lives in Washington, D.C., and in the mid-2000s, in the days before she went back to school to get a master's in political science, she worked as a cub reporter at the *Portland Press-Herald*. Mostly her duties entailed copyediting and coffee brewing, but she was also tasked with screening the local police reports from around the state, looking for any stories worth turning over to the senior crime reporter. She was supposed to find anything having to do with drug trafficking, especially in Lewiston-Auburn, the former logging metropolis that had fallen on hard times and re-incorporated itself as a narcotics depot between the Northeast and Canada. Leah, as instructed, always checked the L-A police reports first, coastal reports last, but at least twice a month, it seemed, there was a significant theft in a large home by the water, and she ignored them all until she couldn't ignore them anymore.

"Are there always this many burglaries?" she asked the senior reporter.

"Burglaries?" he said.

"Yeah, on the coast. Should we investigate?"

"How many we talking?"

"I don't know, a couple a month?"

"That's not very many. Try to find me some drug stuff."

But she kept stumbling across the same reports issued by

different police departments, so she began sifting through old criminal records, finding faint patterns: Over the past decade, there had been hundreds of burglaries, all of them hitting wealthy summer people or recently relocated year-rounders, most of them targeting the house's silver collection, many of them unreported in the press.

She called some of the local police departments, but they all gave her the same line, which was that Kennebunk or Camden liked to present itself as a nice, safe place to live, at least for the summer, because that's what it was, and they didn't want to spoil that for anyone, so if all they were talking about was a little break-in here or there, then they didn't see all that much cause for concern.

Leah wrote up the story anyway, and several days later a headline appeared on the second page of the *Press-Herald:* "Theft a Growing Problem Along the Coast."

The story caught the eye of the president of the Maine State Chamber of Commerce, who called the chief of Maine State Police and said, "This is not good news." Crime along the coast would hurt tourism, which meant that property values could plummet. If the Maine Association of Realtors caught wind of the problem and decided the state's intended countermeasures didn't satisfy, they might raise a serious stink. The chief of the state police, like the senior crime reporter, felt they had larger fish to fry, and by fish he meant drugs, and by fry he meant freebase. Not that he, personally, was freebasing drugs. Junkies were freebasing drugs. On his watch, which drove him apeshit.

Nevertheless a small burglary task force was created, and this task force decided that by and large the break-ins looked random. Sometimes there would be a crime a day, each in a different port. Then the trail would go cold for a month. The only witness to any of the burglaries they could dredge up was an old man on North Haven whose account sounded mixed up to the point of nonsense. Whom he described was not a robber at all; to his mind the perp was more of a masked apparition with rubber pants and a rake, who had dropped in merely to dispense snacks and remind the old man that faucet water was indeed potable.

(Of course, if law enforcement had ever thought to cross-reference the break-ins with the weather, they would have realized that there was absolutely a pattern: The daytime incidents always coincided with heavy fog.)

The state police, with no other leads, produced a map. It was covered in red dots, each one marking a burglary. They sent the map to every police station and sheriff's department along the coast with instructions to post it within headquarters. Some offices followed suit, some did not. In general, the maps were neglected. New incidents rarely appeared on the maps as fresh dots. The map in the Lincoln County Sheriff's Office, for its part, was staying out of the way in a corner of the conference room, rolled into a baton and tucked behind a filing cabinet, under a portrait of an old sheriff, until EJ found it. He had been investigating the office because he was bored. Chief Hunt wouldn't even let him use the radar gun. Once he had unrolled the map, he brought it over to Hunt and said, "What is this?"

She told him it was a map.

"What kind of map?"

She put her pencil down and sighed, as if this intrusion were interrupting something important. EJ looked at her notepad. Everything was upside down, but if he wasn't mistaken, what she had been working on, what was so important, was an illustration of a cat. Hunt removed the notepad from her desk and put it in a drawer. She explained the map, what she knew about how it came into being, and then she talked about criminal activity closer to home, in their county. Actually, there wasn't all that much of it. Which was why it was such bullshit that she was no longer chief of police.

"Let me ask you something," Hunt said, her eyes narrowing. She had an arid voice, like a slough with all the water gone. "Are you sure you're related to your sister?"

"What?"

"You heard me. Your sister. She's like a little"—she waved her hand, looking for the right phrase—"smart person."

"Oh," EJ said. "Yeah. She is."

"Not saying you're dumb. It's just—something happened when she came along, didn't it?" Hunt leaned back in her chair, close to tipping. She had to grab the desk. "Feels like the world just stopped making sense at some point. What happened to honor? Order. Decorum. Stop looking at me like I'm speaking French. Actually, maybe that was French. But you get it."

She was wrong; EJ did not get it, much as he would have liked to. He kept listening as Hunt kept talking about Allie, then Steph, or really Steph's hair, which she "got cut down in Portland for some odd reason," and the Schooner, which had become "too uppity" the moment it started laminating the menus, and then back to Allie, who was the type of daughter, as far as Hunt could tell, who usually only sprang from a line of Goddamn aristocrats.

"Know what I'm saying?" Hunt asked EJ.

"Not really."

"Well, what do you think of the rest of it?"

"The rest of it?"

"Yeah," Hunt said. "Everything I just said."

"Well," EJ said cautiously, "my dad says some people get jealous because he's such a hard worker and my mom's so smart, and also because she works out at the Y every day."

Hunt made a *hmph* sound, and then she informed EJ that he had been good; he could play with the radar gun now.

Later in the afternoon, Hunt checked her watch and said, "Grab your jacket. Let's hit it."

"I don't have a jacket," EJ said.

So she gave him a LINCOLN COUNTY SHERIFFS windbreaker to wear over his sweatshirt and drove him home in an unmarked vehicle, ahead of schedule. EJ tried to exit the passenger's side when they arrived at his house, but the door was locked. "The door's locked," he said.

Chief Hunt was too busy looking at the house to respond. It was small, paint missing, lawn frosty and patchy, sports balls deflating here and there. A faded pink-and-yellow buoy hung next to the front door. Through the windows of the garage, they could see piles and piles of discarded household items and garbage bags.

"It doesn't look like much," Hunt said.

"We only have two bedrooms. Well, three. But I have to share a room with my sister, which is bullsh— sorry. Which is stupid. I try not to get on her nerves, but it's pretty much impossible. This one time I brought home a free turtle—"

"What's a free turtle?"

"Well, there was this box by the road, and it said 'Free Turtles' on it, so I grabbed one, and I found a tank for it at the Pound, and I put it on my sister's side of the room, as a gift, but when she saw it, she freaked out."

"She didn't want a turtle."

"I guess they're hard to take care of, and she thought it was scary, but the point is that everyone thought I got the turtle for myself and that I just put it on her side to mess with her or something. Nobody believed it was a present, even though Allie had been asking for a pet for like three years. We just need more space. I keep telling my dad, let me move into the garage and make it a bedroom."

"Now you're talking."

"But no one's allowed in there," EJ said, meaning the garage. He was getting confused though. He couldn't remember if he was trying to vent to Chief Hunt or defend his parents, so he added, "I guess my dad has his reasons."

"It looks full of shit."

"It is full of shit."

"What kind of shit, that's what I wonder."

"You really think it'd make a good bedroom?" EJ asked.

"Yup."

He heard his door unlock, so he exited, then looked back inside the car and thanked Chief Hunt for the ride. And then, as he walked to the house and through the front door, taking off the SHERIFFS windbreaker as he went, he realized that he had neglected to give it back. His father looked up and over the couch, beard curling off his cheek where a pillow had been pressing against it. He yawned. "How was it?" he asked.

"Fine."

"What'd you do?"

"I don't know. Cop stuff."

"Like what?"

EJ was suspicious. His dad rarely asked follow-up questions. EJ toyed with the idea of staying silent, just to keep the intrigue alive, but he couldn't help it. He had his father's interest, and that was a special thing. He told him all about the day, about the boredom, about the boardroom, about the map, about the conversations, about the chicken salad sandwich he had had for lunch, and about how Hunt agreed that the garage should really be converted into a bedroom because—

"What kind of map?" Ed said.

EJ explained again, in greater detail. He was happy they were talking, but less happy than he might have been because he was hoping to have a rational conversation about the bedroom situation.

"And it was the only map they had?" Ed said.

"That I saw."

"Just burglaries?"

"That I saw."

"Good," Ed said. "Good."

"Why?"

"Why what?"

"Why is that 'good'?"

"It ain't. It's just interesting." His dad faced the television again, faced a stocky Scandinavian man who was straining to place a series of heavy objects onto a truck bed.

"What are you watching?" EJ said.

"Some show about bodybuilders," Ed said.

"Want me to watch it with you?"

"Uh-huh. And if you stick around, you can watch the Celtics game with me and Allie later."

EJ pulled the windbreaker over his head and zipped it all the way to the top. "Actually, I think I'll just go to Uncle Chuck's," he said.

"Suit yourself," Ed said. But then he stood up, circled the couch, and stood above EJ. He put both hands, heavy hands, on EJ's shoulders.

"Hey, EJ," Ed said.

"Yeah?"

"It's good you're doing this."

"Doing what?"

"Working with the police."

"Thanks," EJ said. "But I'm not really working with them. I'm not like a junior detective or anything, shooting guns and solving murders. That's not what police work is."

"Still. Good you took the initiative."

"By breaking a window?"

Ed laughed like EJ had just told a self-deprecating joke and then gave him a big hug.

EJ WAITED FOR HIS MOM outside Chuck's apartment, on the stairs, in his hoodie and SHERIFFS windbreaker. His hands were getting cold, so he tucked them under his jacket, into the pockets of his hoodie, and found the two brownies he'd taken the day before. They hadn't fully hardened yet. He was hungry, so he ate one. It wasn't a matter of courage; he just didn't care anymore. Then he ate the other brownie. The smallest dots of snow began to drift across the sky. There were no clouds, only a sky that looked like a cloud. It was as cold as ever, and yet here it was snowing. Everyone had been wrong about the weather.

Finally his mother showed up.

"Good morning," Steph said once he was inside the Camry.

"Good morning," he said.

"You're chipper."

"Am I?"

"You're smiling."

He was in the passenger seat. He felt his cheeks. They were floating away like hot air balloons. He tried to pull them back to earth, hook them to his jaw. "People smile," he said.

"Excuse me?"

The radio played songs sung by a male vocalist, then a female vocalist, and EJ couldn't say definitively if he had ever heard these songs before, but somehow he knew how the music fit together. He could see every instrument and listen to each string and each chord. He could hear the cymbals vibrating forever, diminishing but not disappearing.

"Why are you humming?" Steph said.

EJ turned slowly in her direction, eyes wide, carefully drawing the hood of his sweatshirt over his head, like a panda bear. Steph kept glancing at EJ, and when they arrived at the sheriff's office, she said goodbye and asked if he was feeling okay. She said it from a distance, as if over a PA system, as he closed the door. He didn't want to say anything weird, so he gave his mom a peace sign, then headed for the station.

Hunt waited inside the entrance, standing by the window, looking through the blinds and drinking coffee.

"There goes your mother in her car," she said.

EJ nodded.

"She bought it new, didn't she?"

EJ nodded.

"How about we take Cliff on a drive?" Hunt said. "To the shooting range?"

EJ nodded again.

The shooting range was outdoors. Was it a shooting range? Not especially, not from what EJ could tell, miles away from any building, no signs, no human-shaped targets. Cliff watched them from the backseat of the unmarked car. They stood behind a table. About twenty yards from the table was a stump with an old paint can sitting on top. It wasn't clear if the can was there for target practice, or if someone had at one time planned to paint the stump. Snow continued to fall, and everything lingered in early shades of white. A pale film lay over all the land, even the air. The hill beyond the end of the range was one of those anonymous hills that goes unnoticed in the summer when its own foliage gets in the way; now, though, it was dead and quite noticeable, a corpse floating to the surface. Hunt taught EJ how to stand with feet shoulder width apart, how to breathe, how to squeeze the trigger with gentle pressure. "You play golf?" she asked.

He shook his head.

"Stop smirking."

How was his face making a smirk?

"Keep your head steady," Hunt said. "A lot of people think the secret is to grip the hell out of the club and swing hard, but that's not the secret."

Part of him worried that this, the shooting range, the gun, the banter, was all part of a not-very-elaborate setup. Part of him worried that Hunt would arrest him for something, anything, for stealing her gun. Part of him also worried that just listening to Hunt, just thinking about her, might cause him to involuntarily swivel the gun in her direction, and by some flinch of his soul, squeeze the trigger, and then the snowflakes would start falling red and EJ would find himself waist deep in the gathering drifts of hell.

Hunt reached over and removed the safety.

EJ's heart was no longer a heart. It was an epileptic squid shimmying down every one of his limbs.

"Fire when ready," Hunt said.

With extreme caution, EJ pulled the trigger. For a moment, then another, nothing seemed to happen. The gun wasn't working. But he kept pulling on the trigger, and suddenly the firearm jumped in his hand and the snow cracked down the middle, the noise ripping through the trees and doubling and receding, waves in a basin.

"Was that awesome?" Hunt said.

EJ nodded.

"You're not talking much today."

EJ nodded. Little did Hunt know. He couldn't talk. He couldn't talk because he was a panda bear with a squid for a heart.

"You can keep firing," she said.

He kept firing, warming to the gun, little by little, round by round.

"So as a cop, you hear things," Hunt said.

He shot at the stump: **BLAM**, *BLAM*, *blam* . . .

"Maybe that's not what I meant. As a person, you hear things. As a cop, you hear them differently. Also, you see things."

BLAM, *BLAM*, *blam* . . .

"Exhale as you pull the trigger. There you go."

BLAM, *BLAM*, *blam* . . .

"And sometimes you think, Man, these things I'm hearing, these things I'm seeing, they don't stack up. What's an example? Here's an example: Say you see a high school dropout like Ed Thatch buying a business here, a business there, you see his wife acting all fancy, and you think, Now, wait a minute, what the hell did they do to earn *that*?"

EJ had never experienced anything so cruel as this. However. He was stoned. He didn't know if Hunt knew that she was being cruel, or even if, on any level, she *was* being cruel. He was too blazed to know what was true, what was in his mind. Maybe someday he would be able to smoke a J and afterwards know how stoned he was and do some kind of arithmetic to understand what was real by subtracting the stoned perception part from the total perception whole. Someday maybe. Not today. He shot again, if only to show Hunt that her words weren't affecting him: **BLAM**, *BLAM*, *blam* . . . This time he hit the can. He would have thought the round would go *ping* but instead it made a heavy, deep *thunk*. If there was any kind of big paint explosion, it was impossible to see beyond the snow. The paint must have been white. Hunt's words were definitely getting to him, the words she hadn't spoken more than the words she had. EJ felt abandoned by the truth. Everyone he knew spoke in half-truths, in half-codes, questioned him for no other reason than to calculate their own answers, which they would not share. He was sick of it.

He turned to Hunt.

"Whoa. Hey," she said.

The gun was aimed right at her hip.

She helped him lay the gun on the table, and he noticed, as her hand guided his, just how hard he'd been shaking.

"I think my dad smokes pot," EJ blurted, and now he could feel hot tears welling in his eyes.

"I don't know, kid," Hunt said quietly, looking across the shooting range. "Something tells me that's not quite right."

THE GARAGE WAS MUSTY AND dark, full of useless stuff, catacombs for the cast-aside. EJ waded and tunneled through bags swollen with clothing, stacks of old patio furniture, golf clubs, fishing rods, life jackets, hunting jackets, CDs, lobster traps, trap lines, trap buoys, a framed watercolor of a gull on a piling, more garbage bags, an air conditioner, a box of air fresheners, a box of unpacked coffee beans, fertilizer bags, mulch bags, and rotted potted plants, all of which must have contributed to the stinging smell. The smell was either unbelievably potent or EJ was still stoned, which he doubted, because the rest of the world, for the most part, had returned to normal.

He worked without pause, moving everything from garage to driveway. He had turned all the lights on, but they were dim. The snow continued to fall through the floods outside the garage. Two dry inches covered the house and the driveway. EJ's father must have been taking a nap because he hadn't come outside to yell at EJ yet. EJ was looking forward to that moment. Finally EJ would speak his mind, say, You know what, *Dad*? Enough is *enough*. He wasn't sleeping at Chuck's anymore, and neither was he sharing a bedroom with his little sister. His confession to Chief Hunt, wrong as it may have been, had cleared his conscience. He was relieved to have spoken what he thought to be true, and even more relieved that she had told him that it wasn't true at all. He felt like he'd become a man in so many ways today. His father and he were closer than ever to being on the same level. He was ready to be more of a contributor around the house, to help his dad *and* his mom, to be less of a punk—but he expected to be treated like an adult in return.

EJ was standing at the front of the garage, waist deep in boxes, throwing everything light enough to be thrown into a heap in the driveway: a coiled garden hose, several shovels, a half-inflated raft, a bucket—

And then, as he flung the bucket over the sparkling snow, he saw his father. His dad was wearing a flannel shirt and a winter hat, and he held a boom box and six Mooseheads that dangled from their plastic rings. Snow was landing and melting in his beard. Ed looked at the garage, looked at the refuse in the driveway, and said, "All right, now *this* is initiative."

"I can't live with Allie anymore," EJ said.

"Yuh," Ed said. "I know. We should have done this sooner."

He went to the corner of the garage and pulled away bag after bag until a workbench came into view. He set the boom box on the workbench, plugged it in, and dialed it to the country station. "Hard labor requires good music," he said.

He tossed EJ a pair of work gloves, then a beer. "Crack it open," he said.

"Really?"

"If you're ready to have a beer, I'm gonna have one with you. No reason to make it some big mystery. That's only gonna make you more interested. It's like having two trays on the counter." Ed paused for a moment, making sure EJ understood. He did. "You can have one beer, that's all. Beer can make you feel pretty good sometimes, but it can also make you mad, or sad, or sick, so it's best to keep an eye on your mood as you drink."

They started working. EJ passed the bags to his father. Once a small mountain had formed in the driveway, Ed brought the truck around and loaded up the bed. They kept listening to the country station as EJ sweat through the cold, under the SHERIFFS windbreaker. He kept his beer on the workbench and drank only when his father drank. EJ had never tasted anything like it. It tasted disgusting and refreshing all at once.

"I know you think I ain't listening sometimes," Ed said. He held a garbage bag aloft, removed a fluorescent-orange hunting cap. "Got this bag at the hospital rummage sale. Got most of this stuff there. Didn't even look to see what was inside the bag, just threw it in here."

"Why?"

"Fill the space." He looked at the hat for a moment longer, then stuffed it in the bag and tossed the whole thing. "Speaking of, if you're going to live in here, it needs to be winterized. We'll go to Poole Brothers this weekend, get some pink stuff. We should do something with the floor, too."

"I don't mind the cement."

"Gotta get a plumber out here."

"I can come inside to use the bathroom."

"Nah," Ed said, shaking his head, looking around the garage, "we should do it right if we're gonna do it."

"It'd be cool if the garage had skylights."

"Yuh."

"And a pool table."

"You can buy that after you buy a window for Chief Hunt's cruiser."

Even after they had filled the truck, they kept removing items from the garage, stacking them in the driveway. The garage was clearing out. The mound had retreated all the way to the back wall.

Ed took two more beers out of their plastic rings. He popped one, took a sip. He held the other one, looked at it, looked at EJ. "As I think you know," he said, "I take most of my parenting tips from your mother because she's smarter than me." He sucked some of the beer out of his mustache. "She believes in letting you and Allie make choices, so I guess I do, too. I think you're bright kids, in your own ways. I'm glad you take after your mother in that respect." He kicked at something furry. A dead animal, EJ thought, until he saw the label. It was an old fur coat. "Anyway," Ed said, "I'm giving you a choice. Two doors. Or you know what? I'll give you a choice before the choice. You wanna hear what I'm about to say?"

EJ said he did. How else could he respond? He felt nervous and kept working if only to do something with his hands.

"All right, door number one," Ed said. "If we keep cleaning out the garage, you're gonna see some things you can't un-see. I think you know what I'm talking about. I'm right pissed at Chuck and Mary-May, but that's not your problem. So one way we can go is to keep unloading the garage, and then you'll know everything. You'd have to promise not to say anything. To anyone. Ever. If we go that route, then it's you and me, and you help me look after your mother and your sister and give them everything they need. By help me, I mean, you know what's going on but you don't say nothing. You don't help in any other way. I won't allow it. So that's one door.

"Now here's the other door," Ed said. "We stop now. You let me clear out the garage—and I will, that's a promise—but you don't see what I'm clearing out. And then you're not involved, on any level."

EJ didn't want to be involved *at all,* even on this level. He
didn't want a choice. His father offered him a second beer. EJ
said no thank you. He longed to put everything back the way
it had been, arrange the bags in their big pile, put the brownies
back in their rightful trays, glue the glass shards back to their
window, enter stage left, tell everyone that he couldn't remember
his lines, shrug, exit stage right. And yet he kept working, faster
than he had all night, pulling bags and equipment and trash,
working without ceasing, unloading the whole place, heaving,
tossing—until he tried to pick up a duffel bag, different from all
the others, now that he looked at it more closely, in that it was
new. And heavy. It wouldn't budge.

"I might have to help you with that one," Ed said.

The squid was back in EJ's heart, seizing his ribs. He knew
what was in this bag. He knew roughly what was in the bag, knew
that it was something he shouldn't behold. He had seen this bag
before, or one like it. He had seen these bags coming off the boats
at the Pound. EJ began to unzip it.

Ed held his wrist. "You sure about this?" he said.

EJ pulled the zipper back. Inside he found gold and silver,
platters and knives, lamps, jewelry, candleholders.

"You okay?" Ed asked.

EJ stepped over the duffel bag and dug under the rest of the
pile. He found more bags like the first. But these weren't heavy.
They were light, almost perfectly rectangular. He opened the first
bag. He smelled it before he saw it. Inside the bag was a sheet of
plastic, and inside the plastic were green clumps of marijuana.
So this was what it was like to see the whole truth, to see the
world as it really was. EJ was too young to know that the world
was what he made of it, that he had a say. He thought he had
discovered everything, all at once, and it devastated him.

He turned and looked at his father. Ed's face was different

than EJ had ever seen it. He was waiting for EJ to make the next move. They might have stayed in that pose for a long time, bags open at their feet, beer can hanging from Ed's hand, clouds of breath lifting between them—they might have stayed like that if a car hadn't driven up the road and turned into the driveway right at that moment, tires flattening the snow. Its engine turned off, but the lights stayed on and something kept ticking beneath the hood, the lights tripling the dim glow of the garage. EJ couldn't see beyond the brightness. He heard a door open. He saw a silhouette step onto the snow, saw the outline of a flat-brimmed hat and wide shoulders. He looked at his father, who was squinting into the light, trying to block it with his hand. His father's face didn't look surprised or scared, not the way EJ knew his own face looked. Ed nodded at the lights. "There's the Chief," he said.

"Why is she here?" EJ whispered.

But Ed didn't respond. He stepped forward, out of the garage, toward the Chief. EJ stood over the open black bag, watching his father shake hands with Chief Hunt and wishing, as he had a thousand times before, that he were old enough to know how other people behaved when he wasn't looking.

7

LATE THIS PAST MARCH, AFTER ONE OF OUR FIRST PRACTICES OF THE
spring, I was taking a lap around Thatch Field, hunting for any
balls that might have gotten lost in the snow. There were high
banks beyond the sidelines, stained black by all the rubber pellets
caught by the plow blade as it peeled off the layers of ice. The
stadium lights were on (we had the late practice that day), a fine
mist was falling, and a frigid wind was blowing over Academy
Hill. I spotted a ball, poked into the bank with my stick, and
dug it out. But as I dropped the ball in the bucket, I began to
sense I wasn't alone. Someone, I saw once I had stood straight
and looked behind me, was walking in my direction from the far
corner of the field. Steph Thatch. I hadn't seen her since the
lacrosse reception. Or no. I hadn't spoken to her since then. I'd
seen her around town, ducking into her car, hiding behind a pair
of giant sunglasses. On this night she was wearing one of those
shiny black parkas, goose feathers stuffed in a tailored Hefty bag.

"I heard you're writing a book about me," she said when we

met in the middle of the field, near the faceoff X. It was a strange way to open the conversation. I'd been leaving voicemails and sending emails for a long time now.

"I'm writing a book about your family, yes," I said.

"Is it a novel?" she asked.

This question always made me wary. Most people, especially my students, had no idea what a novel was. "It's nonfiction," I said.

"Then it's not a novel, is it?"

"I guess not."

"What's your angle?" she asked.

"Angle?"

"You know, slant, spin."

"I don't have an angle."

"Then what's the point?"

I was confused. "Do you *want* me to have an angle?"

She crossed her arms as the wind picked up. "I doubt you have much to go on," she said. "I bet you're just throwing shit at the wall."

"I've got plenty to go on," I said, no idea why, no idea what my angle was.

"Listen, if you don't know what you're talking about, you'll probably end up making up a bunch of BS, so I might as well make sure you get it right. If you're gonna write about us, I'd like you to know the facts."

"And you'll give me the facts?"

"I will."

"And you *have* the facts?"

"I do." She uncrossed her arms and pulled her phone from her pocket, reading a message or checking the time, I couldn't tell, and then she asked if I could come to her house the next day.

I said I would have to check with Maeve, but probably, yes,

and Steph turned and walked away, leaving me on the turf. The mist now looked more like sleet, and it was falling through the stadium lights, turning as bright and white as paper snow in a stage production. Something about the way she left, walking through the gate in the chain-link fence, reminded me of the first time we'd ever met, when she rode away from the lobster pound on the stern of her father's fishing boat. She'd worn a faded stoner hoodie that day, peeled it off when the sun got warm. Now she wore a jacket, one of many, I'm sure, that would have cost more than my laptop.

How had she paid for it? Any of it? This had always been the question, even when Steph could claim it shouldn't have been, that she and Ed had simply strived their way to the top. She still insists that she didn't know what Ed was doing, that her schedule kept her too busy to notice, and while it sounds like a convenient excuse, I can attest that no one was more invested in our community than she was. I'm sure she really did have a lot on her plate. Keep in mind, too, that Ed had explained away their fortunes by the rising price of lobster and his willingness to work long hours, a version of their story that Steph had told often enough to turn it into her own kind of gospel. And we bought it. Why wouldn't we? Just look at the small empire they'd built by the time Maeve and I moved back to Maine: the landscaping outfit, the Pound, the apartments, the boats, the commercial vehicles, all of them painted gray, stenciled with the Thatch name in yellow-and-blue reflective paint.

But what about Ed? How much did he think about his family's place in the world? Well, I know he was proud of it. This was made clear at almost every one of our lunches. He enjoyed paying for me. I saw it even if he never said it. The symbolism. To some extent, I get it. When your head is down, and you're trying to outrun your past, your upbringing, anyone who's ever doubted you, I can see how you might round a bend and enter a straight-away and realize, or fail to realize, that no one's giving chase anymore, that you're the only one still running. Ed was trying to give Steph the life he thought she deserved, and he believed deep down that she deserved everything, so of course he was bound to keep going until he'd acquired all there was to acquire, or until Steph told him, very clearly, that he'd given her enough already.

Take Ed's lobster boat. What it became. Were the changes vital to the family's well-being? Probably not. Ed had converted it from a workboat into a pleasure cruiser. He wanted Steph to be comfortable, he said, to be able to sit on something other than a folding hunter's chair in a boat that smelled like something other than bait and motor oil. The project took two years to complete, and one of the first trips they made on the new and improved *Miss Stephanie* was to Southport for the party Ed had thrown in tribute to their marriage (just because Steph had made an off-hand remark, during an argument about saving for Allie's education, maybe even a wedding reception someday, about how Ed and Steph had never really had their *own* wedding reception, only a poorly attended ceremony in Damariscotta's municipal offices), and on the way to the island, he kept saying, "See? Ain't you happy I fixed her up for you?" even if Steph had never seemed to care all that much about the boat. She was prone to seasickness. She didn't even like going past the end of the river.

It was Ed who wanted to show off the work. At the party in Southport, he brought a half-dozen men and Chief Hunt down to the dock (nearly simultaneous to my smoking the joint on the cliffs) to admire the *Miss Stephanie*'s new look. Most of the others hailed from up-peninsula: Ben Thatch, an attorney named Jamie Kerry, Steph's Pilates instructor, and Allie's former pediatrician. Ed had painted the hull, made her more of a regal argent than the old battleship gray, gutted the cabin and installed a V-berth and a proper head. He had done all the woodwork himself, lining the wheelhouse in glossy teak over the previous two winters. He had installed two captain's chairs, one for him, one for Steph, upholstered them both in white sea-proof leather, and special-ordered matching drop-down seating to go in the back where the bait barrels used to stand. He had ripped out the hydraulic winch and replaced the pulley that hung above the helm with a brand-new stainless-steel model. That and the pink-and-yellow buoy atop the wheelhouse were all that remained to mark the boat as one that had, back in the day, been used for real commercial fishing. "It's impressive," Jamie Kerry said of the boat. "Can't believe what you've done here, Ed. Congrats."

"Real fancy," Chief Hunt said.

"It's beautiful, Ed," the pediatrician said.

There were more compliments paid, but after fifteen minutes or so, once they had run out of boat parts to name and alcohol to consume, the men headed back up the stairs, returning to the bar. Only Ben, Chuck, and Chief Hunt stayed behind.

"Hey, Ed," Chuck said, thumbs hooked in the waist of his pants, bolo tie dangling over a short-sleeved shirt. "Isn't EJ supposed to be taking summer classes?"

"Yuh," Ed said. "He's just down for the weekend."

EJ was enrolled as a parks, recreation, and tourism student at the University of Maine, or at least he lived in an apartment near campus with his girlfriend. It wasn't clear how often he was making it to the lecture hall.

"Seems like he's been getting plenty of sun," Chuck said.

"They get sun in Orono."

"He's got a face full of red everywhere except the eyes. I went up to him and said, 'Where'd you get them Oakleys?' You can still see the lines. He looks like a pink raccoon."

Hunt laughed.

"You ain't one to talk," Ed said to Chuck. "That's how you look every time we get off the water."

"Yuh, takes one to know one," Chuck said, "and I'm pretty sure EJ's been spending some time on the water, too. Jason Page told me EJ helped him with that run up near Bar Harbor."

"EJ did?"

"Yuh."

"He's not supposed to help."

"I'm aware."

"The boy's always wanted to pitch in," Ben said.

"Don't involve him," Hunt said.

"He's not involved," Ed said.

The wake of a distant ferry arrived and started rocking the *Miss Stephanie* against the dock, the lines groaning, the fenders squeaking.

"Ed, here's the thing," Chuck said. "He's already involved. You can only put so much lube back in the tube. At this point, EJ's seen a lot. You might think about bringing him all the way in."

"We don't need him all the way in," Ed said.

"Amen," Hunt said.

Ed glared at her. "Or maybe you could use some help."

"With what?"

"Whatever it is you're supposed to be doing."

"You get what you pay for."

"That's your sales pitch?"

"If you're dissatisfied with my work, Ed, you can put a call in to the Association of Amenable Cops and log an official complaint. Until then, I'm all you've got."

"Speaking of all I've got," Ed said, "'fancy'? What was that all about?"

"I was just saying."

"How is this fancy?"

"Just is." She had something in her mouth, a piece of ice maybe. "Look at it for Christ's sake." Ed did look at the boat, if only to appreciate it again, finding nothing to apologize for. The boat was classy, sure, but not fancy. He turned back to Hunt. She had been his "head of security" ever since she called Ed on her second day with EJ, making vague threats but giving Ed a way out, demanding a cut, promising that if she were on his side, Ed would never, ever receive serious pressure from the law, not when she could warn Ed before the trouble came. Ed had asked her what kind of trouble they might have to face, and as she stumbled through an answer, Ed realized that she didn't have a clue what she was talking about. She had nothing on him—or very little anyway. But then he started to consider the possibilities. He could use someone on the other side of the law. If she was willing, why not? Since then, Ed had been paying her a steady retainer, some of which she spent on a white-hulled fishing boat, some of which she spent on—well, otherwise, Ed couldn't say what she did with her money. Or what she had done, exactly, to earn the money. He didn't like that she had resumed drinking soon after brokering the deal. He felt duped by that. One of her primary tasks was to make sure none of their products ever made it back to Lincoln County, and for the most part their neck of the woods had indeed stayed clean, but Ed had demanded the same assurance from everyone else he did business with, in addition to forbidding his crew from breaking into any homes on either side of the river. They had kept this stretch of the Midcoast safer than anywhere else in Maine, but if anyone deserved the credit for that, it was him, not Hunt.

"It's a workboat," Ed told Hunt.

"Ha," she said. "Not anymore."

"Ed's a successful business owner," Ben said. He coughed and removed a handkerchief from the breast pocket of his blazer.

"Wink-wink," Hunt said.

Ben shook his head, holding the rail of the *Miss Stephanie* to keep himself upright. He stood with a stoop now. He was nearly eighty years old. Discolored spots were spreading across his scalp. "No, no," he said. "Ed has a source of steady income and no reason not to own a few nice things. It would be almost more of a red flag if he didn't own anything nice. As long as he doesn't go overboard with it, and I don't think the boat's overboard— I think it's in good enough taste—he'll be all right."

"This gin's in good enough taste," Hunt said, gazing at the bottom of her empty cup.

But by then Ed had stopped listening. He had caught sight of Steph at the rail by the gazebo, looking in their direction. This was the scene I witnessed from the cliffs, the moment that marked the end of my good time. I remember Ed raised his hand and waved. But Steph didn't wave back. Instead she turned and walked away.

THAT NIGHT, AFTER THEY HAD retired to their suite in the inn, Ed lay on the bed in his suit pants and undershirt, watching Steph take off her earrings and makeup. She was still in some kind of mood, but he made no effort to decode it, which only made the mood more pronounced. The room had a deck that overlooked the ocean, the sliding door jammed open. Outside, the waves were smashing against the rocks and the younger guests were laughing by the firepit.

"Some party," Ed said.

Steph didn't respond right away. She was fiddling with the clasp of her necklace, looking in the mirror.

"I said that was some party."

"Uh-huh," Steph said. "This clasp keeps getting stuck in my

hair." Finally she was able to unhook it. Then she took off her dress, went into the bathroom, started to pee.

"Wonder what Allie's doing," Ed said.

"What?" Steph said from the bathroom.

He said it again, louder, but Steph didn't say anything back. Instead she flushed the toilet and started running the faucet.

"So you don't care?" he asked.

"Care about what?" Steph asked through the open door.

"Allie."

"Oh," she said. "I couldn't hear you."

"But what do you think she's doing?"

"I don't know—nothing. Having fun."

"I saw her talking to Dougie Page earlier."

"So they ran into each other."

"He wasn't invited though."

Steph turned off the light in the bathroom and came into the suite, wearing only her underwear. She leaned against the doorframe and crossed her arms. She started to say something, then stopped.

Ed waited a moment, hoping Steph would drop whatever was on her mind, but she kept staring at him, making it clear that he was supposed to acknowledge the unacknowledged. He exhaled heavily. "Might as well say what you're gonna say."

"Fine," she said. "I will. Chief Hunt was in the Schooner the other night. Refused to pay her bill again."

After a moment, Ed said, "That so?"

"Yup, and here's the thing," Steph said. "It's like she doesn't expect to be asked. Like it's a real *affront* to her sensibility."

"So what—you want me to talk to her?"

"You've asked me that before."

"Just trying to help."

Steph studied him for a moment, then said, "I saw you with her and your brother and Ben on the boat."

Ed pretended to think back. "Yuh, we went down there cuz they wanted to see the changes I made for you."

"For me?"

"Yuh."

"Classic."

"You don't like the boat?"

"I like the boat," she said. "That's not what I'm talking about."

"You're talking about seeing us down there."

"And not for the first time."

"Not for the last."

"What?"

"Won't be the last time, I bet."

"That makes zero sense, Ed."

"Steph," Ed said, "you want me to count all the times I seen you talking to more than one person tonight? That's how a party works. Folks congregate."

"Listen," she said, standing straight, pointing at Ed. "If I saw it, someone else could have seen it."

"So? I was showing em a boat. People wanna watch us looking at a boat? Let em."

"Okay," she said after a long pause. "Fine, Ed. But I'm telling you—I don't like being in the dark. Or getting lied to. Chuck's your brother. Ben's your cousin, or close enough. But Chief Hunt? Hunt's the one I don't understand. And other people are gonna feel the same way. How do you even know her? Why is she hanging out with you, Chuck, and Ben? It's a little odd, don't you think?"

"It's a small town, Steph."

"Exactly." She peeled the coral-print duvet back and slid under the sheets. "The other night, after Chief Hunt was done getting blasted, do you know what she said when I gave her the bill? She said, 'Give it to Ed.' She said you would take care of it. *That's* what I don't fucking understand: Why you of all people would be the one to take care of it."

THE FOLLOWING SPRING, ED DROVE from Bremen to Damariscotta on a rainy day, the clouds hanging low over the river in forlorn communion with the water, lights blazing in all the stores other than Ben's. He was in hospice by then, and the store had been closed for months. On more than one occasion, Steph had remarked that the dark space presented an eyesore and was bad for the whole town's business, but this was her domain, not Ed's. She had an awareness of such things and had turned herself into one of the most vocal members of Damariscotta's town meetings, an advocate for preservation. And modernization. Her plans for the town were what she worked on in the mornings, in her office, with blueprints, notepads, and sketch paper spread around her like the charts of a fifteenth-century explorer. She authored a plan to bring in tourism, homeowners, and tax revenue, and projected a new village full of modern amenities and welcoming storefronts, with green space on the one side, parking on the other. She'd presented this vision to the chamber of commerce in a series of PowerPoint slides, but her audience was hesitant. This was because they were cave dwellers, Steph told Ed, afraid of the outside world. They balked at the proposed budget, even after Steph assured them that the project would pay for itself down the road by expanding the tax base. One of the chamber members worried that the town might become unrecognizable to itself, and in response Steph had blurted out, "Fine!" and the room went silent. As soon as Steph realized her mistake, she tried to take the interjection back, or to explain what she had meant by it: In order to stay solvent, the town had to stay relevant, and in order to stay relevant, it had to adapt with the times. But the damage was done, motion defeated. The next motion she submitted was one to change the town bylaws and allow candidates who weren't residents to run for town manager, but this proposal wasn't likely to pass either. She needed more votes, she told Ed. She needed more people who really understood the complexities of the issue, more people who had seen the world beyond Damariscotta.

Ed was not one of these people. To him, downtown Damariscotta looked pretty much the same as it always had, with everything you might want: a gas station, a post office, a couple restaurants, a couple bars. Actually, it used to have more. It used to have a hardware store and a grocery store. But to miss these things, Steph would say, was to indulge in the type of nostalgic, sentimental thinking she had no patience for.

Over the bridge Ed followed the old, familiar drive past the convenience store, around the softball field, half-covered in snow. He parked in the lot across from the high school gym, walked to the glass doors, and peered inside. He saw boys playing baseball on the far side of the court, lacrosse on the near side (I was in there somewhere, tearing up my practice plan and dodging errant rubber balls). Ed wouldn't have had any way of judging how good or bad the lacrosse was. He had never seen the game before, only was aware of it through infrequent highlights on SportsCenter, thought it was a game for college boys like me. He was surprised to see it played in his old high school (it hadn't been a sport Lincoln offered in his day), and he was disappointed to find that softball tryouts had finished early. He'd been hoping to catch a glimpse of Allie in action.

He went back to the truck and texted Allie: *At Lincoln. You need a ride?* and then he waited, killing time by listening to country music and wiping dust off his dashboard. The Silverado had leather seats, all heated, plenty of cup holders. It belonged to the Pound, technically.

Finally she texted back: *Sorry, went to Subway after practice. Can get ride no problem. See you at home! xoxox.*

WHEN ED CAME INTO THE living room that night, he found Allie holding, instead of a softball mitt, a lacrosse stick. She was on the sofa, her body just another cushion, watching a show about girls in a big city who get internships and complain about their bosses.

"What's that?" he said, pointing at the stick.

"A lacrosse stick."

"Whose is it?"

"Mine."

"What happened to softball?"

"Lacrosse looked more fun."

He picked up the stick, weighed it in his hands, swung it like a baseball bat. "How do you play?"

"I don't know—you try to get the ball in the goal."

"Bet there's more to it than that." He thrust the stick at her like a sword.

"Yeah, we'll see," she said.

Ed went upstairs, carrying the stick, and entered Steph's office. The overhead light was off, the glow of Steph's laptop reflecting off her glasses.

"You hear about this lacrosse idea?" he asked her.

"Sound travels through the vents, so yeah," Steph said.

"What should we do?"

Steph leaned back from the computer and squeezed her nose

beneath her glasses. "I don't know, Ed. This house is too small. I'm getting nothing done."

"What about lacrosse though?"

"What about it?"

"Should we let her play?"

"Of course we should let her play!" Steph said. "Why wouldn't we?"

"I don't know. Just never seen it before."

"How is that a factor?"

"Wouldn't know how to watch it."

"You just stand there and watch it. Sit in the bleachers or get a folding chair. It's not that hard."

The phone rang. There was a receiver on Steph's desk, but she didn't make a move to answer. It rang again.

"Allie, can you get that?" Ed yelled downstairs.

"I'm watching TV!" Allie yelled back.

"I'm gonna blow a gasket," Steph said. "I need some help, Ed. Please."

So he went to their bedroom and picked up the phone. EJ's girlfriend Brittany Dodwell was on the line, calling from her apartment in Orono. EJ was away again, Brittany said.

"Away?" Ed asked.

"Hasn't been back to our apartment in like three days."

"He'll be back," Ed said.

"Maybe four days," she said. "I called Jason but he didn't pick up."

"Jason Page?"

"Yeah."

"Goddammit, EJ."

"You think they're out hunting?" Brittany asked.

"Something like that," Ed said.

"Well, he didn't say nothing. It's weird."

Ed said he would let Brittany know if he heard anything, hung up, and went back downstairs. He had thought EJ's association with Jason Page would be over by now. Jason worked for Ed, ran one of the boats up to Canada and back. He had a younger brother named Dougie, also a fuck-up. Dougie was only fifteen, but, with no other talents or prospects, he was sure to follow after his brother and work on one of Ed's boats someday. He was the type of kid who was always lurking in the background. In more than one photograph from the party on Southport, he'd been the only non–family member facing the camera, his eyes locked on Allie and whatever she was doing.

Ed stopped at the bottom of the stairs. Thought for a second. Now he had a plan.

"All right," Ed said, back in the living room, both hands atop Allie's stick, leaning on it like a staff. "We're making a deal."

"What kind of deal?" she said, eyes on the television, an ad for maxi pads.

"You get to play lacrosse this spring," he said, "but you stop talking to Dougie Page."

"Hang on—what?"

"Take it or leave it."

"You can't be serious," she said, propping herself up on her elbows. "I don't need permission for either of those things."

"Let's face it: Dougie's a loser."

"Yeah, no shit. Everyone knows that."

"Good. Then we got a deal. Watch your language."

"But if I wanted to talk to Dougie Page," she said, "you couldn't stop me."

"You can do better, Allie. That's all I'm saying. He's from down this way, and—"

"*I'm* from down this way!"

"You know we love you, Allie-cat," he said. "But that don't mean you can do whatever the hell you want."

"Oh my God," she said, dropping back into the couch, "do you have any idea how unfair it is when you say the worst things ever and then say 'I love you' after, as if that's supposed to make whatever you said totally *fine*?"

Ed laid the stick against the couch and scratched his beard.

"We good here?" he asked.

"No!"

He went to the kitchen, grabbed a beer from the fridge, then stepped outside, into the cold.

He texted Chuck: *You seen EJ? Brittany says he's missing. Better not be doing something stupid.*

He waited but received no answer, so he put the phone away and stood on the front step, surveying his small property. The only thing he and Steph had brought from the old trailer—over a decade ago now—was the pink-and-yellow pot buoy, which hung by the door, just to Ed's left. *The Thatches* was written in white across the yellow paint, the colors faded. It needed a fresh coat. Ed could do that. He would enjoy doing that. So he removed the buoy from its hook and threw it in the back of the Silverado, next to his toolbox, planning to bring it down to the Pound, where he still had plenty of the old paint.

ONCE ALLIE COMMITTED TO LACROSSE, Ed committed to being a lacrosse dad with born-again devotion, attending every one of the girls' games in a black Lincoln hoodie knifed open at the neck. He'd pace the far sideline, eyes on Allie, only Allie, watching her run, or stand, even when she didn't have the ball. During a game against North Yarmouth Academy, a private school close to Portland, one of the first games Allie ever played, Ed saw right away that Allie couldn't catch or throw, but what she could do—if ever she succeeded in securing the yellow rubber ball in her stick—was turn on the jets and blow past her opponents, leaning forward, protective goggles pointing the way, cheeks red, jaw tight, mouth guard in, gloves on, black leggings pumping up the field, her brown ponytail barely keeping up. Her best runs came after she scooped the ball off the turf, or after the referee had called play dead and Allie could place the ball in her stick with her hand. By the second half against NYA, she was already looking like a natural. At one point she emerged from an improvised spin and found herself out in the open, one-on-one with the goalie, and sure, okay, the opportunity surprised her, and she tried to shoot too late, and by then an opponent had crowded her and the ball had fallen out of Allie's stick and started rolling backwards harmlessly, but still—what a move! Even Ed could appreciate it. It should have been a goal.

"Come on, Stripes!" Ed hollered at the official. "Call something!"

The play was already moving back in the other direction. "Allie, back-check!" Ed yelled, using a term that applies to hockey but not lacrosse.

Lincoln lost the game 17–2.

"Not bad," Ed said to Allie after the game, standing in the middle of the field.

She leaned down and removed black rubber pellets, the artificial turf's artificial soil, from her socks. "Except we sucked," she said.

"You played good."

"That's nice of you, Dad, but you've never seen lacrosse before."

"Seen other sports."

"It's no use anyway. NYA's been practicing outside for a month."

"How come they get to practice outside?"

"Because they have a field that's not an icy swamp?"

Ed looked around, then down, at all the fake blades of grass. He had never seen anything like it. So this was how the private schools got ahead.

"It's a level playing field," Allie said.

"No, it ain't."

"No, I mean, it's like, literally a level playing field. It doesn't have bumps and ditches. I was making a joke."

IN ADDITION TO THEIR TWIN daughters—around Jack's age—Cammie and Colin have border collies, so occasionally we join their family to go cross-country skiing as the dogs dash up and down the trails, belly deep in the snow, and as our children trudge forward on their own stubby skis or get towed behind me in a sled. One day this past winter, Colin was skiing in the lead, laying the tracks, and Maeve was following him, and Cammie and I were farther behind, making sure the kids and dogs didn't get lost in the powder. Cammie's become a serious triathlete (not a pursuit I have any interest in; I sink when I swim) so could answer my questions about Ed and Steph without having to stop and catch her breath. I had asked her about Ben's funeral. She had worked at Main Street Antiques when she was in high school and credited Ben, along with a few others, with encouraging her interest in the arts.

"Oh, yeah," she said. "Weird day."

"Weird how?"

"Just the vibe of it." Her back was to me and she was gliding forward along the trail, but I could see her words taking the form of frozen clouds every time she spoke. "You got the sense that nobody at the funeral really knew Ben. Or at least the ones who knew him best didn't want to be honest about him. Ed's dad said a few things. Steph's dad, too, but he only knew Ben from the Schooner, as a regular."

"Did you talk to Ed?"

"I did, actually," she said. "I talked to him and Steph. We had just moved back to Maine, and I ran into Steph right after the service, so we were catching up. We had come to their party the summer before—the one where we met you guys—but I hadn't really had the chance to talk to her much."

One of the border collies was nipping at my hamstrings. I shooed him away and turned back to make sure the children were still in our tracks, which they were.

"You guys good?" I asked.

"Yeah," Jane said.

"Just let me know if you want to hop in the sled."

It was dragging behind me, empty, but I hoped they wouldn't take me up on the offer. I wasn't sure I could keep up with the others if I had to tow the extra freight, even after losing a couple pounds over the summer and fall—all those afternoon runs around the salt bay.

"Anyway," Cammie said, "I don't think I fully understood how powerful Steph had become. I mean, 'powerful' seems like an insane thing to say when we're talking about Damariscotta, but you know what I mean."

I did.

"I guess I was just surprised to find her giving me advice," Cammie said. "Plus, it was more than advice. It was like, 'Do this if you know what's best for you, if you wanna get what you want.'"

"What did you want?"

"Oh, sorry, yeah—I wanted to find a space for the art gallery. I had been looking all up and down Bristol Road. I thought maybe I could rent a garage or something."

"So it was her idea to take over Ben's space?"

"Yeah. Or no, actually. It was Ed's." She was silent for a moment, thinking back, her skis continuing to swish along the tracks. "He came over to where we were standing, and Steph filled him in on the conversation. Steph was excited about the idea of Damariscotta getting an art gallery, but I could tell by the look on Ed's face that he thought it was the last thing the town needed. Or maybe he was just indifferent. Not that I would have expected him to give a rat's ass. But then suddenly he leans forward and grips my shoulder. Hard. And he goes, 'You're moving into Ben's old store.' It wasn't a question. It sounded like an order. And I said, 'I am?' I thought it was a joke. And he goes, 'Yuh. I'm the executor,' only he pronounced it like exe-*cute*-er. He meant of Ben's estate." She stopped skiing for a moment, turned back. "I couldn't get over that I was standing there, talking to Ed Thatch and Steph LeClair, and they were telling me how to make all my dreams come true."

She faced forward and started skiing again. "But this is the best part," she said over her shoulder, "Ed said he'd give me a great deal on the lease, which was good, because I didn't think I could afford a place on Main Street, but then he goes, 'All you have to do is support Steph.' I thought for sure it was another joke. I asked what he meant. And he said that I had to go to every town meeting, and anything Steph proposed, I had to get behind it. I remember glancing at Steph, hoping she'd be rolling her eyes, hoping she'd be giving me some sign that Ed was kidding. And I guess she kind of was, but she was also looking at me like, *Take the deal, Cammie.*"

"Did you?"

"Of course I did! Are you kidding me? I have the best lease in town. And what do I care what Steph proposes? I pretty much agree with her anyway."

The next morning, when I checked my email, I found the following note in my inbox, subject: *One more thing . . .*

Andrew,

Thought of something else you might be interested in. Sorry it didn't come to me before. It happened by the cars, after the funeral (maybe that's why I forgot to mention it??) Ed was talking to EJ. I remember thinking EJ looked a little silly because he was wearing the same beige suit he had worn to Ed and Steph's party (everyone else was in gray or black). Ed was straightening EJ's tie, even though EJ was obviously a grown man by then. He looked angry but wasn't saying much. Ed was talking to him, very animated, setting his son straight or something, gripping him by the shoulder, jabbing his finger in his chest. . . . I have no idea why, just thought you might be able to make sense of it.

Anyway, fun skiing yesterday! The dogs are all tuckered out. See you guys soon.

Best,
Cammie

I stood from my computer, went into the kitchen, poured a cup of coffee, studied the rooster weathervane atop my neighbor's roof for a minute or two, then circled back to the office. I read the note again. This time it reminded me of something I had learned about the case—but I couldn't remember what it was. I went digging through my stack of notes, looking for the timelines I had assembled for each family member. The timelines documented all the Thatches' whereabouts and activities, anything I had deemed significant or potentially significant. I found EJ's timeline and gave it another look. According to court documents and interviews with members of Ed's crew, EJ had been going out on the boats with Jason Page for over two years by the time of the funeral. This, I'm sure, was why he would disappear for days on end without telling his girlfriend or his parents where he was going. The funeral was on May 5th, 2014. Before that date were several trips to Canada. EJ's presence had been confirmed on each one. But after the funeral, there were no more trips to Canada, not for EJ. Ed must have found out. This may have been the source of the argument Cammie witnessed. Yes. It had to be. I ran my finger down Ed's timeline until I arrived at May 5: *Ben's funeral.* On EJ's timeline was the same notation. But there was something else, just below the funeral, something I had made note of but never thought much about:

May 6: *EJ applies to the Damariscotta PD.*

EJ would no longer be pursuing a degree in parks, recreation, and tourism. He'd be getting a job. Ed was bringing him all the way in.

A WEEK AFTER BEN'S FUNERAL, Ed went to his cousin's old house, just to make sure everything was in working order and nobody had tried to break in or vandalize the place. A real estate sign was already stuck in the grass at the top of Ben's driveway, by the main road. The broker had told him not to expect much action until the summer people arrived, but it was always possible that someone might show up sooner than expected, and if they did, Ed wanted the home to be ready. He parked the Silverado between the farmhouse and the barn. He stepped onto the dirt driveway and looked at the property. On this side of the dock, the meadow was already getting wild. It needed a mow.

Something Ed could do himself. He looped around the farm-house, found a ride-on lawnmower in a shed, and brought it out-side. He drove into the meadow and cut a swath straight down the middle—a long stripe connecting house to river. It took him three minutes just to get from the top of the hill to the shoreline. Then he pivoted and steered the lawnmower back up the incline.

Trimming the meadow took an hour and a half, and when Ed was done, he swept the mulch off his legs and admired the big lawn and the long parallel lines he had drawn. It felt good to accomplish something. The grass was so clean, so neat, it almost looked fake.

Then he stepped inside the house, which was empty of all Ben's furniture. Ed was thirsty, so he turned on the faucet and let it run to cold. He drank from his cupped hands. It was a simple house with neat, box-shaped rooms and plenty of them. Musty though. He should crack the windows, air the place out. The only item Ed hadn't removed, the only piece of furniture, was Ben's workbench, which sat in the middle of the living room. Everything else, including the contents of the old barn, had been sold at auction. Ed leaned back against the countertop and gazed through the house, through the small windows, to the river. There were advantages to living up here, right by town, Ed thought. The house was closer to Lincoln. Closer to Main Street. Anyone who lived here could seek office in Damariscotta. The faucet was still running, so he turned around and shut it off. It kept dripping though. Not good. He tried cranking on the handle again, but all that did was turn the drip into a steady trickle.

He went outside and reached into the back of his truck, into his toolbox, looking for a wrench. But once he had the toolbox slid over to his side of the truck bed, something rolled out from behind it: the yellow-and-pink buoy that said *The Thatches*. He had forgotten all about it, but now, as he looked from the buoy to the house, an idea began to form. He rummaged in the truck's toolbox, removing a hammer and a nail instead of a wrench. Holding the nail in his mouth, the hammer in one hand, the buoy in the other, he went to the front door, removed the nail from his lips, and drove it into the wall. The buoy had a wire loop on it, and Ed hung the loop over the nail. He stepped back to check its height. The buoy still had to be repainted, but it looked natural enough on the white wooden siding. It made the house feel like a home.

Through the windows, Ed could see into the living room. Now he pictured his family in there, sketching their Main Streets, writing their college essays, drinking their coffees on an afternoon break from the Damariscotta Police Department, and he pictured himself, too, coming up from the dock, heading home at the end of a long day. He looked to the kitchen. His kitchen. He looked to the living room. His living room. And then he looked out, over the freshly mowed meadow, to his river, his life drifting by, his life flowing toward the wide, flat ocean.

8

WHEN ED FIRST TOLD STEPH THAT HE HAD REMOVED THE REALTY sign from the top of Ben's driveway, taken the house off the market, and sold it to himself, Steph said, "You can't just buy a house, Ed. There's a whole process. We have to apply for a mortgage."

"I paid cash."

"Cash," Steph said, sounding, she hoped, much more incredulous than impressed.

"Yuh."

"And how exactly did you pay cash?"

"Just wait till you see it."

"I've already seen it."

"Not all empty, when it's already ours."

"Nope. Sorry, Ed. Not this time. I'm out."

She did visit the house the very next day, on her way to work, just to confirm with her own eyes what a huge mistake Ed had made. It was basically a run-down, slapped-together prairie home next to a big gray barn. Apparently Ed's grand plan was for Steph to live like a dairy cow? The door to the farmhouse was open and she was able to walk right in. It smelled like an old man. She walked right back out. No thank you. Then she went to the barn and slid open the door. She was expecting to smell manure or hay but actually it wasn't all that awful. More like wood and varnish. It was a huge space, almost spooky. She walked across the dirt to the river side where there was another set of doors. She opened these doors, too, and let the breeze flow past her. She looked out across the meadow. There was nobody around. She couldn't even see any of the neighboring houses. All she could see was the view of the river, the harbor, the village. Then she started pacing the barn, just to measure how big it was. As she did, she couldn't help imagining the stables gone, replaced with bedrooms. She imagined the walls and roof punched out, replaced with big windows and skylights. She pictured which furniture would go in which corners, in front of which windows, next to which fireplaces. She tried to stop herself, but it was a losing battle—she always saw the potential in a place.

The farmhouse was a disaster, no question. She refused to live in it. But the barn—that was a different story.

Son of a bitch, she thought. Ed had done it again. She was already moving on from how the barn had been bought to how it could help her family. If they relocated, Allie would have better access to school, sports, and friends. EJ could stop by at his leisure. Steph could run for mayor. In the end, it wasn't a very difficult decision to make. It barely felt like she had made any decision at all.

Word spread that the Thatches were heading north, and it was at that point that those less new to the area than Maeve and I began to take note of their rise. It wasn't so much that Ed had purchased all that acreage from his cousin—I think everyone rightly assumed that he would have given himself a good deal on the place—it was more about Ed and Steph's literal ascent up the peninsula. As they approached the heart of the county, they were also edging into the limelight. Ed continued to snap up property, buying more and more real estate on Main Street and Business Route 1. EJ joined the Damariscotta Police Department. Allie made high honors and starred on the varsity soccer, basketball, and lacrosse teams. Steph ran for town manager, and won, and immediately got to work improving Damariscotta. She was still operating the Schooner, and she had to keep her new house in working order, and she had to show up at her daughter's athletic contests to support the team and make sure her husband didn't cross any sidelines or end lines, which had happened once or twice the previous spring.

With so much to keep track of now, Steph needed to organize her schedule down to the minute. When Allie had a soccer game in the neighboring township of Wiscasset, Steph would stop ahead of time at Bon Bon for a coffee but also to replenish the soap from Normandy that she liked to stock in all the bathrooms of the house, and she would bring along her notebook because there was always work to do, both for the Schooner and for the town, work that she could do in the bleachers anytime Allie and the ball were on opposite halves of the field. She had everything all timed out, and she would arrive just a moment before kickoff—

Unless there was a wait for coffee, which there was on this one Saturday in September of 2016, Labor Day weekend. Steph found herself at the end of the line, waiting with soap in one hand, phone in the other, and she knew from experience that this barista—the only one in the county who actually knew what he was doing—liked to take his time. He had a tattered beard, instructions on how to butcher a pig tattooed on his forearm. Arriving punctually to Allie's game was important to Steph, and so too was spending as little time in Bon Bon as possible. The store did have the best espresso around—and the best cheese, olive oil, chocolate—but it was in Wiscasset, not Damariscotta, and Steph didn't like spending money here instead of in her hometown, didn't like worrying that one of her constituents might accidentally wander in and catch her in the act.

She leaned right and glanced forward, trying to make eye contact with the barista to see if he'd recognize her and start preparing her regular drink on the sly, but he was too busy bragging to an out-of-towner about the ethical supply chain of his coffee beans, so Steph checked the time on her phone, swiped out of voice memos (she'd been recording her thoughts as she dressed that morning), then opened Facebook and looked at the "Town Wall." She liked a Rotary Club post about a spaghetti dinner and wrote *Sounds delish!* but no one else had commented, and she had no texts, no missed calls.

The door opened and briefly the noises of the holiday weekend—trucks downshifting in traffic, children hollering to their siblings, John Mellencamp spilling from an open minivan window—washed in and Steph looked to the store's entrance, to the sunshine. Then a man stepped between her and her view of Wiscasset. He paused in the doorway for just a moment, removing his Ray-Bans, familiarizing himself with the store's layout. He resembled any other father who might have left his young family of four in the car while he went in search of caffeine: late thirties, polo shirt, tan, trying to leave work behind, trying to relax, maybe even pulling it off. Steph faced forward again but sensed, almost immediately, that she may have allowed herself to look away too soon. She didn't only see potential in places; she also saw it in people, occasionally to her detriment, and the only proven way to disabuse herself of the most optimistic and wayward first impressions, she'd found, was to stare longer than was socially acceptable, to wait until the person you were trying to see more clearly turned and revealed in this new light that he wasn't quite as symmetrical as he'd first appeared.

She forced herself to keep her attention on the barista. She was fourth in line now. Someone arrived behind her. Someone tall. It had to be the guy from the doorway. After a minute, maybe less, she turned around.

He smiled at her. He had a clipped haircut that showed where the hairline was starting to retreat at the temples but didn't apologize for it. He was well tanned. There were remnants of youthful freckles on his clean jaw. You could see the nuances between the muscles in his neck, and you could see the edges of his clavicle beneath the open collar of his polo, which definition was rare for a man of his age, even if his age, from Steph's slightly more advanced perspective, looked relatively enviable. Steph smiled back. She turned forward. Still fourth in line. The barista scooped foam majestically and slowly.

"Does this guy have any idear we're waiting?" the man whispered.

Steph flushed at the sound of his voice. So she had been wrong on at least one count. He put an *r* on the end of *idea*. He was from around here. "You can't rush great art," Steph whispered over her shoulder. "There's regular coffee by the window next to the soap if you're in a hurry." She gestured to the coffee-pots on a butcher-block table. On the table next to it were giant bricks of rough-edged soap in scents ranging from lavender to sea salt, all nestled in bales of ersatz straw.

"That's soap?" the man asked.

"Yup."

"Does it work?"

"In my experience," Steph said, holding up the block she'd selected, a blend of fig leaf and seaweed. He sniffed it.

"Smells nice."

"It's from France."

"Ah."

They inched forward in line.

"Are you also taking a break from the traffic?" he asked her.

At this point, it seemed absurd not to face him and acknowledge that they were indeed having a conversation, so Steph turned and said, "My daughter has a soccer game today. We live in Damariscotta. She's a senior at Lincoln."

"Oh, good luck to her."

"I'll pass that along."

"You can tell her Nate said that."

"I will, Nate. You should come if you need a respite from your journey." He smiled at the offer, or maybe at her strong word choice, or maybe both. Then he nodded at something going on behind her. Steph had reached the front of the line, apparently. She spun toward the barista. "Hi," she said.

"Hi," the barista said.

She gave him a moment to recognize her and anticipate her order, but he didn't, so she said, "The usual, please."

"Which is?"

"An American. With a little steamed milk. Nonfat."

"You mean, an Americano?" the barista asked.

"That's what I said."

"You said American."

She thought back. Okay, you know what? Maybe she *had* said American. So what? The barista should have known what she meant.

"Your name?" he asked.

He should know that, too. "Steph," she said. "S-T-E-P-H."

After Nate had ordered a double espresso, he came over to where Steph was standing, and they waited there together, or not together but near enough for someone to get the wrong idea, so

Steph drifted over to a table of cookbooks by the window and looked out at Main Street, Wiscasset. There was a long line at Red's Eats, that little shack that served overrated lobster rolls down by the muddy river, and people were sunning themselves on the deck of the café across the street, sucking down Arnold Palmers and car exhaust. The little village was brimming with traffic—license plates from Connecticut, New York, New Jersey, even Delaware. People thought Wiscasset was one of the most charming towns in Maine, but only because they'd fallen prey to the power of self-promotion: Wiscasset's own sign, posted just off Route 1, right after the Ford dealership, said WELCOME TO WIS-CASSET, THE PRETTIEST VILLAGE IN MAINE, and your typical tourist seemed to accept the title without thinking, without comparing it to anywhere else on the Midcoast.

Like, say, Damariscotta! In one of her earliest Facebook posts, Steph had challenged us all to dream about a "36 Hours . . ." featurette appearing in *The New York Times,* and once that article went online, she wrote, appealing to our competitive natures, or possibly just her own, we could finally tell Wiscasset to go shove it.

I'd been following Steph's career as town manager, or mayor, whatever she wanted us to call her, from an amused but supportive distance when she called me out of the blue one day and asked me to submit an op-ed to *The Lincoln County News.* Maeve must have mentioned to Steph that I was a writer, at least by degree, but I didn't know which point of view, exactly, Steph wanted me to espouse in the op-ed.

"Just write about our agenda," she said. "In general."

So what she was looking for was a puff piece. I told Steph that I would think about it, not wanting to disappoint her over the phone, but I knew already that I wasn't likely to follow up. It's not that I disagreed with her message; it's just that I found it, when delivered in speeches or in writing, paradoxical. She would tell us that we lived in the most "authentic" town on the Midcoast and that we had our industrious spirit and our refusal to cater to outside tastes to thank for this designation, but then she would tell us that the time was right to capitalize upon the authenticity by embracing tourism and making a bevy of changes to the way we lived and did business. I understand that progress, as a broad rule, vanquishes tradition, so I get what she was going for, I think, but I would have liked to hear a discussion of how the seemingly contradictory appraisals of our present and future might be reconciled, if only to acknowledge that there was indeed a difference. I guess I could have been the one to make sense of it. I could have done it in an op-ed. What stopped me was that I still felt like an outsider. I hadn't earned the right yet.

Steph felt a touch on her triceps. Nate. He raised his small to-go cup of espresso. "No foam," he said. "Faster."

"Good tip," she said.

"Nice to meet you, Steph."

"You, too," she said, "Nate."

"See you around."

He pushed through the door, and the sun and traffic took his place for a moment, then went away, obscured by the tinted glass as the door returned to its frame. Nate had called her Steph, and yet she had never introduced herself, had she?

The barista called her name. Her Americano was ready. Right. The barista had asked for her name when she placed her order. The whole store knew her name.

She took her drink from the counter and stepped outside, dropping her sunglasses from hair to nose. Once she had walked to her BMW, she took a moment to look from the town hall to the bridge, appraising the neighboring township, wondering where Nate had gone, wondering where he'd come from.

———

AT ALLIE'S SOCCER GAME, STEPH sat in a high corner of the bleach-ers. She had her notebook out, and she was filling the pages with prototypes for a new town sign to go by the Damariscotta side of the bridge. Allie, as the team's sweeper, stayed predominantly on the defensive half of the field, so when the ball went toward Wiscasset's goal, Steph drew signs. She wanted Damariscotta's motto to be something like "Prettiest Village in Maine," but better than that. Sometimes the notebook absorbed her so fully that she missed a defensive possession or two, but sometimes the soccer game held her attention through several back-and-forths, so when she finally turned back to the notebook, her creative momentum had derailed. During one of these moments, as her pencil hovered above a half-filled page, she heard EJ's voice:

"There she is," he said, "scribbling away again."

He sat down next to her on the aluminum bench, and she felt the whole row sag. She tilted the notebook toward her son, who was in his Damariscotta Police uniform. He had taken a style tip from the Staties and put in an order two sizes too small. That EJ had grown into a giant cop never ceased to baffle Steph. That he had come from her was even more mysterious. It shouldn't be possible to give birth to something so much larger than yourself. "I'm trying to come up with a slogan for a town sign," Steph said.

"Why?"

"So people will know what to think about Damariscotta."

"Why can't they think for themselves?"

"Because they'll get it wrong."

EJ was facing forward, watching the game, so Steph also turned to watch. It was 1–1, early in the second half.

"Who's Dad standing with?" EJ asked.

Usually Ed watched the games by himself, but today he

stood next to a thin woman in a purple windbreaker. She wore reflective sunglasses as a headband, pushing her short, frosted tips back from her forehead. "I think she's the lacrosse coach at Amherst," Steph said.

"Someone should tell the Amherst coach that this is a soccer game, not a lacrosse game," EJ said. "Where is Amherst anyway?"

"Ed says they like to see the girls play other sports to see what kind of athletes they are."

"New Hampshire," EJ said. "Amherst, New Hampshire, right?"

"Massachusetts."

"Don't you know someone who went there?"

"Cammie Sweet. I visited her once."

"How was that?"

"I don't remember."

"What do you mean, you don't remember?"

"I was overserved, and it was a long time ago. All I know is Amherst's a really good school, so I'm not sure it's in Allie's best interest to get her hopes up for a place she might not get into. Listen to this: 'Damariscotta . . . The way life should be . . . and always will be.'"

"Mom, I don't know. It sounds fine."

The ball went out of bounds. Ed picked it up and tossed it to Allie, who threw it, overhead, dragging her back foot, to a teammate.

"I hope he's not fucking it up," EJ said. "He's probably overselling her."

"Your dad knows what he's doing."

"How?"

"He's done his research."

Ed was pointing at Allie now, then gesticulating. He held one hand upright, then spun the other one around it, and Steph recognized the pantomime—Ed was telling the coach about the first time he realized his daughter could play lacrosse at the collegiate level, when she was a freshman, when she improvised a spin move out of thin air. Steph had heard the story before. The coach had probably heard it, too. Ed called her once a week these days—called all the NESCAC coaches once a week—to make sure she had seen Allie's new highlight tape or to let her know how much some other coach wanted Allie to play for Tufts, Middlebury, or Wesleyan. Steph couldn't imagine a more invested father. He had his own power ranking of all the schools. When Steph told him she thought Allie was the one who was supposed to come up with that kind of list, Ed said it was a big decision and he was just trying to help. In his mind, Bowdoin College was the obvious number-one, the best combination of academics and athletics, but Steph suspected this preference had more to do with the short commute between Bowdoin and Damariscotta, and when she'd done her own research, she'd discovered that Amherst was ranked highest of all the schools Allie was looking at by *U.S. News* and that its women's lacrosse team had made the national tournament last year.

Steph looked at her notebook, flipped back a few pages. She showed one of the mock-ups to EJ and said, "What about 'Damariscotta . . . It's Vacation-town!'"

"Mom. You're obsessed. Just watch the game."

"I am watching the game. I come to more of Allie's games than you do."

"That's because I have to work. I don't know how you can doodle in that notebook when Allie's playing. I get goosebumps."

"Butterflies."

"Whatever."

"It'd be like Vacationland," she said, "but Vacation-town."

"Uh-huh, I got that."

The Wiscasset goalie drop-kicked the ball, and three girls jumped up and tried to head it, but they all missed.

"Why don't you give your son some credit," EJ said, "and mention that we're the safest little town in Maine?"

"I would if it were true, honey."

"It is true."

"Based on what?"

"Based on maps of criminal activity and such."

"Really?"

"Really."

Steph considered this news, then said, "I'd like to see those maps."

"I'm sure they're on the state website. We have blown-up versions in the department."

"We're really the safest town in Maine?"

"Right up there, anyway."

"That's good, actually," Steph said.

EJ watched the game. Steph went back to her notebook. *Damariscotta . . . The Midcoast's Safe Haven.* She felt EJ looking over her shoulder.

"I wasn't entirely serious, obviously," he said.

"EJ, you just said you were serious. Don't jerk me around, please."

"I'm serious about us being the safest town in Maine, but I'm not serious about you using it."

"Well, *I'm* serious," she said. "I don't know if it works on a sign. But we can put it on brochures. We can put an ad in *Down East* magazine."

"That coach is leaving," EJ said. "I'm gonna say hey to Dad and see how it went." But before he left, he added, voice firm, "You can't say we're safer than other towns."

———

STEPH SHOWED UP AT THE police department several days after Allie's game in Wiscasset with two Chicken Ranch sandwiches from the Schooner, EJ's favorite.

"This is a surprise," EJ said.

They ate the sandwiches. Or EJ did. Steph wasn't hungry.

"How's the weekend looking?" Steph asked.

"What do you mean?" EJ's mouth was full.

"You got any big plans?"

"Nope."

"No dates?"

"Nope."

"You should go down to Portland, hit the bars."

"I'm on duty."

"Well, I don't see how you're gonna meet anyone when you're working every weekend."

"But then if I don't work, I don't have any money to hit the bars—that's the big conundrum, isn't it?"

Steph looked around the office, then suddenly pretended to think of something. "Hey," she said, "you know those maps you mentioned?"

EJ was about to take a bite of the sandwich, but he stopped, put it down. "Uh-huh."

"Think I could see them?"

"They're over there," EJ said, nodding to a wall on the far side of the office. The wall was covered almost entirely in corkboard, and on it were flyers for federal fugitives, missing pets, and the annual Police vs. Firefighters Basketball Cup. But in the middle of the corkboard were two big maps of Maine. One was covered in red dots, the other in blue dots. Steph went to the maps, looked them over.

"What are all the dots?" she asked.

EJ joined her, stood beside her. "Red dots are thefts. Blue dots are significant narcotics arrests."

On the red map, most of the incidents were along the coast. On the blue map there were higher concentrations around urban centers—Portland, Lewiston, and Bangor.

"So this is good," Steph said.

"Sure," EJ said.

"Look at us," Steph said, pointing to Lincoln County on one map, then the other. "Pretty damn clean."

"Yup," EJ said.

"You know who'd be interested in maps like these?"

"Nope."

"New home-buyers."

"I wouldn't know about them."

"I would," Steph said. "Maps like these could really attract interest."

"Who says we want interest all of a sudden?"

"Why wouldn't we?"

He shrugged.

"What?"

"I don't know, I just think most people around here like things the way they are, Mom. Most people aren't trying to bring in all kinds of newcomers."

"Well, what *most people* don't understand," Steph said, her voice beginning to rise, "is that if we want to keep things the way they are, we need a budget to make improvements, and that budget comes from property taxes, and unless we want to pay higher taxes, we need people to buy more property."

"So in order to keep things the way they are, we have to make changes?"

"Exactly."

"Sounds pretty crazy to me."

"Well, it's not!" Steph said, trying not to sound crazy. But this is exactly what she found so infuriating. This inability to see the big picture. Nobody around here understood that she was trying to save Damariscotta from itself. "It's not crazy, it's complex," she said.

"Just be careful, Mom. People don't like complex. People like simple."

"I know what people like," Steph said. "Don't forget—I got elected mayor."

"Manager. You got elected town manager."

Steph took another long look at the maps. "Okay," she said. "So since you understand people so well, tell me why they wouldn't want me to brag about how safe we are."

"Well, I guess it's mostly the other towns up and down the coast you'd have to worry about."

"Why?"

"I don't know, jealousy?"

"Oh, come on—those other towns can blow me."

"Mom."

"I'm sorry. But they can." Steph tried to settle down. But she was getting the runaround. She hated the runaround, especially when it came from her own family. Some things, okay, she didn't have to know about. If she didn't ask, they didn't have to tell her. But when she asked, she expected answers.

"Maybe there's a reason our town's safer than all the rest," EJ said.

"Oh, because you're the world's best cop?"

"No. Not at all. It's just—and maybe it's paranoid—but I don't think we should be shining a big, bright light on ourselves." He scratched at his jaw, as if it weren't perfectly clean-shaven. "I shouldn't even be having this conversation."

"Why not?"

But instead of answering, he turned and went back to his

desk. He tossed his sandwich in the trash and pulled his hat off a hook. "I love you, Mom," he said on his way to the door, "but you better get your head out of your ass."

As he left the station, Steph stood there spinning the ring around her finger, flitting at the silver buoy around her neck, a buoy that Ed had dusted in a coat of tiny diamonds for their twentieth anniversary. She glanced at the maps, then back to the door. EJ was already gone. She'd forgotten to say that she loved him, too, and that she hadn't meant to be sarcastic. He really was a good cop. A good son, too. But he was wrong about her head. It wasn't up her ass. It wasn't up anyone's ass.

STEPH GAVE ME THREE INTERVIEWS, ranging from forty-five minutes to three hours, all with her lawyer present. He came up from Portland and said hardly a word. He wore a dark suit and glasses and took notes on a yellow legal pad, seeming more like a bodyguard or hired muscle than an adviser or confidant. We were in the Thatches' living room and, because we remained seated the entire time, because our conversation constituted the only sound in the place other than the whir of an overhead fan high in the rafters, I was impressed once again, during breaks or when I otherwise became aware of it, by the dimensions of their home, the old barn. Steph claimed that it wasn't until this last stretch of their rise, the final year or so, that she really started to wonder what was going on. It wasn't the big things, like the house; it was the little things. The conversation with EJ. An exchange with Ed. She recounted to me one discussion in particular, not long after EJ had shown her the maps, when she and Ed were lying in bed. They had taken on so many expenses, she said to Ed, that it might be time to come up with a family budget.

"We're fine, Steph," Ed said. "My end of the business is going good."

"How?"

"Just is. Been a nice run."

"But what are you basing this on?"

"Numbers," he said.

"What kind of numbers?"

"Solid ones."

"Show me."

"Show you what?"

"How much money we have."

"You know how much money we have."

"I think I do, but then it always turns out we have more."

"Yuh—that's because we're making money," he said. "That's how it works."

She waited for him to elaborate. Then waited some more. He didn't say a word.

"Ed," she said.

No response.

"Are you a-fucking-sleep?"

He was.

Finally she rolled over, as she always had before, but her eyes remained open. All night long. The next night, too. And soon the nights without sleep began to add a kind of haze to the days that made her even less likely to get to the bottom of whatever was bringing her down. The harder she tried to sleep, the more difficult it became. She would try to concentrate on her breathing, but then she would become fixated on Ed's breathing, and then she would have to go lie on the couch where it was always too bright because none of the big windows had blinds. So then her brain would be humming like an electrical box the next day, so loud that she couldn't slow down or think clearly. Another restless night would pile on. But even sleep-deprived, or maybe *because* she was sleep-deprived, her brain kept working on the problem of how she had come to where she was now. She told herself that Ed wasn't hiding anything, but now that she'd started asking questions, they followed her everywhere, exhausted her, made her disappointed in everything she saw. When she walked down Main Street, she no longer recognized the potential. Or she did, but without feeling any excitement for it. Instead she felt angry that nobody had helped her realize that potential yet.

She flipped on the lights in the Schooner and dropped her bag on the bar. It was 11 A.M., but she felt destroyed from another night without sleep, so she brewed a strong pot of coffee and fixed herself an even stronger Bloody Mary, sipping them alternately, as she prepared for the lunch shift. She popped the sanitary caps off the liquor bottles, took the plastic wrap off the juice pourers. "I'd never felt so out of control," she told me. "I'm used to being in control. I hated it. I've always thought that losing control is a sign of weakness. And it is. That's why I hated it so much."

Lunch guests began arriving, and with them came Steph's father Raymond. He acted more like an honorary master of ceremonies than an employee now, like it should be obvious to Steph and everyone else in the Schooner that the latter stages of his life had afforded him this privilege. The entropy had come on gradually, Steph picking up more and more of the slack until she noticed that she was doing all the bartending, Raymond all the talking. Today he ordered a cheeseburger and ate it standing behind the bar, his long gray hair pulled back in a ponytail to keep it from falling in his meal. He chatted with the construction crew that came in wearing matching T-shirts. They ate Chicken Ranches while keeping their eyes on the flat-screen above the bar, agreeing with Raymond without listening to him. Installing that TV was the last hard work Steph had seen her father do in the Schooner. She had asked him how he was paying for it, and he said, "Ed's got plenty of money."

"Steph," he said now, "can you grab this gentleman another Coke?"

"I'm a little busy," she said. She was polishing wineglasses, getting them ready for dinner guests, just in case anyone with elevated taste accidentally came in tonight.

"You're closer," her father said.

She pushed the half-polished glass onto its rack, apparently less gently than usual, and the stem broke in her hand. Blood seeped from a cut in the crook between thumb and index finger. "Fuck," she said. She wrapped a bar towel around the laceration. "Dad, get your own soda." She left the bar, went into the kitchen, and found the first aid kit.

When she returned, she found her father, to her surprise, working for once. He was sliding a bar napkin in front of a new guest. And this new bar guest—Steph stopped short when she saw him. It was what's-his-name, the man from Bon Bon in Wiscasset. Nate. Nate's sunglasses dangled from the rolled collar of his sweater.

Her father turned to her. "Are you okay?"

"Of course," she said.

Raymond nodded at her hand. A red circle was blooming through the Band-Aid.

"Oh," she said. "It's fine."

"Okay, good. Because our new guest would like a ginger ale." He walked away, past the soda gun, settling across from the construction workers.

Steph fixed Nate a ginger ale and placed it in front of him. "Just passing through?" she said.

"I am," he said. "I go on drives occasionally." He looked around the Schooner. The decor had everything you might expect, local memorabilia from the Red Sox and the lobstering trade, but all of it on the classy end of the bar-and-grill spectrum.

Steph had upgraded the Bud Light Red Sox posters to framed pictures of Ted Williams and Carl Yastrzemski, and the lobster buoys were arranged neatly in a row along one wall, mounted in wooden boxes like butterflies on display in a museum. "This place is nicer than I thought it would be," Nate said.

"So you thought it wouldn't be nice?"

"Well, no—I just had a vague—I don't know."

"But you did have expectations, which means you didn't come here by accident."

He swiveled on his stool, facing Steph again, and splayed his fingers on the bar, like a dealer. "Today," he said, "okay, I confess, I knew I'd find you here."

"That makes me feel a little weird."

"It shouldn't. I googled 'Damariscotta Steph.' A picture of you and 'Town Manager' pops up. You own this place. You have playing fields named after your family. You make speeches in town meetings—"

"Okay, I get it." She gave him a menu. "The Chicken Ranch is the most popular item, but I recommend the Fall Salad."

"I'll have that then."

"Don't do it on my behalf."

"Okay, fine, I'll have the Fall Salad and a side of onion rings."

She wrote his order on a pad, tore off the slip, and passed it through the kitchen window.

"You look tired," Nate said.

"Oh, thanks."

She poured herself a cranberry juice and took a sip.

"Who are you?" she asked him.

He smiled. "I'm from Delaware. Not originally. I grew up in Rockland."

"I noticed your accent."

"You did?"

"I did."

He asked if Steph ever went up toward Rockland, and Steph said not really, but then she remembered that Ed had taken her bike-riding on North Haven once, so she told Nate that she and her husband liked to bring their bikes out to the islands sometimes.

Then she asked Nate why he had moved away, and he said he used to work for MBNA in Camden, until Bank of America bought the credit card company and transferred him to Wilmington. His job was to investigate fraud cases. Sometimes people have their identity stolen or lose their ATM card and they call the bank and say the big tab on their statement isn't theirs. The bank needs someone to look into the claims and find out if it's getting scammed. This was Nate's job.

Steph kept waiting for him to mention a wife, but he never did. Maybe she was dead. That would be an acceptable reason to wear a wedding band *while* flirting. Steph looked over in her father's direction, but he wasn't paying any attention to her. She asked Nate if he had a wife. Yes, he said. And three kids. In Delaware. He sounded reluctant to tell her this. "I'm home for a while," he said, "because my brother died. I'm helping out my parents."

"I'm sorry to hear that," she said.

The construction guys finished their sandwiches, so Steph moved down to their end of the bar and asked her father to step aside while she bussed their plates, and then Nate's lunch came up in the window. She presented him with the plate and a red basket of onion rings. He was a man who ordered onion rings. Nothing about him was as intriguing as she had imagined when he walked into Bon Bon, and really, what she had imagined about him had only taken shape the moment she turned the other way, based on a fleeting and incomplete first appraisal. Nate should have let that be it. He was pretending to be nice and open, but he had a wife and kids somewhere else—and other secrets that weren't even secrets in the place he came from—so in the end he was no different from any other man who tried to keep her from knowing what was rightfully hers to know.

Twenty minutes later, Nate had finished his lunch and crumpled up his napkin. He placed it in the red basket and pushed it across the bar. "So," he said quietly, after finishing his ginger ale. "I'd love to see you when you're not at work. I feel like we have more to talk about."

"I don't think that's possible," Steph said. "You seem like a nice person, but I'm married."

"Me too."

"Right."

He ran a hand over his tan, stubbly head. "Okay," he said finally. "I'll leave my card. I hope you'll call me. I just want to talk." He put his business card on the bar and stood up. He left way too much cash, and then Steph thought he was about to go, but instead he seemed to remember something. "One of those videos," he said, sliding his wallet into his back pocket, "I ended up watching the whole thing. You're a good public speaker."

"Thank you."

"You were talking about the early days, when you were waiting tables and going to college, and Ed was working as a lobsterman, but then the price of lobster started going up, and you guys started making your way."

"Yup," Steph said. "That's how it happened."

"Well," Nate said. "I found the story inspirational. And I don't even think you give yourself enough credit."

"I give myself plenty of credit."

He laughed and said, "Okay, good. Sorry, I just thought it was funny, or interesting, I mean. The price of lobster. I looked it up. It's actually gone down over the years."

"Down?"

"At least compared to inflation. If you guys were making more money—I mean, you say you were hustling like crazy, and I believe it."

When Nate was gone, Raymond asked Steph who he was.

"I don't know," she said, throwing his card in the trash. "Some banker from Delaware."

IT TOOK HER THREE FULL days to clean the house. She threw out old magazines, dusted the fan, dusted the beams above the living room, teetering on a ladder as she reached as far as she could, swept the chimney, checked for loose bricks, rearranged the walk-in closet, refolded all Ed's clothes, threw out all the old shoe boxes. She'd be done as soon as she inspected every plank and nail in the house, she told herself, making sure everything was where it ought to be. Then she would stop. She was far too busy as mayor, restaurateur, and mother to be doing this, anyway. It was just that she knew she wouldn't be able to sleep until she had finished cleaning. And also, it was that she was looking for something. She could admit it. She was looking for something but didn't know what it was.

Once she'd finished with the rest of the house, she went to the master bedroom and stripped the bed and looked under the mattress, but there was nothing there. Nothing anywhere. So, with nowhere left to look, she lay on her bare bed. Outside the bedroom windows, the sun was going gray. A storm was supposed to come up the coast. A great white hurricane was spinning off the Carolinas and it would never make it this far north, but there would be waves marching up the shore, and wind running through the pines, and rain bleeding down the windows. Steph rolled onto her side and thought back to the beginning. She had come home from New Hampshire ready to make the best of her one year at Lincoln. She didn't know anyone, but nor did they know her. She could be whomever she wanted to be, do whatever she pleased. The plan was to kick ass in school and apply to out-of-state colleges like UNH and Northeastern while tearing it up on the weekends, no strings attached. What a joke. No strings. As soon as Ed had shown up at Jamie Kerry's house after the first day of school and found her smoking a joint with Jamie on his bed, she had felt the ties begin to bind, and they had talked for a minute or two, and he had reminded her who he was, that morning on the fuel dock, but Jamie was anxious to get Ed out of there and kept laughing this weird laugh and saying, Well, make yourself right at home, Ed! and then Ed touched the brim of his hat and looked right at Steph and said, Nice bracelet, even though she wasn't wearing a bracelet, and then he was gone, but it was like those lines were already tied tight and he was tugging her right out the door with him. Steph handed the joint to Jamie and said, I'll be right back, but she already knew she'd never return. She caught up to Ed on the dock. He was in his boat, yanking angrily on the engine chain. The sun had gone down by then, so she could make out little more than his dark figure and the scent of salt water, fish, gasoline.

"Hey you," she said.

He didn't respond.

"Why'd you say 'nice bracelet'?" she asked him, raising her voice over the sound of the engine, which had finally come alive. She hugged her arms to her chest to keep herself warm. All she was wearing was a swimsuit and a tank top that said *Old Orchard Beach* in pink cursive font.

"You know why," he said. He was busying himself with the stern line, not looking at her.

"No, I don't." She pointed at her naked wrist. "See? No bracelet."

"I ain't blind," he said.

"Then what are you?"

"Nothing."

"No, you're something."

"What's that supposed to mean?"

"I don't know. Maybe you're mad at me, but I don't know why you would be."

He was about to untie the bow line, but he stopped and stood straight, staring at her from beneath his hat brim. "All right, fine then—I *am* curious—what'd you do with it?"

"With what?"

"You being fresh with me?"

"I'm not, Ed! Swear to God. I have no idea what you're talking about."

He yanked at his hat, looked away, looked back. "You're saying you never got the bracelet I sent?"

"What bracelet?"

"I sent it middle of the summer. Made of twine."

"Twine? Where'd you find a bracelet made of twine?"

"I made it. Tied a monkey fist on one end."

"A what?"

"A monkey fist. A big knot. Put a loop on the other end."

"Like a clasp?"

"I guess."

For a moment they stood silently, staring at one another. Ed had made her a bracelet. Waited for a response. Hadn't heard a peep. It wasn't her fault—but still.

"Ed," she said, "I never got a bracelet. I promise."

"We only met once, so I can see why you wouldn't want it."

"I *did* want it. Or I would have. I'm just—I'm sorry it never got to me."

"Well," he said, "they ain't that hard to make. I could make you another one."

"I'd like that."

He went to the bow and untied the painter but didn't push off—not yet.

"Where are you going?" she asked him.

"Don't know. Home."

They stayed silent for a moment. A bug, too small to see, landed on Ed's neck. He slapped at it, then threw it away. "Why?" he said. "You wanna go somewhere?"

She looked up at the house, back to the boat, then got in and sat on the fore-bench, facing back toward Ed. Soon they were carving away from the dock and heading down the dark river. He kept driving until they reached a soundless cove. Houses shone between the trees on the shore, well away from the boat. Then Ed cut the engine and let the skiff drift.

She could have said no. Or she could have insisted that if they were going to do it, it would be the way she had done it before (quickly, only pausing to yank clothes off and condom on, guy above her, Steph nearly crushed beneath his weight); that would have been fine, too. But what she shouldn't have done, once they had stripped down to their bare skin, at least below the waist, when Ed laid himself against her and started pushing forward, was go along with it. He wasn't wearing anything. All she had to do was say, No, Ed, we wait until you get something. But she couldn't find the words. She didn't want to disappoint him. And she *did* want to feel him inside her—there was that, too. When he entered, it came as a full-body shock. It was like stepping into a frozen lake, waiting for the warmth. The breath went right out of her. They were lying on a bed of oil-stained life jackets in the hull of the Whaler, a sawed-off milk jug rolling around by her head. Sound would travel farther on water than it would on land, so Steph worried that the houses on the shore might be able to hear them, but it was a fleeting concern—soon she'd forgotten all about the people in their houses, forgotten about everyone other than Ed.

That wasn't the only time, and within months she was pregnant and living in the trailer. She remembered being happy. Right? She hoped she had been happy. What she didn't know was if she had been happy since. But nobody's happy all the time. It's no way to go through life. If you're happy all the time, you don't appreciate anything. You have to have contrast, to have low moments to bring out the high moments in relief. And if nothing else, Steph had built a life of high contrast.

A FEW WEEKS LATER, STEPH met with the chamber of commerce and representatives from all the local real estate firms. If her husband and son weren't going to let her in on whatever it was they knew and she didn't, she had no choice but to move ahead as planned. If they wished to keep her in the dark, she would let them.

So, she told everyone, she had good news for the real estate business. The town was embarking on a new publicity campaign—ads in *Down East* magazine and *The Boston Globe,* and a new glossy brochure that would emphasize the authenticity of Damariscotta as well as its safety. She told them about the maps, about how Damariscotta was Maine's "Safe Haven."

Town planning meetings were open to the public, but this one had drawn only a handful of realtors and several senior citizens with nowhere else to go. Cammie was there to keep up her

end of the deal, offering her support and her vote in return for
the discounted lease on Ben's old storefront. EJ was there, too,
sitting at the far end of the table, though Steph had said hardly a
word to him and refused to make eye contact as she laid out her
plans for Damariscotta's future. Steph reminded everyone of her
ambitions for the town and the added revenue they would need
to get there. She reminded them that in today's volatile economy,
they were in competition for every dollar spent on the Midcoast.
And everything was going well, she was receiving in response
to her pitch mostly nods of approval, when she saw someone
who stopped her midsentence. It was Nate, now wearing a red
rain jacket in anticipation of another storm working its way
up the coast. He had let himself in through the front entrance
of the library and taken a seat at the far end of the table. She
hadn't seen him since that afternoon in the Schooner. She hadn't
thought about him either, not for the past few weeks anyway—or
if she did, she assumed he was already gone, back in Delaware.

Now he stared at Steph. Everyone was staring at Steph. But
she felt his gaze more forcefully than all the rest. Faltering and
reaching for the diamond buoy around her neck, she scanned the
note cards spread before her but couldn't find her place. She knew
she was close to the end, approximately, so she said, "Maybe we
should—I guess—let's just open this up to questions."

But she didn't give anyone time to ask anything. She motioned
to vote right away. She was moving too quickly for the seniors to
keep up. EJ stood to go, but now Steph hoped he would stay.
With her eyes she tried to plead with him to remain seated, but
he was on his way to the door, and when she stole a glance at
Nate, the meeting's only nonresident didn't avert his gaze.

"Officer Thatch!" Steph said, but EJ was already gone.

She turned back to the expectant, slightly puzzled faces.
"Let's vote," she told them again, but really there was nothing

much to vote on—what Steph had proposed amounted to a small change in attitude and a subtle shift in the way the town sold itself. The motion passed unanimously and quickly.

She began to pack her things, but when Nate stood from his chair and looked ready to come to her end of the table, wanting a word, clearly, she took whatever she had, leaving the note cards behind, and hustled for the door.

Outside, walking across Main Street, keys in hand, she heard Nate call her name. She kept walking, but then he yelled to her again, louder this time. Finally she turned and saw him jogging down the steps of the library in his red jacket. There was no point trying to run, no point in making a scene. Nate looked both ways as he crossed the street and came to her side—attempting to smile but failing at it. Above his head the clouds were darkening and moving like ships, and the telephone wires were swinging in the wind.

"Thank you," he said. "Sorry. Just wanted to say hello."

"Hello," she said.

"Can we go somewhere?"

"That sounds like more than hello."

"We need to talk."

"How is that possible? What could we have to talk about?"

"That's what I need to explain."

Everything about the exchange felt off-kilter. Steph was no longer attracted to this stranger and couldn't recall why she ever had been. She tried to tell herself that she had remembered their first moment in Wiscasset differently than she had lived it. He had lost his tan since then. He seemed balder somehow. And yet he was promising to tell her something, and she was so desperate to have someone fill her in—on anything—that she asked him where he wanted to go. Anywhere away from anyone she might know, he said. So she told him to follow her.

She opened the door of her BMW and started driving. On her way around the First National Bank, she passed a white Jeep Cherokee with Delaware license plates, which put its blinker on and trailed her up the hill toward the church. Steph turned onto Bristol Road, going faster than the speed limit. The sky overhead was still gray, but as she looked forward, she saw a darker, lower line of clouds forming over the southern horizon. She was close to home now, close to her long driveway, but she didn't stop. This was the safest place in Maine, she told herself, and she needed to know whatever it was that Nate wanted to tell her. She needed to get to the bottom of something, even if it wasn't the right thing.

She kept driving, splitting her attention between the storm filling the windshield and Nate's white SUV in the rearview. She drove until she reached the peninsula's southern tip and the light-house. When she looked at her phone again, it had lost service.

She parked the BMW. The lighthouse beam flashed over the parked cars, then the lawn, the rocks, the sea. Steph had lost sight of the Jeep when she came into the lot, and the sky was dark. There were people on the lawn, storm watchers. They wore foul-weather gear and kept a safe distance from the surf. The wind held them upright as they stood atop a long bladed ridge. The coast here looked ripped apart—its tectonic match gone to the other side of the ocean but the scars still raw and deep. Heavy swells rode in from the horizon and shattered on the rocks, around and over the storm watchers. They all took a step back.

As heavy raindrops pounded the roof of her SUV and washed over the windshield, Steph heard a rapping on the passenger's-side window, and the door opened. Nate settled into the car, rain streaming down the seams of his jacket. He closed the door, and the BMW went quiet again save for the percussion of the rain. Nate removed his hood. Steph could feel wet heat coming off his body, and the windshield fogged over.

"I'd say this is remote enough," he said.

He wiped his hand over his face and pulled rain from his nose and chin. Again, he tried to smile at her and failed. His teeth were beige. "So I guess I'll just start talking," he said. But then he went silent. The rain beat along the roof. Finally he began his story. It was an account of his travels over the last month—for longer than that, actually. Since before they had met. He reminded Steph that his brother had died and that he was home to help his parents. Steph remembered all this. But this time he told her in greater detail about how the brother had passed away. Steph had been picturing the brother as older, but he was younger. The brother had always struggled with the law, authority, drugs. He went to rehab once but dropped out. When he died, he was messed up on pills and dope. And he had been drinking. Steph wasn't sure why any of this was relevant to her. If this was what Nate wanted to tell her, it wasn't worth the trip down the peninsula—he had chosen the wrong person to open up to. Several times she interrupted to ask where this was going—but Nate was intent on finishing and ignored her each time. His parents wanted to blame someone, he said, and he told them to blame his brother. Or his demons, if that made the parents more comfortable. But they said no, no, no—whoever it was that brought these drugs to our town is an evildoer who needs to be brought to justice. Nate told his parents that he knew they were grieving but that they had to try to be reasonable. He asked them what they really wanted. And they—his dad, really—said they wanted the drugs to stop coming to Rockland. So Nate said he would look into it. He said this mostly just to make his father happy. He didn't think he would find anything.

Steph didn't like where Nate was headed—there seemed to be some implied bearing on her own life, and she wanted to keep Nate's story on its own course; this was not the kind of answer she'd been looking for—so she told him that she'd had a change of heart, that she no longer wanted to hear what he had to say, but Nate said Steph needed to hear it, that it was for her own good, and then he said that he'd taken a few long weekends off from work to drive from Delaware to Maine. There was a rumor that the product was coming around the border on boats, but who knew if it was true, and the only mysterious boat anyone remembered seeing (Nate had questioned police chiefs and fishermen in Rockland, Camden, Vinalhaven, and North Haven) belonged to someone who had broken into a big summer home on North Haven about twenty years prior. Nate found this out from the sternman who had seen the boat. The captain he had gone out with that day was dead now. But the sternman remembered the boat as gray and traveling upwards of forty knots. That was pretty fast for a lobster boat, Nate said. Sure was, the sternman said. Nate didn't believe the guy would remember the color of the hull—didn't really believe any of the story and was ready to stop listening because he was more interested in recent crimes—but then the sternman said he knew he was remembering the boat correctly because he had seen it again. Or one just like it. Last year. He had seen the boat tearing past the islands just after dawn, out to sea a ways. The sternman (he wasn't a sternman anymore—he had his own boat—but Nate kept referring to him as the sternman) was returning from a tuna-fishing trip, which was why he was out so far. He had taken note of the gray-hulled boat because it was cruising, just like the one he had seen years before, faster than any lobster boat should have been able to move. The sternman had barely enough time to focus his binoculars before it vanished. And in his binoculars he saw the transom. She was from Casco Bay. He couldn't remember the boat's name, but he remembered that the buoy atop the wheelhouse was black and white.

Still, this was not much for Nate to go on. He filed it away under dead-end leads. He went back to Delaware.

After another few weeks, he returned to Maine, just to check on his parents, and while he was home, Rockland hosted their annual lobster boat race. And it was at this race that Nate saw boats going faster, much faster, than he had ever seen a boat go before. This was interesting. He started thinking. He decided to look up which racing boats had gray hulls, and when he did, he noticed that over the years someone named Ed Thatch had always entered the races, always, according to those who knew, with gray-hulled boats. And when Nate followed Ed Thatch back to his true hailing port, not Casco Bay but South Bristol, and then to his true home address, not South Bristol but Damariscotta, and looked at his new house and the businesses he owned, and Nate saw how beautiful his wife was, Nate couldn't help but think that, for a lobsterman who hadn't graduated high school, Ed Thatch had done pretty well for himself. And when he went down to the docks and looked at *all* Ed's boats and realized they *all* had racing engines, he started to wonder why anyone would need so many boats to move so quickly—certainly not just to get from trap to trap or to compete with one another in the summer races. And so Nate started following Steph because at first he thought she must be in on the family business, but then it became clear that she wasn't; otherwise she wouldn't have held a meeting to tell everyone that her town was the safest on the Midcoast when it was only safe because it was in the eye of the storm, the domain of the man who controlled the weather.

Nate finished his story and the car fell silent. A sheet of rain blew away from the roof, then back onto it.

"Why are you telling me this?" Steph asked him finally. She couldn't believe any of it. It made perfect sense, and she had prepared herself to trust him, and yet she couldn't. This was not what

Ed had withheld from her. He would never build their life upon anything so treacherous. Now she was scared. Scared of what Nate might be capable of and scared of losing her family. Because if what Nate had said was true—any of it—then it was a matter for her to deal with, not him. She wanted desperately to regain control but couldn't think of a way to do so. Her bag was in her lap, and her phone was in her bag, but there was no one to call, no one who could help her, and she didn't have any service anyway.

"I wasn't expecting to like you," Nate said, facing to his right, away from Steph, looking into the storm.

Steph glanced at Nate. She thought of the phone again, and then she reached into her bag, trying to be discreet—

"Wait, back up a second," she said.

"Back up?"

"Yeah," she said, looking down again, tapping the screen, "a second ago, you said you liked me."

"I'm—I just had to say it," he said.

"But when we first met," she said. "It wasn't a coincidence."

"No."

"And you were just doing your job, helping out your parents."

"That's right."

Outside the waves kicked off the rocks, and the observers retreated from the cliff, moving back to the parking lot, their faces all obscured by the rain streaming down the BMW's windows.

"It's just—" Steph said, trying to sound sincere, trying to sound nervous in a way she wasn't, "I thought there was something else that first time we met."

"I thought so, too," Nate said. "Of course I thought that."

"So what—we just leave it like this?"

"Leave it like what?"

"Leave it without—you know—seeing where it goes," she said.

Steph watched him weigh a response. He struggled with her proposal, if that was what it was, for a long time. Then he reached for her hand. His fingers felt somehow wet and cool and hot all at once. "No," he said. "I mean, yeah—I want that to happen."

"Okay," Steph said. "Me, too."

"When?"

"I don't know—now?"

He was staring forward, through the windshield, or at it; there was nothing to see but the thick folds of rain. "Where?" he asked.

"Anywhere."

Steph glanced out the window. A couple in green rain jackets was moving off the grass by the lighthouse and through the parking lot. Hopefully they weren't headed to a car with out-of-state plates. Nate probably wouldn't notice. He was just a bank investigator. The couple would have to do. "Shit," Steph said, ducking.

"What is it?"

"Ed's uncle."

"His uncle?"

"Look away."

Nate did as he was told but said, "You're bullshitting me."

"I'm not. It's a small county. Everyone knows everyone."

"Apparently."

She could feel she was losing him. She didn't want to lose him, and nor did she want to touch him, but this first desire overcame the second. She reached to his crotch, placed her hand on his fly.

"Just not here," she said.

Nate didn't respond. He didn't look toward her. Instead he let himself get erect under Steph's hand. "You drive back toward Rockland," she said. "I'll follow you. There's a motel up Route 1."

He made her wait for a response, and when she withdrew her hand, he leaned over to try to kiss her. She couldn't do it. She stopped him. "Not here," she said. "I don't know where they went." She gestured behind her, at the couple she had accused of being related to her by law.

Nate looked at her one last time, told her to stay close to him in her car, then opened the door as the rain swept in on a gust—

"Wait," she said. "Give me your number. In case I lose you."

He removed another business card from his wallet and handed it to her. "Cellphone's on the bottom," he said.

She waited until he was beyond the rain, and then she went to put her face in her hands to keep herself from screaming. But her hand had been on Nate, and the thought of touching him, then her face, made her gag. So she rolled down her window to gather as much rain in her open palm as she could and rubbed her hands together, as if that might wash off everything that had just taken place.

Even if she also needed to preserve it. She pulled the phone out of the bag, hit the stop button, and scrubbed back to the middle of the timeline. She hit play to test the audio quality:

I thought that, too. Of course I thought that. . . .

A bright light bounced off the rearview. Nate. She hit pause on the phone, pulled out behind the Jeep, and followed him away from the lighthouse, back toward town. She would split off as soon as she could. When they passed from Bristol into Damariscotta, approaching her own road, she entered Nate's number into her phone, called him, and said, "Bear right at the intersection—it's faster," and he did. "Stay on the line," she told him. "I'll give you directions." His Jeep and her BMW went along School Street, by a row of small houses and a farm stand, and then his SUV was passing the police station, in front of which Steph was relieved to see her son's large cruiser. She took a sharp left and pulled in next to it. She could see Nate's taillights up ahead, moving to the shoulder.

Eventually he spoke. "What are you doing?" he asked slowly.

"Going to see my son." She opened her door and got out of the car, walking quickly, hugging her cardigan to her chest with one hand as it soaked through with rain. "My son's a cop," she said into the phone. "As I believe you know. And if he hears the conversation I just recorded, he's not going to be happy. I don't think your wife would be very happy either."

Her hand was on the door of the police station, but she didn't go inside. She watched Nate's Jeep, she listened to the silence on the phone, and then she heard him say, "Fuck you, Steph Thatch." His brake lights went off and he drove back into the road and away from town. Her phone went dead.

Steph waited until well after his lights had disappeared, and then she took her hand off the door and went back to her car. She sat behind the wheel, a series of shallow breaths rattling her chest. When she saw an officer exit the front door—not EJ—she put the car in reverse and headed for home.

The night had arrived with the storm. Steph only thought to turn the headlights on when she realized she couldn't see a thing. Leaning forward over the steering wheel, peering through the overworked windshield wipers, she traced her way to the house. When she arrived in the driveway at last, she turned the car off and looked as far as she could down the meadow. She was parked next to the Silverado, and the lights were on inside the house. She wondered if Ed might have built the first fire of the season in the fireplace, but she wouldn't be able to see the smoke behind the rain. She didn't know what she should do first. Which event she should react to. She took out her phone and thought of all the people she had to call. Everyone who had attended the meeting—she'd have to tell them to forget about Damariscotta's safety record. Forget the vague attitudinal shift. She'd have to call the graphic designers and tell them to remove MAINE'S SAFE HAVEN! from the brochure. But this was not something she needed to address right away. Why had it occurred to her first? She had to deal with her family before she dealt with anything else.

She opened the door and felt the rain on her hair and shoulders. She made it to the kitchen and moved inside, where the hanging lights blazed away above the granite island. Through the speakers on the TV, she could hear the voices of men, but she wasn't ready to approach Ed just yet, so she went to the bedroom and stared at their bed. She looked outside at the relentless weather. She sat in the chair in the corner. She replayed everything she had just heard and said, thought about it, then decided, in the end, that she was not going down like this. No way. She had worked too hard to get to where she was. She needed to find a way to protect herself. Her family. She thought of Ed, thought of turning him in. But calling the police didn't make any sense. There was no reason she should have to throw away the beautiful life she'd made for her family. The life she and Ed had made together.

When she came into the living room, she found Ed with his boots on the ottoman. The television showed rain falling endlessly on a tarp at Fenway Park. He hadn't built a fire. He was drinking a beer. Steph picked up the remote and turned the power off.

"Christ," Ed said, glancing at her for the first time. "What happened to you?"

She sat on the ottoman, on its farthest edge. "I got wet," she said.

"Didn't you have a jacket?"

"I know what you've been doing, Ed."

"And what—"

"Shut up. Shut the fuck up."

He shut up.

"You have to quit," she said. "You have to quit everything you've been doing."

He took his time answering. "It's a little more complicated than that," he said.

"I don't care."

He took his boots off the ottoman now, sitting up. He laid his hat on the table. He was thinking. "This about what EJ said to you?" he asked.

"It's about that and everything else. Doesn't matter what it's about. You have to put an end to it. That's all you need to know."

Ed scratched his beard, then scratched it again. "Can't just snap my fingers, Steph."

"You have to."

"Or else?"

"Or else you'll get caught."

He stared at her. His demise was a prospect, she now understood, that he had already come to terms with.

"And if you get caught," she added, "you'll bring the whole family down."

"That's not gonna happen."

"Yes, it will. I'm telling you, Ed. You haven't considered the fallout."

"Yuh—I have."

"I will divorce you," she said. "Got that? You keep doing what you're doing, we're done."

She waited just long enough for her words to sink in, then rose, placing her hand on Ed's knee and pushing herself up. She went to the master bathroom and flicked on the lights. She started drawing a bath, cranking the faucet to hot. Her fingers, still wet from the cold rain, had taken on an almost translucent quality around the nails and looked ready to molt or peel away. She shed her clothes and stepped into the bath, sinking down low, the water pooling between her legs, rising around her ribs.

9

TOWARD THE END OF OUR FINAL CONVERSATION, I ASKED STEPH IF she ever regretted issuing the ultimatum.

"It wasn't an ultimatum," she said.

"It wasn't?"

"I just told him what the right thing to do was. And what would happen if he didn't do it."

"Sure," I said, "but I guess what I'm asking is: Do you ever wish you hadn't told him anything?"

"You mean, do I ever wish I had turned in my husband?"

"Well, no," I said, hesitating, "unless you do wish that." I gave her just enough time to make it perfectly clear that she did *not* wish that, not at all. "I just meant—" I had to be careful here, because if Steph thought I was assigning any blame in her direction, she would, I knew from previous experience, end the interview with a quick glance at her otherwise silent wingman, the square-rimmed attorney in the corner. "I just meant that you told Ed that he had to stop immediately," I said. "And that caused, you know, some problems."

"I didn't have much of a choice, did I?" She was sitting on the couch, elbow on the arm, high windows and the view of the lawn and the river behind her.

"No, I guess not," I said. "But for Ed, it was hard—it seems—for him to extricate himself from the business right away. Just because he was in so deep."

"He did the best he could. We both did."

"You helped him?"

"I gave him advice. Kept him on track. He told me everything."

And as far as I know, this was true; Ed really had divulged all his secrets to Steph. The majority of what she gave me in fact came from moments that she hadn't been present for, moments that Ed had kept hidden for a long time.

We were both getting tired, so I returned to a few facts in need of checking, and then we were done for the day and I was on my way off the Thatches' property and heading home.

But here's what I was trying to get at:

Steph had acted too hastily, I think. She never should have told Ed so explicitly what he had to do in order to win her back, to stay married and keep his family intact. It was the one thing, in all the years they had been married, that she had never done before. In the past, he had made assumptions and she had never corrected these assumptions, which gradually led Ed to believe, after so many intra-relational transactions had produced the very same results, that all Steph really wanted (which was all he really wanted) was a nice place to live, material comfort, status—all things that he could buy, more or less. But then, in issuing the ultimatum (or whatever it was, however Steph preferred to think of it), she changed the rules. As Ed had tried to tell her, to cease his dealings so abruptly would take a great deal of effort and finesse. Ending the break-ins along the coast was a matter of relative simplicity; Ed would tell his people to stop, and they would stop, unless they didn't, in which case he would make them stop. Ending the relationships with their associates in Lewiston and Canada, however, presented a dicier proposition. Such an extreme revision to the established workflow ought to have been introduced with diplomacy, over a matter of months or years. Ed was not a kingpin. He did not grow or manufacture his product, and he did not sell it on the street. He brought it around the border from Nova Scotia, connecting wholesaler to distributor. How the parties on both sides of the border might react once they lost their middleman shouldn't have been hard to predict; when suddenly a giant lacuna opened up in the supply chain, everyone would lose their shit (as indeed everyone did). Ed knew there would be problems. Many problems. And yet he had always prioritized Steph's desires far ahead of his own, so he tried in earnest to fulfill her demands, even if there might have been a better way to go straight.

When I asked Steph if she regretted making the choices she had made, what I meant was this: She was dealing with a man who, above all else, believed in the virtues of sacrificing his own safety, maybe even integrity, in the name of supporting his wife and family. Perhaps you could call it a noble outlook, but it's also a dangerous one, and doubly so when held by someone who gets away with something for as long as Ed did.

In the end, Ed was determined to change everything, right away, because Steph had asked him to make it so. And that's where, I contend, she may have gone wrong.

MY LUNCHES WITH ED STRETCHED into the fall of Allie's senior year at Lincoln, at which point the Thatches started going on official visits to all those programs that seemed most promising. The first of these trips was to Bates College in Lewiston, and I remember very clearly the exchange I had with Ed once he returned. He told me all about their stay, giving me every detail—or every detail he was willing to share—from the moment they arrived to the moment they left: the drive to the school, the football game, the campus tour, the hotel on the other side of the Androscoggin River.

In early April of this year, I made the forty-five-minute drive up to Bates to take in a men's lacrosse game. I was planning to retrace a few of Ed's steps, imagine the world as it had appeared to him, but the Thatches had arrived on campus in the prime of autumn, on a glorious afternoon, whereas the day I chose was quite the opposite of that, the whole school cast in late-winter grays. When I walked into the stadium, there was a ring of snow around the turf, the sky overhead oppressively dull, and there was not a single leaf budding on any of the trees. All the lacrosse players stood shivering on the sidelines like a herd in peril, huddled close for warmth, their limbs buried in extra layers of Under Armour. I had chosen this weekend in particular because Bates was playing Amherst and I knew that an Amherst parent named Chip Smith would be on premises, watching his son play for the visiting squad. Chip had also been in Lewiston on the weekend in question, when his daughter, Victoria, like Allie, had been a senior in high school and still undecided about which college she would attend (eventually, inevitably, she followed in her brother's footsteps and applied early to Amherst, upholding a family legacy that went back several generations). Chip, I thought, might be able to unearth some clue regarding Ed's behavior during that weekend.

I found him just inside the fence, a purebred Bernese tethered to his wrist. I had spoken to Chip on the phone but never met him face-to-face—unless we had introduced ourselves at the reception on the Thatches' lawn the previous spring and forgotten all about it, which we both admitted was a possibility. I was wearing my dad's old down parka and ski gloves with duct tape around the thumb, this in contrast to Chip who appeared perfectly insulated and appointed in an Irish flat cap, a cashmere scarf, a green Barbour jacket, and an impeccably clean pair of rubber-soled Bean boots. I got the sense that no weather pattern had ever caught Chip off guard, that his wardrobe could handle any occasion in any climate. He's fit for his age, early sixties, his face etched in vertical lines rather than what might look on another man like wrinkles. He lives in Weston, Massachusetts. When I Google-Street-Viewed his house, all that was visible was a stone wall, some treetops, a glimpse of a complicated roofline, a handful of chimneys, and, by the gate, a fleet of GMCs all belonging to the same landscape architecture firm.

We shook hands and exchanged a few words about the game and Amherst's prospects that season—the team was young and talented, ready to make a deep run into the playoffs, Chip told me. He pointed out his son, a midfielder with monstrous calves and, I found out soon enough, a rifle for a shot. We watched the game silently, and then, during a break between quarters, I started asking Chip about the recruiting trip. Chip nodded beyond the fence to the glassy, modern student center. "They had a tent for all the girls set up right there," he said. "But Ed and I had both snuck away to watch the football game, and we happened to be standing near each other. Close to where we're standing right now."

"And Steph was here?"

"Steph was also here. But I didn't know her at the time, so I couldn't tell you what she was doing. Most likely getting acquainted with the other mothers."

"How did you and Ed start talking?"

"His hat," Chip said.

"Oh, right."

When we'd chatted on the phone, Chip had sounded reluctant to speak with me. He wanted to know why I'd reached out to him specifically. I said I understood that Allie and Victoria had become friends and the two families had spent some time together—postgame meals and such. I told him I was a writer who'd known Ed since my days working as a dockhand at the Thatch Lobster Pound. He knew the Pound, he said. He'd been there once a long time ago. He and his wife Sandy used to sail the coast. They loved it. He mentioned Ed's hat, which said THATCH LOBSTER POUND above the brim, told me it was the original connection, which is how I found out that the Smith family had also been in Lewiston when the Thatches visited Bates. When I asked if we could meet in person to continue the conversation, Chip hesitated, then said, "Gladly," and we made arrangements, but it felt like something had changed, like in the course of our phone call, Chip had started wondering if I might be of some use to him.

"What'd you and Ed talk about?" I asked him in April, standing by the turf field, watching his son's lacrosse game.

"Oh, our daughters. The recruiting process. Ed's views on the recruiting process. Sandy and I take a laissez-faire approach when it comes to those types of decisions, but Ed did not. At some point I admitted to Ed that I was an Amherst man, that my son already went there, so I had a personal bias that I had to make sure didn't influence Victoria's decision-making. Ed said, 'So Amherst is your top choice?' And I said, 'Well, no, since I'm the dad, I don't really get a top choice, do I?' But this line of reasoning sunk like a rock with Ed. He was determined to have a say. It made me wonder if maybe Sandy and I had been too lax in our own parenting. Maybe a mother and father ought to be more involved."

"They shouldn't."

Chip smiled. "No, I guess not. But I'm a geezer at this point anyway. I can't tell my children what to do."

"But they both chose Amherst."

"Well, they're bright kids," he said, "despite their old man."

"You said on the phone that you and Ed talked about Lewiston."

"We did, yes. I admitted that I was worried about sending a daughter off to live in a city with such a high crime rate. I don't know if you've spent much time in Lewiston—well, I guess you would know, being a writer from Maine—but it's a little rough around the edges."

I couldn't tell if he'd emphasized *writer from Maine* on purpose, or if I was only imagining it, but he sounded skeptical, like maybe he'd googled my name + writer and nothing had come up. "How did Ed respond?" I asked him.

"He seemed agitated by the notion. So I dropped it. I assumed that Ed was also troubled by the city's reputation, that I was making him think about something he didn't want to think about."

"You probably were."

"Right. At any rate, I regretted bringing it up, and that was just about the end of the conversation. He said he was going for a walk, and we said goodbye."

I looked across the campus. Because there was no foliage, it was easy to see into the distance, all the way to the far side of the quad, where the brick academic buildings ended and the off-campus housing began. On a brighter day, I'm sure the view would have represented an idyllic picture of the collegiate life, but not in early April. Early April in Maine can feel pretty desolate.

"That was the last I saw of him," Chip said, "until the next morning."

"The next morning?" I asked. Chip hadn't mentioned this second meeting on the phone.

"Mm-hm. I was up early, as I usually am. I found Ed sitting in the lobby of the hotel. He seemed a little loopy, but I hardly knew him, so I didn't think much of it. He told me he hadn't slept because he was worried about his daughter, and I took that at face value."

"He seemed 'loopy'?"

"Yes, a little punch-drunk, a little slow. In our previous inter-action, and in all subsequent interactions, I found him to be much sharper. But I figured it was just the sleep deprivation."

"What did you talk about?"

"The lobster trade. I was fascinated. He told me all about it."

We watched the game for a minute or so, but it was as good as over by then. The Amherst players were trying to run out the clock and the Bates players were trying to chop their opponents' arms off.

"It's funny though," Chip said. "Ed didn't remember a word of that conversation."

"He didn't?" I had never known Ed to forget anything.

"No, I brought it up with him at some point. I'd been read-ing up about the lobstering industry. I'd stumbled upon an article and then done a little digging. I'm ignorant when it comes to most subjects, so I try to read up just so I can hold my own."

"Right," I said, but already I was getting wise to Chip's brand of humility. People who self-identify as "ignorant when it comes to most subjects" but then do something about it almost always end up well versed in a great many subjects.

"I had come across a study," Chip said, "that contradicted what he told me—but I found that Ed had very little recollection of our previous discussion. Maybe enough time had passed for him to forget all about it, or maybe I was simply more interested than he was. Still, I thought it was odd."

"Very odd," I said. I was trying to picture that early morning exchange between Chip and Ed in the hotel, but it was hard to imagine Ed acting punch-drunk or slow. I thought back to all the time I had spent in Ed's presence. Even during his long quiet spells at the Pound, I always knew Ed's mind was working on something.

"Huh," I said.

"What?" Chip asked, turning from the game.

"I don't think Ed was sleep-deprived."

"Well, he said he was."

"That's not why he was acting loopy though."

"It's not?"

I shook my head.

"Then what was it?"

"I think he was concussed."

ONCE I HAD SAID GOODBYE to Chip, I walked across the quad until I was no longer on school property. The first few blocks, once you're off-campus, are lined with Victorians, neither perfectly maintained nor falling apart, the banners of various NFL teams hanging in the windows, red plastic cups stuck in hedges, the smell of stale beer wafting from basement windows, hand-me-down luxury cars with out-of-state plates parked in the driveways. This is where Bates upperclassmen find rooms to rent, and the streets feel like any other neighborhood that might surround any other small college in America.

But after a few more blocks, the buildings get a little more ragged. What might be considered "campus adjacent" begins to erode into Lewiston proper: The streets are all one-way, the buildings all triple-deckers, perfectly block-like, slapped together cheaply, some with fire escapes that look ready to collapse in a heap in their cement backyards, held upright by an endless tangle of telephone wires and laundry lines. Dented cars with Maine plates loiter at the curbs, dented beer cans collect by broken stairs. This is the Lewiston that Ed had come to know after doing business in the area for so many years (although it's interesting to note that Ed's knowledge of the city wasn't exactly firsthand; EJ handled most of the interactions with Lewiston while Chuck was the one who dealt with the Canadians).

Their primary counterpart in Lewiston, Ed would later tell Steph who would later tell me, worked out of the stockroom of a liquor store—and it was in this general direction that Ed was headed. He remembered roughly where the store was located but wanted to see how great, or small, a distance separated the students from the dealers, and he also wanted to see if he could find Dougie Page, whose name had come up the day before when Ed was having coffee with EJ in the Schooner. Ed had mentioned their weekend plans and asked EJ if he wanted to come to Lewiston with the rest of the family, but EJ said he had to work. "And honestly," he said, "can't say I'm all that sorry to miss out on a weekend in Lewiston."

"Don't say that to Allie," Ed said. "She's excited about it."

"She is, or you are?"

"She is." Ed pulled at his beard. "She likes their coach. Bates is right near the top of her list."

"The top of 'her' list?"

"I have my own list."

"I'm sure you do." EJ finished his coffee, checked his watch, then pulled his hat from the bar and climbed off his stool. But before he left, he leaned close to his father's ear. "Hey, while you're up there," he whispered, "you might want to say hello to Dougie."

"Dougie Page?" Ed asked. Dougie had worked briefly for the

Thatches as one of their runners, but Ed had refused to take him on full time because he felt the boy was too ambitious, the type to grumble to his colleagues every time he received his cut, which was bound to be thinner than those received by the more senior members of the crew. Ed also thought of Dougie as a suspicious character because he and Allie had spent some time together before the Thatches moved north to Damariscotta. Ed hadn't heard his daughter mention Dougie's name since then, which constituted a minor victory, but you had to stay vigilant with a kid like Dougie or else he'd return again and again like some kind of skin condition.

"Yup," EJ said. "Dougie Page."

"What the hell is Dougie doing in Lewiston?"

"Looking for work, apparently."

"That's the wrong tree to bark up."

"That's what I told him, too."

"So he's with Lew now?"

"Hard to say. But I think he's trying to be. He's up there most days. I'm sure you'll find him if you swing by the liquor store."

"Christ."

"Yeah."

"All right," Ed said, "I'll see what I can do."

So here he was in Lewiston, seeing what he could do, walking several more blocks until he found the liquor store. Across the street from where he stood. There were ads pasted by the entrance for Keystone Light twelve-packs and cases of Malibu rum. This was where Ed, EJ, and Chuck had been just a week prior, telling the man they called Lew, short for Lewiston, that the Thatches would no longer be using their boats to bring product in from Canada. Lew hadn't taken the news well, but Ed had let EJ do most of the talking, and his son was good at delivering bad tidings in the manner of a bored cop, someone who was above the fray.

Now, from where Ed stood on the sidewalk, the liquor store looked innocuous, like any other slum-town packy. To the southwest, in the direction of the river, was a dead industrial desert, flat rooftops and pointed church spires, a black funnel of birds cycling somewhere between the city and the horizon. To the northeast rose the college's green-domed bell tower. Only five blocks stood between there and here, between the dormitories and the liquor store. This was why Bates had never been very high on Ed's list. He agreed with Chip, even if he hadn't said so: Lewiston was no place to send a daughter for four years.

A cloud began to slide across the sun just then and a gust picked up from the direction of campus, flipping a Styrofoam to-go container down the sidewalk toward Ed. He stomped it with his boot, but the box wouldn't dislodge from his heel as easily as it should have, so Ed had to kick it against a telephone pole until it shook loose, and then when he looked up, he found himself staring at Dougie's green Ford Ranger. One block down from the liquor store. There was an old, faded LHS sticker on the back window. Lincoln High School. Rings of rust rimmed each wheel well, and a patch of Bondo had been slapped on the driver's-side door. The Ranger had belonged to Jason Page, but then Jason bought a new Tahoe with money he had earned working for the Thatches and passed the old ride down to his little brother.

Ed and EJ hadn't discussed what to do about Dougie, specifically, but it seemed prudent to appraise the situation before taking any kind of action, so Ed moved away from the liquor store, staying across the street, continuing past the Ranger until he found an uninhabited home. The front yard was choked with weeds and plastic bags, and there were several newspapers, all yellowing with age, scattered across the front porch. On the top step was a flyer for a Chinese restaurant, which Ed picked up and used to wipe away the dirt and dead flies. Then he sat and waited. He could see the front entrance of the liquor store and the alley that led to the back door. He watched for over an hour but saw very few customers go in or out.

A little after three, Ed finally decided to go inside the store and look for Dougie himself, and he was about to rise from the stoop when he saw the front door swing open, and then Dougie emerged, walking and talking with a heavyset young man in a shiny athletic jacket who had black hair that sprang from his head in little corkscrews. Dougie and his friend were heading in Ed's direction but traveling on the other side of the street, so Ed wasn't overly concerned about either of them looking his way, but, just to be safe, he leaned back on one elbow, hoping to make himself look like some kind of porch dweller. He put one hand above the brim of his hat and over the crest, shielding the embroidered THATCH LOBSTER POUND from view. As they passed on the far sidewalk, Ed reassessed the man who walked next to Dougie. He wasn't that heavyset after all. His size, it became clear, was an illusion created by his oversized coat and thick wrestler's neck. Dougie required less of a look. Ed knew the boy well enough. The only thing about him that appeared different was his beard, which grew most prominently on the underside of Dougie's chin and looked from this distance like a shadow of his face. After walking together for a block, Dougie stepped off the sidewalk and cut back to the driver's side of his Ranger. The other man stayed on the other side of the street and turned behind one of the triple-deckers to Ed's right.

Ed's phone began to vibrate. He pulled it from his pocket and checked the screen. Steph. Most likely calling to ask him how he expected her to get to the hotel. Ed silenced the call, but by the time he looked up again, the Ranger was gone and so was Dougie's friend.

ED AND STEPH HAD RESERVED a room at the Hilton Garden Inn on the Auburn side of the river, and that night they went to dinner at Marché, a restaurant Steph chose based on its mostly positive Yelp reviews. I asked Steph at some point how she and Ed could continue to eat out so frequently even after Ed stopped receiving an income from stolen goods and banned substances, but Steph said, "Oh, come on, Andrew," like I was failing to see the bigger picture, before ticking off their various legitimate revenue sources and reminding me of the robust profit margin to be made on every one of them. "And also," she said, "this is Lewiston we're talking about. I know Marché sounds fancy, but it's not. We weren't spending that much money."

Steph ordered two glasses of chardonnay that night, and Ed drank three stouts and then a rum-and-Coke to wake himself up. After dinner, back in the hotel, Steph read in bed—a book about marketing—until she fell asleep sitting up. Once she did, Ed went to the window and peered behind the drapes, across the river toward Lewiston. It wasn't all that late, but the town looked lifeless from his second-floor vantage point. The only movement Ed could see came in the form of the upriver rapids tumbling off the rocks and into the flatter part of the waterway, heading calmly toward the bridge, sliding past the graffiti on the factory walls. Some of the textile mills had been converted into office space but all the windows had gone dark by now, everything tinted blue by the riverside security lights.

Time to go. He dropped the drapes, crossed the hotel room, shut off Steph's lamp, and then he was in the lobby, stepping through the sliding glass doors, entering the clear black night just as a siren flared in the distance and slowly wound away. He climbed into the Silverado. The radio came on, a George Strait

song, volume low. Ed put the truck in gear, and he was about
to back out of the lot and go looking for Dougie Page when he
remembered the other thing he had planned to do—check in
with Allie. So he stopped, pulled out his phone, texted, *Who are
you doing,* and hit send just as he recognized the typo. So he tried
again: *HOW are you doing?*

He waited to see if she might respond right away, but she
didn't, so he put the phone in a cup holder and drove out into
the city.

There weren't many headlights in the streets that night, the
buildings dark and vacant. Ed went along College Street toward
Bates until he arrived at the liquor store, the destination he had
had in mind all along. He parked in front of the same house he
had found before, the one with the overgrown yard and newspapers on the porch. He shut off his lights, waited, and observed,
listening to the country station to kill the time, farting intermit-
tently, watching as the customers, some of them students but
most of them local derelicts, entered and exited.

After thirty minutes, Ed saw the man he had seen earlier—
Dougie Page's contact—appear in the alley. He was shuffling
along the far sidewalk, opening the door to an Acura with tinted
windows and chrome wheels. Ed had always hated Acuras, Steph
told me at some point, recounting the story Ed had given her
sometime after the visit to Lewiston. "He called them Dumb Shit
Cars."

I asked her why.

"Because their drivers were always dumb shits."

The sedan's headlamps came on, and then it pulled into
the street. Ed had slipped out of the hotel to find Dougie, not
this guy, but Dougie's Ranger was nowhere in sight, and it was
possible that the one would lead Ed to the other, so, flipping
on his own lights, Ed guided the Silverado away from the curb

and tailed the sedan at a distance. They went for several blocks toward campus, and then Ed watched as the Acura stopped in front of a residential building, red Budweiser sign buzzing on the third floor, no lights on the second floor, the blue wash of a television swimming between the windows on the first floor. The man walked onto the porch, holding up his beltless pants as he climbed the steps, then vanished inside. A few minutes later, he reemerged and went back to his car.

Ed followed in his truck while the man—Dumb Shit, as Ed was now thinking of him—drove for several more blocks before parking in front of another house, this one almost indistinguishable from the first. Ed rolled down his window and lowered the volume on the radio even further. Again the man went inside for several minutes. Ed looked down the street. The night remained cloudless, the ambient city glow turning the rooftops white but ceding jurisdiction, at street level, to the tall flickering lamps. When the man came out of the house, he got back in his car and Ed put the truck in drive, following him at a distance. As Ed drove and observed the man making his drops, two things must have occurred to him: First, it was possible that whatever Dumb Shit was dealing had come in on Thatch boats. Lewiston might have had a surplus. And if this were the case, Ed should put a stop to it; this is what Steph had demanded of him, after all. But Ed was also struck, again, by how close they were to campus, how close they were to his daughter, and if Allie did end up enrolling at Bates, he wanted to make sure that all the lowlifes—especially those who he had once done business with—had been purged from the region.

The Acura made two more stops, and on the third stop, while the man was still inside, Ed popped open his glove compartment, dug around until he found his black ski mask, and exited the Silverado. He crossed the street and reached the sidewalk just as the

man was coming down the stairs. As Ed approached, he pulled
the ski mask down over his face, unhooked his belt buckle, and
removed the belt from his jeans. The man never saw him coming.
Ed grabbed him by the jacket and shoved him against the Acura,
pinning him against the window.

"Hey, Dumb Shit," Ed said.

"Get your fucking hands off me," the man said, attempting—
but failing—to free himself from Ed's grip. Ed raised the belt and
smacked the man on the side of the head with the buckle.

"What the fuck?"

Ed hit him again.

"You gotta stop," Ed said, through the mask.

"Stop *what*? *You're* hitting *me*." The man struggled to break
free again, but he couldn't. Ed swung the buckle and it glanced
off the man's ear and put a crack in the window of the Acura.

"You gotta stop what you're doing," Ed said.

"The fuck does that mean?"

"Take a guess."

"You don't know shit about what I'm doing."

"Yuh," Ed said, "I do." He moved his free hand to the man's
clavicle and dug his thumb deep beneath the muscles, digging
toward bone. "I know all about it," he said. "And you gotta stop.
Let everyone you work with know they gotta stop, too."

"Fuck you," the man wheezed.

Ed squeezed harder. "And you know what else?" he said.
"You should get a belt."

"Fuck you!"

Ed swung the buckle at the man, again and again. "Belts," he
said, "are very," between blows, "frickin handy."

Dumb Shit slumped, his back sliding down the window of
the car, his arms overhead. "Just *fucking* stop already!" he said.

"Yuh," Ed said. "I'll stop if you stop." The man was groaning, clutching at his ribs. "You're gonna get in your car and drive away now. You're gonna flush that shit down the toilet or toss it in the river—whatever you gotta do to get rid of it. You got me?"

The man tried to swing at Ed's face, but Ed blocked him, then hit him with the belt buckle three more times.

"I'm gonna ask you again," Ed said. "Do you. Got me?"

This time the man didn't respond.

"That a yes?" Ed asked.

The man couldn't bring himself to utter anything else, but Ed felt he had been understood.

"Good," Ed said. "Now get in the car."

He released his hold on the jacket and waited until the man started moving, until he opened his door and slid gingerly behind the wheel. After a moment, the car turned on and pulled away from the curb. Ed watched him go, then hustled across the street to his Silverado. He was breathing hard now. He took off his ski mask, threw it in the backseat, and turned on the truck, putting his blinker on, then speeding until he caught the taillights of the Acura. It turned left, then right. Ed did, too. It accelerated and decelerated. The driver seemed to know that Ed was behind him, seemed to be trying to lose him.

"Go home, ya dumb shit," Ed said out loud, knowing the man couldn't hear him, realizing it probably wouldn't have mattered even if he could. The man wasn't going home. He was circling the same neighborhood, lapping the same blocks, driving more and more slowly. And then, after a meandering chase that brought them right back to where they started, the Acura stopped. Ed hit the brakes, too, his fender nearly bumping the smaller vehicle's taillights.

"What are you doing?" Ed said to his windshield. "Don't do this."

The driver's side of the Acura opened, and the man came

back toward Ed's truck, his movements halting, glancing over his shoulder, reaching behind him and pulling something from his waistband. A black pistol, a nine-millimeter. Ed stayed frozen, staring straight ahead. Dumb Shit tapped the muzzle of the gun against Ed's window. Ed put his hands up but didn't say anything. After a long moment, the man's breath rising like smoke, he started nodding, as if he had made himself clear. Ed saw this out of the corner of his eye. Before the man turned away, he dragged his gun across Ed's door, from high to low. Ed couldn't see it, but he could hear the metal scraping across metal. Then the man went back to his car, climbed in, and started to drive away.

Now, as Ed watched the sedan turn left onto a one-way street, he felt angry. He had circled this neighborhood several times by this point, once on foot, then in his truck, and he had become familiar enough with the layout. Some of the streets were dead ends. Some went in a loop. Where the Acura had gone, there was only one way out. Ed put his truck in reverse, then turned left on a parallel street, ignoring the red-and-white DO NOT ENTER sign. He turned a corner, drove past a sloped driveway, then backed into it, all the way to the garage. He shut his lights off, his fists wrapped around the wheel, squeezing hard. About twenty yards separated the grille of his truck from the street. The driveway was protected from view by a row of scraggly hedges and a chain-link fence with, on the driveway side, a BEWARE OF DOG notice clipped to the wire. This street was still and dark, all the residents asleep for the night. Ed's phone vibrated and he looked down to find a message from Allie: *Haha, not doing anyone. Just having good clean fun ;) Get some sleep, old man. See ya tomorrow! xoxoxo.* As he was reading the text, headlights turned onto the street, and Ed put the phone away. Here came Dumb Shit. The Acura's lights swept against a telephone pole just across from the driveway. Ed waited until the lights came strobing through the gaps in the bushes, and then he hit the gas. The Silverado's tires spun against the asphalt, then caught. He accelerated down the driveway just as the sedan emerged from behind the hedge—but from Ed's angle the motion looked reversed, as though the passenger door of the Acura were speeding toward him. In the middle of the street his front fender slammed into the side of the sedan and plowed it into the telephone pole behind it. The Acura's car alarm went off as Ed's airbag exploded in his face, pounding him in the forehead.

After a brief moment of darkness, Ed blinked. Something blocked his vision. Clung to his face. He couldn't see. He beat at the thing in front of him—the airbag, that was it—until it began to deflate. He could see the front of his truck now—and a car. Almost directly beneath him. He saw blood at the shaved hairline of the driver, and he saw the driver spit out more blood. Ed put his truck in reverse and backed up. His head felt full of a heavy, sloshing liquid, but he was pretty sure his best option was to drive away. And as he brought the truck down the street and turned on his headlights, he could see where he was going but couldn't remember where the road came from or where it led. He checked the rearview mirror and saw nothing. The car alarm continued to blast, honking and whining but receding as the truck left it behind. A piece of Ed's truck was dragging along the pavement, but otherwise the vehicle drove fine, and he traveled a mile in the direction of the river before pulling over to inspect the damage.

When he stepped down from the truck, he found that the fender had detached at the left corner. The Chevy crest had fallen off the bashed-in grille. The driver's-side blinker was smashed out. There was a long gouge in the door. Otherwise the truck had survived. Ed lifted the droopy side of the fender and jammed it back in place. It bowed unnaturally but wouldn't rub on the asphalt any longer. Ed stared at his truck, trying to remember how he had broken the fender. He was in Lewiston, he knew that much. He climbed back inside and sat with the deflated airbag in his lap. It wouldn't stay in its compartment when he tried to stuff it back in place, punching it like a sleeping bag, so he pulled his jackknife from the center console and slashed at the bag until it ripped free. Mounted on the dashboard was a GPS system, and when Ed scrolled through all the Recent Destinations, he found the Hilton Garden Inn, which, he decided, must be where he was staying.

ED NEVER WENT UP TO his hotel room that night. Instead he remained in the lobby, sitting in one of the vertically striped, high-backed chairs, until the sun edged its way through the blinds and Chip Smith came downstairs. Chip said good morning to Ed and asked if he could take the seat across from him. They drank complimentary coffee as Chip read the Sunday *Globe*. Ed stared straight ahead. After several minutes, Chip put the newspaper down and asked if Ed was feeling all right.

"Oh sure," Ed said.

"How'd you sleep?"

"Didn't really."

"Me neither," Chip said. "I never sleep well in hotels."

"Yuh."

"Especially when I'm worried about my daughter."

"You said it."

Chip folded the paper in his lap. "Now, your family owns the Thatch Lobster Pound?" he asked Ed. "Do I have that right?"

"Yuh," Ed said. "I own it."

"And you're a lobsterman by trade?"

"Yuh, pretty much."

The conversation continued along these lines until eventually

Ed began to speak more freely, almost drunkenly (I know how this can go; I once took a shot to the head during a lacrosse game against Syracuse and babbled on and on to my teammates during the bus ride home, knowing full well that I should stop talking but not knowing how to put an end to it). In response to Chip's increasingly specific questions, Ed told him exactly how the lobster traps worked, how the cages were a marvel of sustainability (I presume this was Chip's phrase in the retelling, not Ed's), catching the older, legal lobsters while nourishing all the younger lobsters. Most small creatures, according to Ed (according to Chip), could enter the trap, eat bait, and exit without getting hooked by the netting. He and Chip went on discussing aquaculture until Steph came downstairs and Ed said goodbye to his new friend and went out to the truck with his wife.

"Great guy," Ed said to Steph.

But instead of responding, Steph stopped short. They had arrived at the Silverado, and she was now confronted with the broken grille. By this point, Ed's wits were beginning to return, and he felt exhausted from a sleepless night but less disoriented than he had been immediately post–airbag deployment.

"What the hell," Steph said.

Ed stared at the truck. He did remember an accident. He remembered following Dumb Shit but couldn't connect the event with the man. The day was breaking bright and cloudy, and Lewiston across the river presented a rising slope of white light and silver shadows.

"Ed," Steph said. "Would you like to tell me what happened?"

"Just went for a drive," he said.

"And then what?"

"And then I hit a car."

"Which car?"

"Just some car. Don't worry about it. It's all over."

He had his keys out, ready to open the driver's-side door.

"Ed, stop," Steph said. She walked to him. She lowered his bearded chin and looked into his eyes. "You're all dilated," she said. "I think you're concussed."

"Nah," he said, reaching for the door handle.

"You're not driving," Steph said. Her hand was out, palm up.

Ed shrugged and gave Steph his keys, and then she pointed at the passenger seat, so he crossed to the other side of the vehicle and climbed inside.

As they drove toward Bates, Ed took off his sweatshirt and balled it between window and headrest.

"You can't fall asleep," Steph said. "It's bad to fall asleep if you've got a concussion."

When Ed opened his left eye, Steph was glancing over at him, frowning. "Yuh," he said, but then his lids started to close again and he felt himself nodding off as the truck headed over the bridge, toward Bates. Then the truck was stopping and Steph was gone, and a few minutes later both Steph and Allie were back in the truck, Steph to his left, Allie behind him. Some kind of conversation must have taken place outside the cab because Allie seemed to know already that Ed was in a strange place. "Dad, are you okay?" she asked him.

"Yuh," he said, opening his eyes. "A-okay. How you doing?"

"Good," she said, still looking concerned.

"You have fun?"

"Yeah. I would love to go here." Now she was addressing Steph more than Ed. "The team is ridiculous—in a good way, I mean."

"Did you drink?" Steph asked. They were driving now, away from campus.

"A little," Allie said, "but apparently a recruit got really drunk last year and went home with a boy and puked in his bed and the coaches found out, so now they're being super strict about how recruits aren't supposed to drink at all, but my host was pretty cool."

They were already turning onto Route 196, the road that would take them back to Damariscotta.

"Okay," Allie said cautiously. "Just a hypothetical: What if I like the other schools just as much as I liked Bates?"

"I'm sure you will, Allie," Steph said, splitting her gaze between the road and Ed.

"But what if—" Allie hesitated. "What if the school I like best isn't in Maine?"

"That's up to you."

"Dad, you wouldn't freak out?"

"Nope," he said. "Don't think I would." Then he thought it over. He had always hoped that Allie would stay close to home, but Lewiston, despite all his efforts, would remain a dangerous place. In fact, all of Maine, everywhere other than Damariscotta, could be considered dangerous, at least when you knew as much as Ed did. And hey, if a school like Amherst was the best option for the daughter of a man like Chip Smith, then it couldn't be the *worst* option for Allie. "Know what?" Ed said. "Might not be such a bad move. Can't live your whole life in Maine."

"Really?"

"'Magine."

Slouching in his seat, looking out the window, all Ed could see were the inverted arcs cut by the rising and falling telephone wires against the sky. He let his eyes close and felt the sun coming through the window, landing on his skin. He refolded his sweatshirt against the door, shifted his back against the seat, and got himself as comfortable as he could for the ride home. He began to drift, remembering the sounds of the football game, whistles and cheers—

But then he felt a tap on his shoulder, from behind. Allie. With an effort, he opened his eyes and looked to his left. She was leaning forward, between the seats, holding something in her hand.

"Why is there a ski mask?" she asked him.

10

AT FIRST, WHEN THE AMHERST PRESIDENT GAVE ALLIE AND FIVE HUN-
dred of her classmates "unequivocal permission to be exceptional,"
Allie felt flattered. But then, when she thought about it, she felt less
flattered. She started thinking maybe the president was overselling
the point. All the freshmen and their parents were sitting on white
folding chairs in long rows, under a breeze that slowly shuffled the
green leaves and made the PA system alternately clear and hard to
hear. Everywhere she looked, there were freshmen. So many freshmen. They couldn't *all* be exceptional, could they?

　　She enrolled in four classes that fall, one of them a survey of
classic British literature. The professor spoke casually and engag-
ingly and assumed all the students knew the difference between
Old English and Middle English. Everyone did other than Allie.
Therefore Allie became a careful recorder of handwritten lecture notes while the other students went online shopping or social
networking instead, chatting with one another through their lap-
tops as they sat side by side:

so, so hungover right now. please help
weed helps . . .
weed helps everything
i wish
wish what
wish i was high
hahaha i knoooooooow

Allie was neither hungover nor high. Whom would she drink
with? Smoke with? Who were all these kids who already knew
each other? The only students Allie had met were her roommate, a nocturnal, self-assured, sleepy creature, and the girls on
the lacrosse team, all of whom had introduced themselves at a
welcome-to-Amherst BBQ, and all of whom had, since then,
dematerialized. Oh, and there was Allie's RA, who on day one
had promised to show Allie and all the other freshmen where to
go and where not to go, who wore overalls and a messy bun, who
every now and then would use the bathroom when Allie used the
bathroom, who'd rub her dark eyebrows in the mirror as Allie
looked into that same mirror, but who never said anything on a
Friday night other than have fun and be safe out there. If only
Allie had been assigned a roommate with prep school credentials
and a ready-made understanding of the campus's social ebbs
and eddies. A roommate with an older brother, a junior on the
men's lacrosse team, a roommate like Victoria Smith. Hey, Victoria (thanks for stopping), did you know that I imagine the two
of us just shooting the shit when I look in the mirror sometimes?
Just, you know, being roomies?

V: Okay, so it's Thursday night. Where should we go? What
should we do?
A: Too many options. You choose.

V: I would say let's go pre-game in my brother's apartment, but I think he has a crush on you or something because he always acts, like, giddy when you're around.

A: He seems normal enough to me.

V: Of course he seems normal to *you*. You're only around him when you're around him. Ninety-nine percent of the time he's an asshole, and then you show up, and suddenly he's this gentleman.

A: (*inspecting self-esteem in the mirror*) I kind of doubt it, Victoria.

V: Fine. I want you to doubt it. Oh! Okay, so Kim said we could come over to the seniors' house and drink with them.

A: And get hazed.

V: Yeah, and get hazed.

A: Which, what, you *like*?

V: I like drinking. And then we'll go out.

A: Out where?

V: Out to the Owl? Out to a bar?

A: Yeah, so that's not gonna work for me. No can do *sans* ID.

V: But . . . isn't it your birthday?

A: My birthday's not until February.

V: That's funny, because according to the state of New Jersey, today is, in fact, your twenty-second birthday.

A: No. Way.

V: (*presenting an ID-sized envelope with "Allie" and two hearts scrawled on it*) Happy birthday!

They hug.

As soon as Allie stepped away from the mirror, she felt like flogging herself. She hated the way she sounded in her own head. She also hated that Victoria, or someone like her, wasn't her roommate. Lauren was. Lauren was an Alaskan who didn't bother to decorate her side of the room. She went to bed at four in the morning. She FaceTimed with her family on Sundays.

Lauren was an engineer, a member of some kind of robotics team. She hung out—or at least built things—with fellow engineers in the science lab on most weeknights. Since Lauren was always off testing robots in wind tunnels, Allie could study by herself in the dorm, a better option than going to the library because in the library there were all those separate study halls and some were for upperclassmen and some were too crowded and cliquey, so why wander around looking for a seat, disturbing the peace? Lauren went to Cambridge in late October for an engineering convention at MIT. Lauren was soooo exceptional.

And Allie was fine. Just fine. Her clothes were fine. Her willingness to have fun was fine. Her face was fine. Adults called her pretty. Maybe they liked not being threatened by her. Maybe she was leaving parties too soon, before anyone young and drunk enough had time to make a move. Nobody talked to her. Nobody took her home. Nobody took her anywhere.

CHRISTMAS. HOME IN MAINE, SHUTTING herself in her room for three days, listening through headphones to music by a dead folk artist, the one whose songs had always reached out and grabbed her by the rib cage, shaking it until she trembled. Used to tremble. Not so much anymore. Eventually she made a phone call. She drove to Pemaquid Point, got high in Dougie Page's truck, had sex with him in his bedroom in the apartment he shared with his older brother. Dougie, nineteen, his room like a boy's. One poster on the wall. A quarterback at the fifty-yard line and behind him lightning bolts electrifying a set of goalposts. This hadn't happened since senior year. This wasn't happening, she told Dougie. She used to see him once or twice a month at a party and end up at his house later that night, even when she told herself she wouldn't. Dougie was always in possession of good pot, devoted to Allie like a stray, ragged dog.

"Maybe I can drive down and see you," Dougie said as she lay in his bed, counting the minutes until she could leave, counting the days until she could go back to school and vanish like a ghost.

"I don't know," Allie said.

"You could take the bus to Portsmouth, we could meet there."

"I don't think the bus runs between Amherst and Portsmouth." She pulled her underwear over her calves and thighs, wriggled the band around her waist. She'd refused to let the underwear leave her ankle. She'd refused to let Dougie remove her bra. She dressed and reached for the door as Dougie removed something from under his mattress. It was a large plastic bag, at least an ounce of pot. He handed it to her.

"Dougie, what the hell? I'm not even smoking right now. I'm supposed to be getting ready for lacrosse season."

"Take it," he said. "My gift to you. You'll be the most popular girl on campus."

She did take it, just to shut him up, just to make things less complicated, and she put it in her duffel bag, which rode in the back of the Silverado as her dad drove her to Amherst. They listened to bad country music while the dirty snow on the sides of the highway raced by and turned to slush. In Damariscotta, Allie was the smart girl, 30 on her ACT, off to Amherst. At Amherst, she was the girl who had gained acceptance, despite below-average board scores, only because she was an allegedly good athlete hailing from a town with an unpronounceable name in a state with not many applicants. She was like the recipient of a nameless grant, an outreach case.

"All right," Ed said, hand on the wheel.

"Dad—"

"What?"

"Can we not do the big speech?"

"You don't know what I'm gonna say."

"Yes, I do."

"We're just proud of you."

"I know," she said.

"So why can't I say that?"

"Just—I feel enough pressure already."

"It ain't pressure."

"It *is* pressure. You don't decide if it's pressure. I do. If I feel pressure, there's pressure."

"But you don't gotta think of it that way."

"Look," Allie said, "do you realize that going to college isn't even a big deal anymore? Other kids just . . . go?"

"It's a big deal for us."

"Yeah. I *know*. That's what I'm saying. We're like tourists taking pictures of stuff that's not even famous."

"Who cares if it's famous?"

"I care."

They drove in silence, waiting for Amherst signs.

"That was clever," Ed said. "What you said about the tourists."

They pulled into the lot behind her dorm, and Allie thanked her father for the ride.

"Wait until lacrosse season rolls around," he said. "We'll be here all the time."

"Oh, great," she said, but deep down, not even that deep, she was looking forward to it. Her three weeks in Maine had been mostly good ones, all told. Her parents seemed to be entering some new stage together. It wasn't uncommon for empty nesters, Allie knew, to find that they had nothing left in common once their kids departed, but somehow her parents seemed to have grown closer than ever before. Not, like, intimately close. Allie didn't even want to think about that. It just felt like they were on the same page about stuff. They agreed with one another, even about simple things, like who should run to the store for the milk they had forgotten to buy. They were the opposite of all those other middle-aged parents, and maybe it was because they weren't all that middle-aged yet. Allie wondered if she should take offense, then decided no, let it go, she should be happy for Ed and Steph.

SHE SOLD ALL THE WEED, or most of the weed, to kids in her dorm. She divided the big bag into eight smaller bags, nine if she counted the one she kept for herself. An older boy on her floor who spent his summers following around a jam band, experimenting with psychedelics, bought three of the bags. She gave him a discount. She gave everyone a discount. She just wanted to be rid of it. When he handed over the cash, he also asked her if she liked Thai restaurants or movies by this one Danish filmmaker. She thanked him for his interest but said she didn't know much about either, and he shrugged and said, "Cool." She closed her dorm room door and leaned against it, realizing that she had nearly, almost accidentally, made a friend.

She studied hard for her exams and scored one B-plus, two A-minuses, and an A, every one of her marks a notch or two better than the class median. Maybe, in the end, all those online shoppers and chatters in her English lecture hadn't really understood what the professor was saying; maybe they were every bit as lost as Allie but unwilling to admit it or address it. Maybe their grades didn't matter. At any rate, Old English was basically just a burlap sack full of different dialects. Middle English was more like French without the gendered nouns. An anonymous author wrote *Sir Gawain and the Green Knight*. Chaucer wrote *The Canterbury Tales*, and the Wife of Bath was a modern-day heroine living centuries before her time. Allie hadn't known any of this in September. Now she knew it.

But she also knew, or was coming to know, that she did not belong in a room with the women's lacrosse team. At their first official meeting, the girls sat in chairs connected to desks and faced Coach Morris, who told them they were all exceptional in their own ways and spoke about maintaining high academic standards and resisting the temptations of collegiate life and . . . But Allie was too enthralled by the other women to give Coach Morris her full attention, too in awe of their easy confidence—

And then she heard her own name, heard it spoken in praise. Best grades in the freshman class, Coach Morris said. Everyone clapping. Allie wishing they would stop. She wasn't exceptional; she worked hard. There was nothing worse than working hard. Nothing worse than trying, and Allie had definitely had to try.

That night the older girls invited the younger girls to their off-campus house for a party. Allie went and got drunk and sat on a couch upholstered in beige leather and duct tape. She didn't talk to anyone unless they talked to her. Everyone was cool but non-committal. The men's team came late, Victoria's older brother Trip, too. He caught her staring at him. She looked away. He had a familiar face, like the way pictures of young men at war always look alike. He probably had a crush—not that he would call it a crush—on Bonnie from Baltimore. Bonnie had a way of looking up at guys to make delayed, shy, fuck-me eye contact. Allie fixed herself another vodka-cola and watched Trip and Victoria Smith interact next to a fish tank and wondered if they would get it on if they weren't related. They would, she thought. They were matching siblings. He had light brown hair. She had blond hair. They both had gray eyes. No, blue eyes. They were just light blue eyes.

After the party, or after she was done with the party, Allie walked home alone and held her own hair back as she vomited in a bush. She felt better after puking and congratulated herself for doing it all by herself. But then the bush went white. Headlights were on, and a car door was opening, and pretty soon Allie was being escorted to the infirmary, checked in by purple-parka'd Amherst Security. "I'm fine," Allie kept saying, but nobody would listen to her, and a mark went on her disciplinary record. Parents were called. Allie was put on something not called probation but which was basically probation. She was embarrassed, but oh well. She was done partying.

Or trying to be. If only Dougie would stop shipping packages, unsolicited, ignoring her texts, which asked him to stop. The first box arrived in the school post office just after the winter break. Allie knew immediately what it was. She didn't want it. Couldn't keep it. She dug through the coffee beans, pulled out the plastic bag, broke the weed into eighths again, keeping nothing more than the dregs. The boy in her dorm bought three more eighths and asked when the next shipment might be arriving. This was not a "shipment," Allie said. It was a burden, just something she had to unload.

EARLY MARCH NOW. ON THE ROAD. Gettysburg. Dinner at Kim Cicarelli's home the night before the game, a mansion in a gated community, the landscaping perfectly maintained, clean lines between the lawns and sidewalks. All the streets named after military ranks. Kim lived on Colonel's Courtway. In the living room was a line for food, and Allie was standing in the line, and Coach Morris was approaching her, then placing a hand on her shoulder and saying, "Remember to load up on carbs."

Load up on carbs? Why? So she could warm the bench tomorrow? Wait. Might Allie play . . . ?

But Coach Morris was already moving down the line, touching all the other players, saying load up on carbs, load up on carbs. Everyone should be exceptional except in their diet and how they lifted weights and what shade of purple they wore. Allie shoveled pasta onto a paper plate and set off to find a small, personal realm of solitude, which she located in the farthest corner of the house, in the kitchen.

She ate slowly while looking through the back-door windows to the Cicarellis' driveway. Her father's truck was out there, comically huge, able to crush all the other cars, looking oddly generic without the Chevy crest on its grille. She pressed her forehead against the windowpane and found the temperature neither warm nor cool. Beyond all the cars, above the rooftops of the neighboring mansions, the sun was going red and splashing like lava on the lowest, flattest clouds. The trees had just begun to bud. Spring felt attainable. The end of the school year felt attainable.

"There's our star midfielder," Allie heard from behind her. She turned to find her father, then her mother walking into the kitchen. Ed held a plate full of spaghetti, on top of chicken parm on top of lasagna on top of garlic bread.

"Your dad just volunteered to host one of these receptions," Steph said.

"They asked us," Ed said, "because we're so close to Bowdoin."

"We're not that close to Bowdoin," Allie said.

"We already explained the idea to Coach Morris."

"What idea?"

"A lobster bake in the backyard," Steph said, jerking her thumb at Ed like he was a lunatic while somehow also looking on board with the idea. "Your dad wants to take people out on the boat. You could use the hot tub. It might be fun, I don't know. It's up to you. I think it's crazy, but it's up to you."

"We told Coach Morris to have everyone pack bathing suits," Ed said.

"Hold on," Allie said. "This is just a reception where we eat and then thank the parents and then go back to the hotel. It's not a slumber party."

"Coach Morris said it's fine to do a lobster bake as long as we got pasta."

"We're thinking of asking the Smiths if they want to stay in the guest bedroom," Steph said.

"The *Smiths?*" Allie said. "Do you even know the Smiths?"

"Your dad and Chip send each other emails about the team," Steph said.

"And other things," Ed said.

"Please tell me you don't forward him the racist stuff," Allie said.

"It's not racist."

"It *is* racist. It's even worse that you don't realize it's racist."

"Well," Steph said, "we haven't met Victoria's mother Sandy yet because she's been sick, but she's doing better, apparently." Then she whispered, "It's lupus." She went back to normal volume: "Chip says her fingers are so swollen she can't wear her wedding band. You probably know all this. You're friends with Victoria."

"No, I'm not."

"Well, she's your teammate."

"Yeah, I *know*—but hang on—can we go back to the part where it's really up to me?"

"Oh, and I talked to Coach Morris about your playing time," Ed said. "She says you're working hard, and good things will happen to those who wait."

"Okay, so that's useless."

"Sounded encouraging to me."

"But what she said is just a trite thing people say when they're put on the spot."

"I think she meant it."

"Oh my God," Allie said. In moments like these, she dreamed of going to Europe, Barcelona, Paris in the springtime—or the fall time. The winter time. Whenever. But instead she went to the bus, to the hotel room, to her cot, where she tossed all night long. Kelly Cooley's snoring was unprecedented. Or no, there was precedent—EJ's snoring, the snoring she used to hear as a little girl. In the hotel, their beds were near the highway and headlights kept searching across the ceiling. There were trucks all night long, shifting gears all night long.

ON BOTH SIDES OF EVERY road game were the bus trips. The long, long bus trips.

"We need to work on our base tans before spring break," Kim Cicarelli said to the flock of young laxers in the back of the bus. Kim knew the ropes—her currency—and bartered this wisdom for popularity amongst the lowerclassmen.

"You're Italian though," Victoria said.

Allie tried to think. She tried to understand. She was always playing catch-up, always having to make sense of these jokes before she knew to laugh. Italian. What did Italian mean? It meant pizza, wine, fast cars, expensive shoes, expensive suits, dark skin—*skin!* Okay, so:

If Kim = Italian = a person with darker skin = Kim doesn't need to get a base tan . . .

The bus rumbled along, especially in the back. It had the electric blue smell of lavatory chemicals. Midterms were coming. Then spring break. Florida. Two games, lots of practice.

"*Half* Italian," Kim said. "Didn't you see my mom? She's a

Viking. I *need* to work on my base. Dana's the one who doesn't need a base. She's Mexican."

"I am?" Dana said from the dark. "I thought I was Spanish, man." She said it with a heavy accent that made everyone laugh.

"Same thing," someone said.

"Oh, that is fucked up, man," Dana said, accent even heavier now. Her mother was an orthodontist in the Bay Area. Her father was a painter. Houses, mostly. Canvases when he could. "I'm gonna take you back to my dad's car wash and run you through the fucking twirly-brushes till you don't got a fucking face no more, man." She sounded more like a Cuban coke dealer than a Spaniard now. Everyone laughed again. Allie had never met anyone so funny as Dana.

"If you ran someone through a car wash," Victoria said, "wouldn't you just be making them . . . cleaner?"

"I'm more worried about Allie," Dana said, back to her native California pitch. "It's dark like twenty-two hours a day in Maine. She'll fry in Florida."

A factual inaccuracy! And yet—Allie was thrilled. Just to be mentioned. She felt so included that she decided to speak up: "How do I get a base tan?" she asked.

Quiet.

Then Victoria: "Uh, you go to the tanning salon."

Allie had to speak over the laughter: "No, I know, but I mean, *where*? Like, how do we get there?"

The laughter subsided.

Kim told Allie very matter-of-factly where the cheapest tanning salon was. A lull followed. Bus noises. Bus smells. A new conversation. Allie listened. She learned. She worked hard to see where she had gone wrong.

———

AND THEN IT WAS SPRING break. The campus emptied out, but
the team stayed on. They felt like caretakers. The school—its
greens, its purples, its brick-red dorms and libraries—appeared
more worthy of respect, more hallowed, now that there was no
one else to revel in its debasement. They were looking forward
to the flight to Florida. The campus was giving them the creeps.
For the third day in a row, they were the only ones in the tanning
salon. In her UV bed, amidst the buzzing of the tubular lights,
amidst the pulsing, Allie could hear the emptiness of the place.
When her time was up, she stood and looked in the mirror where
she saw herself, her old self, only browner and lit neon. Her eyes
looked radioactive. She was in a bathing suit. She was leaner,
with abs all of a sudden. The positioning of the overhead light,
that was what gave her the abs. She also had lats though, those
dorsal muscles tracing the outside of her ribs. Since when? Little
dents to the interior of her hips where her muscles pushed the
bathing suit out from the skin. This was either sexy or beastly.
What would Smith think? Trip Smith. Victoria, next door, would
know. Allie snuck into her teammate's tanning booth and found
her staring into the neon glow through her little space goggles.
Victoria lifted the cover of the bed and leaned out so she could
prop the goggles on her forehead.

Allie pointed to the dents in her pelvis. "Do you have these?"
she asked.

"Have what?"

"These dimples. I didn't have them before, but now I have
them, I think from all the weight lifting and core strengthening."

Victoria looked at Allie's waist. Her shoulders began to
shake. She closed the hood of the tanning bed, chuckling in her
chamber.

At Chipotle, Victoria told everyone what Allie had said in
the tanning salon. Allie rolled a crumpled-up ball of aluminum

foil across the table, feeling how it resisted at the ridges, and said, "I'm serious, you guys. I have muscles in places I didn't even know existed."

"You're so jacked," Dana said, squeezing and admiring Allie's forearm.

"So I'm the only one?"

"Everyone gets it," Kim said, sliding her burrito bowl onto the table, joining the conversation late but knowing roughly where it was headed. "It's like the freshman fifteen, but for athletes it's just weird muscle. You'll get used to it. You won't look like a woman again until after you graduate, but you *will* get used to it."

That night, alone in her dorm room, Allie received a text from an unknown number, a Massachusetts area code:

Hey, it's V. We should make brownies :)

Allie stared at her phone. The text worried her. She wrote: *With what?*

Hmmm, thought you had a hookup. My bad if not.

Don't really have a hookup :(

But as soon as she sent the text, she regretted it. It wasn't true. And it would put distance—or keep distance—between her and Victoria. So she texted again: *But I do have enough, I think. Let's do this. All we need is a kitchen.*

IN FLORIDA, THE DAYS WERE mostly rainy, then mostly sunny. The team beat Buffalo State and William Smith. Allie played almost a full quarter in the first game, almost a full half in the second. Practices were balmy, held under a wash of watercolor clouds, drenched in sunscreen. The girls sang along to mindless Top 40 songs that played through a portable speaker standing by the benches.

On their last night in Florida, friends of a senior showed up in a convertible and a minivan borrowed from parents with a plan to drive to South Beach. The women ran from the hotel lobby to the cars, under bending palm trees, streetlamps and fast-food signs burning on the strip in the distance. All the lights looked far away but close, the night sky warmed by its blinking belly. In Allie's hand was a paper bag. In the paper bag was trail mix. In the trail mix was a crumbled-up brownie. Several brownies. She watched her teammates clamber into the minivan and the drop-top, all those big shoulders in thin straps, athletic calves over high heels. Allie was next to Victoria, who wore a short white dress, the muscles in her thighs pushing at the silk, her freckled breasts propped up. Allie was wearing a black dress that she had bought with her mother's credit card.

She made a joke about feeling like a cross-dresser, which wasn't quite true, but which worked, and then she doled out the trail mix, and soon they were standing between the seats and rising through the sunroof, on their way to fountains and gold lights and heat, the tumble of distant waves breaking against the beach. They went to a club where the music poured down the walls and across their skin like sweat. Bodies were moving shoulder to shoulder beneath a fog of lasers and lights, the music in their lungs. The songs ran together. The lights ran together. Allie's life, finally, was running together, not in a blur but in harmony. It was so overwhelming and new that she had to leave the club to find air and clarity, and once she was outside, she found herself coming out of a spin and facing the other girls. Allie was confused. They looked ready to leave and unsurprised by Allie's presence. Maybe this was the plan. Allie couldn't remember. The contents of the night were spilling from her memory, sifting away like sand in a riptide. She fell asleep in the van, and when they arrived at the hotel, she fought her way up the wavering, off-white stairwell to her floor, past fire extinguishers and exit signs. Her room card wasn't in her clutch. She knocked on the door. Nobody answered. She knocked harder. Still no answer.

She awoke to the sight of Coach Morris, squatting next to her, wrists resting on her thighs. "You're on the wrong floor, Allie," Coach said.

"Okay," Allie said.

"You should take a shower."

"Okay."

When she stood up, her dress was all wet.

A disciplinary violation. Breaking team drinking rules. After what happened in the fall, and yes, Coach Morris knew what had happened in the fall, Allie was lucky she wasn't getting suspended. She would run her ass off instead. But Allie had already been running so much—more running felt good. She didn't mind at all. She deserved it.

SPRING WAS OPENING UP ON the Amherst campus, not all at once, but little by little. Faces were becoming more familiar. There was a certain rhythm to the season, but one that evolved late enough to never stop feeling strange or exciting. It had been almost a month since Dougie's last package arrived at the post office, and Allie was glad he had stopped sending her the shipments—they *were* shipments, she could admit—and glad she had run out of weed. The team was winning. They beat Tufts in a midweek game, and afterward took the bus to Weston, through old farmhouses and newer villas with gabled roofs that stood still, stood watch, as columns, gates, and hedges raced before them and hid the lower floors from view. The women climbed out of the bus and walked up and up and up the Smiths' long driveway. This was Victoria's home, her childhood room stuffed with stuffed animals and trophies and posters of world-class soccer players standing in dimly lit fields in their sports bras. Victoria showed Allie the room quickly, ushering her out the door, as though its continued existence were something to be ashamed of.

They walked downstairs, where Allie talked to parents, accepting all their congratulations, discussing every significant moment from the earlier game. She saw her father disappear with his new best friend Chip down a hallway, into the kitchen, and Allie was about to ask Victoria where they might be going when a teammate found the two of them and leaned in close and began to whisper urgently. There was a crisis back on campus, she said. This teammate had broken off from a larger group, but almost immediately those other girls reconvened around Allie and Victoria. There wasn't any weed in Amherst. This was the crisis, they said. Allie listened blankly. It took her a moment to understand that they were addressing her more than they were addressing Victoria. There was something solicitous in their tones; they expected her, Allie, to fix the problem. Allie looked to Victoria, then back to their friends. She didn't care about the pot, not anymore. She didn't care if they smoked or didn't smoke. The dispersal, or disposal, of the marijuana was one of those things that, somewhere along the way, had become, without her noticing, pretty easy. She could handle it, she realized.

"I'll see what I can do," she said to the group. The other girls took a step back and Allie slid between them, toward the floor-to-ceiling glass doors, which opened onto a patio, then a floodlit lawn.

She walked down through a rose garden to a whitewashed gazebo. The heavy grass was wet, although it hadn't rained that day. The night had taken over most of the sky, but there were no stars, only black and the faint tint of city light. As she pulled out her phone and rang Dougie, she imagined him sitting at home, watching TV, on his couch, basketball shorts on, shirt off, hand down his pants.

"Allie," he said after one ring.

"I know I shouldn't be calling just because I need something," she said.

"No, it's cool. How's it going?"

"Fine. Sorry, I just—everyone's low on weed at school and I thought maybe you could help."

She listened through a long moment of silence. He started to speak, then hesitated. "I don't know," he said. "Something's come up with your dad. I have to be careful."

"With my dad?" Allie said. There was no reason for her dad and Dougie to cross paths, ever.

"No, I mean, he just knows I'm seeing you, I think."

"You're not seeing me."

"Right, I know that. That's what I told your brother. But it's like—if your dad found out I was sending you pot, he'd murder me."

"How would my dad find out?"

"I don't know. But I'm serious. He would kill the shit out of me."

"Dougie, I'm not planning to tell my dad that you sent me weed."

"Oh man, I *definitely* can't send it anymore. That's the other thing. Too dangerous."

"I'll pay for it this time," Allie said. "And for shipping and handling or whatever."

"I could drive it to you. Maybe. I mean, it's the only way."

Allie contemplated hanging up. "This was a bad idea," she said. "It's okay. I'll figure something out. Thanks, Dougie."

She walked back inside. If anything, she was pleased that it hadn't worked out. She had done her part, tried her best, but sorry, she couldn't help. She slid aside the patio door and broke back into the noise and warmth of the reception. She wandered around, speaking to a coach, then a parent, then several of her friends, until her father blindsided her with a hard, meaningful hug.

"What was that for?" she asked him.

"Just proud of you," he said. He looked around at the party, breathing it in.

"Please don't."

"Please don't what?"

She was about to tell him not to be proud—but before she said it, she stopped herself; the response was automatic, the rehearsal of a part she'd been playing for a long time. Too long. If her dad wanted to be proud, he could be proud. "Never mind," she said. "All good."

AND JUST LIKE THAT, THE spring was almost over. On Saturday morning, the last home game of the season, Allie walked to dining hall wearing shorts and an Amherst Lacrosse hoodie, her number, 22, printed on the sleeve. The campus was budding and bursting. Sections of lawn were cordoned off for growing sod, and the air had a note of fertilizer in it, but also a note of optimism. Or maybe it didn't—maybe Allie was simply walking in the sun, feeling like she knew where things were now, like she knew where she was going. This was her new life. It felt as separate from her old life as a distant galaxy, with its own bright sun and its own pure air.

They beat Williams that day and went out to a late lunch with Allie's parents and Victoria's parents, just the girls, no older brothers. Victoria's mother was doing better, she had more energy now. Chip asked Ed and Steph how they first met, then kept peppering them with follow-ups until it was time to pay the bill and Sandy said, "Okay, hon, I think we've badgered them enough already!" At some point during the retelling, Allie realized that she didn't have to be embarrassed by her family's humble origin story anymore, and if the Smiths were willing to hang out with her parents, then there was no need for Allie to continue to think of Ed and Steph as the outcasts of the parent group.

When, after the meal, Allie went to thank her mother and say goodbye, it took her a moment to get Steph's attention. Her mom was lost in thought, looking down the sidewalk, into the bright blue sky above Pleasant Street.

"Mom," Allie said again.

"Hm?" Steph said.

"You okay?"

Steph turned, her gaze faraway and unfocused. "Oh, I'm fine," she said. "Everything's just—exactly the same."

"As what?"

"Well," she said. "As I imagined it, I guess. I don't know." She gave Allie a hug. "Have fun tonight. Be safe."

And then the young women headed back to the college and drank in their dorms before making their way to a room party on the other side of campus. The night had turned cool, but the dorm room was dark and hot, everybody pressed back to back under the blinking Christmas lights. Allie knew just about everyone in attendance. Amherst was a small place. Its smallness was what made it exceptional. Trip Smith was one of the ones who had come to the party, one of the few she hadn't officially met yet. She studied him, even after he looked her way. He talked to someone, then someone else, then came to her side.

"You're Victoria's friend," he said.

"You're her brother."

"Trip."

"Allie."

She touched her plastic cup to Trip's, he asked her about the Williams game, and she said they won, and he said he couldn't hear her, so from then on, when they spoke, they spoke into each other's ears. When he had something to say, he put his hand on her back. And when she had a response, she held his wrist. He asked if she wanted to take a shot, and she said no thanks, shots made her stupid, so he shrugged and stood next to her, then went his own way, and then returned to say he was leaving and she should come, too. They left with his friends, some boys, some girls. They stood outside the library, which was modern, a flat intersection of rectangles like a spaceship drawn in the '60s, and which, on this night, looked to Allie like something that didn't belong with the other buildings on campus. She finished her beer and chucked the bottle. It shattered against the bricks. They stood there watching the shards fall to the ground like sleet. Then they all looked at each other and ran.

After sprinting for what felt like a mile, Allie found herself out of breath, alone with Trip, between the roots of a maple tree. She pushed him in the chest, pressing his back against a burl, just to show him how strong she was. Then she kissed his lower lip. "I like you," she told him.

He pulled a Magic Marker from the pocket of his pants.

"Do you always have that?" she asked him.

"No."

He pushed up the sleeve of her coat. Along her forearm, in a black scrawl, he wrote his name, the letters growing smaller as they neared her hand. Then he drew a heart behind his name and crisscrossing bones behind the heart. "Heart and cross-bones," he said.

"This is so badass," she said, examining it.

"I'm glad you think so."

"It's my first tattoo."

They held hands as they walked back to her dorm, where she said good night. Trip asked her if she was sure—three times—but she kept nodding and shaking her head. Yes, he could *not* come in. She was a little drunk but in control and saying no to Trip Smith, just for now. She opened the door, but he remained there, standing. She asked him if he was planning to stay there all night or what, and he said no, he would leave as soon as she disappeared inside, and she said that was sweet but he should go now and then wave when he arrived at the sidewalk. He did as he was told. She waved back, then walked through the door. She didn't realize she was smiling until she stepped inside, onto the marble, until she looked across and saw Dougie Page sitting at the bottom of the stairs, a backpack to his side, the scraggly hair on his chin propped in the palm of his hand. The light in the dorm was pulsing and blinding, and Dougie looked sad enough to make Allie feel guilty for whatever she might have done to ruin his night. "Who was that?" he asked her.

"A friend," she said. "When did you get here?"

"Earlier."

"You should have called me."

"I did. A bunch of times."

This was true. She had ignored his calls. She unwrapped the scarf from her neck, then unzipped her jacket. She exhaled and invited Dougie upstairs, but only for a few minutes, she said. Then he had to go.

ALLIE CHANGED INTO SWEATPANTS AND came back into the common space. Lauren was away at a robotics tournament, so Allie and Dougie had the room to themselves. Now that she had had a moment to come to terms with Dougie's presence, in her dorm, in

her room, in her night, the guilt began to diminish and she went
back to feeling the way she had as she opened the dormitory door:
a little faded, a little overwhelmed, but like she had seen parts of
the campus she'd never seen before, parts of herself she'd never
known existed, seen a future that held the promise of more nights
like this one. Her whole life suddenly trembled with potential.

Dougie took his hat off, the shadow of the hatband still stuck
in his hair. He tried to smooth it out with his hand but the indent
wouldn't go away. They went to the futon and Allie crossed her
legs beneath her, sitting straight-backed and at a distance from
Dougie. There was a plastic bag of weed on the chest in front
of the futon. He had brought her a stubby glass bong, too. He
packed a bowl, and Allie said no thanks, but then gave in and
smoked anyway. It didn't matter if she smoked, and he would
take it as an insult if she made him do it alone.

They put on a movie, but she didn't pay attention to it once
it was playing. She checked her phone and found a text from
Victoria: *where are you???* and when she looked up, she realized
that Dougie wasn't watching the movie; he was watching Allie.
She put her phone away. She held his hand for a moment, and
he edged closer on the futon, but her eyes, by now, had found the
television and declined to return his gaze. She loved Dougie, she
supposed, but only in the way she loved maple syrup, blueberries,
fog, her dad's beard, the SCHOONA vanity plate on her grandfather's car, the stories about made-up cities full of skyscrapers
that her mom used to tell her at bedtime, wool sweaters, flannel
sheets, snow blowing over the rocky coast . . . She loved Dougie
like a picture book from her youth.

"If I'm not staying," Dougie said, with an effort, "I guess I
should go."

Allie nodded. But then she said, "Wait. Just—sleep on the
futon. You can't drive home tonight."

He weighed this option. "Can't I sleep with you?" he asked.

She shook her head and stood. She pulled out the futon frame, and he helped her lay the mattress across the wooden slats. On the mattress she tossed a blanket and one of her own pillows. She gave Dougie a hug, then went into her room and closed the door.

WHEN SHE AWOKE IN A bedroom that smelled of down and her own heat, there was soft, early sunshine outside the window. For a moment, she felt disoriented, but then fragments of the previous night started coming back, and she started smiling despite herself. She knew she would go back to bed, back to sleep, but she had to pee and felt thankful for this brief exposure to the morning. She stepped toward the window in her underwear and T-shirt and caught her reflection in the full-length mirror as she passed. She flexed her biceps. Trip's name was still on her forearm. It had smudged slightly overnight, but remained, for the most part, intact. She flexed again and watched the way her muscles stretched the crossbones and wondered how long the ink would last. Outside, the sky was the lightest shade of blue and the grass was green and the buildings were red, all so perfect and exceptional. She felt powerful. She looked down through the window to the small parking lot. Dougie's Ranger was out there, an orange parking violation tucked beneath a windshield wiper, but her view of the Ranger was soon obscured by another vehicle, this one on the move, then stopping in the middle of the lot. A vehicle with lights on the roof. A cop car, the door opening. A large man in plain clothes exiting. She wondered why a cop car would be in the parking lot and then she felt anxious.

The previous night—a new, more broken set of memories— now assembled in her mind, and Allie wondered if she had made a misstep—or if Dougie had made a misstep. She pulled on a pair of sweats and opened the bedroom door and found Dougie, sleeping facedown, the blanket wrapped in a tangle around his jeans. He was clutching the pillow like a life preserver. The weed was on the chest in front of the futon, and so was the bong. This was it. Someone had seen him waiting in her dorm. Someone had smelled the smoke. Or someone had seen her throw a bottle against the library.

"Dougie," she whispered. She tugged on his foot. "Wake up."

He roused. "Hey," he said.

"There's a cop outside."

"Why?"

"I don't know, but we need to put everything away."

"Okay," he said. "Give me a second."

He stood and stretched and tried to put the futon frame back in its upright position, but he kept fumbling it and only got half-way there.

"Jesus, Dougie," she said, "I don't care about the futon."

There was a knock on the door.

She and Dougie both stood still. They heard another knock. She nodded at the bedroom door. Dougie understood and went inside and closed the door behind him. Grabbing the bag of weed, Allie looked around, then stuffed it in the top drawer of Lauren's desk, no, her own desk. She picked up the bong and searched for a spot big enough to hide it. The knocking grew louder and more insistent. She tried to jam the bong in the space behind the futon, but there wasn't much room and the edges of the frame were hard and blunt, so the bowl cracked against the wood and the bong smashed in her hands and fell across the floor, the water spreading like an oil spill. A piece of shrapnel landed on Allie's foot, and a dapple of blood bloomed in its place. There was more knocking on the door, and then Allie heard her name.

She stood straight and looked to the door. This all felt unfair. All she needed was a little more time to get her affairs in order, a little more time to piss and wake up, for Christ's sake, and if this officer would please only stop knocking and saying her name over and over, then she could say to anyone listening with total confidence, almost total confidence, that she would be able to take everything she had broken, solder it back together again, and make it even stronger than before.

11

AS I SORT THROUGH THE EVENTS OF THAT SPRING, I'VE FOUND IT HELP-
ful to keep a copy of Allie's lacrosse schedule tacked above my laptop, there for consultation whenever I'm struggling to remember
what happened when, or who was involved where. Ed and Steph
eventually organized so much of their own lives around Allie's athletic career, I figure it makes sense to arrange my own notes along
the same lines. Here, then, is a brief summary of the final two
weeks of the Amherst regular season (home games in caps):

Wednesday, May 14th — Tufts
  - reception at the Smiths'
Saturday, May 17th — WILLIAMS
  - dinner w/ the Smiths
Saturday, May 24th — Bowdoin
  - reception at the Thatches' on Fri.

After that victory over Tufts, at the party held in the Smiths' home, Ed had been drinking a beer and talking shop with another lax dad who owned a chain of pain centers near Fort Lauderdale, when Chip approached the two men and asked if they wanted to step away from the living room and head for the den. The Floridian checked his bulky watch and apologized—he had a plane to catch—so Ed shook the man's hand, finished his beer, placed it amongst all the crab cakes on a surprised caterer's tray, and told Chip to lead the way (Allie, you'll recall, noticed them slip away from across the room, then was quickly ambushed by her teammates).

Chip brought Ed down a hallway, where several of the players were helping each other connect a phone to a stereo dock, then through the busy kitchen, past mixing bowls and cutting boards and row after row of purple-frosted cupcakes, before taking him through a door that seemed destined to reveal a pantry. Chip let Ed go in first and closed the door behind him. The door was heavy and landed flush against the frame like the hatch of a space station, sealing out the din. Chip twisted a knob, and amber light and pitchy shadows sprang from a lamp and landed on the room—not a pantry at all. More like a secret office. Bookshelves lined two walls. Sailing pictures and diplomas covered a third wall. The fourth wall had windows, and through the slats in the shades they could see the Smiths' pool, lit from beneath the surface and glowing under the dusky sky. In front of the windows was an impressively sturdy desk, hewn from the wood of some kind of glossy red tree. Facing the desk were two black chairs with golden Amherst crests stamped onto the backs.

"Where'd you get the chairs?" Ed asked.

"The Jeff chairs? They were my father's."

Ed said he was gonna buy one for his own office.

Chip laughed. "You should," he said, before gesturing

elsewhere, to a set of clubhouse seats in the corner. "But sit there for now. More comfortable."

Ed sat, unzipping his Amherst Lacrosse windbreaker, leaving his hat on.

Chip poured two brandies, handed one snifter to Ed, and brought the other over by the windows, where he made a stool for himself out of the corner of his desk. He had been imagining three fathers, not two, when he extended the invitation to come to the study, so the setup felt much more intimate than intended, as if Chip could only have brought Ed here to pose some kind of urgent question. The old grandfather clock was ticking loudly and slowly next to the door, and Ed kept glancing over his shoulder at a bookshelf; behind the bookshelf were all the young women, and it seemed obvious that he was missing the noise and camaraderie, wishing he could rejoin his daughter and her friends. But it would have been even more uncomfortable— for either of them—to admit that breaking off from the rest of the group had been a bad idea, so there was nothing to do, really, but drink their brandy and, in Chip's case, think of something to say. As it happened, Chip had read an article in the *Times* earlier in the spring about fisheries and climate change, and it had sparked his interest enough to seek out two or three more articles on the subject in online journals. It felt relevant to Ed's business, so—

But Ed misunderstood. "My business?" he said.

"Oh, I—"

"Nothing very interesting about my business."

Chip didn't know what he'd said to make Ed so defensive, but he was determined to be a good host, and he tried to explain to Ed that all he wanted to talk about was how many lobsters remained in the sea and what plummeting pH levels might do to their habitats. Ed nodded warily. He seemed reassured, at least moderately, but the fact was, the two men were destined to have a halting conversation, no matter how Chip approached the subject, because Ed couldn't remember their previous interaction, the one that had taken place early in the morning when Ed was concussed. It took some time for Chip to backtrack, but this is not how good conversations are supposed to go. This was no river. It was a sputtering, broken sprinkler.

Chip did the best he could, talking about fish and lobsters and lobster traps, and as he did, Ed rose from his chair to take a lap around the room. He walked to one of the walls, a wall filled with books. The titles, I'm sure, meant nothing to Ed. Mostly they were law texts. In the spaces between the leather spines, there were silver plates, chalices, miniature sailboats mounted on wooden bases. Ed studied the trophies as Chip talked. Chip was trying to tell Ed that he'd read something surprising, that the way Ed had *said* lobster traps worked wasn't quite right. He had to remind Ed what Ed had said in the hotel, that lobsters go into a trap to eat the baitfish and then get caught in the netting and can't leave. Ed said he knew all this, and stood by it. Well, but what Chip had discovered, he said, or what marine biologists with underwater cameras had discovered, was that the lobsters *could* leave the traps. They went in, ate the fish, left when they felt like it. Getting plucked out of the sea was just a matter of chance then. If you were in the trap when the sternman started cranking on the line, you got caught. On the one hand, it was funny because the way lobster traps had been designed wasn't how they really worked. But on the other hand, the traps were accidentally brilliant, perfectly built sustainability machines. They fed the lobsters, the lobsters grew, and somehow it all worked out so that the lobstermen always, or almost always, hauled just enough from the sea to make a living without decimating the population.

By then Ed had arrived in front of a picture: Chip and Sandy when they were younger, sailing and sitting on the windward rail, hair whipping in the breeze, smiling back at a photographer who must have been sitting in the cockpit. The cockpit of a large sailboat. Waves and blue sky filled the rest of the frame. "This your boat?" Ed asked.

"It was my father's," Chip said.

"Looks nice."

"It was. He kept it in Newport. Sandy and I used to take it on cruises up to Maine. We used to go to the Midcoast, to your neck of the woods. That's why I recognized your hat when we were visiting Bates."

Ed didn't respond—his mind had already drifted away from his own line of inquiry, it seemed—and Chip had nothing more to add. Both men had finished their brandy by then, so it felt like they'd done enough to suggest making a return to the party without losing face.

But something gave Chip pause. Ed had gone very still. He was staring at the wall. At what, specifically, Chip couldn't tell. Chip looked at the photos, too, just to see if there was anything he was missing. He had hung them there—some older, some newer, some taken from the deck of the boat, some from a helicopter—but typically when he was in this room, he was working, paying no mind to the decor. Even upon this fresh appraisal, there wasn't much to see, nothing revealing. The yacht was navy-hulled. Ninety feet long. There was a painting of it, too—oil on canvas, the yacht gliding behind its taut rainbow spinnaker. Ed was standing closer to the wall than Chip was, and he had tugged the brim of his hat down low, so it was impossible to see Ed's eyes, impossible to know what had captured Ed's attention so fully, at least not at the time.

As I've already mentioned, when *The Boston Globe* first ran the piece about Ed's original heist, Maeve and I discussed it with

Colin and Cammie over dinner, as we discussed every new rev-
elation about the Thatches in those days, as our whole town did.
But we weren't the only ones interested in the story. Down in
the suburbs of Boston, that issue of the *Globe* had also made it
to Chip and Sandy's house, and when Chip found the article, he
went straight to his den. There was nothing he needed to see—at
some point, he'd already figured out that it would have been Ed
who came aboard the yacht that night—but he felt compelled to
regard his own office from Ed's perspective anyway, to see what
he'd missed the first time around.

Chiseled onto the placard beneath the painting of Chip's
father's yacht was the name of the boat and its hailing port:

NEPTUNE & MERCURY

NEWPORT, RI

This was the yacht that Chip and Sandy had guided up the
Damariscotta River in the fall of 1992. On their second night in
town, Ed had climbed over the stern, gone to the master cabin,
and stolen Sandy's diamond ring.

THE PAPERS NEVER CONNECTED THE boat's owners to the boat's
owners' grandchildren, teammates and friends of Allie Thatch.
I only learned of that scene in Chip's study when I visited the
Smiths' residence myself, just last month, on my way to a wedding on Buzzards Bay. Why Chip chose to tell me then was only
as mysterious as the choice not to tell me on the phone or in Lewiston, only as mysterious as his absence from any of the initial
accounts. The Smiths, I gathered, were the type of old-money
New Englanders who'd been brought up to look down upon any
public affirmation of wealth (as if their mansion, summer home,

and yacht weren't all the affirmation we'd ever need). When I called Chip out of the blue, he must have assumed I'd discovered this other connection to the Thatches. I hadn't. And I was still clueless when I showed up to his mansion in Weston. I doubt he thought all that much of me as a writer, but maybe he'd been convinced, by then, that I was a hard enough worker, willing to show up and do some digging. I'd made it to his home. He might as well show me the walls.

ON THE DRIVE TO BUZZARDS BAY, I mused out loud to Maeve about what a crazy coincidence it had been that Ed eventually became friends with Chip Smith, captain of the *Neptune & Mercury*, but Maeve didn't seem nearly as impressed.

"It's a small world," she said.

"Not that small."

We were traveling a highway already flanked by the low scrubby pines and blond soil indigenous to the Cape. One of my former students was getting married in Marion, and I was wearing a bow tie because this student had always worn bow ties, and I was also wearing a new suit that I'd purchased, on a whim, on my way back from the visit to Bates. This wedding was looming, and suddenly I didn't want to bust out the same linen blazer and the same wrinkled slacks that I'd worn to every other wedding and probably this same student's graduation over a decade earlier. The Freeport outlets were on the way home from Bates, or close enough, and as I entered the store, I must have had the look of a man who does not often shop for himself because the salesman approached me cautiously, like a park ranger trying to coax a scared raccoon out of an outhouse. I told him I was a 42R, 35 waist, but he looked at me skeptically and brought me a 40R with a 33 waist, which fit just fine. Maeve said I looked good in my new suit. I said she also looked good. She'd cut her hair short, and it was down, her dress made of some kind of synthetic feather, blue jay or peacock.

"Okay," Maeve said, gesturing to the road ahead of us, "we're on our way to this wedding, right?"

"We are."

"And one of your old students is getting married to a girl who went to Tabor, which is why the ceremony's in Marion."

"True."

"And Tabor is also where your dad went to school."

"True."

"Is that a coincidence?"

I thought about it, then said, "Not really. Not a big one anyway."

"Right, and when we get to this wedding, you're probably going to run into someone you weren't expecting to see, or at least one person who knows someone you went to school with, or someone you played lacrosse with."

"Maybe," I said, although I could calculate the odds just as well as Maeve, and of course she was right—but what made me hedge was this conversation's familiar contours. Were we about to have the same old argument? Maeve worries that I'm planning to ship Jane and Jack off to Exeter and Dartmouth and turn them into well-rounded zombies. I'm resentful because if she thinks that's what I want, then she doesn't know what I want (even if I do want that, but only if *they* want that).

"Look," she said, "I'm not trying to make this about your evil network or anything."

"You're sure?"

"Yeah, just listen," she said, shifting in her seat to face me. "What I'm saying is, Ed and Steph were starting to enter a society—*this* society." She gestured to the space between us.

"I'm including myself here. Okay? They were gonna run into someone, sooner or later. You know how it is: There was a one hundred percent chance that the Thatches would meet someone at one of these *receptions* or whatever, who was like, 'Oh, you're from Maine? I have a summer home in Maine. Someone robbed it back in the early 2000s.' And then Steph would be like, 'Hey, that's funny—my husband used to *rob* summer homes in Maine. Maybe he even robbed yours. Where's Ed? We'll have to ask him if he ever broke into your house. Hey, Ed!' "

"Or your yacht."

"Or your yacht."

"I don't know," I said.

"They were in the enemy's lair, Andrew. It was bound to go south eventually."

I almost missed the exit to 195 and had to veer across two lanes, so Maeve turned forward and gripped the dash, and from then on, we spoke only of our own affairs. But I kept thinking about Ed, wondering if it had occurred to him that by gaining entry into this world that had always been denied to him—*your kind of people, Andy*—he'd also increased his chances of crossing paths with someone he'd done some harm to back when he was a younger man. Yes, I decided. He was too sharp not to understand that he was chasing his own bait, lingering in his own trap. He might have even taken pleasure in it. He had always loved a challenge, always loved proving the doubters wrong. No one ever thought he'd start showing up at lacrosse receptions; we didn't have to say it for him to know it, for him to believe that his very presence at the Smiths' home was a victory over expectations. As for the painting of the *Neptune & Mercury,* when Ed first discovered it in the Smiths' home, he must have gone on high alert—but only for a moment, only until it became clear that Chip didn't know a thing. Ed had penetrated the "enemy's lair" and lived to tell about it. By the time he and Steph crossed the border to Maine, the satisfaction of escape would have overcome any remaining nerves. He had survived once again. Which only made him that much more convinced that he would continue to survive, no matter who or what might come after him next.

The road that he and Steph drove upon that night was mostly deserted. Not many Mainers are still awake at 11 P.M. on a Wednesday. Ed listened to the country station but not loud enough to rouse Steph, who slept in the passenger seat under Ed's Amherst windbreaker. Occasionally a pair of headlights on the far side of the median flashed by, but the gaps between cars were widening by full minutes now. He ascended the bridge over the Kennebec River and looked past Steph, down to the naval yard. The cranes were all lit up. Two military ships—stealth destroyers—hugged the edge of the river. One destroyer was finished, one was awaiting further construction, its hull floating in the darkness. There was a deck and a bridge, but the turrets were missing.

The cup holder began to rattle.

A text from EJ: *Need to meet.*

Ed texted back: *Why?*

EJ: *Just come to the gym.*

THE CANADIANS, ONCE THEY COULD no longer rely on the transportation system previously supplied by the Thatches' boats, had quickly found a Plan B. They established contact with an outfit in New York that's been accused by the DEA of having Sinaloa ties and swiftly pioneered creative ways to cross the border, sending seaplanes into northern lakes where there's no one within a hundred miles and all the towns have numbers for names. The New Yorkers picked up the packages there, on logging routes, for distribution across New England. They had other ways, too; just the other day, I read about a crateful of Pakistani rugs confiscated at the border (heroin had been woven into the threads somehow), and I wondered if any of Ed's former associates had been involved. Perhaps the Canadians. But definitely not the Mainers. Lew and his people had been unceremoniously cut out by their northern neighbors. With the Thatches no longer in the picture, Lew was left to scramble for inferior product, and to make matters worse, as he was pondering what to do next, one of his dealers had been approached by a man in a ski mask who told the dealer he better shut down operations for good. And then, just to make sure the message had been heard, the man in the ski mask rammed the dealer's Acura with his truck, nearly killing the dealer in the process. Lew may have suspected the Thatches, but it wouldn't have made much sense (he would have had to assume that Ed was acting irrationally or on behalf of indiscernible forces), and at any rate, even if Lew did have a hunch, he was slow to act on it. For months, his crew lay low, waiting to see if there would be any further action, which there wasn't.

So, from Ed's perspective, the collision had achieved its desired effect, at least temporarily. He had never told Chuck and EJ about what he had done because there had been no real need and because he wanted to project himself, especially after Ben's death, as a voice of reason. His actions in Lewiston, were Chuck and EJ ever to discover them, would contradict the measured exit strategy Ed had been promoting for over a year now. Besides, the Silverado had been repaired before anyone other than Steph or Allie saw the damage. The only thing missing was the Chevy crest, which couldn't be replaced; the grille still had a dent that the body shop had failed to notice until Ed arrived to pick up the truck, by which point it was too late to fix because Ed needed to get to one of Allie's soccer games.

After the reception at the Smiths' house, when Ed met EJ

and Chuck in the weight room at Lincoln High, he found the two of them on or near the bench press. The room was cold. The rubber mats stunk like used truck tires. EJ was thrusting the bar upward, exhaling sharply on each rep, two forty-five-pound plates clamped to either side of his fists. Chuck was standing behind him, leaning on a radiator with arms crossed, in the spotter's position without bothering to spot. He wore a black crew-necked sweatshirt, the eye-patched mascot of the Portland Pirates, Maine's old minor league hockey team, scowling out from the chest. Ed waited until EJ dropped the bar back on its mount, then told him that Steph was outside in the car, so it would be appreciated if they could make this quick.

EJ toweled off his forehead. Over the past few years, even as he had put on muscle, his face had retained its round shape. He looked young for his age. "We got a call from Lewiston," he said. "They're getting anxious again."

"Nothing new there," Ed said.

"They want in with Canada."

"Nope—ain't happening."

"I know. But Lewiston already bought their own boats. I saw them."

"Well, you're just gonna have to talk to Lew again."

"And say what?"

"I don't know," Ed said. "Sound helpful."

"How?"

"Explain the way we did things."

"I've done that. A hundred times."

Ed thought about their position. He liked their position. It was high above the sea of bullshit that he used to have to wade through. "What kind of boats?" he asked EJ.

"What kind of *boats*?"

"Yuh. Sport fishing? Inflatable?"

"Dad, I don't know. They're white. Okay? They float. I only saw them for a second at the docks. They look like—like, I don't know, regular old speedboats."

"They're white?"

"Yeah, they're white."

"All right, there you go. Tell them to paint them dark gray, not white. For the fog. Find out what kind of engines, too. Whatever they got, tell them they need bigger ones."

"This is not what they're asking for, Dad."

"Well. It's all we got."

EJ dropped back on the bench. He throttled the bar and banged out another three reps. He sat up again. "The guys aren't gonna like it," he said, flexing his hands.

"The guys?" Ed said. "What guys? We don't got 'guys' anymore."

EJ looked up at Chuck.

"What?" Ed said.

Chuck uncrossed his arms, put both hands on the broken radiator. "Nevertheless, some of them are getting restless."

"We're not saying they have a leg to stand on," EJ said. "Just saying we have a situation."

"A Dougie Page situation," Chuck said.

"Not that kid."

"It seems," EJ said, "that Dougie borrowed a boat. He took it up the coast and broke into a house. We think someone saw him on his way out, and he neglected to put the dummy name and hailing port on the back of the boat. They left a note in one of our traps."

Chuck handed Ed the laminated piece of lined paper. Salt water had leaked through the plastic and made the ink run. In blocky letters, it read: HAUL YOUR OWN TRAPS. STAY OUT OF OTHERS.

"There's a rumor that someone saw a boat from Rockland

down near the Pound," EJ said. "Probably they're the ones who left the note. We've got the guys on the lookout for it."

"Rockland's where Dougie broke in," Chuck said.

"At least they think he was hauling traps," Ed said.

"For now they do," Chuck said. "Yeah. But we need to keep an eye on that kid."

"LET ME PROPOSE SOMETHING," ED said to Steph as she rinsed out a coffee mug in the kitchen sink. It was Thursday morning, the day after the Tufts game, two days before the Williams game, nine days before the Bowdoin game. "We got so much to do to get ready for this lobster bake—what if the Smiths stay somewhere else?"

"What?" Steph said, turning around. "No, Ed. You're the one who invited them, and I'm not reneging when Sandy's been sick. No reason to stress her out about finding a place to stay."

"We could find the place." Ed held up a to-do list, written on a notepad, that detailed everything that needed to be bought, rented, or repaired between now and the reception they would host the day before the Bowdoin game. He wanted Steph to see how long the list was. She removed her glasses from her bag, placed them on her nose, studied the notepad. Then she started crossing off items: paper towels, ice, keg, pasta—

"We need that stuff," Ed said.

"I can get most of it through the Schooner."

"By next Friday?"

"By next Friday. Relax, Ed."

She slid her scarf off a stool and pulled it around her neck, ready to go to work. Something occurred to her though. She looked at the list again.

"You forgot lobster," she said.

"I didn't forget lobster. It's a lobster bake."

Steph eyed her husband.

"What?" he said. "I got a plan."

"A plan, huh?" She put her hand on his chest, patted it twice, then headed for the door. "Okay, you're in charge of the lobster."

Once she was gone, Ed sat on the stool and looked at his list. He had to call the pool guy and make sure the hot tub got maintenanced. He had to make sure the gravel outfit from Nobleboro was still planning to regrade the driveway over the weekend. He had to call the tent company and the bouncy castle company. He had to call Brittany Dodwell, EJ's ex, and ask if she and her brother might be interested in running the lobster bake. He picked up the phone.

"You wanna do lobsters, clams, the whole shebang?" Brittany asked him. Ed could hear her typing on the other end of the line. "Now you're getting into Deluxe Lobster Bake territory."

"How much?"

"Um, lemme look it up. Hang on a sec." Ed heard her coughing. She cleared her throat. "Seventy a head," she said.

"That some kind of joke?"

"Ask for the Deluxe, get the horns."

"We're supplying all the lobsters," Ed said. "All you gotta do is throw em on the grill. How about I give you and your brother five hundred bucks?"

"Each?"

"Total."

"EJ gonna be there?"

"Maybe."

"Be nice to see him after all this time."

Ed heard a beep: call-waiting. He asked Brittany to hang on a second and hit the flash button. Had he known it was Bev, their nearest neighbor—she lived on her own driveway, but their properties were separated by a long, high fence—he wouldn't have answered. She was always calling about flinty-tasting water, backed-up sewage, deer in her garden. She lived alone.

"Hi there, Ed," she said. "You know I hate to bother you with these things, but the fence has gone and broken itself again."

"It's your fence, Bev. You built it."

"But you're the one who insisted on it being tasteful looking, no?"

"Steph did," he said, moving out from behind the stove and its hanging hood to glare through his windows at the descending fence and Bev's white house looming above it.

"And why?"

"Because we gotta see it every day."

"You won't take an eensy-weensy look then?"

"I'm looking at it right now."

"And fix it, I mean."

"Bev—"

"*One* look."

"Goddammit, Bev. Fine. Yuh, I'll fix the fence. I gotta go."

He hit the flash button again.

"So he'll be there or what?" Brittany asked.

"Who?"

"EJ."

"At the lobster bake? I don't know. He should be."

"Guarantee he'll come," Brittany said, "and we'll do it for fifteen hundred."

ON FRIDAY ED WAS OUT all day, running errands, buying anything Steph couldn't acquire at a discount: indoor/outdoor lights for the tent, oil for the lawnmower, oil for the boat, oil for the tiki torches that he planned to plant along the path to the dock. I happened to run into him at Damariscotta Hardware that afternoon. He was wearing dirty work boots, carpenter jeans, and a hoodie. He would have looked like any other lobsterman along the Midcoast, except the sweatshirt was purple and said AMHERST LACROSSE across the chest. This was during my lunch break from school, and I was there to pick up paint, rollers, and drop cloths for a project I had vowed to take on that weekend, a redesign of Jane's bedroom.

Nine months had passed since Ed and I last spoke. Now that Allie had enrolled in college, there was no reason for us to continue our monthly lunches. I said hello, then Ed said hello, and I asked him how life was. He told me all about Allie's achievements on the lacrosse field. I congratulated him, and then he talked about the lobster bake he was planning until it was his turn at the register. I waited as he paid with cash, and then we said goodbye. But just before he left the store, he turned and said, "You and the fam should come on by. Gonna be plenty of your kind of people, Andy."

"My kind of people?"

"You know—Benzes and filet mignon."

It was an old joke, from when we worked together as teenagers. He used to accuse me of knowing everyone who arrived at the Pound via sailboat, anyone who looked like they might have a German sedan waiting at the dock, ready to whisk them off to a candlelit dinner at a fancy restaurant. "Sounds like they're more your people than mine," I said, "but thanks for the invite. I'll run it by Maeve."

He touched the brim of his cap, went through the sliding doors, and I turned my attention back to the cashier, who was waiting to scan my items. When she asked me how my day was going, I said, "Good enough," which was true, or had been true only a few minutes earlier, up until my encounter with Ed.

———

EARLY SATURDAY MORNING, THE DAY after I saw him, the day of the Williams game, one week before the Bowdoin game, Ed went to the Pound. There, he picked up three empty traps. The idea was to fill them with lobster, sink them in the river, take the lacrosse players out on his boat, and haul the traps before steaming the lobsters—make a big show of it.

Once he dropped the traps at his house, he and Steph drove to Amherst for Allie's game. Afterward, the Thatches and Smiths went out to a late lunch and Chip asked Ed and Steph how they first met, how it all started. The two families split the check. Ed and Steph said goodbye to Allie, and then, on their way back home, once night had fallen and the Thatches were driving through Falmouth, Steph received a phone call. She showed the screen to Ed. It was Bev. Their neighbor.

"Don't answer," Ed told Steph. "I already told her I'd fix the fence."

"What fence?"

"Her fence."

Steph picked up anyway. Ed listened as he drove, as his wife said *Uh-huh* and *Mm-hm* between long periods of silence. Then she began to adopt a tone of concern, or feigned concern. "Really?" she said. "No, that's good to know." And then, "Well, it's not hunting season, but I'll have Ed or EJ look into it. Thanks for calling, Bev."

She hung up.

"Hunting season?" Ed said.

"I mean—take it with a grain of salt."

"Or a shaker-full of salt."

"Yeah, well, she claims she heard shots somewhere near the house, not too long ago."

"Must be hearing things."

"Probably. I'll call EJ, just to make sure."

She dialed their son, but after waiting for half a minute, she said, "He's not picking up."

"He had to go down to Lewiston today," Ed said. "Might be out of range."

When they arrived back in Damariscotta, they had to get groceries (butter, coffee, beer, and granola, as confirmed by receipts and the supermarket's security footage), so they drove through town to Hannaford, which meant that, once the groceries had been purchased, Ed and Steph took an alternate route home. The fastest way from the store to the Thatches' is to take School Street, and School Street joins Bristol Road a half mile south of their driveway. Therefore Ed turned right onto Bristol Road, heading north toward the big hill that looms above the hospital. The sun was long gone, the temperature had dropped, but it was mid-May now and Ed wanted to drive with the windows down. Steph had her seat warmers on, the heat on her side of the truck set to seventy-eight, which was how they often drove. The exterior lights on the houses along Bristol Road had come on, and hundreds of blackflies were darting in and out of the glow. But there were two more lights—or really two pairs of lights—that neither Ed nor Steph expected to see. Headlights. Two vehicles. They were leaving the woods that marked the entrance to the Thatches' road. Ed and Steph noticed the lights at the same time, as their Silverado came down the hill, about a quarter mile from the driveway.

"That's weird," Steph said.

Ed thought so, too. He leaned forward and squinted through the windshield. It was weird to see the lights because the only house on the driveway belonged to him and Steph. The cars were too far away to recognize by model, and they were headed in the other direction, toward town. The white headlights were soon replaced by red taillights, which accelerated and rounded the bend in the road, disappearing.

"Who do you think it was?" Steph asked.

Ed wasn't sure. He thought back to all the calls he had made that week, all the requests for service. Then he remembered the road crew. They had been scheduled to come earlier in the day. "Must be the gravel outfit," he said.

"Here this late?"

"Guess they were running behind."

By then Ed and Steph had reached their mailbox, the end of the road, so Ed flicked on his blinker and made the turn. Sure enough, the dirt was fresh, rough, and soft; the road crew had come and gone and done their job. Ed and Steph could hear the tires sinking the stones beneath the new surface. Everything looked fine. Until it didn't.

"Whoa," Steph said.

She pointed forward, but Ed had already seen it—four long lines in the road. He pulled over and kept his brights on. The lines ran in pairs, deep gouges like the tracks a giant skier might draw through dark powder, ending abruptly.

"Skid marks?" Steph asked.

"Yuh. Wait one sec," Ed said, opening his door. "I'll check it out."

Steph wasn't inclined to wait though. She got out and walked alongside Ed to the first set of tracks. Ed looked down the hill, through the trees, to their house, which was dark. A breeze crackled the branches and rustled out the smell of pine.

"Two sets," Steph said, walking along the tracks. "This is so strange."

Now Ed joined Steph in examining the tracks. The uphill pair ran parallel to the right shoulder of the road, before ending in deep divots. About ten feet from the end of the tracks, the new set began—or ended—and these downhill tracks hooked across the road, almost perpendicular to the first. Ed squatted and ran a hand over the upturned dirt.

"What are you doing?" Steph asked him.

He didn't answer.

"You think you're some kind of tracker now?"

"No."

"Then what are you doing?"

"Thinking," he said.

"About what?"

"The tracks."

"Was it hunters?"

"It wasn't hunters."

"Then who was it?"

"That's what I'm trying to figure out—dammit, Steph. Gimme a second."

He stood and looked back toward the main road. He was trying not to be overly concerned about the tracks, not yet, but he did wonder about EJ. His son had met with Lewiston, per Ed's instructions, earlier in the afternoon, and it was possible that he had come to the house afterwards and maybe slammed on the brakes when he saw a wild animal—a raccoon or a deer—crossing the road, but this theory would do nothing to explain the second set of tracks. Or the gunshots—if gunshots were indeed what Bev had heard. Ed wiped the dirt on his pants and walked back toward the Silverado. "Must have been the gravel outfit," he said again. "I'll call my guy."

"Wait," Steph said. "Why is it the 'gravel outfit'?"

Ed was already climbing in the truck. Steph joined him in the cab, on the passenger's side. "You think EJ's okay?" she asked.

"Yuh. He's got nothing to do with this."

"But what about the gunshots?"

"That's just Bev starting rumors."

"And you really think it looks like the road crew made these marks?"

"Yuh."

"How can you be so sure?"

Ed put the truck in drive. "Because nothing else makes sense."

INSIDE THE HOUSE, THE AIR was still and dark, the windows blue and violet, the walls black. Ed hung his keys on the iron hook shaped like an antler as Steph undimmed the lights in the kitchen. Once they could see, they noticed, sitting by itself on the granite countertop, a small square envelope. Ed picked it up. It seemed to hold something bulky, bulky but light. Steph came to his side and watched as he tore through the envelope. When he emptied the contents on the counter, they found a yellow folded note and a gold plastic Chevy crest, the kind that might go on the grille of a Silverado.

They read the note, a message from their son. EJ always wrote in short sentences. Everything was an incident report.

Mom, Dad—

Sorry I missed you. Dad, picked this up for the truck. Call me before you put it on.

—EJ

Ed and Steph exchanged a glance and then Steph pulled out her phone. Again, she called EJ. Again, he didn't answer. This time the call went straight to voicemail.

——

BY THE END OF THE next day, EJ still hadn't answered his phone or even turned it on, and by Monday, Ed decided it was time to pay a visit to his son's apartment. He had been downplaying his concern to Steph, even going so far as to lie and tell her that he and EJ had already spoken and that everything was fine. At some point I asked Steph if she was mad that Ed had misled her about something so important to both of them, but she said, "Of course not. He was just trying to protect me."

"And you're grateful for that?"

"He was doing his best. He didn't want me to worry."

EJ lived above the post office in a building owned by Ed, so Ed let himself in with the landlord key. The apartment was neat and nearly empty. It was a one-bedroom. On the dresser there was a picture of EJ and all his buddies from the police academy on the day they graduated, but otherwise all the pictures were of family. A framed print of that French lighthouse getting crushed by a huge wave hung above a black leather couch in the living room. There was nothing else on the walls. Ed was standing in the doorway between rooms, his hands against the top of the frame. EJ used to be famous for his disappearing acts. He would go missing for days on end, so frequently that Ed had stopped worrying about his whereabouts years and years ago. But that was before EJ had started working for him, before EJ had agreed to always let his dad know when he was headed off somewhere and to report back as soon as he made it home.

Ed made a final lap through the apartment, then went back out to the hallway. He locked the door behind him, and then he stood there, staring at it. He tried to convince himself that his son would turn up soon, and when he did, and when Ed admitted that he had been worried about him for a second or two, they would laugh about it. Ha ha ha. And then Ed would tell EJ he wasn't to deal with Lewiston, Canada, or anyone else, ever again. He would be a cop, a good cop, and nothing more.

AT VARIOUS LOCATIONS AROUND THE property, Ed had buried safes. One of them was in the garden by the back deck. The soil in the garden was damp and cool. Ed reached into it, digging until he hit the door of the safe. He wiped it off and dialed in the code. He pulled out ten thousand dollars in cash, locked the safe back up, covered it with dirt. He had texted Chief Hunt, checking in, asking if she had heard anything, and she had suggested they meet in person. He drove to Wiscasset, through its Main Street, past the sign thanking him for visiting the prettiest village in Maine, and after three more miles pulled onto the road that used to lead to the nuclear power plant before the state shut it down. The road ran alongside a clear-cut swath of boulders and grass, overgrown now, where the electrical wires had once run. He stopped on the road's shoulder and waited.

Fifteen minutes later, Chief Hunt arrived in an unmarked sheriff's vehicle. She climbed out and circled to the front of her car. Ed left his truck and they stood on the sandy pavement together.

"Chief," Ed said. He handed her the cash, wrapped in waxed paper from the Pound. "A little extra."

She weighed it in her hand.

"EJ still hasn't turned on his phone," Ed said.

"I know that," she said. "The Damariscotta station's looking for him, too. His cruiser's gone."

"Can't they track it?"

"Not if someone ripped out the GPS." Hunt removed her shades. Her eyes were dilated, and she blinked as they adjusted.

"Hang on." She went back to her car, reached inside the passenger's-side window, and removed a manila folder. Before she handed it to Ed, she said, "Maybe you already know what you're about to see, but if you don't, I just want you to know that EJ's not one of those in the car. Don't go having a heart attack when you look at the pictures."

Ed flipped open the folder and stared at the glossy photographs. He was looking at a torched car in front of an abandoned factory, and then he was looking at the incinerated corpses they'd found inside the vehicle.

"Who are they?" he asked.

"So you don't know?" Hunt asked.

"Nope."

"You're sure?"

"Just tell me, for Christ's sake."

"They're a couple a thugs from Lewiston. No one's connecting the dots."

"You're connecting the dots."

"Not really," she said. "I don't know what the hell's going on, and I don't wanna know. I just thought the timing was coincidental. No one else knows what I know anyway. If you think about it, I'm pretty much the only one who could do what I'm doing right now—put that in your pipe."

"When did this happen?"

"Saturday night. They were found Sunday morning. You think EJ was involved?"

Ed didn't respond. He just closed the folder and held it at his side. "What else you got?"

"Nothing really."

"Nothing really?" He pointed at the cash in her hand.

Hunt looked back toward the road, then out into the scruffy clearing where the electrical wires used to run. "Well, there's a

rumor," she said. "Supposedly the DEA knows how stuff is coming into the state."

"When'd you find that out?"

"While ago," she said.

"Why didn't you tell me?"

"Didn't think it was relevant," Hunt said.

"You know damn well it's relevant."

Hunt took a deep breath, put her hands on her lower back,
leaned her hips forward until her spine cracked, then circled
behind the open driver's-side door. "It's a good thing for you I
like EJ," she said. "He's always been a good kid." She was holding the top of the door but hadn't ducked inside yet. "You know
what I'm hoping EJ did? I'm hoping he took off. Just got the hell
out of town and rode into the Goddamn sunset."

And then she lowered herself into the cruiser and turned the
key. She must have been listening to the classic rock station on
her way to meet Ed because "L.A. Woman" came on mid-song.
She closed the door, muffling the big keyboard solo, and then Ed
watched as Hunt drove away, in reverse, all the way up the hill
to Route 1.

12

ON THE AFTERNOON OF MAY 17, A SATURDAY, RIGHT AROUND THE TIME
that Allie's lacrosse team was playing Williams two states away, EJ
Thatch, wearing plain clothes, went to meet two representatives
from Lewiston halfway between him and them, in a town called
Lisbon Falls. They were already waiting when he arrived in his
cruiser, a white Explorer marked with Damariscotta Police decals.
He tucked his service weapon in the pocket of his canvas jacket,
opened the door, and stepped outside. They were in the parking
lot of an abandoned railroad station, an island of blight where
weeds and vines were taking their revenge on cracked pavement
and empty windows. A handless clock. EJ headed for a silver Lincoln sedan, the only other vehicle in the lot. A crow flapped up
from a tree by the Androscoggin, the river hidden from view, moving somewhere behind the railroad station and a tangled thicket.
Otherwise the day was still. Warm in the sun.

EJ climbed into the back of the Lincoln and worked his large
body to the middle of the bench, sliding his hamstrings across

the leather upholstery, his knees pressing against the seat backs. There were two men up front. The man on the right, the one who always sat on the right, wore oval, thin-framed glasses. This was Lew. The driver EJ had never seen before, but the drivers were always different. This one had dark hair that sprang off his head in corky nubs, and he wore a brown sweatshirt with a gold, sequin-lined hood. Puerto Rican or Dominican, EJ guessed. The breeze outside tussled the leaves behind the railroad station, but the air in the car remained stuffy and stagnant, steeped in cigarettes and cowboy cologne, Lew's scent like the open back door of a midmorning dive bar.

Lew turned, gave EJ a nod, and faced forward again. Then he asked about the Canadians.

"We're working on it," EJ said. Other than the jacket, he wore a flannel shirt, blue jeans, work boots. He kept his fists in the pockets of his coat, right hand on his service weapon, although he didn't anticipate having to use it. He gazed through the window at the sun reflecting off the hood of his cruiser, waxed earlier that morning. He was only allowed to meet with Lewiston on his days off. His workdays were supposed to look like any other cop's, preserve the routine. This was his father's rule. Now everything was changing, though, had changed already, and after so many years working with his dad and his uncle, taking so much pride in Ed's confidence—ever since that snowy evening in the garage—EJ sometimes struggled to imagine what he might do next. The only way he could think to spend the free hours was by going to the Lincoln gym twice a day. But there were only so many dumbbells to lift, only so many times he could pull his chin up to a bar. Given a choice, he would have said no to dealing with Lew ever again, but it wasn't up to him, and actually he'd been looking forward to the meeting, to the purpose it gave his day.

"We need product," Lew said.

"I hear you."

"Has to happen. You can't just back out and let everything fall to shit. That's not how it works."

EJ looked around the car as Lew went on about the ill fate that had befallen his business, covering all the territory that had already been covered, mounting an argument that, in essence, balanced upon the honestly very cruel *unfairness* of it all. EJ nodded and said *Uh-huh* as Lew spoke, making gestures of sympathy without capitulation. There were rosary beads hanging from the rearview, a wooden cross dangling from the beads, and something in one of the cup holders—a plastic crest, the kind you might find on the grille of a Chevrolet, the shape of an italicized plus sign.

"Ask him about demand," Lew said to EJ.

"I'm sorry?"

"Ask him." Lew nodded at the driver. "About demand. You know, supply and demand? Ask him about it."

EJ asked the driver how demand was.

"Same as fucking ever," the driver whispered. EJ wasn't especially interested in the answer but found himself leaning forward to hear the driver's voice. It had a harsh quality, almost a hiss. "Except we got nothing to sell."

"Why are you whispering?" EJ asked.

"He crushed his vocal cords in a car accident," Lew said.

"Not an accident," the driver said. His eyes flashed upward, meeting EJ's in the rearview. He looked angry; he would have been yelling if he could, but the effort had an inverse effect on the whisper, lowering it further. "Fucker rammed me on purpose."

"His throat hit the steering wheel," Lew said.

"That can mess with your speech?" EJ asked.

"Sounds like it," Lew said, finding the impediment amusing, apparently. He lit a cigarette and rolled the window down just enough to ash through the crack.

"Anyway," EJ said, "about your boats."

"Our empty boats."

"Can't help you there. But I'm supposed to tell you to paint them gray."

"Gray," Lew said.

"Yeah."

"Well, they're not gray. They're white. Who gives a fuck the color."

"I don't know, makes them blend in with the weather, I guess," EJ said. "That's Today's Hot Tip. Listen, I feel like we're just talking in circles at this point. You know we have to back away for a while. We know you want to take over the import. That's fine. We support that. But while you were lying low, the Canadians found other distributors to work with. We're trying to help you change that. We are. But for now, we're stuck. And you're stuck because you don't want our heat. So let's just call it what it is and know that we're all working toward the same goal here."

Lew rolled down his window all the way. He hacked and spit, then tossed his cigarette outside and rolled the window back up. "This is a waste of time," he said.

"You're the one who wanted to meet," EJ said.

"You get us a new supplier—or more product—or we're coming down to the Midcoast and kicking shit around until we find what we're looking for. You hear me?"

"Yeah, I hear you," EJ said. He started dragging himself back across the leather seat toward the door, but on his way he happened to look forward, between Lew and the driver, to that Chevy crest. "Hey," he said to the kid. "Where'd you get the thing?"

The kid glanced in the mirror. "What thing?" he whispered.

"Where'd you get the Chevy emblem?"

It took a moment for him to answer. "Just picked it up."

"Just picked it up."

"Yeah."

"Where?" EJ asked.

"The street."

"So you just saw it on the street and thought, 'Hey, I want that'?"

"Yeah. I did," the kid said. "That a problem?"

EJ waited, but a deeper explanation didn't feel like it was forthcoming, and the conversation, now that EJ had a moment to think about it, had probably gone as far as he wanted it to go, maybe farther. Probably EJ shouldn't have asked about the crest. His father was missing one. The driver had one. For no reason.

Time to go. EJ had forgotten how little he actually enjoyed these meetings. He felt glad to be leaving and glad his family was leaving the business for good. He didn't like having to think one thing, say another. He slid to the door, opened it, and left. The sun was fading behind a wide gray cloud, and the afternoon felt suddenly cool.

But then he heard a voice coming from behind him, a strained whisper: "Yo."

The driver. EJ turned. The kid was standing outside the Lincoln. He held up the crest. "I can't use this shit," he said. "It's for a truck. I don't got no truck."

EJ didn't move. He kept his hands in the pockets of his coat, right hand gripping the firearm.

The driver frisbeed the crest at EJ. The breeze caught it, knocked it down at EJ's feet. He crouched slowly and picked it up, keeping his eye on the driver, and then he finished the walk to his cruiser.

IN A DRAWER IN HIS parents' kitchen, EJ found an envelope and tucked the crest inside. The spring sunset was going dark, the only light in the house falling from the recessed overheads in the kitchen ceiling. He knew his parents were on their way back from Amherst, and briefly he considered waiting, but the encounter in Lisbon Falls had left him feeling unsettled, and he wanted to keep moving. On a piece of yellow notepaper, he wrote:

Mom, Dad—

Sorry I missed you. Dad, picked this up for the truck.

—EJ

He took a step toward the door but glanced one last time at the envelope. It struck him again as strange, really strange, that Lew's driver had been in possession of the crest. It was also strange that he had given it to EJ. Or thrown it at him. Like a test almost.

He thought for a moment, then grabbed the pen and added one more sentence to the note: *Call me before you put it on.* Then he slid the note inside the envelope and went to the door. He would go to the station, he decided, and look up incident reports from across the state, starting with Androscoggin County. If the driver, the kid with the whisper, had been in an accident that crushed his windpipe, and if it had happened in Maine, then a write-up ought to exist somewhere. As soon as he found something, and as soon as his dad was home, they would talk it over.

He left the house, closed the door behind him, climbed into his cruiser, and pulled forward along the gravel. The road had been resurfaced that afternoon, so EJ—knowing that his parents would be hosting Allie's team later in the week and that they would want the driveway to stay pristine between now and then—drove more carefully than usual up the hill, toward Bristol Road. After a cold winter, the leaves were just starting to bud, and EJ could see all the way through the woods to the main road, where headlights flashed behind the tree trunks—

Then one set of headlights turned onto the Thatches' road. EJ watched the car through the windshield as it weaved through the trees, toward his own advancing vehicle. At this point in the evening, he knew, the headlights would almost certainly belong to his mother or his father. Or no, that couldn't be right—Steph had texted on their way out of Amherst to tell him that Allie's team had won. That was only three hours ago. His parents couldn't be home for another half hour—and that was if they drove without stopping and made good time. The headlights emerged onto a straightaway just as EJ came onto the same length of gravel. EJ blinked his lights on and off. If it *were* his mom or dad, arriving earlier than expected somehow, they would pull over and he would slide his window down and they would say hello, talk about the game, and he would tell them about the crest he'd left in the envelope. But the other headlights never blinked back. The car rolled closer to EJ, and as it did he could finally see past the lamps—the grille, hood, and windshield all unblinded for the first time—and see that it was not his father's Silverado. It was a silver sedan. A Lincoln.

Both vehicles approached each other cautiously—but even so, EJ had barely more than a second to determine what to do before the cars passed each other. Fifty yards separated the two cars, then forty, then thirty. Abruptly EJ cut the wheel and hit the brakes, sending the SUV into a skid across the fresh dirt. The sedan braked, too. If EJ acted efficiently, he felt sure he could take the other car by surprise. He opened his door and walked around the front of the cruiser, toward the Lincoln. He tried to look through the headlights, but they were too bright, turning the night almost entirely white. He could make out the silhouettes, nothing more, of the driver and the passenger. Pulling the gun from his pocket and releasing the safety, he fired one round at the driver, another at the passenger. The shots echoed off the bare tree trunks. The passenger went instantly still, but the driver kept moving, grabbing at his shoulder or the door handle. It looked like he was trying to say something. EJ took another step forward and fired two more rounds at the driver, whose mouth finally stopped moving, his body motionless.

IN MY SECOND INTERVIEW WITH Steph, during a discussion of the earliest days of her marriage, we had a small misunderstanding. I asked her if she thought EJ had ever felt guilty, I meant about Steph's decision regarding her unborn child, whether to stick around Damariscotta or resume her previous course and apply to colleges, but she said, "For what? What happened to those lowlifes? No. No way. That was their own fault."

"Oh," I said. "Sorry. That's not what I meant."

"What did you mean?"

"I meant: Did EJ ever feel guilty for diverting you from your dreams?"

"He didn't divert me from anything," she said.

"He didn't?"

"Why would you blame him?"

"I wouldn't," I said. "It's just—sometimes people blame themselves for things their parents do, even if they shouldn't, even if it's beyond their control."

Steph waved away my theory. "That's a little too Freud for me," she said. "EJ knew that he was lucky to be on the planet. When your parents are only eighteen years older than you, it's not hard to do the math. At some point, he realized he could either feel unwanted or he could feel lucky. I mean, you're saying he should blame himself—"

"I'm really not—"

"But honestly, he should *congratulate* himself. Think about it. If it weren't for EJ, we wouldn't even have a family. And you know what? He would even say that sometimes. He would come up to me and give me a big hug and say, 'Aren't you glad you had me?' And I would say, 'I sure am, EJ.'"

It was one of the only times I didn't believe Steph. It's not that I thought she was misrepresenting her son or her relationship with him; just that I didn't believe that the specific moments she seemed to be recalling had actually happened.

Didn't matter what I thought though. Steph kept plowing ahead: "He would say the same thing to Allie, you know. He would look at her and say, 'I'm so proud of you, sis.'" At this point she started nodding, thinking back, or appearing to think back, through years and years of memory. "And then he would say, 'But just remember, if it weren't for me, you wouldn't even exist!'"

She kept nodding, more and more vigorously, I think to prevent me from noticing that her eyes had begun to tear up. And then she excused herself, left through the sliding glass doors—the former barn doors—and walked onto the porch, where she stayed for the next ten minutes, just barely in view, staring at something in the sky.

EJ PLACED HIS WEAPON IN the passenger seat of the cruiser with a shaky right hand. He turned that hand into a fist and held it in his left palm, squeezing until the tremor subsided. He was breathing sharply, shallowly. He forced himself to draw in a deeper lungful of air. The breath snagged, but he tried again and continued to try until the breaths finally stretched down and filled his chest, his heart rate slowing to a manageable pounding. He looked through the passenger's-side window at the sedan. He had seen worse. Had he? He could imagine worse. From what he could tell, the bodily evidence remained in the car, which was fortunate. Now that the night had gone fully black, EJ should be able to drive the sedan under the cover of its own headlamps without anyone noticing the damaged windshield. But he couldn't leave his cruiser here. He would need help.

But not from Ed or Chuck. He wanted to protect his family for as long as possible, so he texted Jason Page instead: *Can you come down to my parents place? Need you ASAP. Important.*

Then EJ turned on his police scanner, black numerals assembling on the red screen. He split his gaze between the sedan and the main road, watching cars on the far side of the trees to make sure their paths stayed perpendicular to the driveway.

After several minutes, Jason texted back: *On my way.*

EJ stayed in his seat, staring at the stage made by the cruiser's lamps, until finally he remembered that time was passing—and passing quickly—so he forced himself to leave his vehicle.

He opened the front door of the Lincoln and checked for pulses but found nothing, found himself holding warm, lifeless wrists. He wanted to keep everything in the car if possible, but the bodies couldn't stay in the front seats, not if he planned to move the vehicle. So he eased himself into the backseat. He pulled the passenger's shoulder toward the shifter, yanked on him until he was sideways, the torso slotted in the gap over the park brake. EJ hauled on the man, gripping from under the armpits, then dropped him in the backseat. The corpse lay awkwardly across EJ's lap now. He was heavy. The new position granted EJ a clear view of his face. He was not Lew. He was just a young kid. White. EJ didn't recognize him. The bullet had folded his right eye inside out. The socket looked like crushed raspberries. His left cheek was remarkably clean but pitted, either from acne or meth or both. Back to the eye. It was sickening. EJ had seen enough of it. He shifted along the seat and let the corpse fall to the footwell. He kicked the body until it was deep beneath the level of the seats. Nobody would see it unless the car was stopped and someone looked through the windows and down—but the odds of that happening were reliably low at this time of night in this part of the world.

EJ dropped the backseat, opening a channel to the trunk, then started heaving at the shoulders of the other body. The driver. This one EJ recognized. He was the kid with the crushed vocal cords, the one who had given EJ the Chevy crest. EJ pulled him all the way across the backseat before shoving him in the trunk. Then he heard something. The police scanner, crackling from inside the cruiser. He jogged back.

The dispatcher, Connie, was asking one of the two on-duty officers to drive down Bristol Road to see about a report of gunshots.

EJ picked up the handset. "This is Thatch," he said. His voice sounded dry, so he cleared his throat and glanced around the cruiser for water, but he hadn't brought any. "Where on Bristol Road?"

"One five seven Bristol is where the nine-one-one call was made," Connie said. "Resident thinks shots came from north of there."

"You know what? That's over by my folks' place, and I'm heading there anyway. I can poke around. Probably just kids shooting at a mailbox—I don't mind writing it up."

"If that's what it is," Connie said, "maybe we should send someone else so they can make sure the kids stop shooting at mailboxes, know what I mean?"

"I can take care of it," EJ said.

"On your day off?"

EJ told Connie it wasn't a big deal, he didn't mind, and then he hooked the handset back on its cradle. He checked his coat for blood, saw that the left sleeve was stained dark red but the right sleeve was still clean, and wiped this sleeve across his brow. He had begun to sweat. He didn't like that the cruiser was facing the Lincoln, so he turned the key and backed up his vehicle, steered around the sedan, pulled a U-turn, and parked behind it. On the off chance someone drove down here before Jason Page arrived, EJ could claim he had stumbled upon the crime scene, that it had taken him by surprise. It wasn't a solution that would last, definitely not, but it might buy him a small window in which to operate as he looked for a better way out.

His phone lit up. A call from his mother. EJ silenced it. But it was a reminder that his parents would be home soon, and he needed to make sure everything was gone before they made the turn onto their long, dark driveway.

As he waited for Jason, he used the time he did have to write an incident report in his head, to imagine what he would think if he found the vehicle in its current state, the bullet holes in the windshield, the two bodies in the back. More importantly, what would the state detectives think? They would focus their investigation on other dealers in Lewiston, EJ was almost sure. Nobody on the law side would know to connect EJ with the missing bodies—just so long as he relocated the evidence.

Ten minutes later, headlights flashed in the rearview.

EJ reached for his weapon, hid it in his jacket. The lights caught up to EJ's cruiser, slowed alongside it, stopped. Jason rolled down the window of his Tahoe, turned down a Phish song, and said, "What's up, big guy?"

EJ nodded at the sedan. He told Jason what had happened, and then he laid out the rest of the problem. It was like a brainteaser: three cars, two bodies, two drivers. One car and both bodies had to be torched, somewhere far from the scene of the crime. Nobody could know.

"You cool with this?" EJ said.

Jason glanced at the Lincoln, back to EJ. He looked much less happy to be here than he had when he first arrived, but he signaled that yes, he was basically cool with it, and then they started moving.

AFTER PARKING JASON'S TAHOE IN a back row of the hospital lot (EJ drove the Lincoln there and back) they returned to the Thatches' road and picked up EJ's cruiser. Now they were ready to head for central Maine. EJ remained in the sedan, the bodies behind him in the backseat and the trunk, while Jason drove EJ's cruiser. They had made it this far without drawing any scrutiny. But as EJ steered up the driveway one last time, then onto the main road, he saw a pair of headlights to his right. When he turned left, he looked in his rearview and saw that the car's blinker was on. Someone was slowing down, preparing to turn onto the driveway. Their driveway. It had to be his parents. EJ had left just in time then. They wouldn't see a thing. No glass, no blood—

And then EJ remembered the tire tracks. They would see the tire tracks.

He reached for his phone.

On his way over the bridge, EJ threw the phone out the window, into the river. The current was ripping around the cutwaters, white rapids charging out to sea.

THEY WATCHED FROM EJ'S CRUISER, parked behind a scuttled paper mill east of Augusta. The sedan looked like it wouldn't light, and EJ was about to open his door and add more gas and strike another match—when the fire leapt up and out of the windows, throwing off a burst of heat that reached all the way to the cruiser.

He and Jason waited as the car burned, turning black beneath flames that twisted ash and smoke above the mill, into the sky.

"Ready?" EJ said.

"Ready," Jason said. He looped a finger inside his lip, scooped out a wet wad of tobacco, and threw it out the window, onto the pavement, which was reflecting the flames from the car like the floor of a blacksmith's forge.

"Seriously?" EJ said.

"What?"

EJ nodded out the window. "That's evidence."

"Oh," Jason said. He opened his door, leaned down, and shoveled the dip into his palm. "What should I do with it?"

"Whatever you want."

Jason stopped and thought. Then he put the wad in the pocket of his corduroy jacket. The scent of used wintergreen filled the cab as EJ put the car in reverse, wheeling back from the mill.

"Jesus," Jason said. "I can't believe we just did that." His knee was bouncing. He slapped his hand against the knee.

"Calm down," EJ said, looking over his shoulder.

"Holy fucking shit."

"Just relax."

"Holy. Fucking. Shit."

Jason slapped his knee one more time, then bit his finger-nails as he stared through the window. The cruiser was moving forward now, back toward home.

THE EVENTS OF THESE FIRST few hours have been reconstructed using Jason Page's testimony, which was provided to the district attorney as part of his plea bargain. We know which actions he and EJ performed and which words were exchanged—or at least which words Jason said were exchanged—while they were still together. But once EJ dropped off Jason at his Tahoe in the hospital parking lot, EJ was on his own and there's no first-person account of his next movements, so some level of speculation, for those of us intent on re-creating the case down to the most granular of details, becomes an inevitable part of the process. Where EJ went, when he arrived and departed, what the checkpoints were—this is all documented clearly. Why EJ chose to take this path is more of a mystery.

The first move EJ made was to head south, out of the state, through New Hampshire. Then he took 495 to 90, heading west through Massachusetts. All these decisions make sense, more or less; EJ was trying to get as far away as possible. At around four-fifteen in the morning, he passed the green sign welcoming him to the Empire State. At this point, it seems that EJ ran out of steam, because shortly after crossing the border, he checked himself in to a motel. It's highly improbable that he would have stopped—anywhere—unless he absolutely had to, so he must have been falling asleep at the wheel or seeing double as he peered into oncoming traffic; otherwise I'm sure he would have tried to put more distance between him and Maine. Unless he had already decided that, come morning, he would take a detour.

There was a Knights Inn just off the highway, south of Albany, and EJ took a room there. (I've been to this place, just to see it. Maeve and I and the kids were driving home from Ohio after spending Christmas with her folks, and I pulled off the interstate and exited the car, standing near the lobby entrance on a frigid, uniformly bleak day. There was no snow on the ground, no foliage on the trees. There was a minivan parked in front of one of the rooms, a steady cloud puffing from the exhaust. Judging by the flat brown stones glued to the carport supports, the area around the motel's lobby had been designed with a medieval concept in mind. The Knights Inn sign was supposed to look like a castle's turret. I would have gone inside but Maeve wouldn't let me. I heard her calling from the open window of the car, saying the motel was giving her the creeps—and the children, too—so I went back to the driver's side, slid behind the wheel, apologized to everyone for bringing us here, and then we continued on our way.)

If EJ was able to fall asleep that night, it wasn't for long. After two or three hours, he was awake, according to motel security footage, and back in his cruiser, heading for the highway.

But here's the strange part: He didn't go west. He went east. The wrong way. He was giving up the very ground that he had won the night before. We know where he was going—Amherst College—and we know whom he visited there—his sister—but it's hard to say why he would have decided to derail his own momentum just to see Allie. Some people speculate that he left something with her, some piece of evidence perhaps. Others are convinced that it was the other way around: Allie had something to give to EJ. But I'm skeptical of all such conspiracy theories. The Thatches had worked so hard to inoculate Allie from the truth of her own family, I can't see how she would have been able to contribute anything to EJ's escape.

I have my own thoughts about why EJ went back to Amherst. Remember: He had no idea when he was coming back. He didn't even know *if* he was coming back. To my mind, there's only one explanation, and it's pretty simple: EJ wanted to say goodbye to someone he loved.

WHEN EJ PARKED IN THE lot outside his sister's dorm, the sun was lifting above the roofs and dormers, the day turning bright and blue already. A sign specifically forbade nonpermitted cars from parking behind the dorm, but any security officer who came across a cruiser, even one from Maine, would probably leave it alone, at least for a little while, and EJ didn't plan to stay long anyway. The door to the residence hall was locked, but a sleepy girl happened to walk by on her way to or from the bathroom, and when EJ knocked on the windowpane, she let him in without a word. He asked her if she knew Allie Thatch, and she said third floor, pointing vaguely above her and behind her.

EJ climbed the stairs and found a door with a whiteboard that said, *Allie, where r u, bitch <3,* in a girl's handwriting. The hallway smelled of dust and old carpeting. EJ knocked. There was no response, so he knocked again. Now he heard a rustling inside. Whoever was in the room seemed to be avoiding him, so he called his sister's name and knocked a little louder. Then he heard a muffled thud and a crash. He pounded on the door again. "Allie?" he said.

After a long pause: "Who is it?"

"It's EJ." He looked down the hallway.

"Who?" It was Allie's voice, definitely, and she was closer to the door now.

"EJ," he whispered loudly.

The door opened, and in its place stood EJ's little sister, different from the way he remembered her. She looked tan and fit—but also crazy. Her ponytail was falling loosely to one side. Staticky hair reached for the ceiling. Last night's makeup was smeared around her eyes. And then she started to cry.

"Whoa," EJ said. "What's going on? Hey, it's okay."

He gripped her by the shoulders, pulled her in for a hug. She let her arms dangle limply at her side as she cried into his chest, and then she stepped back and pushed him. "I thought you were a cop!" she cried.

"I am a cop," EJ said.

"That's not"—she hiccupped—"even funny."

EJ caught a whiff of bong resin, he thought deriving from Allie's hair—but when he brought his nose down, closer to her, all he could smell was sleep. He guided Allie across the threshold, into the room, and heeled the door shut behind him.

"Did you just smell me?" she asked him.

"No."

"Yes, you fucking did."

EJ looked around the room. He hadn't been in a college dorm since his days at UMaine Orono, but this one was much the same, exactly as he might have expected: a small TV and a roll of paper towels balanced on a mini-fridge; a chest serving as a coffee table. On the far side of the chest was a half-assembled futon, and from under the futon, a large black water stain was spreading across the carpet.

"As you can see," Allie said, "I broke the bong."

"You what?"

"I *broke*. The *bong*." Her eyes were getting red again, tears about to form.

"Okay," EJ said, "just calm down. That's no big deal. Happens to the best of us."

He circled the chest and found the shattered bong on the floor, an explosion of glass shards, all with interrupted green swirls, dozens of glass pieces stuck in the carpet.

"What happened?" he said, turning to Allie.

She threw her hands in the air. "I told you! I thought you were a cop. What are you even doing here?"

"Take it easy," he said. "I was passing through, and I wanted to say hi and apologize because it looks like I can't go to your game at Bowdoin next week."

"Oh," Allie said. She sniffled. She pulled the hem of her T-shirt up to her nose, wiped the snot away. "Why are you passing through? What fucking time is it, by the way?"

"I tried calling but you didn't answer."

"Probably because I was sleeping, you know?"

"Sorry, Allie. I just wanted to say hello."

She shuffled to the mini-fridge, opened it, and pulled out an orange Gatorade. EJ watched her chug half the bottle in one pull, then burp. "What?" she said. "I'm hungover."

EJ became aware of two more physical changes in his sister. One was a large tattoo on her forearm—or no. It wasn't a tattoo. It was drawn in marker. It said TRIP, and around the name someone had drawn a heart and two crisscrossed bones. Allie was also bleeding from a cut on the top of her right foot. EJ pointed at the cut.

"It's from the bong," Allie said. She wiped at her eyes again. She was calming down. She took another sip of Gatorade.

"You okay?" EJ said.

"Yeah. You just surprised me, so I panicked and dropped the bong."

"Sit down," he said. "Careful of the glass."

"Fine," she said. "Just let me go to the bathroom first."

While she was gone, EJ folded the futon back into a couch, and when Allie returned, she sat down on it. He grabbed the paper towels from the mini-fridge and ripped off a few panels. After stanching the bleeding around her foot, he examined the wound, which was still open and in need of a suture or two. The stitches would have to wait. EJ wrapped a fresh length of paper towel around Allie's foot, then placed it gently on the chest. "Keep it elevated for the time being," he said.

He found a waste bin by one of the two girls' desks and brought it to the edge of the futon. He placed the larger pieces of glass in the bin, then used a paper towel to pick up the smaller pieces. "Do you have any type of detergent?" he asked.

"No," Allie said. "My roommate has like Windex to clean her computer monitor. Oh, and I have laundry soap."

"Liquid?"

"Yeah. In the closet." She nodded at a door. EJ opened it and found rows of jackets, shirts, skirts, layer upon layer of jeans. Amidst the pile of shoes on the floor EJ saw a laundry bag and an orange bottle of Tide. He took the Tide and sat next to Allie on the futon, pouring the blue liquid on the stain, letting it seep into the carpet, the smell of fresh sheets comingling with the resiny odor.

"You've got a lot of clothes," he said.

"I don't have that much. Mom just sends me most of it anyway. It's not like I buy it all."

"That's nice of her."

"I guess. What is this? Some kind of hangover intervention? I'll have you know I was doing awesome this morning until I saw a cop car outside my dorm."

This reminded EJ that he was parked illegally and needed to get back on the road. He had no idea how much time he might have left, and the arbitrary clock in his head felt stolen from a bad recurring dream.

"Finish your Gatorade," he said. She downed it. He put his arm around her back, which he noticed was quite muscular now. He squeezed her left biceps. "You've been working out," he said.

"Obviously."

"Curls?"

"Other stuff, too. Rows, pull-ups, medicine ball."

"Nice," EJ said.

"Can I sleep some more? We can meet for brunch or something. This is ridiculous."

"I'd love that, but I have to go."

"You do?"

"I do."

She looked around her room and said, "Thanks for cleaning everything up. I guess. It's basically your fault there was a mess in the first place, but thanks for dealing with it. This was a really weird visit."

He nodded, then glanced through the window. "Maybe I should go back to school."

"What?"

"Maybe I should get some kind of degree."

"You don't want to be a cop anymore?"

"I'd still be a cop. Just feels like my role's changing anyway, so maybe if I went someplace like this, I could, I don't know, study something and get ahead."

"Sure," Allie said. "I'm not sure if someplace like this has exactly the kind of program you're talking about, but yeah, that all sounds good."

"Does it? Or does it sound dumb? I don't know where I'd get the scratch."

"Mom and Dad."

"They're paying enough already."

"Right."

"Right?"

"You don't have to remind me how expensive Amherst is."

"Allie—"

"Seriously, it stresses me out."

"No one wants you to feel stressed."

"Well, good." She glanced at him distrustfully. "I'm not fucking up, by the way. You can tell Mom and Dad that."

"Nobody thinks you're fucking up."

"I don't know if that's true. But honestly, if I *were* fucking up? It would be because this is exactly the kind of pressure that none of my friends have to deal with. Like, most of the other kids here? It's not that big a deal that they're at Amherst. Their parents went here or somewhere like it. It's just taken for granted. They're not supposed to be extra appreciative or anything. They don't have their parents looking at them like, 'Don't blow it, Allie!'" She was getting animated, her voice rising. "I *know* way too much of our money is going toward my tuition. I know it, okay? And I don't want to blow it either. But sometimes it feels like everything Mom and Dad do is for me, and sometimes it's easier not to think about it than it is to think about letting them down. I'm jealous of you. You get to do your own thing. You're like, outside the family, almost. I'd kill to be outside this family."

"No, you wouldn't," EJ said.

"You get what I'm saying though."

EJ's right hand was starting to shake again. He closed it in his left hand.

"What's the matter?" Allie asked him.

"Nothing. I have to go. Give me a hug."

They hugged while sitting on the couch. They both looked at the bloody paper towels around her foot when the hug was over. "Take care of your foot, okay?" he said. He squeezed her thigh.

"Looks like the bleeding stopped, at least," she said. "Thank you."

"Sure."

He lifted himself from the futon, stepped over the chest, went to the door, but stopped. "Allie, where'd you get a bong?"

"It's not even mine."

"Where'd you get the weed?"

She stared at him. She didn't want to say. She didn't have to say.

"Don't get it from home anymore, okay? I mean that."

She nodded. "Don't worry," she said. "You scared me straight."

"Love you, Allie."

"Love you, too."

"Who's Trip?" he asked.

"I don't know," she said, trying not to smile but smiling anyway. "I don't know why he wrote this on my arm."

IT'S TOO BAD EJ NEVER saw Dougie's Ranger. Had he noticed it in the dormitory parking lot, the LHS sticker in the rear window, the orange parking violation tucked under the wiper, he could have circled back to Allie's room and asked if Dougie was in there somewhere, and then Allie could have sheepishly pointed to the bedroom, and EJ could have questioned Dougie until it was revealed that he had been hiding there the entire time, listening to the exchange between brother and sister. EJ could have told Dougie that he was not to say a word about this visit to anyone—*anyone*—no matter who was asking. Dougie might have resisted at first, because it was in his nature to resist—he was a punk—but eventually he would have caved. Then, as they were reaching an understanding, EJ could have heard the vibrations coming from Dougie's pocket, and he could have asked to see the phone. EJ would have recognized the Lewiston number glowing on the screen. He would have silenced the call. Maybe even destroyed the phone.

But none of that happened because EJ never saw the Ranger. When Dougie's phone began to ring, he was alone in Allie's bedroom sitting on the edge of her bed, and Allie was alone on her futon drinking a second Gatorade, and EJ was alone in his cruiser, heading for the highway, driving west once again.

HE DROVE THROUGH ALBANY, SYRACUSE, and Buffalo. He stopped
at a gas station and bought a postcard and a stamp. The postcard
had a picture of Niagara Falls on it. He wrote:

> Mom, Dad—
>
>> Had to leave town. Wanted to say I'm fine but lost my
>> phone. Will call when I'm settled.
>> Stopped by to see Allie.
>> Who is Trip??
>> Love you both.
>
> —EJ

He dropped the card in a mail slot and kept driving, toward
a sun that went down in the haze between Cleveland and Toledo.
EJ glanced in the mirror from time to time but saw no cars that
looked familiar. He switched lanes, got off the highway, then back
on, but no one seemed to notice or care. He watched the rearview until all he could see were headlights, and then he faced
forward, faced the great dark plains. Tomorrow he would find
a small city with an auto mile. Somewhere with used-car deal-
erships all in a row. He would go to a bank, withdraw enough
cash to buy a used truck. Go to Walmart, buy some new clothes.
Leave the cruiser in the woods or lock the shifter in drive and let
it tumble into a quarry. Drive west into the sun, into the Rockies,
into the desert. West until he hit the other ocean.

Beyond Toledo, he pulled off the highway to fill up on gas
and take a piss. The bathroom was behind the store, and when
he located the door, it was locked. It was easier to piss in the

bushes than return to the store to find a key. A paved road layered in dirt circled the building. EJ found a shrub on the far side, in the dark. He had thrown his jacket away in a dumpster behind the motel, and now he was underdressed, so he shivered as he pissed. He had imagined it would be balmy by now, this far into the journey, but it wasn't. He wasn't traveling south—he was traveling west. Of course it wasn't balmy.

He zipped his fly, took a step toward his cruiser, and then he felt, though nothing made contact right away, movement behind him. He was about to turn when something hard, like iron, struck him in the ear. He swung up his arm instinctively, but he was already falling. More iron hit him. Boots, too. He tried to protect himself, but his muscles were no match for this hard thing, which kept hitting him. All he could think about was getting hit. There were multiple hard things. EJ tasted a metallic flood of blood in his mouth, and then one of the hard things landed another solid blow to the back of his head, and then the night swept in and never left.

13

WHEN MAEVE AND I WERE STILL LIVING IN MASSACHUSETTS AND JACK
was just a few weeks old, we went to a Red Sox game on Patriots'
Day, also known in Boston as Marathon Monday. A good friend
from Exeter, who at the time worked in the front office of the
Tampa Bay Rays, had given us tickets in the grandstand. Jack
slept through most of the game, cradled in our laps, bundled in
three or four layers of wool and fleece, and Maeve and I took
turns walking Jane around the concourse, feeding her hot dogs
and cotton candy. After the sixth or seventh inning, we left with
the rest of the crowd and descended upon Boylston Street. As
we approached the finish line of the marathon, close enough
to feel the energy of the race but not quite close enough to see
the competitors, we found ourselves jostling along increasingly
crowded sidewalks. Neither Maeve nor I felt it was worth it to
keep walking only to stand behind rows and rows of spectators,
shielding the kids from stray elbows and shoulders, so we ducked
into a bar called Bukowski's and hunkered down in a booth and

ordered poutine. Fifteen minutes later, two homemade bombs, pressure cookers loaded with nails and ball bearings, exploded about three blocks from where we sat. But the bar was so loud, we couldn't hear the blasts. We only learned what had happened when a neighboring table shushed us and told us to look at the TV. On the monitor we saw aerial footage of the finish line, smoke wafting through the air, and then when we looked through the windows of the bar, we saw real-life runners and fans fleeing past.

It was a near-miss—there's an alternate reality where the four of us keep walking and end up standing right by the explosions—but, in the end, our experience was hardly any different from someone who watched the events at home or on a monitor set to CNN in an airport. We were close to the incident, but we were never really in danger. Having Jack and Jane with us made the retrospective threat feel more heightened, but this is the kind of localized fear that all parents are forced to confront at some point.

A little over a decade prior, I went on an overnight camping trip near Big Bear with a dozen students from a charter school in LA. One of my buddies was a math teacher, and he asked if I would help chaperone the trip. He knew my hours at the restaurant were flexible, and I'd tutored at the school once or twice the previous spring so had already passed a background check. We were out there for three nights, hiking during the day, building campfires at night. We emerged from the woods on September 13th, 2001. The high school's vice principal—who had also been leading a trip—was waiting for us at the end of the trail, near the school bus. He had something very serious to tell us, he said. He then relayed what had happened in New York and Washington (although, because he had only recently been informed of the news himself, and it was so difficult to process, he got many of the facts mixed up and said that fighter jets had taken out the Twin Towers, and that America was at war already. It took me a day or two to understand, even on a surface level, what had actually transpired). The good news was that the school had contacted close family and friends, and none of us had been directly affected by the attacks. Everyone we loved was fine. If any of the members of our trip had been personally impacted, the school's administrators would have found us in the woods and brought us out right away. The message seemed mostly directed at my friend and me, perhaps because we were the only adults in the group, or perhaps because we were both from the East Coast and therefore more likely to be implicated than the students, whose relatives lived predominantly in Central and South America. I sometimes tell people that I must have been one of the last people on earth to find out about the attacks.

I guess my question is: Why do I feel the need to distinguish myself at all? Why would I ever wish, if not for a deeper relationship with a tragic event, for a more unusual relationship with a tragic event? At the time of that camping trip, I was in my midtwenties, ostensibly an adult, and yet I experienced what I would call a very puerile reaction to the vice principal's announcement. Some part of me wished that in fact I *had* known someone who had been on a plane, or in the Towers, or in the Pentagon. Some part of me wished that the school *had* interrupted the trip—for me—because I, the friend of the teacher, knew someone who was yet to be accounted for or because my brother (and I don't even have a brother) had been working in Tower 1 that day. To be clear, a *larger* part of me knew that this first impulse was morbid and solipsistic, and that I should be relieved to discover that everyone I knew was okay (and I *was* relieved, definitely), but still—what's with this first part? Why do I have it? Why does anyone have it?

I don't know, but maybe, or definitely, it has something to do with storytelling. When we narrate the past, it helps to place ourselves as close as possible to the center of the action. But the problem is: The vast majority of humans, or maybe just well-to-do Americans, never get all that close to the center of anything.

Instead we get this other life. One I try to be grateful for. I, Maeve, Jane, and Jack feel at home in Damariscotta—even if I always believed that to stay on the Midcoast, or even to return to it, would mean that I'd given up on the pursuit of something greater. Which may well be the case, but at a certain point the hardest thing about so much of your ambition going unfulfilled becomes finding out that you're basically okay with the way things have gone. And while it could be said that I haven't been at the center of any story that anyone would find very interesting, it could also be said that I've been near enough to a few of them. And I think—or hope—that all that matters, returning to that impulse I've been trying to identify—the desire to be somehow near-*er* a tragedy—is what I feel when I've achieved some distance from the episode, and the way I feel then is relieved. I'm happy I have what I have. I'm happy I haven't lost any of it along the way. I could have risked more—and perhaps lived to tell about it and therefore had *more* to tell—but with all apologies to my younger self, I can't think of a single instance from my past that I wish had gone another way.

ON THE MAY AFTERNOON OF the lacrosse reception held in the Thatches' backyard, our little village looked every bit as perfect as the ads in *Down East* magazine make it out to be. We left our home just after 4 P.M. that day. Maeve was in the passenger seat, Jane and Jack in the back. There's a sign now, just after the bridge, that says, WELCOME TO DAMARISCOTTA . . . MAINE'S

VACATION HAVEN, and at first the slogan struck us as a little phony and ridiculous, but then, after a couple hundred times driving past the sign, we stopped noticing it, stopped thinking of it as something that didn't quite fit. Over dinner recently, talking to friends from New York who were staying in our guest room (actually, Jack's room; we don't have a guest room), we inevitably started ticking off all the things we missed about the city, but as the list grew lengthier I felt we might be losing sight of the way we—or I—truly felt about our urban-to-rural decampment, so I said, "Well, hang on—we should acknowledge that we're in Maine's 'Vacation Haven' right now. I mean, that's a *pretty* big deal." Our friends laughed. Maeve and I only ever used Steph's moniker facetiously. But moments later I found myself defending the title. Look around, I told our friends: Our village still has the same old rustic charm—but with upgrades! Main Street's been freshly paved, the sidewalks trimmed in granite. The restaurants are—well, they're not *awesome*—but neither are they as uninspiring as they used to be. On the river side of Main Street, the parking lot still exists—Steph never succeeded in ripping it out and turning it into green space (mostly because—where would all the cars go?)—but skinny young maples have been planted by the water, their knobby trunks staked and guyed to the soil, and the town dock and boat ramp have been replanked and resurfaced, respectively. Next to the dock is a rock with a plaque on it. It's called the Raymond LeClair Municipal Pier now (Raymond's still alive—don't worry—it's just that Ed made the largest donation so got to pick the name). The pier is the place to be during Pumpkinfest, which has turned into an annual, well-attended Columbus Day event. Pumpkinfest features the traditional dropping of a 1,200-pound pumpkin onto a rusty Windstar minivan, and it also features the Pumpkinboat Regatta, a race around the harbor in which all participants drive hollowed-out giant gourds with outboard engines bolted to whichever end most resembles a stern.

While you're watching the regatta, you might notice black steel waste bins around the lot that beseech you to "Pitch in and keep the Coast CLEAR," and in general, the town feels clean and well maintained. If you look around the harbor and down the river, you can see a few new buildings—including a red condominium structure that seems a little too fancy to attract anyone we might approve of—but basically this stretch of coastline looks just the same as it would have a long, long time ago, back when the locals—the original locals—named our estuary the River of Little Fishes.

We were moving onto Bristol Road now, leaving Main Street behind, passing by the old colonials and through the shade of freshly blooming trees. Everything was a bright, almost neon, shade of green. The day was just right for a lacrosse reception, and I was glad that the Amherst players, parents, and coaches would get to see the Midcoast in full splendor.

YOU MIGHT REMEMBER THAT AT the reception Maeve and I split up (she was detained by the superintendent; I ran into Steph) and that when I finally found Ed, he was alone in his living room, staring at the photographs in the manila folder, looking for previously undetected clues, I presume. As I watched him, then as I slid the door open, I felt sure that I was interrupting some indiscernible, private train of thought. Now, though, looking back, that train of thought doesn't seem quite so indiscernible. After all, Ed was under siege. The DEA—with the help of the FBI and the Coast Guard, as it turns out—was investigating his former business. His neighbors to the east, lobstermen from Penobscot Bay, had launched an informal investigation of their own, according to the reports delivered by Chuck and EJ. Then there were Ed's old business associates in Lewiston, who had threatened to come down to Damariscotta in their new white-hulled boats at any moment and leverage their way back into the distribution network. They had made this threat to EJ, and then EJ had disappeared. For the last week, Ed had heard nothing, or next to nothing, from his son, and it was this mystery, above all else, that must have been occupying Ed's mind. All the other dangers would have seemed trivial in comparison. EJ had sent no word other than the postcard from Niagara Falls, which arrived in the middle of the week, and Ed, by then, must have begun to consider the possibility that his son was not coming back.

In fact, Ed did seem worried about his family when we spoke on the deck. He made sure Steph was looking for him, not EJ, and I think this was to gauge his wife's concern and make sure she wasn't as anxious about their son's whereabouts as Ed was. Then he asked me about the name Trip.

For three days, Ed had been wondering what it meant and why his son had phrased this one hint (and Ed was convinced that it *was* a hint) so cryptically. He had asked Chuck and Chief Hunt to look into the matter, see if anyone north or south of the border had a Trip in their organization, but their search had turned up no leads—as it never could have. They were investigating the wrong type of organization. They should have been checking the rosters of college lacrosse teams. Trip was just an Amherst junior whose name EJ had read, written like a tattoo, on Allie's forearm.

When I explained what I thought the name meant, Ed seemed to relax. Then he squeezed my trapezius muscle, hard, his grip as painful as a lobster's (every show of goodwill always accompanied by a corresponding show of strength) before he walked away, into the fog.

It should be noted that I'm not the only one who observed that Ed seemed a little off that day. Many of the visiting players, parents, and coaches likewise detected a distance. Keep in mind: They were expecting their host to be convivial and jovial, the only way they had ever known him to be. At all the previous receptions, he had been one of the most noticeably engaged parents, never the loudest voice amongst the boosters—at least once the games were over—but amongst the most devoted. Not the day before the Bowdoin game though. And who could blame him? I may have helped him solve a central enigma—*Who is Trip??*—but plenty of other, more substantial mysteries remained unsolved. By removing that one source of anxiety, I had also robbed him of his only clue.

ED DIDN'T GO TO THE dock right away (where Steph was most likely to be found, waiting with the others to take the boat out) but instead went to the big black grill at the bottom of the meadow and stood there watching Brittany Dodwell, who was smoking a cigarette and poking at the seaweed.

"Ed," she said after a while.

"Brittany."

She would later tell a DEA agent that she thought Ed seemed preoccupied, like a man who had meant to ask a question but couldn't remember what it was (it's possible he had intended to ask Brittany about the pasta, a dish that he had promised Coach Morris would be served, but which, for the record, was never served).

"You okay?" Brittany asked him.

"Yuh."

"You gonna get me that lobster soon?"

"Yuh."

The smoke was rising out of the seaweed, drifting into the

air and upriver on a southwesterly. Downriver, the sky was taper-ing into its own kind of smoke—cold fog, billowing up from the ocean. Ed glanced along the path of burning tiki torches, down the pier, which appeared to fade into the distance. Tied to the float, his lobster boat and the faint lines of its antennae were just barely visible. The deck was already full of young women, a few of their parents, too. They were supposed to go out on the river and haul a string of traps, the ones that Ed and Chuck had already preloaded with lobsters.

"Now would be good," Brittany said, nodding at the weather. "Don't wanna lose your way out there."

"I know my way," Ed said.

She shoveled at the seaweed, took a drag from the cigarette. "EJ here yet?" she asked.

"Not yet."

"I was hoping to see him."

"Yuh—me, too."

Ed gave Brittany the same goodbye he gave me—a squeeze above the collarbone—and then he went down the ramp to the *Miss Stephanie*.

Those already on the boat saw Ed go to Steph, who was standing by the bow, holding the line, and engage in a brief, hushed conversation, but the engine was on, rumbling loudly, so no one could hear what was said.

Steph would later recount to me that she was expressing con-cern about Allie: "She had just showed me a gift that Dougie Page gave her. Allie asked me what she should do because it was a nice gift, but she wasn't interested in Dougie."

"What kind of gift?" I asked her. This was in our final interview.

"A necklace," she said. "I bet that kid didn't even know how much it was worth. I don't think Allie did either. She thought she did, but it was even nicer than that. There was a diamond on this thing you wouldn't believe."

"What'd you end up doing with it?"

"What did *I* end up doing with it?"

"Well, yeah. Or—what happened to it?"

"I wouldn't know."

I waited.

"It was Allie's," she said, speaking very deliberately, looking almost offended by the idea that she might know more about the necklace than she'd already divulged. I stared at her for a moment, trying to decide if she could really be so oblivious to the implication here. If what Steph was saying was true, it was entirely possible that Allie *still* had the stolen necklace. I hoped— I really hoped—that she didn't. "What did Ed say?"

"Nothing, really. I asked him if he thought the necklace was stolen, and he said he didn't know, but that it might explain the boats. 'Which boats?' I said, and he told me the boys had been seeing lobster boats lurking around the peninsula. They weren't sure who they belonged to, but maybe someone had seen Dougie and come looking for him."

"Ed didn't say what he planned to do about it?"

"He said he'd look into it."

"And then you got on the boat?"

"And then we got on the boat."

Once they were aboard, the lines were dropped and Chuck steered the vessel into the river. At some point, Ed took the helm. He pushed the throttle forward and powered through the river in a wide arc, heading south. High tide was approaching. Some of the girls were on the bow, and Ed asked them to sit low so he could see the buoys as they flashed toward the boat. They were running right down the middle of the river—from where they were, they couldn't see either shoreline.

"I've tried to navigate the Midcoast in a thick fog," Chip told me over the phone during one of our interviews. "It's hard. Even with modern technology. Ed wasn't even using his GPS. I was watching him closely. He just knew where to go. It was quite the feat of navigation."

Those players who weren't on the bow were sitting on the white bench in the stern, where the lobster barrels used to go. The women were shivering and huddling close to one another but laughing and shouting over the loud twin engines. More women and parents stood between them, the wind bending around the wheelhouse and blowing their hair back. Chuck stood in the center of the deck, wearing his orange rubber overalls and boots, a cut-off sweatshirt showing off his hairy arms. He wore black rubber gloves, ready to handle the lobster. Behind Ed, Steph sat in one of the captain's chairs. Sandy Smith sat in the other captain's chair, and Chip stood in front of her.

When I visited the Smiths' house—on our way to that wedding in Massachusetts—Chip met me in the foyer, wearing a faded polo and a beard of white stubble. He looked freshly showered, comb lines still etched in his hair. He led me through the kitchen to the den, flicked on the lights, and there it all was: the pictures of Chip and Sandy, pictures of the boat, the oil painting. I looked around at the bookcases, the trophies, the grandfather clock, the Amherst chairs. And then Chip told me about the conversation that had taken place with Ed in that very room, told me about returning to look at the painting when he read the article in the *Globe*. I had a notebook, and I was jotting down everything I could, too excited to keep my letters from smearing across the page. When he was done with the account, I thanked him again and again and said I would be on my way now but then remembered I had a few more questions to ask and also needed to snap some pictures. He said go ahead, so I photographed the walls with my phone. I would study them when I got home.

On the way back through the kitchen, passing a marble island the size of a parade float, I asked Chip how old the house was and he said not as old as it felt, and then as we walked through a hallway and past a watercolor portrait of all four Smiths posed on a silver couch, Victoria and Trip much younger, I asked how his kids were doing, but instead of replying directly, Chip reminded me that I had wanted to know about Ed's behavior on the day before the Amherst-Bowdoin lacrosse game, and I said yes, thanks, I did. Steph had insisted that Chip and Sandy arrive in advance of all the other guests. She wanted to give them a guided tour of our town. It was the Smiths' first trip to the Midcoast in over two decades.

"Well, he seemed quiet," Chip said.

"Yeah, I thought so, too," I said. "Did he say anything in the car?"

"Not really. But maybe because Steph was doing all the talking."

"What was she talking about?"

"Oh, just—this improvement, that improvement."

"It's come a long way, hasn't it?"

"What, Damariscotta?"

"Yes."

"I suppose." But this was all he gave me. I expected him to pay us a few compliments—as anyone who had ever been to our village tended to—but Chip seemed reluctant to place Damariscotta in a more positive light.

"You didn't like the changes?" I asked. We were back in the foyer by then.

"No, no, I did," he said. "It's just—well, first, I should admit that I was a bit preoccupied that day."

"By what?"

"Oh, just—here's the thing: Damariscotta was very different from the way I remembered it. I guess one of the things Sandy and I used to love about the town was how untouched it seemed."

"Steph says that all the time."

"And yet she touched it."

"Right," I said. "No, I know. She definitely touched it."

He started to say something, then stopped. He appeared to be weighing his words carefully. "There used to be something a little more authentic about the *lack* of amenities," he said.

"That's probably true."

"Now it feels more like the Cape or the Hamptons. Or other towns in Maine. I guess that's the way it always happens. Visitors go to the Midcoast because they think they want something rustic and industrial—the way life should be and all that—but really what they want is rustic and industrial *plus* one good coffee shop, and if they're staying for longer than a weekend, then they want all that plus *two* good coffee shops, because the first one gets boring after a while—"

"It really does."

"I understand. But then the tourists also want a T-shirt shop that sells gifts to bring home for the in-laws, and then a designer boutique because they weren't expecting it to get so cool at night and because they've talked themselves into spending more money than they'd budgeted for just because they're on vacation and because it'd be nice to find a knit sweater that matches exactly with their notion of what a well-heeled mariner on the Maine coast might wear on exactly such an evening, and so the town tries to provide all these services until, before you know it, it's made enough concessions, on behalf of convenience and some imagined version of the town that only exists in brochures—to eventually, not that anyone's really noticed, because it takes place over years or decades—trade 'authenticity' for what feels more like an airbrushed portrait of itself. A caricature. Buildings shaped like factories but containing everything someone from out of town thinks they don't want but do want, or thinks they do want but don't want."

"So Damariscotta should have stayed in its lane," I said.

I meant it as a joke, but Chip seemed to take it seriously. "You know, it probably should have," he said.

Sandy came down the wide staircase right at that moment, wearing tennis whites, descending like the commodore of a yacht club. "I'm heading to the court," she said to Chip, once we had introduced ourselves. She stood with her hands on her waist, legs shoulder width apart—the stance of a jock. She wore tight shorts instead of a skirt. On her right wrist, she wore a terry cloth wristband. And on her left hand, she wore the most eye-catching diamond I have ever seen attached to another human. I couldn't have guessed how many carats were welded to that platinum band, but Maeve's diamond is a half carat, and Sandy's stone had to be ten times the size of it. Slowly I realized that I was staring at the ring, and that the Smiths were waiting patiently for me to bring my eyes back to conversation level. So I did. And yet, I had questions about that diamond. It looked exactly like the one I had seen in the case files (where the owner was listed as Sandra Richards, Sandy's maiden name). But it couldn't be the same diamond. Could it? Was it a replica? Paid for by whom? Insurance? Insurance. However, in that case, when had they replaced the stolen ring? And had Sandy ever worn the diamond around Ed? Or Steph? Had her illness—the lupus—made her joints too swollen to slide her rings on? And was there ever a moment in which Steph and Sandy were wearing different versions of the same ring at the same time? There must have been. Maybe on the boat. But no one had ever noticed. Or at least, no one had ever let on that they noticed.

Another grandfather clock in the foyer was telling me that it really was time to go, time to pick up Maeve in Boston and head to my former student's wedding, so I thanked Chip and Sandy for having me and said I'd show myself out, but Chip insisted on walking me to the car. He held the massive door open, then followed me down the pebbled walkway.

I had parked in front of their three-car garage, so had to execute a five- or six-point turn to get the Subaru pointed in the right direction. As the metal gate was sliding itself open, I rolled down my window and waved to Chip. He waved back, but then he held one finger in the air, as though something had just occurred to him.

He took a step toward the car and called out, "I don't know if you're aware, Andrew, but the statute of limitations in Maine is six years. So we couldn't have pressed charges, even if we'd wanted to."

"Oh," I said. "No, I didn't know that."

"Just an FYI. For your book."

"Okay," I said. "Appreciated."

He waved again and smiled—his first real smile of the day—then told me to drive safely on my way to the wedding.

IT WASN'T UNTIL RECENTLY, WHEN I was writing about that visit to Weston, that I went back to the notebook I'd had with me that day and found Chip's parting words, which I'd recorded right away but forgotten about in the intervening months. He'd chosen a strange tense, I realized: Instead of *We couldn't press charges*, he said, *We couldn't* have *pressed charges*, implying an earlier time frame than I'd first understood, a time frame that had closed at some point. Probably the distinction didn't matter. But the slim possibility that it did kept bothering me. I called Chip, but he didn't pick up, so I sent him an email, asking if he'd meant to use that tense and also when, precisely, he'd looked up the law on Maine's statute of limitations, because even if he and Sandy couldn't have pressed charges, there were other measures they could have taken, as I was sure he was aware.

I'm still waiting to hear back.

FOR WHAT IT'S WORTH, WHEN I asked Steph if she knew that she was in possession of Sandy's ring, she looked down at her left hand and said she had owned what she was wearing for over twenty-five years. Therefore it was *her* ring. Sandy had her own ring, she said.

"Well," I said.

"Well what?"

"Nothing—I just—I'm not sure if Sandy would see it that way."

She shook her head. "I don't know how Sandy would see it, but that's none of my business." She looked out the window, then across the room, at Ben's old workbench. "And also, you're missing the point."

"I am?"

"Yeah."

She stood and went to the workbench, opened the top drawer, removed something, and came back to the living room. In her hand was a small white box, Scotch tape keeping the lid on. She handed it to me and sat down.

"Go ahead," she said, "open it."

I unsealed the tape and lifted the lid. Inside was an object, or the ghost of an object, that I hadn't seen for over a quarter century: a bracelet made of twine. Back from the dead, I thought. But no, it couldn't have been the bracelet I'd thrown in the dumpster. It had to be something else, a newer version. Steph had already told me about her conversation with Ed on the Kerrys' dock, Ed assuring her that he could make her another bracelet, but she hadn't told me that he'd actually done it. The twine had dried out by now. I could still smell the sweet wax, but only faintly. The bracelet, like the ring, was a replica, although when a replica outlasts its original by so many years, it's hard to argue that it's not the more important artifact. This was the point Steph was trying to make about the ring, I guess, but the bracelet had been lost, whereas the ring had been stolen and destroyed, so to my mind the analogy didn't fit, not the way Steph would have liked.

"Ed gave me that bracelet when we were teenagers," she said.

"But you know," I said cautiously, "that this isn't the original, right?"

"Well, of course I know, Andrew. I mean, that's *kind of* how Ed and I got together. He thought I'd just ignored this nice thing he made for me, and I felt bad about that, and it was like the easiest way to make him feel better was to just let him make me a new bracelet and tell him I loved it."

"And you know what happened to the first one?"

"Ed said he gave it to you, and you sent it to me, but it never got there. I guess the post office must have lost it."

I hesitated, a little stunned to hear this version of the story. "That's what he told you?"

"Yup."

I stared out the window, unable to speak. If Ed had really believed that I'd sent the bracelet, not lost it, then he'd been treating me with much more trust than I deserved.

"Anyway," Steph said, looking at me like maybe she should ask if I was feeling okay, "the point is: That bracelet is way more

important than any piece of jewelry. Ed *made* the bracelet. I did
love it. I've always loved it."

ED BROUGHT THE BOAT INTO Seal Cove, where the loaded traps
had been sunk, and then he pulled back on the throttle. The fog
was thicker than ever, and for a moment the visitors on the boat
felt certain they were lost. They were surrounded by pot buoys,
none of them, it seemed, painted yellow and pink.

Normally Ed would have used the small rock island in the
center of the cove as a directional marker, but by now it was
high tide, and the island was submerged. He guided the boat in
a circle. They couldn't see more than ten feet.

"Hey!" one of the young women shouted. She was pointing
at a dark shape in the river, which seemed to be resting, somehow, just beneath the surface. A seal. On the island. It slithered
on its belly and dipped into the water. For Allie, the seal was no
big deal, but for many of her teammates it was the highlight of
the ride thus far. (I'm not sure which lacrosse player saw the seal
first—both Dana and Kim told me they had been the one to get
everyone's attention—so maybe they saw the seal simultaneously.
Maybe it was a tie.)

The seal indicated to Ed where the island was, and once he
knew that, he could find his traps. He steered in their direction,
then saw a marker, the one he had been looking for, materialize
from the fog. He went to it, letting the buoy bump against the side
of the boat, idling and waiting as Chuck leaned over and grabbed
the long wooden stem. Chuck pulled on it and lifted the slimy
green line from the water. He brought it to the stainless-steel pulley, which had never been used—it was part of the *Miss Stephanie's* renovations, there only for show up until that point—and he
looped the line over the wheel and asked the girls to help him pull.

On a real working lobster boat, there would have been a hydraulic hauler, but Ed's boat was a pleasure cruiser now, not a commercial fishing vessel. However, with all the women pulling—all of whom had been building their cores since the fall, getting stronger and stronger—they could replace the force of the hauler, and it was shallow where they were—Ed and Chuck had picked this location on purpose—so within a minute, the first trap was looming up from the darkness, breaching the surface and swinging toward the gunwale. It was loaded with blue flapping and snapping lobsters.

"Keep pulling," Chuck said. "Lift with your backs, not your legs."

The women pulled on the line again, and the second trap emerged, full of lobsters.

"And that," Chip Smith told me, "was when we sensed the presence of the other boat."

It didn't take shape right away. There were those on the *Miss Stephanie* who claim they heard it before they saw it. Ed cut the engine, and the cove went silent. Chuck kept hauling on the line with the girls, but he looked at Ed, brow raised, questioning. Now that the cove had gone so quiet and calm, they could hear the other boat again. It was at a distance, dampened by the weather, higher in pitch than the *Miss Stephanie*'s outboards. The third trap was up on the rail now, and Chuck was helping the girls bring it aboard, but he was still looking at Ed. Steph stood from the captain's chair and said to Ed, "Who is that?"

Ed must have been running through the possibilities. It could have been a local lobsterman, a day cruiser, a small yacht from a more southern state (although it was early in the spring for that), but it would have seemed to Ed that the boat was much more likely to be coming from Lewiston, or the nearest Coast Guard station, or whichever town Dougie had visited last.

And then the boat finally appeared. It was heading straight for the *Miss Stephanie*. As it whined closer, they could see the white hull. It moved quickly through the fog, and all the guests on Ed's boat were watching it now, frozen and silent. The boat exploded from the mist—it wasn't a lobster boat, nor was it a Coast Guard cutter (there were no orange or blue stripes on the bow). There was no wheelhouse, just a stand-alone center console with a steering wheel and a low windshield and someone manning the wheel and throttle. The boat began to turn, white foam leaping off its hull, began to slide parallel to the *Miss Stephanie*.

Those who knew the boat's captain could recognize her by now: Chief Hunt. She was standing at the wheel, wearing a yellow raincoat over her uniform.

She brought her throttle down and slid sideways into Ed's boat with a thud. "Coming in hot," she said. Then she saluted the other guests aboard the boat and said, "Hey there, folks," before turning her attention to Ed. "Ed, can I talk to you for a quick sec?"

NOBODY KNOWS WHERE CHIEF HUNT is now, so it's impossible to say precisely what she told Ed once he stepped foot onto her boat. None of the Thatches' guests were able to hear the conversation. But it's not hard to guess. Hunt had just learned that EJ's cruiser had been found, burned to black in a forest in Ohio, and that EJ's body had been discovered inside it, and that identifying it—officially—was only a matter of formality at this point. At their house, once the lobstering expedition was over, there would be state troopers waiting to speak with Ed and Steph. The police would investigate EJ's death. They would associate it with the two corpses found in the sedan—also burned to black, coincidentally, or perhaps not—in the parking lot by the old mill in

Augusta. More questions would follow, and if Ed didn't want to face those questions, now was the time to make his exit.

And then Ed was back on his own boat, pulling his hat down low, not even acknowledging that he had any passengers, just pushing the throttle forward and swinging the boat around. As Chief Hunt tore off into the fog, Ed went in the other direction, back toward home. According to Chip, Steph and Allie both went to Ed. They wanted to know what Chief Hunt had said, but from what Chip could tell—and this has been corroborated by everyone else on board—Ed didn't say a word to his wife or daughter in response. The boat was going faster and faster, racing through the fog, buoys ripping by on either side of the boat.

"Everyone was a little scared by then," Chip told me. "We didn't know what was going on, and the boat seemed to be going dangerously fast considering the conditions. I leaned toward Ed and asked if everything was all right—but Chuck grabbed me by the arm and told me to stop talking. Actually, he told me to shut the fuck up."

IF YOU HAD CUT TO ME, at that very moment, you would have seen me standing in the Thatches' meadow, serving as assistant coach while one of the Amherst players instructed Jane and Jack how to throw and catch a lacrosse ball. I had decided not to tell Maeve about the photographs I'd seen until later, until we were off the Thatches' property, but half my mind was still sorting through every possible explanation. The Amherst player and her friend, neither of whom had gone out on the boat, had noticed Jane eyeing them as they threw the ball back and forth. Amy was the player's name—she was a senior, not someone with whom Allie was particularly close—and she was standing behind my daughter, showing her how to pull with the bottom hand, push with the top hand. Jack was also holding a crosse, but I had made the mistake of telling him it was a girl's stick—the men's game allows for a deeper pocket—and since then, his interest had faded. Maeve was standing by, taking pictures with her phone. Jack and I were next to each other, angled in the direction of the river. Jane and Amy were facing us, Amy in a crouch, carefully placing my daughter's hands in the correct positions on the stick. I remember Amy smiling at the progress they were making— Jane is not a quick learner but she does put the work in—and then pointing at my son, showing Jane where to throw the ball. But when Amy looked in our direction, her smile began to wane. Something had caught her eye. She stood straight and looked behind us, up the hill. That's when I turned, too, and saw the line of state police cruisers, five in all, burning down the driveway, emerging from the trees at the bottom of the hill, then stopping in front of the house.

The officers left their vehicles—some in uniform, some in plain clothes, wearing police badges on chains around their necks—and fanned out. Several officers headed for the house, several others walked straight onto the meadow.

Three of them came in our direction. The man in front, a tall mustachioed cop wearing a black windbreaker, jeans, and black sneakers, asked me if I knew where Ed Thatch was.

"He went out on the river in his boat," I said. "He'll be back. What's this about?"

The officer nodded behind him at one of his colleagues, who pulled out a walkie-talkie, stepped away, his back to us, and said something into the receiver. Though I didn't know why they might be looking for Ed, I presumed the officer was alerting his colleagues farther down the coast, telling them to keep an eye out for a boat. That would be no easy task though. Ed's boat was the same color as the weather.

Clearly Ed was a person of interest, already; otherwise the police wouldn't have been rolling so deep. Whatever they were after, the three men started walking downward, toward the pier, and as they left, Maeve came to my side. Jack hugged my leg, and I held him by the shoulder. "What's going on?" Maeve asked me.

"I don't know," I said.

"I hope everyone's all right."

"Me, too."

As the three officers disappeared into the mist, I began to see other people appearing from the direction of the pier, coming uphill between the glowing tiki torches—players and parents who had gone out on the boat. Just before I lost sight of the officers, they said something to the first group of women, and the women pointed, and the officers started jogging. Then they were gone.

"I'm gonna see what's up," I told Maeve, and I started walking toward the shoreline. As I passed the young women, they looked pale and serious. I asked if everything was all right, and they told me they didn't know.

Each step toward the end of the meadow extended my vision by a corresponding foot or so. First I saw the pier, then I saw the dock, and then, once I had stepped onto the top of the ramp, I saw the rippled surface of the river—just barely. There were five shapes on the float: three officers, Steph Thatch, and Allie Thatch. But there was no boat. No Ed. No Chuck.

If what Steph has told me is true, Ed never informed her or Allie that EJ was dead. He couldn't bring himself to do it, apparently, or didn't feel he had the time. I don't know. All I know is that he let the officers deliver the news to Steph and Allie— I watched it happen. I saw them collapse into each other. I saw them learn that their son, their brother, was dead. They learned this as Ed guided his boat onto the river and into the fog.

_____

THEY WERE HEADING SOUTH BY then, carving through the traps. The tide was going out and gave the boat an extra knot or two. Ed and Chuck needed all the help they could get if they were going to reach the mouth of the river before the authorities moved out and blocked their passage. Ed gave the engines more gas, as much as they could take. The *Miss Stephanie* could still motor as fast as or faster than any other lobster boat on the coast. They hit forty knots, then forty-five, the boat lifting, planing, and leveling, the engine roaring against the walls of gray, traps bursting from the ether, racing past the hull, tumbling into the wake. If they could make it to the open sea, they could get lost out there—this must have been the plan. I'm sure Ed was already telling himself that he would send word to his family from whichever coast would have him next. It's even possible, by now, that he's already done so, and that Steph's already heard from him. For all I know, there's a time and place where they're meant to reunite, to live onward together—I can picture them in the Caribbean or in the Gulf of Mexico or in Southeast Asia, posted up at a beachside bar, drinking whatever the local beer is, whatever native cocktail comes in a coconut. Ed has shaved his beard. Steph has cut her hair and dyed it blond or black. They're in a place where there's a kind of camaraderie amongst the locals and the expats. Ed and Steph have been there long enough to become a part of the economy, to see a newcomer as fresh blood, or someone to be wary of. On this beach, under the mountains, at the edge of the jungle, Ed and Steph are amongst fellow fugitives. It's like Alaska but hot, full of sunburned Kiwis and Aussies in Croakies and short khaki shorts. Finally Steph has built a new life for herself, somewhere other than Maine, surrounded by people who are not Mainers. That Ed is there, too, would surprise her younger self but probably not her older self. At this point, after spending so much of their lives together, she wouldn't know how to pass her days with anyone else.

She'll tell Allie, maybe, but no one else. She'll wish she could tell EJ—wish she could tell him a lot of things—and then she'll wish she was the type of person who believed that he was still listening. When it's time for her to leave, and she determines that the coast is clear, she'll go without a word, and the house will be empty and our town will be without a mayor (which it will be shortly—the process of removing her from office has already begun. Although I'm not sure impeaching Steph Thatch is in our best interests. She's done a good job, despite everything).

Once Steph has finally left us for good, our world will go back to normal. We'll have to find something else to discuss at the dinner table. I'll have to find something else to do with my days. And that's another process that's already in the works. Now that my investigation into the Thatches has effectively come to an end, I'll be moving on, which feels like a relief. For a while there, I was having nightmares. Sometimes I arrived in scene to discover that I was playing the role of a loyal Thatch minion, sometimes Ed and Chuck were coming after me because I had broken into the lobster pound or stolen one of their boats, but the dreams always ended the same way: At some point, I would turn, and Ed would be pointing a gun at my forehead. Then I'd wake up.

Now that I'm done, or almost done, I've been trying to put more energy into teaching. This year I'm running a creative writing workshop, seniors only, and we've established a few rules. One is no dream sequences. Another is that you're required to splice at least a little of your own DNA into everything you write. In this directive, I'm trying to correct an early trend, especially apparent in those short stories written by my male students, an attentiveness to plot that was overwhelming any sense of humanity. In just five pages, quarterbacks were driving pickup trucks off bridges, breaking up with improbably perfect girlfriends, winning state championships on ninety-seven-yard romps that unfolded over the course of a single sentence. Hoping to inspire a deeper look inward, I had all the kids bring in some small personal object, something that they, and only they, would find important. I brought something, too: the pen I'd given to Maeve the first time we ever talked, the one that still says RIOTT instead of MARRIOTT. I'd put it in my bedside table that night, forgotten all about it, then found it again when we moved to Boston. Any story I'd ever want to tell, I told my class, no matter how crazy, where it was set, who the main characters were, would include this old pen, or something like it. The pen's not worth a penny, I said, no more than a piece of twine, but if you write about what's meaningful to you, even if you're just some nobody from Maine who's not doing all that much with his life, who's watching other people do a whole lot more, then your readers might be able to connect with your story, even if they're nothing like you. You can make something from whatever's on hand, I told my class, and if you do, you'll find that a piece of you has ended up deep in the fibers.

Next weekend, a long weekend, Maeve and I have a trip planned to New York, just us, no kids, something we haven't done for a long while. We'll be staying with old friends in Brooklyn, and I found discount theater tickets and made a reservation at a restaurant that had nothing available before ten-thirty on a Friday. When we're not traveling, I'm planning to fix the window in the office and vacuum the living room and—who knows— maybe even stake out a garden for next summer. A small one. Just a few heads of lettuce and some eggplant. I like eggplant. Right now we get it at the farmers market. It's a good farmers market, established just a couple years ago after Steph dreamed it into existence. She found space for it in the field behind Lincoln

High—the fields our teams used to play on before the artificial
turf went in. This all happened when the town budget was running at a deficit, but Ed had his crew build two dozen stalls for
the vendors out of plywood, and his team installed them all, free
of charge. Ed was happy to help, he told me over lunch at King
Eider's Pub during one of the rare occasions when we spoke
about something other than Allie's lacrosse career. It was our last
meeting. Ed drank two beers. I drank three. Allie had already
sent her application in to Amherst, and I'd spent the early part
of our lunch reassuring Ed that it was a smart decision, that
she'd be fine there, that he had nothing much to worry about.
Fall was upon us, and there was a gray mist overtaking Main
Street. No one else was in the restaurant. The silence of the off-
season was like a rustling of fallen leaves: a pot clanking in the
kitchen, the ice melting and resettling in the bar, Ed thumbing
cash onto the table to pay for our meal. He didn't really care one
way or the other if the town had a farmers market, he said, tuck-
ing the cash into the checkbook and sliding along the shellacked
wooden booth, snugging his hat down low as he went, but he'd
made a promise, a long time ago, to give Steph everything she
deserved, so if this was what she wanted, then he wanted her to
have it.

Acknowledgments

When a book takes eleven years to write, you end up saying thank you (and sorry) to a lot of wonderful people. So here goes:

Thank you to Mom and Dad for loving me always and trusting me to find the right path, even when that path was taking me straight from jazz band to hockey practice. And thanks to the rest of the family for being there right from the get-go and/or down the home stretch. (Grammy and Papa, Judy, Michael, Brian, Daria, Corinne and Jason, all the Whites, all the O'Briens!)

If I hadn't been randomly assigned Mark Sweeney as a roommate, or hadn't taken a class with George Mangan, Ernest Hebert, or John Rassias, I might never have become a writer.

Thanks to those I met at Columbia, particularly my classmates and workshop professors: Sam Lipsyte, Jonathan Dee, David Ebershoff, and Mark Poirier (who might be more responsible for this book's publication than anyone).

Early readers gave me encouragement and some really valuable notes, so big thanks to Dean Adams, Sean Cleary, Ronnie

Fletcher, Sarah Fuld, Rachael Dillon Fried, Jesse Klempner, Andrew Martin, Caitie Parker, and Dave Smith. Matt Lally showed real courage by reading countless versions of this novel, and Alex Plapinger gave me a boost when I needed it most. Matt Heineman has helped me in every way possible, including giving me a job when I had foot surgery and couldn't wait tables anymore. Captain Dodwell put us up—on a smelly fishing boat, but still—and gave us work when Erin and I were clearly pretty desperate.

There's an excellent book on the history of Maine called *The Lobster Coast,* which informed some of what my characters say about lobstering, so thank you to that book's very knowledgeable author, Colin Woodard.

Thanks to Richard Ford, Doug Preston, and David Benioff for all their good advice on writing and the business of writing.

Thanks to Kirby Kim for taking me on and making the book readable and getting the right people to read it, and thanks also to Eloy Bleifuss for all the hard work and especially the smart and thoughtful notes.

Thank you to Jillian Buckley for finding this novel and helping to make it just what it always wanted to be—but better than that!—and for getting everyone else to believe in it, too.

Thank you to St. Sebastian's School for letting me share my love of writing in a place that thinks it's just as important as I do. And for funding a sabbatical that allowed me to spend time with family and finish the novel. Students and colleagues, thanks for all the conversations. I've learned a lot. Go Arrows!

Thank you to Leo for liking my stories and telling me I'm funny. You're the best guy ever.

And this book is for Erin, my favorite writer. Dear Dolphin Stryker, thanks for everything. Love, Ice Dawg.

THE MIDCOAST

Adam White

A Book Club Guide

A CONVERSATION BETWEEN ADAM WHITE
AND DAVID BENIOFF

David Benioff is the bestselling author of the novels *The 25th Hour* and *City of Thieves*, and co-creator of *Game of Thrones*.

David Benioff: You first began writing *The Midcoast* in grad school, and ultimately it took you ten years to complete it. How did the book evolve over time? How did you grow as a writer?

Adam White: It was actually eleven years! I serialized chapters of my first draft in workshop and had a full manuscript by the end of my MFA program, but that early draft was written entirely in the third person. I had told the story of the Thatches, and to some extent I had built the world, but the novel wasn't where I wanted it to be yet. And other readers— friends, family, an agent or two—seemed to agree. I kept working on it, but eventually I decided that what was missing was more of my own voice and point of view. So that's when

I decided to introduce the first-person narrator. I rewrote everything from this new perspective, and I gave Andrew, my narrator, a biography that was similar to my own, so that I would always be confident that he was seeing the world the way I'd see it. My feeling was that if he felt real, or if the lens that he was looking through felt authentic, then it would make the Thatches' more extraordinary story feel real, too. It was important for Andrew to be the same age as the Thatches, but the Thatches were older than me, so at first I felt like I knew Andrew as a younger person but had to imagine who he might be as a married father of two. Of course, the more I worked on the novel and the more time passed, the closer I grew to Andrew. I got married and had a kid. After a few years, he wasn't that much older than I was. So I was putting more and more of myself into the novel, my anxieties about not having finished it included. I would've loved to write the book faster, but it wouldn't be the same book, so in a way, I'm glad I had to take my time with it.

DB: Switching from third person to first person must have taken a lot of work. How did it affect the novel?

AW: Well, I already had the story of the Thatches, which hasn't changed all that much. Some sections of *The Midcoast* still feel like they're told in the third person. These are the scenes that Andrew's reconstructed using interviews and research. Of course, Andrew's own story is new, and I wanted him to be implicated in the Thatches' rise on some level, so I placed him on the dock when Ed meets Steph, and I had Ed give Andrew the bracelet intended for Steph. But mostly what Andrew adds is context, perspective, and more avenues through which to explore all the big themes I was interested in.

He allowed me to access more of the texture of Damariscotta and the surrounding towns and counties. Once I started writing in the first person, I realized that I was having more fun, and also that I was able to keep the story intact while adding the depth and thematic complexity that I'd been looking for.

DB: Andrew, like you, is a teacher and lacrosse coach. What has lacrosse taught you about writing and storytelling? And what has writing taught you about lacrosse?

AW: I don't know that the skills I employ as a lacrosse coach are all that transferable to writing, but that's actually one of the best things about coaching lacrosse. When I'm on the sidelines, I'm using a very different part of the brain. That's not to say that playing lacrosse and coaching lacrosse haven't impacted my writing. Obviously the sport plays a large role in the novel. Lacrosse felt like the perfect sport for Allie to pick up because it's viewed as such a symbol of privilege in certain circles. Even though the sport's played much more widely than it was when I was growing up, it's still considered a prep school pastime. So bringing in some of what I've observed as a lacrosse coach helped me get at the class dynamics that I wanted to discuss, especially in the later chapters as Allie turns into a star athlete and heads off to Amherst.

As for what kind of impact my writing has on lacrosse, I don't know, maybe none? Although I like to think I'm relatively creative for a coach. Every year we have a different theme for our team, and I probably put more energy than I should into designing what our shooting shirts will look like. A couple years ago, our theme was the wolf, and I had a lot of fun mocking up wolf shirts with lightning bolts and a giant moon. Did this lead to our team having a better record? I don't think so.

DB: As Andrew says on the first page, people make all sorts of assumptions about Maine. What makes Maine so compelling—both as a setting for a novel and in people's psyches?

AW: Well, I think one of the things that made me want to write this book was that I felt like people often have no idea what it's really like to live year-round in Maine. And I should say, full disclosure, that I haven't been living year-round in Maine since I was a teenager. But I think people visit Maine in the summer, and the state is just what they want it to be, maybe just what they want America to be, like a Rockwell painting. Or a Hopper painting. And Hopper is someone who in fact spent a lot of time painting the Maine coast. In the summer, the weather is close to perfect, cooler than wherever the tourists are coming from. Many parts of Maine feel untouched. Yes, there are some touristy towns, but it's not hard to drive down the peninsula and end up at a harbor that remains unmoved by the outside world. Which is what people come for. One of the characters, Chip Smith, delivers a monologue toward the end of the book about what a visitor thinks they don't want but actually do want, which is for a town to cater to their desires. Most visitors to Maine want to believe that they've arrived in a place where they might live if only they could quit their job and embrace a more elemental existence. It all looks beautiful, and the more degraded the lobster boat or the fish pound, the more perfectly rustic everything seems. Everyone likes to imagine having a beer after a long day on the water, working hard, but the big question is: Who's willing to put in that day of hard labor? Or day after day of it? Not me, that's for sure. It's a hard life. And even if lobstering isn't what you do for a living, Maine in the winter and early spring isn't for the faint of heart. The sun goes down in mid-afternoon, and the trees don't begin to bud until it's almost June. There's something mysterious about Maine because it's a big state with not all that many people, far away from most of the rest of the country. But there's also something aspirational. People want to imagine that they have what it takes to rough it there, to make it as a true Mainer.

DB: When you started writing, did you always know you would write about Maine? Or did you resist the pull of your home state?

AW: As a kid I was pretty intent on getting out of Maine, so when I left for school, I mostly put the place behind me. I wrote about it once in college and people seemed to like what I wrote. It was a column for the school paper, and it went viral by 2001 standards, which I guess just meant that people were sharing the hyperlink with each other via email. But I heard from friends that the article had been shared with them at the Maine college they attended, or I heard from friends from home who had found it at whichever out-of-state school they went to. I liked that people were reading something that I'd written, and maybe it occurred to me that people seemed intrigued by the state if they weren't from there, or, if they were from there, they appreciated that somebody had put some of what they knew to be true on the page. But it was just a light comedic thing, mostly jokes, and I didn't take what I'd written all that seriously, and I didn't think I'd return to Maine as a setting for my fiction.

But then in grad school I needed to figure out what to write, and I had a professor, Benjamin Taylor, who made an offhand remark about writers always writing about their home; it just takes some writers some time to get to that point, he said. They need to get some distance from wherever they're from. I perked up when I heard that. And I suppose I'd been thinking more about class issues, too, because I had had the opportunity to go to college and eventually grad school, but there were people I'd gone to school with or worked with during my summer job at the lobster pound who would never get that opportunity. Not because they weren't as smart as me, but because the path hadn't been presented to them early on as an option. So I started wondering what it might take to jump from one track to another. That's how Ed and Steph Thatch were born.

DB: The American Dream is the novel's great subtext. Why this theme? Have you always been interested in it?

AW: Damariscotta is a tiny place, so everyone grows up together. They go to school together, they work together. I didn't think anything of it until I went to boarding school and realized that most places aren't like that. And I also realized that affluence in my little town was very different from affluence in other parts of the country. So maybe I felt like I was straddling the fence; I grew up with many more opportunities than some of my classmates back home but was blown away by the wealth and privilege I encountered at prep school, then college.

We all know that the American Dream's getting harder and harder to achieve. *The Great Gatsby* is all about characters from the working class who get punished for aspiring to something more, and that book was written almost a century ago! It's only gotten harder to break into the upper class. To have a shot, you generally have to decide really early on that that's what you want, and you have to set yourself in motion toward the top, and then you have to get lucky. I grew up pretty lucky, which actually, in my case, probably means that the traditional American Dream is unavailable to me. My grandfather already lived some version of it, so now it's up to my generation not to screw things up, not to backslide. It's on us to do some good in the world.

But if you're starting from the lower class and trying to work your way up, especially if you decide this is something you want a little bit later in life, like Ed Thatch, then it makes the American Dream almost impossible. At least without cutting some corners. Because of the level of urgency that goes into Ed's decisions, he's forced to commit crimes. And again, I return to how different the choices are for a guy like Ed and a character like Andrew, who comes from a background much more like mine. Andrew would never have to make the decisions Ed makes. If Andrew needed a diamond ring, he could probably borrow money from his parents. Andrew could do well for himself, but I'm not sure "doing well" qualifies as living the American Dream—not for Andrew. He'll never be upwardly mobile unless he becomes obscenely rich. So even though Ed has to resort to criminal behavior, there's something romantic about starting from the bottom and aiming for the top, and especially if he's doing it all for his family. There's a reason Andrew feels some level of envy toward Ed.

DB: Reviewers have invoked books like *The Great Gatsby* and shows like *Ozark* when describing *The Midcoast*. What were some of your sources of inspiration?

AW: After so many years, I'm sure I've forgotten most of the sources of inspiration, but definitely *The Great Gatsby* was a prominent one, especially once I decided to rewrite the book with the first-person narrator. I reread *Gatsby* to see how Fitzgerald introduces Gatsby and how he transitions into the brief glimpses we get of Gatsby's past. Those are moments that the narrator Nick Carraway wasn't present for, but he finds a way to report on them anyway, typically through witness accounts. I wasn't trying to emulate Fitzgerald's writing style (that would have been dangerous), but I did look at the structure.

I don't know if my crime scenes bear any resemblance to Richard Price's, but he sets the gold standard, so I wanted to get those scenes right in the way that he always gets them right. His books might revolve around a crime, but they're always about much more, and they have such a strong sense of place. In a way I think of the crime label as a Trojan horse. In *The Midcoast*, the mystery of the Thatches' rise propels the story forward, but the book's really about these two families and what it's like to make a life in Maine.

Then there's the small-town stuff, and the very specific sense of humor that goes along with it. I'm sure I had *The End of Vandalism* by Tom Drury in mind as I was imagining some of the local color and all the randomness of living in a very small town.

Like everyone else, I've read plenty of autofiction over the past decade—novelists like Ben Lerner and Rachel Cusk. I can't do what they do, and I'm not really trying to, but some of those books probably gave me the permission I needed to write from a perspective not all that different from my own.

DB: What has screenwriting taught you about storytelling?

AW: There are stricter parameters in screenwriting. You only have so much space to tell a story, around one hundred pages for a screenplay. There's no cheating or convincing yourself that maybe the screenplay really needs to be two hundred pages, the way a novelist might convince himself that his novel is a masterpiece that can't be appreciated in fewer than 550 pages. Because of the compressed nature of the screenplay and because viewers of movies or shows generally come to the experience with more rigid expectations, most screenwriters learn little tricks of the craft, or maxims, that might be considered gauche in fiction writing. My experience is that writers of literary fiction tend to play by feel more than follow a certain structure or formula. And I think that's mostly a good thing. But there are times when I'll look at a piece of fiction that I'm working on through the screenwriter's lens and realize that I don't have any conflict in a scene, or that one of my characters doesn't want anything. I don't approach writing fiction the same way I approach writing a script, but sometimes it's good to have my screenwriter self on standby as an editor.

DB: How do you really feel about lobsters?

AW: Like, as a food source? They're good. I didn't love them as a kid, but one of the benefits of living outside the state is that lobsters become something to look forward to on visits to Maine. I'm willing to work for my meal every now and then. But I don't need it breakfast, lunch, and dinner. And I don't need a McDonald's lobster roll. Nobody needs that.

And as a driver of the economy, lobsters are great. We need them to keep thriving. Please don't go to Canada, lobsters. I know the water in the Gulf of Maine is getting warmer and warmer, but we need at least a few of you to stick around and make a home on the Midcoast.

QUESTIONS AND TOPICS FOR DISCUSSION

1. "We weren't friends with the Thatches. The Thatches didn't have friends," Andrew says. How are the Thatches viewed within Damariscotta? Early in the novel, did you see them as friendless because they were ostracized, because they were elitist—or something else? Did your opinion change in the course of the book?

2. Andrew and Ed's conversation about the nicknames "Trip" and "Chip" nicely and quickly encapsulates some of the differences between the two men. In what ways do they differ and in what ways are they similar? What is the source of the friction between them?

3. *The Midcoast* moves back and forth in time. How did this shifting timeline affect your reading experience?

4. Consider the robbery scene in which Ed helps Frank, the elderly man, with a snack and sets him up in the bathroom—while robbing him. What does this tell us about Ed's character?

5. Did you find yourself sympathizing with the Thatches? Why or why not?

6. What do you think was the turning point for the Thatches? When did things finally go too far?

7. Does Andrew feel more empathy or envy toward Ed and Steph? Talk about Andrew's complicated relationship to the Thatches.

8. Do you think anything in these characters' lives would have changed if Andrew had sent Ed's bracelet to Steph like he promised?

9. "If you're happy all the time, you don't appreciate anything," White writes. "You have to have contrast, to have low moments to bring out the high moments in relief." Do you agree? Why or why not?

10. White writes that in Damariscotta, Allie was the smart girl. But at Amherst, she was a below-average student who was accepted only because she was an athlete from a small town. How does this contrast affect her? How does your opinion of yourself change in different settings or in different crowds? What have those experiences been like?

11. Discuss EJ and Allie's relationship. How do their parents put different expectations on each of them? How has this shaped the young adults they've become?

12. What did you make of EJ's involvement in Ed's operation? What was Ed's responsibility as a father in this situa-

tion? How much blame can we place on the police? How complicit is Steph?

13. How has the story of the Thatches challenged, changed, or validated your understanding of the American dream?

14. "Why do I feel the need to distinguish myself at all?" Andrew says of his 9/11 story. "Why would I ever wish, if not for a deeper relationship with a tragic event, for a more unusual relationship with a tragic event?" Have you ever experienced this desire, or an urge to connect yourself to a tragedy? Why do you think we tend to do this?

15. Did you find the ending ambiguous? What do you think happens to everyone in the end?

PHOTO: MOLLY HAMILL

ADAM WHITE grew up in Damariscotta, Maine, and now lives with his wife and son in Boston, where he teaches writing and coaches lacrosse. He holds an MFA from Columbia University. *The Midcoast* is his first novel.

About the Type

This book was set in Baskerville, a typeface designed by John Baskerville (1706–75), an amateur printer and typefounder, and cut for him by John Handy in 1750. The type became popular again when the Lanston Monotype Corporation of London revived the classic roman face in 1923. The Mergenthaler Linotype Company in England and the United States cut a version of Baskerville in 1931, making it one of the most widely used typefaces today.